THE HOUSE AT WATCH HILL

ALSO BY KAREN MARIE MONING

THE HOUSE
AT
WATCH HILL

A Novel

KAREN MARIE MONING

WILLIAM MORROW

An Imprint of HarperCollins*Publishers*

THE HOUSE AT WATCH HILL. Copyright © 2024 by Karen Marie Moning, LLC. All rights reserved. Printed in the United States of America. No part of this book may be used or reproduced in any manner whatsoever without written permission except in the case of brief quotations embodied in critical articles and reviews. For information, address HarperCollins Publishers, 195 Broadway, New York, NY 10007.

HarperCollins books may be purchased for educational, business, or sales promotional use. For information, please email the Special Markets Department at SPsales@harpercollins.com.

FIRST EDITION

Designed by Bonni Leon-Berman

Library of Congress Cataloging-in-Publication Data has been applied for.

ISBN 978-0-06-324921-9

24 25 26 27 28 LBC 5 4 3 2 1

This one is for my wonderful, witchy mother, who saw the ghost, too. In loving memory of Janet Louise Moning, December 30, 1939–September 15, 2023.

For my tribe: Sara Smith, Kimberly Cousins, Sally Short-Blondiau, Nora Luna, Andrea Sullivan, Dawn Mosley, Nicole Garcia, Sue Ramjatan, Alicia Emley, and Anne Wessels-Paris for standing steadfastly by my side, through the darkest years of my life.

For Carrie Edwards, Brenda Steele, and Jeanne Meyer, who were there in the beginning, decades ago, supporting my freshman efforts to write a novel with their unwavering belief, enthusiasm, and friendship.

For Stacy Testa, Genevieve Gagne-Hawes, and May Chen, my dream team, who waited with extraordinary patience, compassion, and support while I fled murder house after murder house.

I wouldn't be here today if not for the helping hands of strong, brilliant, talented women.

I know this: If you bring forth what is within you, what is within you will save you. If you do not bring forth what is within you, what is within you will destroy you.

I know also the power of a "coven"—a gathering of like-minded women who passionately support each other's hopes and dreams through trial and triumph.

United, we are capable of wondrous magic. United, we are capable of *anything*. And so we are feared.

And so we have been burned.

In the beginning, God created Man.

However, contrary to the common telling,
God did not say, "Man, thou must have a mate."

God said, "Oh, *shit*, what did I just *do*?"

So, God created a better model and said unto his
initial creation, "Behold, I have created People 2.0,
with fewer bugs and glitches. I give you Woman."

And Man was *pissed*.

—*It's a Wonderful Wiccan Way of Life*

Sacred is the soil

Holy is the sky

Divine is the water

Hallowed is the fire

Above is the Cailleach

Whose breath is life

Below is the darkness

We are the light

Blessed be my life

—A light witch's prayer

THE HOUSE AT WATCH HILL

PART I

There are few things more intrinsically debilitating than feeling simultaneously as if you've escaped hell yet been evicted from paradise. Sometimes it's an intimate relationship that does it. You despise what they did to you, yet ache for the love you thought was real. You never suffered such agony, yet never felt more thrillingly alive. You love, and you loathe, with the same breath.

In my case, it was a House, with a capital H.

And even now, far removed from that exquisite, terrible place and time, some nights as I drift to sleep, dreams reach for me with dark, ravenous tentacles, and, suddenly, I'm in the rear courtyard of the house at Watch Hill, poised with my hand on the knob of the conservatory door, admiring, despite my horror, the glassy pool reflecting gently swaying oak branches hung with sprigs of drying lavender tied with ribbon, cobalt bottles clinking on jute cords, and strands of fairy lights.

I smell the rich, earthy dampness of leaves and coffee grounds composting in the garden, the drugging opulence of night-blooming jasmine, I feel the unevenness of cream and slate pavers, warm beneath my bare feet, note cobwebs that need sweeping from the cubby above the door, the wisteria draping the garage that wants trimming, and it's all so lovely and real, it terrifies me, as if the house is trying to suck me back to it because it's not done with me.

It will never be done with me. I was the sweetest thing the evil in those walls ever tasted.

It frightens me so much that I refuse—even in dreams—to enter my beloved greenhouse, where once I crushed herbs and mixed potions, practicing the ancient magyck of the Cailleach, while Rufus whuffed softly, watching from his perch in the jackfruit tree.

I jerk myself violently awake, deathly afraid and utterly certain, should I step through that dream door, I'll wake up at Watch Hill, only to find I never escaped at all—that my freedom is, in fact, the dream.

FRIDAY, MARCH 25

THE HOUSE AT WATCH HILL was a patient beast, born of dichotomy, a familiar stranger, a beautiful monstrosity. It seduced before it terrified.

But back then, I knew little of the dangerously fine line between good and evil, and I'd yet to suffer betrayals so staggering, so utterly unforgivable they make you willing to cross it. Nor did I know anything of traps so exquisitely baited you'd march straight into hell with a smile on your lips and wonder in your heart.

I knew only that my life was an endless shitstorm of problems, and if I didn't solve the immediate one of needing a new job, yet again, it was going to get infinitely worse. "But the sign outside says you're hiring," I said with an edge of desperation in my voice that I despised. "And your hostess, Claire, said you're down two waitresses."

The man behind the desk, in an office wedged into a corner adjacent to the walk-in freezer at Sophie's House of Pancakes, looked nearly identical to the one I'd just left at the Scrambled Diner, and the one before that at the Saucy Egg Café. Same longish crew cut, dingy white shirt, and stained tie, same quick slip of his gaze to the left as he replied, "I forgot to tell Claire I filled both those positions this morning."

"You're lying," I said softly.

Tightly, he replied, "I am *not*."

He was. And I was beyond weary. Four prior interviewers had also miraculously secured new employees moments before I'd walked in, and service positions weren't easy to fill around these parts. "Mr. Schumann, just tell me the truth. If you're not going to hire me, that's the least you can do."

My fifth interview today was going to end in a no too, and I dreaded the thought of having to go all the way into Indianapolis to find work. With traffic, it would take me over an hour to get home and gas money I couldn't afford, and the further into the city I went, the more likely they were to insist on references.

"It's because you heard my mother's ill, isn't it?" I pressed when he made no reply. Small towns gossip endlessly. Someone's husband knows someone's cousin two towns over, who knows someone's girlfriend three towns to the east, whose brother one town over is the sheriff, and the next thing you know, they're discussing your personal business on the police scanner, a thing Mom and I try really hard to avoid.

He shifted uncomfortably behind his desk, choosing his words with care. "Ms. Grey, your mother isn't just ill. She's dying of cancer, and while I'm very sorry about that, there's not a town within sixty miles of Frankfort willing to hire you. You don't show up for work. You leave in the middle of shifts. You beg for extra shifts, then don't cover them. How many jobs have you lost in the past year? A dozen? Two? I need waitresses I can count on."

Mr. Schumann was exaggerating. No one would hire me within thirty-seven miles, which was twenty-three shy of his alleged sixty. Carmel, Indiana, where I was currently trying to get a job, *any* early morning job, to supplement my afternoon and evening jobs cleaning houses, offices, motels, and anything else I could get paid to clean, was forty-two miles from my house. Whenever I got fired, I expanded outward in the smallest increments possible. The further I worked from home, the longer it took to get back to Mom when she needed me.

"I'm not irresponsible," I said. "I only miss a shift when I have to take Mom to the hospital. I'm a hardworking, committed employee who's grateful to have a job and does everything in her power to make each shift."

"I'm sure you do. But trying," he said with a patronizing smile, "and succeeding are two very different things. I didn't *try* to go to college to earn my business degree. I showed up every day and did the work. It's not fair to the other waitresses to have to pick up your slack. I run a business, not a charity."

Bet you didn't have a dying mother you had to support while you were privileged enough to take those classes! I wanted to retort, but that would destroy any chance I had of changing his mind. I counted to ten before replying firmly, "Yes, I've had to rush home to take my mother to the hospital, and I've even had to miss shifts on occasion if they change her chemo appointments. But I'm willing to work doubles to make up for it. If you've heard about Mom, then you also must have heard that I'm a terrific waitress. The customers love me, and so do the other waitresses." They knew I was in an impossible position and hated seeing me get fired. Women got it; we'd been caretakers since the dawn of time, when Adam, convalescing from his missing rib, conned Eve into climbing a tree to pick him an apple, and the fairer sex has been taking the fall ever since. We knew life was challenging and could be deeply unfair. Compassion went a long way.

He said curtly, "What's the point? If I hire you today, we both know you'll only end up getting fired. I've heard sometimes you don't even last two weeks. All that paperwork alone is an inconvenience. Then I have to start the hiring process all over again, which means more forms to fill out. It's not just the waitresses you burden."

Sometimes I hated my life. Especially on days like this, sitting across the desk from a man maybe ten years older than me who, by dint of an associate's degree in business from a local community college, was manager of this store and two others, as he'd loftily informed me when I'd walked in the door, whereas I—twenty-four years old, with no college degree, few saleable skills, and no time to acquire new ones—was reduced to pleading my case in order to keep food on the table and a roof over our heads while watching my mother die slowly and in escalating pain. How dreadful that Mr. Schumann might be inconvenienced by *paperwork*.

I clipped out, "The *point* is that, at least during those two weeks, I can afford to buy my dying mother food and medicine. That might be a small thing to you, but it's everything to me." Dying of cancer was one thing. Dying in pain or of starvation was another. Not on my watch.

He opened his mouth and closed it again, eyes narrowing, resenting that I'd just made him feel like a callous asshole.

He was a callous asshole, and I didn't care what I made him feel, so long as he hired me. This was my only day off; I took one every three weeks, and I was supposed to be spending it at home, with Mom, cherishing what little time we had together, trying to cram a lifetime into those hours. But I'd lost yet another job yesterday and didn't dare go home until I knew I had something slated for tomorrow morning that guaranteed us a paycheck, especially since I'd dropped my cell phone in a deep fryer two days ago and had to spring for a new one. Even the cheap dumb phone

I'd replaced it with was an expense not remotely in my budget. I was still pissed at myself about it, but it had been my third shift that day, I was clumsy-tired, and I couldn't be without a phone in case Mom needed me.

"I'm sorry, but the position isn't available."

To you, he didn't say, but we both heard it. I wasn't above pleading. I wasn't above anything when it came to my mother. "Mr. Schumann, please, just give me the cha—*ahhhhhh!*" I doubled over in my chair, clutching my head.

"Spare me the hysterics," Mr. Schumann said tightly. "I won't be manipulated into hiring you when I know I can't count on you. I have budgets to meet, profits I'm expected to turn. Franchises don't run themselves. I'm on the fast track to owning my own stores." When I remained hunched over, twitching and jerking silently, he growled, "*What* are you doing?" Then, sounding ever so slightly, and quite belatedly, in my opinion, worried, "Do you need a doctor? Answer me!"

I was pretty sure I did. But answering him was out of the question. I felt simultaneously as if my head might explode, an elephant was standing on my chest, and the skin all over my body was about to burst into flames, while deep in the pit of my stomach something enormous and searingly hot had begun whipping its head from side to side, a great fiery dragon rousing from sleep, only to find itself trapped in a cage. Pain was stabbing, burning, and exploding in every part of my body, and I had no idea why.

I tried desperately to inhale, but my lungs were tight and hot, burning as if blistered, and refused to inflate. I did, however, get a sudden rush of the acrid smell of smoke and the bitter taste of ash on my tongue. It occurred to me I might be having a heart attack or a brain aneurism, which, as young and healthy as I was, seemed highly improbable and unequivocally unacceptable.

Panicking, in agony, I lurched from the chair, staggered about in a wobbly circle, then crashed to the floor where I lay writhing, flapping at myself as if trying to put out flames, thinking with horror, *This can't be happening. Mom needs me. She'll die without me!*

That she was going to die with me, too, was something I fully understood.

But I was her Charon, ferrying her across the river Styx, with all the tenderness and love in my soul, and I would, by God, see her safely and gently across that dark divide.

That was my last thought before I passed out.

WHEN I REGAINED consciousness, Mr. Schumann was looming over me with a scowl.

"Bob, what on earth is going on here?" exclaimed a woman beyond my range of vision, sprawled as I was half beneath the desk, staring up at the underside, observing with vague disgust the gum stuck to it in multiple places. Either I'd continued flopping around after I'd passed out or he'd tried to toe me out of the way. I'd have believed either.

"I didn't touch her," he said defensively, glancing at whoever stood in the door. "I don't know what happened. She had some kind of fit and fell down. She landed like that. *Exactly* like that," he stressed.

I performed a hasty mental check: my head felt normal, my heart was beating as regularly as a metronome, my body was no longer a marshmallow toasting over open flame, and my lungs were working again, but that fiery dragon still raged in my stomach, tail whipping acid and nausea into a froth. Groaning, I inched from beneath the desk, leveraged myself into a sitting position, and scraped hair from my face.

Mr. Schumann—clearly as inconvenienced by my "episode" as extra paperwork—said stiffly, "Can you get up now?" In other words, could I get the hell out of his office before I caused any more problems for him? Although I couldn't imagine how I'd made any problems for—oh!

Yanking my skirt back down and smoothing it, I glanced hastily at the door to determine who else had seen my underwear.

Another waitress, fifty or so, with kind, concerned eyes. "Are you okay, honey?"

I nodded. "I think so."

"I'm Mae. Here, I'll help you up," she said, stepping into the office and offering her hand.

Accepting it gratefully, I rose and quickly locked my knees to steady myself. I didn't feel so hot.

"Can I call someone for you?" Mae said.

I shook my head gingerly, hoping it wouldn't spike that hellish headache again. Who would she call? I had no family other than Mom, and no time for socializing. Este was the only friend I'd managed to keep through the years of incessant moving. "I'm fine. I must not have eaten enough today. Low blood sugar."

Gently, Mae offered, "Buy you lunch?"

I winced inwardly, hoping I didn't look that broke. I wasn't. I had a meager nest egg tucked away, enough that if we ended up on the street, I'd be able to get Mom back off it while I lived in my car. Pasting a bright smile on my face, I said, "I'm good, Mae. Thanks, though. I really appreciate it."

Deciding the presence of a waitress with obvious seniority—she'd called him by his first name—might be enough to guilt him into reconsidering, I turned back to Mr. Schumann and said fervently, "Please, Mr. Schumann, I need the job. Just give me one week to prove to you that I—"

"If you're well enough to walk, there's the door. Use it." He cut me off sharply, gesturing at the exit. I think Mae must have shot him a dirty look, because he added grudgingly, "Though, if you're not well enough . . . of course we would call you an ambulance." His words trailed off to an indistinct mutter, so deeply did he resent saying them, but he could hardly permit a woman who'd been seen in his office passed out on the floor with her skirt up to die on the premises. It might require some kind of paperwork.

The dragon in my stomach chose that moment to snort a burst of flames, and pressing a hand to my abdomen, I braced myself for the return of the crushing migraine and pain of being burned, but it didn't come. Locking gazes with him, I said in a rush of quiet ferocity, "I'm a good person and a hard worker. My mother's illness is not my fault, nor is it hers. I'm just trying to take care of her until I no longer have that privilege. You *will* hire me and you *will* give me a chance to prove myself!"

"Hire her, Bob," Mae said quietly. "We'll figure it out."

Oh, God, something was seriously wrong with me, I thought, horrified, because for a moment, I thought I saw flames shimmering in his eyes. Then they were gone, but his gaze seemed strangely glassy as he said, without inflection, "Of course, Ms. Grey. Can you start tomorrow? Breakfast shift?"

The thoughts *Maybe I have a brain tumor* and *Wow, Mae has major pull with the boss*, collided inside my head. If I did have a tumor, it'd damn well better be slow-growing. "Oh, yes," I exclaimed. "Thank you so much. I won't let you down."

We both knew I would. It was only a matter of time. Mae knew it, too, yet I suspected, like me, she'd once desperately needed a helping hand. I hoped she'd gotten it and also hoped, one day, I'd be in a position to repay her kindness.

Gathering my purse and keys, with a warm smile, I thanked the older woman profusely as I hurried out.

BY THE TIME I got to my car—an ancient Corolla with 177,000 miles on it, dents galore, and a missing fender—I was fine.

Mostly. I was still feeling uncharacteristically, wildly emotional. Even when I had PMS, I only got a smidge testy. We Greys were steady, pragmatic women; no extravagant feelings, no fiery she-dragons in our bellies.

As I opened the door and got in, carefree laughter rang out, and I glanced through the windshield to see two women a few years younger than me getting out of a shiny BMW they'd just parked a cautious distance from my beater, wearing Purdue sorority jackets with outfits that would have bought me and Mom groceries for a month, carrying purses I'd have pawned in a heartbeat.

I stared, trying to imagine what their lives were like. No dying mother. No crushing debt. Working toward a degree, partying with friends. Free. Light. Virtually weightless; bright, buoyant feathers drifting on a summer breeze infused with abundant opportunities and limitless choices.

I couldn't begin to fathom the kind of world they inhabited, any more than I could stand listening to happy, mindless pop music, and there was no point anyway. My life was what it was. I cranked the key the requisite three times to get the engine started, and as it sputtered to life, my phone rang.

"Is this Zoey Grey?" a man asked when I answered.

Something in the tone of his voice sent such chills up my spine; I didn't even snap my usual caustic *It's Zo. Like* no, like I did every time someone messed up my name. "It is."

"This is Tom Harris with the Frankfort Fire De—"

"I know who you are. I used to serve lunch to you and your crew." Four jobs ago. "What's wrong?"

"You need to come home. Now."

I VIOLATED EVERY traffic law known to man as I pushed the Toyota's beleaguered, straining engine, zigging and zagging through traffic with reckless audacity.

Tom wouldn't tell me anything on the phone except they'd been called to my house for a fire.

I spent the frantic forty-two-mile dash assuring myself it was merely a small kitchen fire, easily contained. Since I'd lied about having renter's insurance—okay, so I'd also forged paperwork, but dying mother, remember—to secure our current lease, I'd have to figure out a way to pay for repairs. As I pondered various methods of increasing my income and dealing with the landlord (who would learn of the fire soon enough, everyone talked about everyone in our town), somewhere deep inside me, in a place that was frighteningly dark and still, I knew I was only buying time, minutes and miles, to continue pretending Mom was alive, cradled in a firefighter's arms or tucked beneath blankets on a stretcher, waiting for me. Life would go on, and nothing else would happen to further fracture my fragile hold on hope or sanity.

At a stop sign two blocks from our house, I nearly broke down. Put on the brake and sat, choking on suppressed sobs, blinking furiously, trying to pull it together while drivers bottlenecked behind me and began honking angrily.

Finally, I moved forward again, only to find my street barricaded, three fire trucks blocking it, and a dozen firefighters standing in a weary, sooty half circle, staring across the street at the charred wreckage of my house. Gawking neighbors milled about on lawns, shaking their heads. *That poor Zo Grey,* they would say. *She never had much, and now she has nothing, nothing at all.* And feel better about their own lives, such as they were.

It took me repeated clumsy attempts to unfasten my seat belt and open the door, my hands were shaking so badly, but I finally managed and began to walk unsteadily down the street, gaping, with shock and horror, at the smoking ruin of our home. A total loss, the insurance company would call it. Provided the landlord actually had insurance and wasn't already planning to sue me. He could get in line.

The fire chief hurried forward to meet me. "Zoey, honey, I'm so sorry," he said quietly.

Dragging my gaze from the smoldering heap, I searched his eyes. "But you haven't found—" I swallowed several times before I was able to force out, "A body?"

Tom opened his mouth and closed it again, glancing over his shoulder at the still-popping, hissing remains, before looking back at me, hoping I wouldn't make him say it.

Fisting my hands at my sides, nails digging into my palms, I said more strongly, "Did you find a body?"

He exhaled gustily. "It burned too hot. Too fast. Didn't stand a chance. We did everything we could. The roof and three of the walls had already collapsed by the time we got here. The fourth went while we were getting the hoses ready. No, we haven't found a body. Yet. But, Zoey," he added softly, "we will."

"Zo," I corrected him numbly. "Like *no.*" I knew they would. Mom had difficulty walking unassisted; the cancer had spread to her bones. She no longer cooked, and she never left the house. She wasn't about to give me more to worry about.

I'd kissed her cheek that morning, promised her Alfredo pasta for dinner—always high calorie, cancer is a hungry bitch—and ice cream topped with the final jar of strawberry jam we'd made last summer. Told her to call me if she needed me for any reason, however insignificant. I'd apologized for having to go interview on what should have been one of our rare days together, and she'd apologized for being so sick that I needed to. There'd been so much love in our house this morning. There always was.

I stared past Tom at the embers of my life, the heaps of splintered, blackened trusses and beams, the ashes listing soddenly into a leaden March sky, trying to process that my mother was no longer dying of cancer.

Joanna Grey was dead.

I had no place to go, no bed in which to sleep, no idea what to do next. I had nothing but the clothes I was wearing and the purse on my arm. I got briefly fixated on the inane observation that I had no toothbrush, tampons, or Q-tips, no soap or shampoo— and God, those things were so expensive—then detoured into tallying the myriad painful absences in my world that actually mattered.

All trace of our life together was gone. Our photo albums, our ancient laptop, my diaries, the cheap mementos and magnets we'd collected at various Cracker Barrels as we'd traveled from state to state, the birthday cards, the steno notebooks of silly notes and drawings we'd left each other over the years when we'd been on different shifts, before she got too sick to work. Oh, God, my old phone! Mom had ingrained her deep distrust of cloud storage in me. Every photo of her, every voicemail and text she'd left me was gone, destroyed the moment I'd dropped the only smartphone I'd ever owned into a vat of boiling oil.

It was as if my mother had finally been fully and completely erased from the life we'd taken such diligent pains to erase ourselves from, time after time, as we'd fled from town to town, careful to leave no trace behind. It was too much to bear. I didn't even have a piece of her clothing. Nothing to bury my nose in, inhale the scent of the woman who gave me life, an exquisite perfume of safety, love, belonging, home. Nothing to remember her by or clutch to my heart while I sobbed.

Everything—ash.

"Your mother died of smoke inhalation, long before the flames reached her," Tom said gently.

Balling my hands into fists again, I smiled faintly, bitterly at the kindness of his lie. Tom Harris was a good man.

But I knew better.

What I'd felt in Mr. Schumann's office was the death my mother had suffered. The sensation that my body was about to burst into flame, lungs tight and hot, burning as if blistered, refusing to inflate, the acrid smell of smoke and the bitter taste of ash on my tongue. Impossible though it was to explain, I'd experienced my mother's death, as if our love was so deep, so strong that I'd empathically shared, to a lesser degree, the final, horrific moments of her life. I could find no other explanation for what I'd suffered at the precise moment our house was being devoured by flames.

My mother hadn't died easy.

Like witches of yore, Joanna Grey had burned alive.

"Mom," I whispered, and began to cry.

2

Alisdair

Once I wore my past, *a crown of thorns, a cloak of penitence.*

I killed those who did not deserve to die, coveted what they had, and took what should never have been mine, pillaging without a backward glance. A brute of a man, I hammered my way through the centuries, pounding to dust all that did not yield to my will.

Now, with nothing but time to contemplate those centuries, I see myself for who and what I am, and know I deserved my fate. Yet not at my enemy's hands, for my enemy is no better than I. In truth, my enemy merits far greater punishment.

Still, once, we were two of a kind.

I suspect, were humans confined to solitary, as I have been, and forced to face themselves for a long enough period of time, they would either descend into despair and terminate their miserable existence or get a fucking clue and evolve.

I met despair unwillingly, was dragged kicking and raging into that dark, devouring vortex until the time came when I craved nothing more than to cease to exist—a release I am forever denied.

I reviled despair, held it in contempt, perceiving it as I did all emotion: weakness. I struggled against it, swinging my mighty hammer to obliterate it.

The harder I fought, the more obdurate despair became.

At last, weary of battle, tired of closing my eyes to avoid the bloody wreckage of my life, I dropped my hammer and opened them. Wide.

The abyss of despair stared at me, and I stared back, unflinching. Then, with a snort of laughter, I leapt into that bottomless gorge of madness.

To my surprise, I found the abyss had a bottom and, in the depths of that merciless chasm, I discovered the still place.

There, I came to understand one does not do battle with despair.

One must walk differently within it. One must step sideways, lightly, as if passing over the surface of quicksand, and as you continue stepping sideways, it becomes a sort of instinctual dance, older than time itself. A dance that can carry you beyond the moment, through the dark night of your soul, into the dawn.

For as your spirit moves in those slow, certain steps you were born knowing, steps imprinted in the very essence of your being, you begin to remember the finest of who you are, who you might have been were circumstances different, and who you might yet be, because it's possible—each fragile fresh dawn you draw breath—to choose again.

Impossible, however, to forge a new path wearing the accoutrements of self-inflicted punishment, regrets for deeds that can't be undone. You must relinquish the past, never forgotten, eternally part of your spirit, but only in the manner the cocoon precedes the butterfly.

Some deem stillness and dancing opposites.

They are two sides of the same coin, and that coin is the currency of life.

You must learn how to be still. You must remember the dance.

Then, to do more than exist—to truly live—you must learn how to do both at the same time.

The young witch who approaches Watch Hill has mastered stillness.

But she has not learned to dance. She can't even hear the music in her blood.

My enemy awaits her.

It amuses the fiend that the fledgling Cailleach will never once see me, although she will certainly behold me.

I—who was once the most deeply feared warrior on any battlefield, in any century—am powerless to help her, and soon she will know life as I do.

Hell without end.

3

SUNDAY, APRIL 10

I WAS A KNOT OF dark, tangled emotions when my plane touched down in New Orleans. Since the day of the fire, they'd been raging out of control. Gone was pragmatic, steady Zo. From the ashes of my mother's fiery grave, a wild thing had arisen.

The horrific, wholly inexplicable sensations I'd experienced as I'd somehow shared my mother's death hadn't revisited me, but the crusty dragon birthed in my belly at that moment had neither departed nor calmed. Rather, she grew testier and more volatile with each passing day. I attributed the fractious inferno to grief, as I did everything lately.

The evening sky was indigo and orchid, and the city, silvered by recent rain, was lavender grit, bougainvillea, neon signs, and gently decaying architecture. As we taxied through the narrow cobblestone streets to the Hotel Monteleone, where I'd be spending the night before leaving for Divinity, Louisiana, tomorrow afternoon, I listened to my cab driver tallying the places in the city I should take care to avoid. New Orleans was magical, with countless experiences to be savored, but a solitary traveler, he warned, should give wide berth to certain pockets of the city. I took mental notes of those areas, although I had little intention of leaving my hotel.

If tonight was anything like the nights preceding it, I'd be in bed, crying, trying to decide what to do next, pretending I had a choice, any choice at all, other than lining up three new jobs and working to exhaustion to pay Mom's medical bills for pretty much the rest of my life. They'd begun refusing treatment until I'd agreed to leverage my future, putting all accounts in my name. At least now I wouldn't get fired all the time. There was that depressing bright spot.

The Monteleone soared up from the grimy street, an elegant ivory Beaux-Arts hotel embellished with elaborate moldings, attended by impeccable doormen who ushered me inside. After registering at the front desk and peeking into the rotating Carousel Bar & Lounge (very cool) and the restaurant, Criollo (way above my pay grade), I was surprised to find the accommodations James Balfour had reserved for me were luxurious. The attorney had spared no expense on my trip from Frankfort, Indiana, to New Orleans, coupling a business-class ticket with the Eudora Welty suite. I wandered in bemused silence from spacious bedroom to marble bathroom with a deep garden tub to the inviting parlor that looked out over the Mississippi River, pausing occasionally to pass a wondering hand over the cool crystals of a lamp, the plush velvet of a chair.

Mom and I never had much, and now I stood in an elegant Old World hotel room furnished with antiques and chandeliers, about to journey to a small town a few hours from New Orleans where—according to Mr. Balfour—a distant relative had recently died, leaving me an inheritance the attorney was unwilling to discuss by phone.

I'd been uneasy until Mr. Balfour clarified that the line of descent was maternal. Mom never talked about family. I knew nothing of my grandparents on either side, and one of the few things I knew—or rather suspected with a high degree of certainty, both from things Mom had said and *not* said about my father—was that he was the reason we'd been on the run for the first fifteen years of my life, moving constantly from one small town to the next, a state over, or up three states before down to a new town, always in the northeast of the country and usually in Midwestern farmland or the foothills of the West Virginia mountains.

The mere mention of my father would bring darkness to my mother's eyes that lingered for days. Then something happened—I assumed he'd died and she'd learned of it—and we began staying longer in the same place. I'd spent all of my junior and senior years at the same high school in Brownsburg, Indiana, where I'd once attended part of fourth grade and all of seventh.

When Mr. Balfour insisted that I come meet with him, after researching to ascertain the firm and town existed—although there'd been little information online about either—I decided I had nothing to lose and possibly something to gain. It was conceivable a far-removed cousin on Mom's side had left me something.

Desperate for a distraction from grief, and in no mood for another night in the cramped, unfurnished studio I'd leased after the fire, where I'd been tossing and turning on a blowup mattress on the floor, I'd decided it was possible, however implausible, the trip might yield a small financial gain. I could certainly use it. When they'd found the remains of Joanna Grey, despite it being a fraction of a full-size body, the funeral home had still charged me full price for the cremation, nearly wiping out my nest egg.

I dropped my duffle onto the bed, hung the few clothes I owned in the closet, arranged my toiletries in the bathroom, and gently placed the urn holding Mom's ashes on the dresser. It was all I had left of her, and I'd been unwilling to leave it behind in the impersonal, empty studio, unable to quell the irrational fear someone might take that from me, too. Sinking to the edge of the bathtub, I buried my face in my hands, aching to crawl into a real bed for the first time in weeks, where I would weep until exhaustion deepened to fitful slumber.

More agonizing than the grief I felt were the shameful waves of relief that sometimes crashed over me, for the fire that had ended my mother's life had also ended my incessant, gnawing fears about which part of her body cancer might attack next, how badly she would suffer, how much more painful her life and mine would become. Whether it would progress, as the doctors assured us it would, to her brain. She'd been so terrified of that, as was I. Our situation was bad, destined to get worse before it was over.

It hadn't.

It simply ended in the middle, abruptly and without warning, a bookmark halfway through a novel on a bedside table we'd had every intention of finishing. I'd been so focused on the death I knew was coming for her, I'd not once considered some other death might take her away from me sooner. It wasn't fair. It was bullshit. It made me so angry at times I felt my head might explode. I'd been cheated; she was stolen from me before her time. I'd understood the parameters of our life: Mom had cancer and at least another year to live. We'd had *plans* for that time. We'd gotten none of the lingering goodbye we'd expected. She'd promised to tell me more about my father, said there were things about the Greys I needed to know before she died.

A blessing, I would muse eventually in the bleary-eyed, cotton-brained hours of dawn, after I'd wept myself dry. I knew the horrors the future held for her, for both of us, had she lived.

Still, there are blessings that flay to bone.

You must promise me, Mom had begun insisting in recent months, *that you won't grieve me when I'm gone. You've paid too high a price already. Live, my darling Zo. Live. Be irresponsible for once in your life. File bankruptcy and seize every opportunity that comes your way. Find a husband, have babies. You'll be such a wonderful mother!*

Mom had wanted desperately to hold a grandchild before she died, avidly encouraging it. She'd made it clear she had no issues with me having a baby without a husband on the horizon. It would be just us, three generations of Grey women. Before she'd gotten so sick, I'd often thought I might one day do that. I loved our life. Wherever we landed, in whatever town, we always found a bit of land, grew a garden, and found some kind of work. I loved the bond we shared, her uplifting way of looking at the world no matter how hard things were, and I looked forward to being a mother. I imagined the joy of holding my own child might eclipse all other joys, and there would be nothing I wouldn't do for my daughter or son, no price I wouldn't pay to see them grow strong and thrive, love and be loved. To share that experience with my mother had been a nearly irresistible pull in my blood.

But Joanna Grey, quiet and grateful for life's many gifts, haunted and hunted yet cheerful and kind, frail in body yet formidable in will, would never hold a grandchild. I'd failed to grant that wish, and countless others. I'd failed to save her. I'd failed the devotion of being at her side, holding her hand, assuring her of how deeply she was loved, that she was the best of mothers, so that the last earthly words she heard were ones that warmed her heart and comforted her soul. I failed to ease her gently into that good night.

I tossed my head, shuttered those thoughts. I knew they would return all too soon, with a thorny cluster of others I couldn't deal with, so I pushed up from the edge of the tub and stared at my reflection in the mirror. Glittering amber eyes stared back, and I knew the edge in them, the wildness, the hunger. As close to need as I ever got. I'd learned to need nothing at a young age; it was easier when your life was always vanishing in the taillights of a hastily packed car.

I made the impulsive decision to treat myself to dinner downstairs at Criollo, further proof of my volatile emotions. I should have been hoarding every cent I had, but *should* didn't carry the same weight it once had. Easier to take risks when you were the only one who might suffer for them and could live on cans of tuna and boxes of crackers for a few weeks to recover from the splurge.

I showered, did my hair and makeup, then slipped into one of the two new dresses I'd bought on sale. I had two pairs of jeans, five shirts, seven pairs of underwear, and two bras, one white, one black. I could travel carrying everything I owned. It was a strange feeling. No family, few possessions, no home. I simply couldn't conceive of a world without my mother in it. I felt invisible. I hungered to be seen. Touched. Made to feel alive to counter how dead I felt inside.

Around my neck, I dropped the amber pendant I'd been wearing the day of the fire, added the matching earrings, slid into sandals, grabbed my purse, and headed downstairs to the hotel restaurant, where I would eat crab cakes and crawfish, maybe try Criollo's legendary bread pudding, have a drink, and find something luscious and chocolatey on the menu.

I'd not been able to promise Mom I would be irresponsible. I'd been taking care of us for so long, I knew no other way to be. Nor could I convince myself to weasel out of debt by filing bankruptcy because, well, I wasn't a weasel. Yet. Perhaps, after a few years of drudgery, I'd grow whiskers (and balls) and slink away any way I could.

Not grieve her? Impossible.

But I could fulfill the most important part of what she'd asked of me. What I knew deep in my heart was all that mattered to her, if somewhere, unseen, she lingered, watching over me.

Live, my darling Zo. Live.

LATER, I WOULD recall that when I walked into Criollo that night, I felt strangely as if I were attending a debutante ball and, for some inexplicable reason, I was the diamond. I would also know why.

As the hostess escorted me to my table, eyes followed me, and I was gratified to see many of the men watching me were the type I found attractive.

I never had time to date. The loss of my virginity was a dreadful, awkward affair I preferred not to think about, but it hadn't dissuaded me from trying again. Rather, it refined my selection process. No more boys. I liked men, even then. I'd never had bad sex again. I'd decided then and there that in the future, I would make sex all about me, what *I* wanted it to be.

I had no time for a relationship, but there were nights I needed something for myself, something that was all my own and only about me, and I'd hungered for it so badly, I was nearly wild with it.

Sex had proved a viable petcock for a system about to blow.

I hadn't needed it often. Sometimes I'd make it six, seven, even eight months before the pressure built again and I hungered to feel seen, caressed, cherished for a time, if only my body and only an illusion. On those nights, I'd prowl, tense and volatile, searching for the right man, one that made lust burn in my veins, was willing to exchange first names only, no personal talk, no strings attached, and most definitely, no tomorrow.

They weren't easy to find. I have a type; I like self-possessed, strong, magnetic men, and I like them to have a bit of an edge, a hint of wildness. Hidden depths, layers, an indefinable quality of . . . *more*. I also like them tall, dark, and muscular. On the rare occasions I indulge, I shoot for the stars.

Sometimes, it took me days to find the elusive fruit for which I hungered, but tonight I marveled as I glanced around the restaurant; I seemed to have fallen in the berry patch. Either that, or men just came darker, hotter, and more to my liking in the Deep South.

Ever vigilant of wasting time, I'd perfected a siren's call that never failed me. Once I made my decision, I gave the man what I thought of as the Look, and we'd end up in his bed, or up against a wall, in a bathroom stall, anywhere that wasn't home with my mother.

I don't think I'm all that, but men seem to appreciate my tangle of long coppery chestnut hair and unusual golden eyes. I have clear, healthy skin, and I've always been mostly happy with how I'm built. My body is strong from hard work, lean and proportionate for my five-foot-eight frame. However, I don't think my success rate has much to do with how I look. Men are kind of . . . well, easy. We women know, for the most part, if we want to get laid, we can. Men don't have that assurance, and a lot of them seem to have figured out that hitting on a woman too aggressively can get them in loads of trouble these days. So I take the risk out of it for them by making the first move. I like doing it. It makes me feel strong, a woman making her own choices, in control.

It's a simple look, really, easy to put into my eyes, perhaps because by the time I get around to doing it, I'm a gasket about to
blow. I'm surprised more people don't do it. Especially women.
I once tried to explain it to a co-worker, who'd stared at me, baffled; said nobody could read a look and eyes didn't talk.

Yes, they do. Saying too much, too often. I rarely meet a person's gaze, preferring to focus on noses, blurring the irises and
pupils. On the rare occasions I do lock gazes with a person, I
tend to get hit with a messy tangle of emotions, sometimes images, rarely pleasant.

If a man ever gave me such a blatant, sexually loaded, I-want-
to-devour-you look, I'd be lost. None ever has. Yet, I hope.

Over an appetizer of shrimp, blue crab, and avocado, I studied
the room, gaze drifting from table to booth, peering into the
smaller, more private dining rooms on the sides, never lingering
overlong. For a change, the dragon in my belly seemed . . . placid,
content, even, as if rumbling soft approval of my plans. Probably
just grateful I was finally about to do something besides cry. If
so, it was a sentiment we shared.

I had a luxury suite upstairs, a king-size bed, a Jacuzzi bath
large enough for two, plus an enormous walk-in shower. I wasn't
about to waste it all. Mom herself had encouraged me to seize
my opportunities, and Criollo was certainly teeming with them.
I was finding it difficult to narrow down my decision, and I'd
never had that problem before. If Frankfort was famine, New
Orleans was feast.

There was an older man, forty or so (age doesn't matter to
me; it's what they exude), thick dark hair touched with silver at
the temples, wearing an elegant suit, yet I could tell his body
was strong and rugged beneath it. The dichotomy intrigued me,
made me think all civility might fall away with the shedding of

that suit and he'd be pure animal in bed. Plus, I could count on him to be experienced.

Then there was the man seated near the bar, in his late twenties, who I decided was Mediterranean, wearing a muted scarf with a collared chambray and jeans. He had a lean, athletic build, and I knew he'd be pretty much the perfect casual sex but not necessarily the best sex. Still, the waitresses were lingering nearby, vying to bring him his next drink. He, too, had presence. I was surprised to realize most of the men in the restaurant did. I'd never been in a room with so much palpable masculine energy before.

At a table near the door was a man, probably thirty-five, with short black hair, the shadow of a beard framing his wide jaw, and a mouth I could kiss for hours before unbuttoning that crisp white shirt to drag my tongue across his beautiful dark brown skin. There was something watchful and refined about him that intrigued me. His gestures were fluid and precise, he was kind to the staff (always a big hit with me), and I got the sense he was a man who concealed his strengths, played his cards close to the cuff in public, which made me insatiably curious to know what he was like in private.

Then there was a man unlike any I'd chosen in the past, perhaps thirty, blond with ocean-blue eyes, leaning back, legs outstretched in a booth in one of those side rooms with the dimmed lights. He intrigued me, despite my preference for dark men, because of something in his eyes and the way he moved, with power and grace. He wore faded jeans, a blue T-shirt, and boots. As I stole another glance at him, he stood and stretched over the table, accepting a bottle being passed from booth to booth in that private area, and his shirt slid up, affording me a glimpse of his cut stomach. My gaze lingered appreciatively on the leanness of his hips, the muscular ass, the broad shoulders. He threw his head back and laughed and, before drinking, shouted out a toast with a sexy Irish accent. I wasn't entirely sure what he'd said, but I liked the sound of it and decided perhaps it was time for something different.

When the waiter returned to take my entrée order, I declined to place it and requested my bill. I'd order room service later. My appetites had changed.

I waited until the blond sat back down and let my gaze rest on him. The moment he turned my way, my chin would notch down, I'd glance up from beneath my brows with a sheen of challenge, the promise of a wild side. I would put all I felt into my eyes, let it gather intensity and radiate toward him. The hunger, the frustrated energy that desperately needed an outlet, the pain, the grief, the passion, the loneliness born not of weakness but from the appetite of a strong young woman seeking an equal in sensuality, intellect, and competence. I wouldn't send it to him wending gently around guests, delicate and inquiring.

I'd slam it into him.

I'd say with flat ferocity, *I want you. Come to my bed. No apology, no ego, no games. Only hunger and lust and the burn of my passion, and I will be kind though not necessarily gentle, and you will never forget this night.*

The blond man's head began to turn toward me, and tensing with delicious anticipation, I notched my chin down.

As his gaze was about to collide with mine, abruptly another man slid into the booth next to him, obliterating my view of the blond with his dark, powerful frame. He said something to the man, punched him on the shoulder, as if in consolation, then turned his head and locked gazes with me.

And I do mean *locked.*

I was caught, trapped, ensorcelled, spellbound, powerless to look away. I stared helplessly into eyes dark as a raven's wings, into a face more formidable than handsome, and the instant he knew he had me bound, he caught the tip of his tongue between his teeth in a smile that dripped challenge, and flung his words across the room at me, sharp as knives.

He said, *I want you. Come to my bed. I know how wild you hunger to be. I'll meet you in those untamed lands, and I'll be kind but not gentle, because gentle isn't what you want. You want to feel intensely, dangerously alive, to recover dreams you've been forced to abandon, faith you've lost, power that's been stripped from you by the incessant, mundane demands of the world. Fuck me, woman. I'll give you all that and more, and you will never forget this night.*

The breath whooshed from my lungs in an incoherent sound, and for a moment, I couldn't form a thought.

Then, as my brain cleared, my first thought was incensed: How *dare* he interfere with my strong, aggressive woman-in-charge-of-her-own-life moment? I was as offended as I was—

Oh, God, he was rising, collecting his drink, and heading toward me, and I had no idea how I'd failed to see him while scanning the restaurant. The presence he exuded was staggering, more than the other four men combined.

Dozens of heads swiveled to follow him as he strode my way, and I got the sudden impression that something was going on in Criollo tonight that I didn't understand. As if threads of cohesiveness stitched together each moment that had passed since I'd entered the restaurant, with each person in that room, and everyone else could clearly see the fabric of this night but me.

Then he was at my table, staring down at me, and the fanciful thought burned off, mist in the sun.

I said before that I have a type. This man typified the type.

This man was the mold for it, and they'd broken it after they'd made him, and every other man I'd chosen in the past had been only a shadow of him. The kind of edge I looked for—this man had in spades. His edges had edges. There was a kind of . . . were I fanciful, I'd say an aura that surrounded him, silvery and seductive and stitched somehow of both luminosity and utter absence of light, as if he wore a full moon's brilliance purled to midnight as a cloak.

"I'm Kellan."

"Stop," I said hastily, before he could say more. "No last names."

"I had no intention of offering you one."

I scowled, both pleased (he knew the rules) and irritated (he seemed to be the one making them). I'd always thought I would savor it, absolutely lose my mind, if ever a man gave me the kind of look I used.

I thoroughly resented it.

Would I have chosen him, anyway, if I'd seen him? Yes. That wasn't the point. The point was, *he* chose *me*; it chafed, and now there was no way I was going to have sex with him, despite the fact that the blond was currently gathering his coat to leave and the Mediterranean man was already gone.

Then there was the fact that the bastard's look had been so much more polished than mine.

"They always come when you summon, don't they?" Irish accent, like the blond. Sexy as hell. When he twisted a chair around and dropped into it, it creaked beneath his weight. Maybe six foot five, two hundred and forty pounds. I like big men; they make me feel like I can go crazy on them in bed and not worry about hurting them. My mouth went dry.

"I didn't ask you to join me," I said flatly.

"Nor have you told me to leave."

"Leave."

He stood instantly.

"Sit down," I snarled.

Amusement glittered in his dark gaze. The chair creaked again. My mouth was absolutely parched.

"You prefer to choose," he murmured. "It makes you feel strong."

That was it exactly. I'd been in control of so little in my life, I needed this one thing. And I hadn't fully understood it until this moment, when the man made the choice for me.

"Losing control because the world has taken it from you in infinitesimal degrees, without warning and without your consent, in demeaning ways, is one thing. Losing control because you choose to, because you've met someone you can let go with, break free, obey no rules, tithe to neither god nor demon, that's entirely another."

"And I suppose you think you're that someone."

"I was watching you from the moment you walked in and knew exactly what you were looking for. Ian, the blond you'd settled on, is a good man, without question. I'd want him at my side in a fight, and I trust him running several of my companies. But he'd leave you just as unsatisfied as they always do. My guess is that's how you prefer it. Playing it safe. You never choose anyone you might want to see again. How's choking down that same bland appetizer, over and over, working out for you? Ready for a meal yet?"

Implying he was the meal. And how subtly he'd just made it clear he was wealthy and Ian worked for him, not vice versa. "Oh, fuck you," I growled.

Wolfishness and mockery shaped his smile. "Your suite or mine?"

"You think you know me. You don't know me," I shot at him.

"You don't know you," he fired back.

It's funny. We think we want a man who sees us. Who gets us. But wheel that rarity up to the table, and we get downright defensive, erect barricades left and right. He was correct. My life had been composed entirely of responsibilities, bills to pay, too much to do, too few hours in the day, a dying mother, no time to wonder what I wanted or might one day become, if given the chance.

I'd *wanted* Joanna Grey to live. I'd *become* what she'd needed me to be.

Without her, I was floundering.

In a strange way, it felt as if, the day she'd died, I was born. That she'd had to become a thing of the past for me to become a thing of the future; for me to even understand I could have a future. It was the only explanation I could find for the countless volatile emotions waking up inside me. I must have put myself into a shallow trance to survive. Numb was eminently capable. Empty of want, of need, one could give endlessly, completely. And I didn't regret it. I'd do it over and over again.

Yet here I was, a blank slate at twenty-four. Each day I awakened, my brain kicked on, and the only thing I had to ask myself was: What do I want to do? Granted, I was buried in debt and didn't have all that many choices, but suddenly, there was nothing and no one else to consider. I had no idea how to live this way. I'd become obdurate as ice to deal with my reality. Thawing was a melty, messy process I was rather beginning to despise.

"I'm Zo," I said irritably.

He laughed. "Could you sound any pissier telling me your name?" Then his smile faded, and his gaze darkened with challenge and frank carnality. "Tell me, Zo—what do you *want* to do?" he said in a low, rough voice.

I wanted to stand up, tell him to go to hell, and walk away. Yet I knew, even from our brief exchange, this man wasn't the kind to offer anything to a woman twice. And since the moment he'd dropped into that chair across from me—no, from the moment he'd knifed into my head with his damn look—I'd been burning with lust. The dragon in my stomach was snorting and stomping and turning in voracious circles. We were in complete agreement about this man, and I was the new Zo, who was going to live and not miss opportunities.

I leaned forward and told him in exacting detail what I wanted to do. What I wanted him to do to me.

Muscle working in his jaw, eyes glittering, he rose and offered me his hand. I shivered when he laced his fingers with mine.

Presence was an understatement. People make so much noise about IQ: intelligence quotient. I've never found myself impressed by that number. I look for AQ: awareness quotient, and Kellan's was off the charts. He saw. He knew. He put things together, divining patterns in the smallest of details. Later, I would learn his IQ was astronomical, too, so much so that he had difficulty communicating sometimes and could work himself into a lather about it. Later, I would learn many things about Kellan, some of which I would refuse to believe, for if I did, they would terrify me.

I didn't emerge until late the next afternoon, barely able to walk and barely meeting my driver in time.

Kellan fucked as if I were both woman and wolf, lady and whore, hummingbird and hawk.

He saw me. The good and bad, the selfless and selfish. The woman who'd bled out, without reservation, for the mother she loved, and the quiet rage it made her feel at pretty much the whole world. The lonely orphan and the she-dragon that needed no one and nothing but the chance at command of her own destiny and soul.

He saw the hunger and fear and pain, and the unbreakable vow I'd made to myself that all I had been to date in my life was *not* all I would ever be.

He was, hands down, the best sex of my life, making good on his promise that I would never forget this night, and I've had my share of good sex. It's the only place in my life I've permitted myself to be selfish and utterly unrestrained. To take as I desire, to give as I choose, to demand and bestow explosively, pouring through my hands, from the very core of my being, an inferno of passion, releasing the countless things I don't permit myself to say and, often, refuse to acknowledge I feel. The anger, hope, joy, fear, every shade of emotion—I drench their bodies with it. I forget myself. Nothing exists but the moment, their body, mine. Releasing all that pent volatility recharges me. I stand up from sex-soaked sheets far stronger than I got into them.

Kellan was dangerous.

He fucked like I did. As if it was all about him. He took and gave the same way, his touch electrifying, laced with the same explosive charge. His lust was equally bottomless. We burned up that bed, we knocked over tables and chairs; I'm not entirely certain we didn't shatter the glass door of the shower. He seemed to flawlessly intuit each nuance I was venting, throwing it back at me, egging me on, pushing for more. At times, it became a flat-out battle to outdo, to *undo* each other.

He reached inside me with his strong hands and searing kisses, with the burn of his big, hard body against mine, to expose parts of me I'd refused to see. It was raw, it was fierce, it was frighteningly intimate. I left hungering to see into him as clearly as he seemed to see into me, each brilliant and every shadowy, demon-inhabited corner of his soul.

I wanted more. Of *him*. I'd never felt that before.

I left feeling as if his every touch had been somehow seared, with the chafing permanence of a brand, deep into my skin.

I left—no, I *fled* while he was in the bathroom, hastily snatching my clothes and donning them as I raced for the door—without his last name, without giving him mine.

4

How many people live in Divinity?" I asked my driver, Evander Graham, a burly man with silver hair who looked to be in his early sixties, as I stared out the sedan's window at the passing landscape.

"'Bout twenty-five thousand."

Kellan's dark head between my thighs. Challenge blazing in his eyes as I gripped fistfuls of his hair, bucking against him as I came.

The unbidden image brought a flush to skin that still bore his scent, spicy and intoxicating. There'd been no time for a shower. I needed one, as soon as possible, to wash away all memory of that man. Last night, and well into the day, had been merely a nameless one-night stand, no different from the others, never to be repeated, never thought of again: one of my many unbreakable rules—never take the same lover twice. I'd never wanted to. Until now.

Twenty-five thousand was roughly ten thousand more than Frankfort, closer to the size of Brownsburg, where I'd finished high school. It was a comfortable size, large enough to offer amenities, small enough to feel cozy and navigable. "Everybody knows everybody, don't they?"

"Pretty much. There's a lot of history in Divinity. It was settled in the late sixteen hundreds, and we've dozens of families that trace their roots back to those early settlers. Folks take pride in our town, work hard to keep it nice. It began as a planned settlement, stayed small until the late eighteen hundreds. Got a lot of fancy houses in the Queen Anne style, some Colonial and Antebellum. Streets are the prettiest I've ever seen. No real pollution.

In my opinion, it's the best town in the whole damn country to live. We don't advertise the fact, though. Towns get attention, they start drawing the wrong kind of folk. Got no crime to speak of, work's plentiful, though some keep offices in New Orleans. Mostly we stay to ourselves."

Sounded too good to be true. All towns, no matter their size, had dark sides: drugs, homelessness, racism, economic inequity, religious intolerance. Although, when I was younger, I'd hated being constantly uprooted, torn away from new friendships again and again, my sense of loss was ameliorated by the endless discovery of new towns and new people. I hadn't gotten the best schooling, but I'd acquired resilience, curiosity, and an open mind from our nomadic lifestyle. The only thing I'd missed was my best friend, Este. When Mom let us stay in Brownsburg for two years, I'd been ecstatic, especially since I knew, for reasons beyond my fathoming, Mom didn't like Este any more than Dalia Hunter liked me. They'd barely tolerated our friendship—and they'd not tolerated each other at all, unwilling to share the same room. Hell, they wouldn't even occupy the same city block, which had only made me and Este more protective of our friendship.

Este and I had been inseparable from the moment we met in fourth grade, when I was the new kid once again and both of us were outsiders. Me because I was always moving, often hastily, in the dead of night, and Este because she was brilliant, fierce, and—in a town that was 95 percent white in blue-collar jobs— biracial and from an affluent family, a singularity in both grade and high school. I still remembered what I was wearing the day we met, as I sat alone in the cafeteria picking at a greasy corn dog and fries on an orange plastic tray: jeans that I'd grown too tall for, so Mom had sewn bits of a flowered pillowcase to the bottoms, with a faded pink T-shirt that had only the tiniest of tears near the hem. I didn't look bad. I merely looked what we were: poor. Not Este. Her folks had money, lots of it, and it made her even more of a misfit at school.

Casting a glare about the cafeteria that had kids ducking their heads to avoid her withering gaze, nine-year-old Este swaggered to my table, plunked down her tray, flashed me a smile as warm as her cyan glare was icy, and said, *Name's Este Hunter. I'm going to be a famous artist someday, and everyone will know my name. You look like you have the balls to be friends with me. Do you?*

I was a goner. Only nine years old, and she'd said *balls* like she owned the word. Este did everything like she owned it. There was no "Zo, like *no*," on my lips that day. Este was then and has always been able to blast through my countless barriers.

I smiled at the memory, gazing out the window at the passing scenery. Louisiana was subtropical-lush with trees and flowers I'd never seen before. The abundance of greenery was a feast to my winter-starved eyes. It was sunny, the sky cloudless, the temperature seventy-five. I hoped whatever local hotel Mr. Balfour had put me in had a pool, that prior to heading back to New Orleans to catch my return flight, I could have breakfast outside and soak up the sunshine before returning to a town where the only flowers brightening the dreary landscape were listless daffodils, assured of another killing frost, devoting scant effort to their pale blooms. In the Deep South, the foliage exploded with brazen audacity, exotic and wild, while I, feeling too much like those wan Midwestern daffodils, would droop home tomorrow to the same chilly terrain I'd left, with the same bone-deep chill in my heart. For a moment, I imagined living down here, never shoveling snow again, never de-icing my car as I shivered in the early morning gloom, never having to watch the world go colorless and cold around me for six long months, until the relentless gray of the sky was so similar to the roads, I might drive into the horizon without even realizing I'd left the ground. Then I sighed. I couldn't afford to move. I was so deeply in debt, dreams were beyond my budget.

When we passed the sign that announced we were entering Divinity, I sat up straighter, hugging my purse, gripped by a sudden tension and apprehension I attributed to the unknowns of the meeting I was about to have. I wondered if I really did have relatives, if the last one had recently died or if some remained and I might find family here. It was strange to be so alone, and I hadn't wrapped my brain around it. I could feel the awareness of it, far off in the distance—*You, Zo Grey, have no family in all the world*—but it drifted aimlessly beyond a cyclone of grief.

Mr. Graham wasn't exaggerating. Divinity was the prettiest town I'd ever seen. The streets were immaculate, the centuries-old houses faultlessly maintained behind cast-iron fences, their bright Victorian facades painted in historic shades, some with fluted columns, others with whimsical romantic turrets, lace curtains fluttering in the afternoon breeze. Nearly all had inviting porches and lawns bursting with bougainvillea, crepe myrtles, and magnolias.

As we entered the town commons—a one-block square of park hemmed on three sides by shops, with a fountain at the center and benches dotting the hawthorn-hedged green—I gestured to an unusual building that resembled an old-time theater, modernized with a striking cerulean and chrome facade. "What's that?"

"The Gossamer. It's a popular club with the young folk, live music and such. Then there's the Shadows at the south end of town, where a more adult crowd gathers."

We passed dozens of quaint businesses, restaurants, a bank,

a retro pizzeria, the post office and local gym, two coffee shops, and three bars. Then we were turning off the main thoroughfare and down a maze of cobbled alleys before exiting onto another main road and pulling into the circular drive of the Balfour and Baird Law Firm, which occupied a stately Colonial home, entry framed by tall white columns.

"Do you know where I'll be staying tonight?" *Not with Kellan. Never with him again.* My unbreakable rules are essential for navigating my life. I'd begun making them young for good reasons.

Mr. Graham got out of the car and opened my door. "I imagine Mr. Balfour will be telling you that."

As I stepped out, a sultry breeze lifted my hair and a sudden chill pierced the nape of my neck, burrowing to bone. My spine constricted with a violent shiver, as if an icy airborne dart came concealed within the draft.

Later, I would understand I'd begun feeling the house at Watch Hill long before I saw it, the moment we'd entered the intangible but oh so carefully guarded boundaries of Divinity, a cold, disturbing burn in my blood. When I stepped from the car, we got that much closer to each other. I just hadn't understood what was happening.

Some things should never be awakened. Joanna Grey knew that.

Home to three centuries of secrets, blood, and lies, the mansion on the hill was a dark, slumbering beast.

Come to me. Know me. Live in me.

Shivering again, I tipped back my head, feeling irresistibly compelled to glance up and to the east.

Beyond gnarled, moss-draped limbs of centuries-old live oaks, an enormous hill hulked over the town of Divinity. At the crest of the hill, behind an ornate black cast-iron fence that was nearly swallowed by vines, crouched a dark, forbidding edifice flanked by turrets at the north and south ends. It peaked at five stories, its west-facing windows blazing like hellfire with afternoon sun, and, despite the brightness of the day, the fortress loomed, a stygian citadel on a high promontory.

It appeared to have been added on to multiple times. The vertiginous lines of the roofs soared and fell, veering off at opposing angles, creating heavily gloomed niches between. It was a colossal structure, sweeping from grand porch to tall chimneys, from turret to balcony to rooftop garden, hemmed by oaks twice the size of any I'd ever seen, their long, wandering, moss-fringed branches brushing perilously near windowpanes.

Crouching high above Divinity, an uneasy blend of whimsical Victorian and funereal Gothic, painted pewter with ebony trim, it squatted, a venomous spider presiding over the town, studying its meticulously spun web of streets below. The structure fascinated and repelled me in equal measure. I wanted to explore the oddity; I never wanted to set foot inside it. I shuddered, hoping I wasn't expected to stay there tonight. "Is that a hotel?" *Please say no,* I willed silently.

Mr. Graham laughed softly. "Private residence."

I hadn't realized I was holding my breath until it exploded in a sigh of relief. I wouldn't be sleeping there. Good. "That's a *house?*" More a mountain of malevolence, watching Divinity with shuttered eyes. "It's enormous."

"Oldest in town, built on the spot the first settlers chose. The original, centuries-old cabin was incorporated into it. The first families still hold their funerals in the cemetery up there."

I forced my gaze away from the house with reluctance, with relief. The chill retreated as the ordinariness of the day washed back in, and I was suddenly embarrassed by how spooked I'd become. "I didn't think there were any hills in Louisiana." This was coastal plain, renowned for its unbroken flatness.

"We got a few. Watch Hill's the tallest in the state at six hundred fifty-four feet above sea level. Divinity's fifty feet above sea level, then there's New Orleans at eight feet below, which causes countless problems. We don't advertise our hill either. Louisiana's pride, Mount Driskill, is only five hundred thirty-five feet, and folks flock in droves to hike it, litter it up, and spoil the beauty."

One day I would marvel that the largest hill in the state of Louisiana had been kept so secret that only Mount Driskill appeared on maps, but by then it would seem trivial compared to the countless other impossibilities I was facing.

When I withdrew some of what remained of my dwindling store of cash—a waitress never fails to tip—he waved away my money, assuring me Mr. Balfour had taken good care of him, and directed me to the door.

"Will you be driving me back to New Orleans tomorrow?"

"Welcome to Divinity, Ms. Cameron. It's good to have you here," Mr. Graham replied, as he got back into the car.

"Grey," I corrected. But the door was closed and he was already driving away.

JAMES BALFOUR WAS a distinguished gentleman of seventy-six, though he didn't feel a day over fifty, he told me, blue eyes twinkling. He had the bearing of a retired actor aware of his every move, an abundance of white hair, a ready smile, and genteel manners. Fit and trim, he moved with the easy grace of a man decades younger, gesturing expansively as he talked. It was my guess he'd been a trial attorney at some point in his career, arguing cases with dramatic flair. His dark blue tailored slacks, light sweater, and expensive watch made me grateful I'd slipped into my other dress instead of jeans. Before getting down to the business at hand, he insisted I indulge in a glass of sweet tea and a thick wedge of the seven-layer caramel cake his wife, Lennox, had baked that morning.

By the time he set aside his plate and rose to gather a leather attaché from his desk, I was in the throes of a sugar rush and more than ready to find out about my alleged inheritance so I could go to my hotel and shower. If I didn't wash the smell of Kellan off me soon, I was afraid I might devise a loophole to one of my inviolate rules, return to New Orleans, and hunt him down, telling myself I deserved a fabulous farewell fuck before flying back to my miserable life. I was already halfway sold on the thought.

Throughout the day, flash after flash of our night together had slammed into me, virtually blanking my mind each time. I'd caught myself losing focus on the driver's conversation, wondering where Kellan lived, how he lived, what kind of businesses he ran, what style of house he lived in. What music he listened to, if he read books, what he did in his free time. Did he date often, casually, indiscriminately? Or was he picky, like me? Did he always fuck like that? Was last night as different for him as it had been for me, or was I the inconsequential recipient of what I'd so recklessly bestowed on others in the past? Had the best sex of my life been nothing more than a never-to-be-repeated, meaningless one-night stand to *him*, or had I gotten under his skin as deeply as he'd gotten under mine? Was he thinking about me today?

I felt like such an idiot! I was actually wondering if a man was thinking about me today. What was wrong with me? I'd never wondered such things before. It was mortifying. I didn't like this Zo at all. I entered clean and swift and exited the same way.

Too clean, darling, Mom would say. She'd blamed herself for my lack of boyfriends. There was truth to that. When you know upon arrival you won't be staying long, you unpack only what you need, acquire no knickknacks, hang no pictures on the walls. Nothing is permanent. You know it, you adapt.

"As I told you on the phone," Mr. Balfour said, resuming his seat on the sofa opposite me, placing the attaché on the coffee table between us, "you've been left an inheritance as the deceased's sole living heir."

So swiftly was the hope I'd been clinging to dashed—I would find no family here. I'd had a single other relative, but that person was also dead. I truly was an orphan, the last of my line. "There were no children?"

"A daughter, but she died long ago."

"How were we related?"

"I'm not privy to that."

"But it's definitely my maternal side, not my father's?"

"I believe."

"Believe?"

"Upon review, I found nothing in my file. Juniper must have mentioned it; I merely failed to notate it."

"Surely you need more verification than someone's say-so that we're kin."

"If Juniper said you're related, you are. I had the privilege of working for her for fifty-two years. She made no mistakes, left nothing to chance."

There wasn't a person alive who'd made no mistakes. "How did she find me?"

"I'm not privy to that either, but she assured me the genetic testing was conclusive. You are unequivocally related."

There went my inheritance, whatever it was. "I've never done genetic testing."

He arched a brow with a wry smile. "That you know of."

I arched a brow in return. "What's that supposed to mean?"

"Do you get your hair cut in a local salon? Take your trash out to the curb overnight?"

My eyes narrowed. "You're telling me this Juniper of yours would have pilfered my trash, hunting for . . . I don't know what, Band-Aids or hair?"

"She'd have pilfered more than that, Ms. Grey. Although I find it more likely she had her private investigator follow you to a hair appointment and collect samples from the floor when no one was looking. She'd been hunting for blood kin for decades."

"When did she die?"

"Nine days ago."

Six days after my mother.

"Juniper found your mother through hospital records. I understand she was ill and then . . . the fire. I'm so very sorry for your loss."

"Medical records are private. But I suppose the kind of woman that would steal someone's hair wouldn't balk at illegally accessing medical records. Sounds like a real winner, this Juniper of yours."

He laughed. "*Your* Juniper. She's your relative, and I see it in you already. You've got the same take-no-guff attitude. You also narrow your eyes the same way when your temper rises."

"I, however, don't believe the end justifies the means," I retorted, unaware my assertion would soon be put to the test, and I'd find myself willing to employ any means, any at all. No line of demarcation between light and dark, right and wrong. Funny how swiftly survival instinct breaches what you once deemed unbreachable.

"Perhaps you've never had as much at stake. Once you've signed the papers, the settlement is incontestable, not that there's anyone to contest it. I set up the trust myself, and it affords protection for both your interests. You're welcome to have an attorney of your own look over it before you sign, and, in fact, I encourage you to do so. However, the contingencies of the inheritance are nonnegotiable. They must be met with no deviations or infractions."

That sounded ominous. I was bristling again. The astute Mr. Balfour noticed and offered, "As for the details of how you're related to Juniper, it's likely you'll find that information somewhere on the estate, in her paperwork. I'm not withholding facts from you, Ms. Grey. In my role as her solicitor, I'm simply not privy to them." He frowned, then added, "She said there was a necklace worn by various branches of the family and your mother might have had one?"

"Nothing comes to mind."

"She didn't have a favorite necklace?"

"Mom wasn't much for jewelry," I said. "Now we'll never know. I lost everything in the fire."

Not quite everything. Tom Harris had phoned a few days ago to tell me they'd salvaged enough to fill a small box. A fireproof safe in mom's closet had been crushed by falling debris, but the contents were intact. I'd made plans to collect them upon my return. I suspected I'd find little more than paperwork, but hoped there would be more; special photos Mom had tucked away, loving mementos that had survived the fire that I could clutch while weeping. A scarf she'd worn, to which clung the priceless scent of my mother. I didn't have a single picture of her. I ached to curl

in bed, laughing, weeping, reminiscing, but had only my duffle, an urn of ash, and memories that would grow increasingly
blurred around the edges with the passage of years.

"It was a small seven-pointed star on a delicate chain."

"I'm surprised Juniper didn't have people break in to search
our house for it," I remarked caustically.

"Juniper was an exceptional woman, brilliant and devoted to
this town, but she'd known she was dying for some time. She
would have been one hundred and three years old this year. She'd
grown desperate to find an heir. She had no wish to leave her estate to a stranger or have it fall into disrepair. It meant everything
to her, and it means a great deal to our town, too. She was deeply
loved, and her passing is deeply grieved. Juniper was a generous
spirit and committed to those she cared about. Yes, Ms. Grey,
she was ruthless about finding you, but if she hadn't been, she'd
have died heirless. When she confirmed you were related, I'd
never seen her happier. She hoped to bring both you and your
mother here."

"Why didn't she contact us herself?"

"She slipped into a coma. I phoned after she passed. When
the call to your home didn't go through, we knew of no other
way to reach you, so the investigator flew back up, only to learn
your house had burned to the ground. We feared we'd lost you
both, but when Chuck went to the fire station, they told him you
weren't home when it happened and gave him your cell phone
number."

I was abruptly exhausted, as if the past few years had caught
up to me all at once, leaving me hollow and drained. "What is
this inheritance?"

"It's complicated."

"Why doesn't that surprise me?"

"Juniper wasn't looking merely for someone to whom she might leave her estate. She hoped her heir would love it as much as she did and choose to live in Divinity. Could you see yourself living here, Ms. Grey?"

I stared at him blankly. I couldn't see past the next five minutes. "I have no idea. I've been here all of an hour."

He said gently, "It's not as if you have a home to return to."

There was that. I wasn't looking forward to sleeping on a blowup mattress in an empty studio again. "I take it she left me a house." Could be a blessing, if it was livable and had furnishings, even if they were as sadly outdated as they were bound to be, given her age. I envisioned worn carpeting, tattered upholstered chairs, a yellow Formica dinette set in the corner of a tiny linoleumed kitchen. I didn't care how old the bed was or what it looked like, so long as it had a mattress.

"She did. But you must live in it to inherit."

"How long?"

"Three years."

"*Years?* It's not mine until then?"

"I'm afraid not."

I surged to my feet, strode past the desk, and stood at the window, staring out. Though I despised winter and loved what I'd seen of the climate in the south, it would be a drastic change. I might be an orphan, but at least back home I knew people. Down here, I wouldn't know anyone, except a dangerously seductive man in New Orleans I'd prefer to stop thinking about. There was comfort in familiarity, in navigating habitual landmarks, and Este lived less than an hour away from Frankfort. Was I expected to pay rent? How much was the mortgage? What if it needed costly repairs?

"That's ridiculous," I clipped over my shoulder. "What kind

of person forces you to live in a house for three years before you even own it?"

Mr. Balfour said, "During that time, all bills, utilities, and maintenance will be paid by the trust. Additionally, you will be given five thousand dollars a month to cover living expenses, for an annual total of sixty thousand dollars."

I gasped, stunned by the amount. No bills to pay plus an income of sixty thousand dollars?

That was life-changing!

If I stayed the entire three years, I'd receive one hundred and eighty thousand dollars. I could barely fathom it. I could get a job and save every penny, set up a long-term payment plan with my creditors. I'd actually *own* a house! I'd never asked myself what I wanted to one day be, what college major I might choose. Those thoughts were too painful when I knew they would only become reality if Mom was dead.

One hundred and eighty thousand dollars meant I could go to college in three years. Or, if there was a university nearby, I might even take a class or two while I was here. With a degree, I'd qualify for a job that paid well and eventually be able to dig myself out of debt, build a life.

Dreams I'd refused to let myself entertain exploded in my mind. My passions were baking, nature, and animals. I could go to culinary school, study horticulture, or pursue a degree in veterinary sciences. If I couldn't get a scholarship for graduate school, I could at least become a technician while taking classes at night. My world was abruptly, dizzyingly rich with possibility.

"At the end of the first year, you inherit one million dollars."

I whirled to face him, blood draining from my face. Maybe there wasn't a yellow Formica dinette set in the kitchen.

"At the end of the second year, you inherit another million."

My heart began to pound, and my knees were suddenly weak. Maybe that kitchen had a dishwasher, a really nice stove with a gas range and those pretty red knobs. Carefully, I made my way back to the sofa and sank onto it. "And at the end of three years?" I managed to say weakly.

"At the end of three years, you inherit the house and the entire estate, the liquid portion of which is currently valued at one hundred and forty-seven million dollars."

I opened my mouth and closed it again, sagging limply against the sofa, the unfathomable figure echoing inside my skull.

One. Hundred. Forty-seven. *Million*. The liquid portion. What the hell was the nonliquid portion?

"The nonliquid portion will take a bit of an education to understand," he said, as if reading my mind. "The estate's investments are complex."

"Is this some kind of joke?" I finally managed to whisper.

"Absolutely not. Perhaps now you understand why she was ruthless about finding you."

I certainly did. If I were leaving that much to an heir, I too would have stolen DNA and accessed private medical records. It took me several long moments to say weakly, "And you're *certain* we're related?"

"Unequivocally."

I locked eyes with him and searched his gaze intently, opening that inner part of me that sees too much in people's eyes. I discerned no hint of falsehood. He genuinely believed what he was saying. If there was any deceit in this situation, both of us were being fooled.

"Juniper made alternate plans, with which she was satisfied in case she was unable to locate a living relative. Under no circumstances would she have bequeathed her estate to a stranger. She'd have employed the alternative."

I fished for something intelligent and composed to say, but all that came out, so faintly it was little more than puffs of air with a hint of vocalization, was, "Okay. Then. Well."

With one hundred and forty-seven million dollars, I could buy a culinary school, a dozen veterinary practices! I cast about desperately for something more substantial, perhaps even intelligent to say, finally seizing upon, "What can you tell me about the house? Where is it?" With luck, it was one of the pretty Victorians on the main thoroughfare.

"You might have noticed it on the way in."

My hopes soared.

"It graces the peak of Watch Hill."

"That *monstrosity* is my *house*?" The primitive, instinctive response exploded from my mouth before I could stop it.

Graces was hardly the word I'd have chosen. I'd have gone with *looms diabolically*, perhaps *postures predatorily*, even *a menace to the town*. The only thing I'd seen in all of Divinity capable of icing my blood and striking dread into my heart was the very thing that had been left to me.

Mr. Balfour's nostrils flared. His gaze chilled, and he took several measured breaths before suggesting tightly, "You may not have looked closely, or perhaps the light wasn't quite right. Cameron Manor is the most gracious, inviting home I've ever seen. You haven't been inside yet. *Do* try to keep an open mind."

I'd been grateful I didn't have to sleep there tonight. Now he expected me to sleep there.

Alone.

For three years.

Still, I'd insulted the home of someone he'd cared deeply

about, and Mom had raised me better. "I'm sorry; I'm certain you're right, I must not have gotten a good look at it." I wasn't certain of that at all, but it was the thing to say.

Stiffly, he replied, "I'm afraid I've overwhelmed you, Ms. Grey. Perhaps you'd like to adjourn for dinner, have a glass of wine, relax, and let your mind settle a bit."

Belatedly, I understood my driver's parting comment. "That's why Mr. Graham called me Ms. Cameron. She was Juniper Cameron of Cameron Manor."

"He shouldn't have addressed you as such. There's no codicil in the will that requires you to change your name. Juniper hoped you might choose to, but only of your own volition. Evander is a good man who dearly loved Juniper, and he spoke from grief. We miss her, and you're her kin. We hope you decide to stay with us, but every bit of this is your choice. You can leave tomorrow and never look back. You can stay as long as you wish while you make up your mind. You can live at the house for a year, and if at the end of that time you no longer care to remain, you leave with a million dollars and the estate passes to the alternate."

A million dollars. My God, the things I could do with it. Live anywhere I wanted, do anything. Be free, light, weightless, a buoyant feather. Feeling mercenary but compelled nonetheless to clarify, I said, "Unencumbered in any way?"

"Of course. It's all spelled out in the paperwork you'll sign. If you stay two years, you'll leave with two million."

I'd lose my mind doing nothing for two years. I needed a job.

I hadn't realized I'd said it aloud until Mr. Balfour's eyes were again sparkling and his tone warm. "You're two of a kind. Juniper couldn't stand an idle moment either, although she found running the estate and heading her charities and committees a full-time occupation. Still, I'm certain any establishment in town would be delighted to have you. I could put out feelers, see who's hiring, if you wish."

"Thank you, but if you don't mind, I'd like to go to my hotel now." My head was spinning, and I needed to be alone.

"Oh, my dear, I'm afraid I didn't . . . You see, I thought . . ." Mr. Balfour trailed off.

"I'd stay . . . *there*." I couldn't bring myself to say the words *Cameron Manor*. It would make it too real. Live in that enormous, shadowy citadel all by myself? "How big is the house?"

"Square feet?"

I nodded.

He frowned. "Truth be told, I have no idea. It's never been on the market. I don't believe it's ever been measured."

"Do you know how many bedrooms it has?"

He shook his head and said, with unconcealed disappointment, "I was never given a tour of the entire manor."

"Twenty-five, thirty thousand square feet?" Our house in Indiana had been barely a thousand. I was offering numbers I couldn't comprehend. My guess at the size of it made me feel ridiculously small. I could only imagine how Lilliputian being inside the monstrosity would make me feel.

"Quite likely more. The fifth floor is small. It used to be the maid's quarters, but Juniper had it sealed off, as it wasn't structurally sound. There's a basement—with a marvelous wine cellar, by the way—that adds considerable square footage, and an expansive conservatory, which houses exotic flowers and trees. Juniper hosted parties at the manor all the time, threw a fabulous annual Halloween bash for the town. I imagine you'll find photos of that and many other celebrations at the house. She hired a professional photographer for such events."

"She lived up there all by herself?" Over a hundred years old in the macabre old mansion? If she could do it, so could I. But I'd rather not do it alone.

"Yes, although in later years, she had a nurse on-site."

"If I choose to stay, could I have someone live with me?"

"I'm afraid not. Guests are acceptable but no full-time residents for the first three years."

"Any limits regarding guests?"

"Daily visitors at your discretion. You may have one overnight guest, two weekends a month starting Friday at six in the evening, ending Sunday at the same time."

"I find that disconcertingly controlling." Not to mention, bizarre.

"Juniper was heavy-handed when it came to the passing of her estate. I disagreed with her on the guest issue. After a bit of time, say six months, I won't monitor the comings and goings of your company, so long as you don't breach it so flagrantly it becomes difficult to ignore. After three years, the contingencies no longer apply; the estate is yours, and you may do as you wish. A daytime staff cares for the manor. We've several wonderful local chefs if you'd care to retain meal services. There are maids, carpenters, pool crew, gardeners, and the like. We've had the pantry stocked, and Lennox took the liberty of placing a few casseroles that just need heating in the fridge, along with an assortment of essentials. The house is clean, ready, and waiting for you. If and when you've a mind, my wife—my better half, we've been married since graduating high school, and she's a gem to have put up with me this long—would love to meet you, show you around town a bit. Lennox knows everyone, can help you get a feel for Divinity."

We sat in silence for a time while I tried and failed to wrap my mind around a single element of what he'd said. "You're absolutely *certain* I'm Juniper Cameron's relative?" I said finally. I couldn't shake the feeling this was some kind of prank, but I couldn't see what anyone stood to gain from it.

"Juniper was, and that's all that matters. The papers are drawn up, awaiting your signature. Once you sign, the transfer of the estate is irrevocable so long as the contingencies are met."

I lapsed into another silence. Half of me was insisting I leap up, pounce on the papers, and sign this very instant before such a stupendous opportunity was snatched away. The other half was telling me to run like hell and pretend none of this had ever happened. The inheritance, like the town, seemed too good to be true. Life didn't work this way for Grey women. I understood hardship, running, sacrifice, and premature, painful goodbyes. I understood attaching to nothing, putting down no roots, erasing myself again and again. Struggling to survive. Not a life of luxury, settling somewhere permanently, people seeing to my every need, with more money than I could spend in a hundred lifetimes.

Mr. Balfour said gently, "Ms. Grey, I don't know you, but I get the feeling your life hasn't been easy, and you may find it difficult to believe that good things happen to good people. Life isn't always hard. What do you have to lose? Give it a try. Go see the house. You might find you love it here in Divinity. You and I may not be relatives, but Juniper was family to us, and that means you're family too. Welcome. We hope you choose to make our town your home."

The grief I hadn't allowed myself to release last night was building pressure in my chest. Mom would have loved Divinity. If Juniper Cameron had found us sooner, we'd have had money for the best of care, I'd have had more free time to spend with

Mom, and she wouldn't even have *been* in our house when it burned. She'd still be with me.

God, when would this pain ever stop? Would it, or was there to forever be a Mom-shaped hole in my heart?

"Would you mind driving me up the hill?"

He beamed, eyes twinkling. "I was hoping you'd say that. It would be my pleasure. The view of town from Watch Hill at twilight is divine. We can meet tomorrow and discuss things further, or you can take a few days to relax and think things over. The pool is ready, and you needn't worry about mosquitos. There's a constant breeze on the hill that proves quite the deterrent, plus the landscapers planted abundant floral repellants. The wetlands are a different matter. Do take the time to coat yourself in spray if you go hiking. Perhaps a few nights, even a week in Juniper's lovely home will change your mind."

I wasn't sure my mind needed changing. A million dollars for a year, two million for two, plus sixty thousand annually; if I worked to pay for food and miscellaneous expenses, that would give me another hundred and twenty thousand dollars in addition to whatever I saved. I could pay all of Mom's medical bills and have a fortune left over.

Three years? I couldn't wrap my brain around the possibility of committing to it, or the outcome: one hundred and forty-seven million dollars, ownership of Cameron Manor and whatever the nonliquid estate was.

I was certain, however, that despite my first impression of Watch Hill, for one million dollars, I could survive a single year on the cusp of hell itself.

Of course, at that moment, I had no idea I'd be doing just that.

5

A NARROW ROAD SNAKED UP the steep face of Watch Hill, winding back on itself in hairpin bends. Although I've been called an aggressive driver, Mr. Balfour guided the Mercedes roadster up the peak at a speed that intimidated even me. A time or two I was certain we would roar out of a blind curve and vault airborne off the cliff's edge, but he handled the subtle bank of each turn superbly, accelerating with precision, decelerating rarely.

"The manor you stand to inherit," Mr. Balfour told me with pride as we scaled the ascent, "stands on five hundred and seventy-two acres. Most of it is virgin forest, with spectacular live oaks that have been standing for centuries. The Sylvan Oak is the eldest, at three to four hundred years, with a limb spread of nearly two hundred feet."

I'm not a woman prone to gaping; at least I wasn't before to-day. The largest yard my mother and I ever had was half an acre, and we'd gardened every inch of it, putting up corn and squash, canning beans and pickles. Nearly six hundred acres seemed an entire town to me. I could get lost on my own "lawn."

Oblivious to my shock, he breezed on. "We can discuss the details of Juniper's investments and business concerns, and the trust she established, once you've settled in. The estate itself is a lot to absorb. The manor occupies the west face of the hill. The old cemetery, Watch End, is out to the east. Watch Marsh is a hundred-and-twenty-acre wetlands preserve to the north, and Watch Burren is a cluster of caves—do be careful to let some-one know if you go exploring—to the south. Don't hike too far past the cemetery, or you'll find yourself in the Bottoms with the Littlehollows, which is never a pleasant experience." He grimaced. "We tend to avoid that area. That town—and I'm being generous calling it such—is as dark and unpolished as Divinity is bright and inviting."

"The Littlehollows?" I echoed.

"A family those of us in Divinity tend to give a wide berth. Their ways are not ours."

As we coasted through an elaborate gate that opened via a key fob he passed to me after using, I was surprised to find the courtyard within the Gothic enclosure welcoming, with a tiled circular drive that looped about a mossy three-tiered fountain surrounded by flowers.

I stepped from the car and moved to the fence, pushing my hair from my eyes and twisting it back into a knot, as there was, indeed, a bracing breeze at the peak of Watch Hill. Grasping the iron rails, I peered between them and caught my breath at the picturesque sprawl of Divinity, tiny and tidy, far below. As I'd imagined earlier, the house presided over the town, an imposing sentinel: Watch Hill watching every detail.

Laid out with mathematical precision, the streets ran crisply parallel, divided into neat blocks. At the center of the town was the Commons, through which I'd passed earlier. The spires of four churches loomed, sharp and dark against the gloaming, and lights in the windows of countless homes twinkled. It was charming and idyllic, just the type of town where one might raise children and enjoy a good quiet life. *No crime to speak of,* Mr. Graham had said.

I was turning to tell Mr. Balfour the view was as spectacular as he'd claimed when something exploded from the sky, descending on me, battering my head and clawing at my shoulder. I flung up my arms to protect myself, ducked and shook vigorously, but was unable to dislodge the attacker, so I fisted a hand and took a blind punch at it.

Mr. Balfour cried, "Ms. Grey, that's Rufus! He won't harm you. Don't hurt him. Calm yourself this very instant!"

Something about being told to "calm myself this very instant" tends to have the opposite effect on me, but I went still, doubled over, protecting the sides of my face with my fists while the creature shifted awkwardly on my shoulder and growled. "What exactly is Rufus?"

"An owl. Rufus was Juniper's pet."

I exhaled slowly, collecting myself before straightening. As I stood, the raptor stabilized on my right shoulder, and I turned my head to inspect it. The owl regarded me intently with a single fierce bloodred eye. It had a positively demonic face, its long black ear tufts fluttering in the breeze. *But of course*, I thought dryly, *why would I expect the old woman's pet to be any less forbidding than her house?*

"That's not an owl. I've seen owls, barn owls, snowy owls, great horned ones. They don't look like that."

"Rufus is a Stygian owl. They're unique, and in certain light, their eyes appear crimson. You'll find his are actually a warm yellow-orange in daylight, not that he often opens them in daylight."

The raptor rotated his head in the uncanny way of owls, swiveling to regard me with first one disturbingly scarlet eye, then the next, before leaning in to peck my head. "Ow!" It didn't hurt so much as it startled, but rebuffed by my cry, the owl pushed off my shoulder and flapped to the cleft of a nearby oak, where he sat ruffling his feathers and *whuffing* softly. I cast Mr. Balfour a dark look. "Warn me next time."

He raised his hands in apology. "Had I any idea Rufus might

descend to perch on you, I'd certainly have cautioned you, but I've never seen him approach a stranger before."

"Does he live inside the house? Am I expected to bring him in at night?"

"No. He roosts in the conservatory during the day. Devlin must have let him out for the evening. He'll return near dawn."

"Devlin or the owl?"

"Rufus. He knows to wait in the cubby outside until someone lets him in. Whenever you normally get up is fine. He's a nocturnal beast, his comings and goings crepuscular." He paused before adding with some irritation, "Much like Devlin's."

I'd inherited a monster owl along with a monstrous house. "Who's Devlin?"

An expression of distaste was quickly masked behind what I suspected was his courtroom smile, all teeth and not much else. "He does carpentry about the estate and he's often just . . . around, as if he considers himself entailed with the property. He's not. He's here at your discretion," he added, cutting me a sharp look. "And he works only on the exterior of the house. Any interior work you want done, call me. He does *no* work inside." Then his gaze warmed as he fretted, "I do hope Rufus doesn't frighten you away from us, my dear. You must at least see the house."

"Not at all. I'm just tired. It's been a long day."

"Come. I'll show you in," he said brightly.

"No need. I'll let myself in, grab a bite, and go to bed. I'm sure I'll feel better in the morning." My desire to be alone so I could ponder my unfathomable situation was only slightly greater—and I do mean infinitesimally so, by perhaps a hair—than my dread of walking into the dark, forbidding house by myself. Since learning of my alleged inheritance, not a single flashback of sex with Kellan had crashed, uninvited, into my mind; I was *that* stupefied.

"I'll give you a proper tour," he insisted. "I know the manor and can show you how everything works. The house, landscape, and pool are controlled by a Lutron lighting system that offers a variety of themes, but the panels that operate it are a bit complex."

"Thanks, but I'll give it a go tomorrow and call you if I have questions." I was so overwhelmed that I was going numb. Even my she-dragon was slumped in a silent stupor.

His features tightened at my refusal, and he hesitated a moment before saying, "But of course, Ms. Grey. I'm sorry. On the heels of such a tragic loss, I've given you quite a lot to think about, and, my dear, you must be overwhelmed and exhausted, wanting your privacy. Do try Lennox's chicken pot pie casserole with a side of biscuits before you nod off. It's good old-fashioned comfort food. You'll also find a pan of shrimp and cheese grits with pork chops, and if you've a mind to fry eggs and slice tomatoes, you'll have a proper southern breakfast. Lennox tucked slices of red velvet cake into the freezer if you find yourself peckish for a sweet. Forty-five seconds in the microwave warms the cream cheese frosting to perfection. Till tomorrow, then." He handed me the keys to the house, got in his car, sped about the circular drive, and roared back down the hill to Divinity.

I peered up past heavy drapes of Spanish moss fluttering in the breeze, into the tenebrous depths of the oak. Two eyes stared back, round, vermillion, and unblinking, reflecting the light cast by the lamps behind me, which had flickered on when we arrived.

"Sorry about that, Rufus. You startled me," I murmured. I loved animals and had always wanted a pet, but we'd moved so often and I'd had so little free time between school and work, it was never an option. "Stick around. I could use a friend."

The owl blinked twice, made a loud *clak-clak-clak* sound, and thrust aloft to soar beyond the treetops, vanishing into the caliginous sky.

Bracing myself, I turned to face the other beast at Watch Hill. The House.

Its macabre presence was amplified by proximity, and—so much for Mr. Balfour's glowing tribute to the beauty and charm of Juniper Cameron's manor—the fortress was no more inviting up close than it was from a distance. The turrets were ears on a face as dark and demonic as the owl's; the windows sinister, pale eyes; the double doors a mouth with fangs that might snap me in two were I foolhardy enough to attempt to enter.

It towered over me, jutting into the sky, shades of obsidian against cobalt, and I had a sudden premonition of how inconsequential I was going to feel wandering around inside alone. I decided I would leave the lights on all the time, and if the estate had a problem with the utility bills, perhaps they'd reconsider my desire for a roommate.

I thought back to the details Mr. Balfour had provided on the drive. The original cabin, built over three hundred years ago, was preserved within the house, precisely as it had once stood. The manor had been added on to repeatedly, revamped and expanded in the late eighteen hundreds, expanded and updated again in the nineteen twenties. The exterior was refreshed, and the main floor had been extensively renovated five years ago, along with much of the second floor, but at ninety-seven years of age, Juniper had lacked the stamina and patience to continue, and more than half the house remained as it was over a century past, with the exception of the costly addition of central air. He'd warned me there'd been a "small bit of a charring" due to a rapidly contained fire and parts were in dire need of repair; a few million should cover it, he'd told me, and the estate would see to the expense should I choose to commence the work during my initial three years.

"A few million," I whispered, as I stood staring at the house. He'd mentioned the sum so casually, a pittance. I supposed the return on investments of 147 million dollars might reach that figure annually, making no dent in the principal.

Lamps lit the walkway to a set of wide, curving stairs bracketed by enormous oaks dripping silvery moss, at the top of which a shadowy porch stretched north and south behind an elegant cast-iron balustrade draped with wisteria. The double doors were topped with a stained-glass transom and matching sidelights. Above an assortment of wicker patio furniture, a gently whirling ceiling fan suspended from a tropical blue beadboard ceiling lent the porch an inviting air. If only the house weren't so ominous.

I strode briskly forward, heels tapping on smoke and cream pavers, ascended the stairs, and was halfway across the porch to the door when a flicker of movement to my right wrenched a startled cry from my lips. I whirled, bracing myself for another attack by Rufus.

"Easy, Ms. Grey," a man murmured, approaching with his hand outstretched in greeting. "I didn't mean to startle you. I'm Devlin Blackstone."

I hadn't seen him in the shadows. Shirtless, glistening wet, and beautifully muscled, he had a deep voice with the trace of an accent, not quite Scottish, not quite British, but a blend of things, similar to Este's, as if he, too had been exposed to multiple dialects at an early age. For a moment I simply stared wordlessly. In the vicinity of thirty, give or take a few years, he was tall and broad through the shoulders with the lithe yet powerful build that wasn't found in a gym, but rather laboring in a field or on a construction site. His arms were sleeved in ink and, beneath a six-pack, a T-shirt dangled from the waistband of his jeans, tucked in by a corner. His hair was dark as coal and slicked back as if he'd taken a recent swim. Though decidedly masculine, his face was beautiful, nearly otherworldly in its symmetrical perfection. Something about his eyes, besides their unusual color—a rich burnt umber, blending whisky with copper and a kiss of sun—held an attribute I found equally striking. Mom used to call eyes like his those of an old soul.

He flashed me a smile that nearly made my toes curl. "I'm accustomed to using the pool in the evenings, but as it's yours now, I'll curtail that habit. If you wish. I hope to continue, if you don't mind."

I hadn't yet decided if I planned to stay; I couldn't conceive of this place or the pool as mine, and it was instinctive to be polite and protest he needn't give up the liberty, but his jeans weren't wet, I spied no trunks laid out to dry, and the last thing I needed was this man swimming nude beyond my bedroom window, especially with my volatile emotions. I wondered if the 103-year-old woman had watched with aged eyes and failing body, desire burning in her veins, if we held on to lust that long. "Thank you."

As our hands connected, our eyes locked and something passed between us. A nearly tangible current, like a shock of recognition, familiarity. Yet I'd never seen him before.

"Does that mean I can or can't continue to swim?"

He was so damned beautiful I imagined women granted him whatever liberties he wished and had done so all his life, which made it easier for me to grant him none.

"It means no swimming," I said firmly.

Despite the disappointment in his gaze, he inclined his head and said, "As you wish. Mr. Balfour told me you'd be arriving tonight. I suspected you might find the house overwhelming."

"A bit."

"Most do, at first. It's a lot to take in. Then you fall head over heels in love, and wild horses couldn't drag you away." He noted my expression and laughed. "With the house, not me."

I said dryly, "But I imagine many women do. Fall in love with you."

Smiling, he employed a thick brogue. "Aye, the lassies do seem a wee bit fond o' me, Ms. Grey, I'll no' be lying tae ye about that. It's a hardship I try tae bear with grace."

I laughed. "Are you from Scotland?"

"I've passed a fair measure of time there. Women have a thing for the brogue, especially of late, and accents come easy to me."

"So, Mr. Balfour was the official and you're the unofficial welcoming committee."

"Something like that. Rest easy tonight with no worries on your head. I'll be here if you need me."

"You can't mean the whole night."

"I do."

"That's not necessary," I said with a conviction I didn't entirely feel. "I'll be fine."

"I've no doubt of that, Ms. Grey. You've a look of fierceness about you."

I glanced at the wicker sofa. It was too small for him and there were no pillows or throw. "I can't have you sleeping on the porch the entire night. That's absurd."

"I don't sleep much. Besides, I'll be working out back in the garage most of the night. I'll give you a tour of the manor, if you'd like me to accompany you in?"

I arched a brow. "Perhaps I find you scarier than the house."

"Not possible," he said, and we both laughed. "How about the tour? Would you like me to come in?"

I shook my head.

"Well, then, go on, have a look about. Lock up and relax, knowing you're not alone your first night on the hill. I wouldn't be comfortable coming here for my first time at night, staying by myself in the manor. I'm not sure anyone would."

"So, it's not just me. The house really is big and dark and scary."

"Humor me. Go back down on the walkway."

I glanced askance but did as he suggested.

"Turn around and look up at the house."

I did, and there was that damned instinctive shudder again.

He noticed it. "Now picture it painted white. Or, if you really want to neutralize it, paint it a light green or lilac."

My eyes widened. It felt like an entirely different house, merely by mentally changing the paint color.

"The townspeople never stopped trying to get Juniper to repaint it, but she was wed to history, and those are the original colors. Perhaps you'll make the change. It's the size, the height of it, the towers coupled with the darkness that's so off-putting. Until you discover what lies within. Then you see the beauty. Appearances can be deceiving."

I ascended the stairs. "Thank you. You helped me see it as just a house."

"I wouldn't go that far," he murmured. "Sleep easy, Zo Grey."

"You too." *Devlin Blackstone*, I didn't say. I liked his name. I liked his accent. I liked his body. A lot. And he knew it. I'd have to curb my interest around him. Impossible to flash him one of my seductive looks, unless I fired him afterward, which wouldn't be fair. As a woman who'd lost her job too many times to unfair circumstances, that wasn't a line I'd cross. Yet another of my unbreakable rules.

I pine for the days I used to have them.

He was smiling faintly, as if he knew exactly what I was thinking about him. "If I can do anything, Zo, *anything* at all to help you settle in, feel more comfortable, less alone, you've only to say the word. Whatever you need. I'm here for you."

"Appreciate it. Good night." I injected the coolness of dismissal into my tone. The man was too attractive for any woman's peace of mind, and I was too overwhelmed, too exhausted by a sleepless night last night, to deal with him.

Amusement glinting in his gaze, he inclined his head, turned, and loped down the stairs, disappearing around the corner of the house.

I glanced at the door and paused a long moment, bracing myself. Then I slipped the key into the lock, turned it, and slowly pushed open the door. It slid soundlessly inward, revealing a grand, high-ceilinged foyer with a marble-topped pedestal table adorned with a large crystal vase of cut flowers.

As I took my first step across the threshold, I was assailed by sudden severe vertigo, and, to my astonishment, I fainted.

It was brief, so transient a lapse some would have dismissed it as a stumble of exhaustion, perhaps low blood sugar, but it was more than that. I felt the complete and total interruption of circuitry in my brain, and the instant it happened, I pivoted sharply, positioning my back toward the jamb so the frame might break my fall and prevent serious injury.

That was all the time I had before the darkness at the perimeter of my gaze expanded, obliterating my vision. Blackness swallowed me, and I knew nothing more.

Then I was there again. So temporary was the disruption, I'd only had time to slump against the jamb and melt halfway to the floor. Much to my surprise, my eyes were still open. I was simply there after having not been, as if I'd been vacuumed from my body, then shoveled swiftly back in.

I continued my descent to the floor and sat motionless, assessing myself, unwilling to rise if there was a chance I might faint again. I didn't feel weak in any way. The moment had seemed more mental than physical, for I'd had an explosion of thoughts as I stepped through the doorway: of Mom's death ending the only way of life I'd ever known, and this strange, unexpected, mind-boggling new beginning; of inconceivable sums of money, cemeteries and swamps and caves; of perhaps finally having a place where I might get to stay and belong; of forked paths, roads traveled and not taken, choices and consequences, accompanied by a ponderous sense of finality and inevitability, as if deep in the marrow of my bones a voice had whispered, *But of course, all roads lead here.*

As I pushed up from the floor, I decided perhaps there'd been so much going on in my brain that it had simply shut down, a physically mandated time-out, the shock of so many recent changes congealing in a moment of incapacitation.

"Strange," I muttered, closing the door behind me.

CONCEALED IN SHADOWS on the lawn at Watch Hill, a man said quietly into his cell phone, "It's too late. She crossed the threshold. She staggered, but caught herself and, after a few moments, closed the door. All the lights in the house flickered, but I don't think she noticed. Whatever spell they placed in the entry worked."

A pause, then he growled, "I'm aware it needed to be done before she entered the manor. But Balfour was with her, and I couldn't get close. You know I don't have the power to go up against that one."

He listened a moment. Then, "We tried at the hotel. That rogue bastard got in the way. There wasn't a single house that didn't have witches stationed at the Monteleone, awaiting her arrival. Some for her life, others for her blood. Most wanted both."

After listening again, he replied, "They'll accept her. With Juniper gone, they know the danger they face. The carrion creatures have begun to flock. Some have arrived." He laughed. "And, as you know, some of us were already here to begin with."

Another pause. "Yes, he's on the grounds. Nothing we can do about it. There's never been any controlling that one. Of course, I understand how much is at stake. I'll keep you apprised."

6

I STOOD IN THE FOYER, duffle in hand, free hand opening and closing reflexively, as if grasping at everything and nothing. It's an
old habit of mine when I'm uneasy, reaching for something that
isn't there or perhaps bracing to fend something off. Mom used
to try to get me to stop, but it never worked. After a short absence, the habit always returned.

"Mommy," I couldn't help but whisper, feeling like a little girl
lost, perched on the threshold of an unfathomable new world.

The interior of Cameron Manor was illuminated by amber
radiance from wall sconces, and as I glanced left to right, I saw
the same soft glow in each room. It was a nice touch, just what I
needed to find my way about at night without stumbling through
dark, unfamiliar rooms, crashing into furniture, especially since
I had no clue what a Lutron lighting system was, and figuring
out how to work complex electronics was one of my weaknesses,
as we'd never been able to afford any.

Directly ahead, beyond the table, a wide dark staircase of polished mahogany, tread carpeted with a faded Persian pattern,
ascended within an elaborately carved banister. As I approached
and tipped back my head, the staircase unfurled above me in a
dizzying, seemingly endless rectangle of frames. At the top of
the first landing was a large stained-glass window featuring a
woman in a grove of ancient trees standing between two young
children, holding their hands, beneath which was a plaque pro-
claiming *The Lady of Cameron Manor*.

I supposed that was me now, assuming I decided to stay.

I placed my duffle on the bottom stair and decided to turn left and navigate the main floor in a clockwise fashion until I found the kitchen, where I would heat something and take it upstairs to eat in whichever bedroom looked most welcoming. I had neither the desire nor the energy to explore the house until tomorrow in the daylight. My goal was to see as little as possible before securing the comfort of walls closing in around me and a locked door behind which I might forget the cavernous enormity of the house expanding in all directions. Forget everything. Mom's death. My current mystifying situation. A man who'd reached too far inside me and left me ravenous for more of him.

First was a sitting room, and I registered little more than that it was stylish and elegant before hurrying into a second sumptuously furnished sitting room (how many did a person need?), ignoring, from the corner of my eye, a gloomy corridor stretching an impossible distance, doors on both sides, that branched off into a pitch-dark corridor, ending eventually, I supposed, at one of the turrets.

I was a woman on a mission. I wanted the kitchen and a bedroom, and I wanted them fast. I kept bearing to the right, hoping I was corkscrewing into the center of the house and, in normal house fashion, the kitchen would be at the heart of it.

More dimly lit rooms—a dining room, a butler's pantry with cabinets all the way to the high ceiling, a second, smaller dining room—then I was at the rear of the house, staring past a bistro table and chairs, out a wall of floor-to-ceiling windows at a large illuminated pool, hemmed by a patio of cream and smoke pavers, framed by trellises of lush flowers and vines, sheltered by magnolias and oaks, their boughs bending and swaying in the ever-present breeze, strands of twinkling fairy lights and clusters of blue glass bottles dangling from their limbs. The view was magical, more than I could absorb. I was a starving street urchin, invited to a royal feast, being told not merely to eat my fill, but that I now owned everything I could see. I was rubber-necking, at breakneck speed, between disbelief and jubilation, suspicion and hope. Could all of this truly be mine?

Beyond the pool lay a flower garden, and beyond that, a garage with seven bay doors, a lacy tumble of wisteria falling from the roof to spill down the side, and a pool house with an outdoor clawfoot bathtub and open shower. No sign of Devlin, although I briefly envisioned him there, emerging nude from the pool, water dripping from his dark-skinned body. Once I'd quelled the hot rush of hormones, I acknowledged that I did feel much more comfortable knowing I wasn't completely alone on the hill.

Then I pictured myself waking up here in the morning, going for an early swim, followed by an outdoor shower in the sunshine and jasmine-scented breeze, living in this place, hiking, garden-ing, taming the exotic black owl, getting another pet or two or ten, perhaps even horses. Feeling suddenly light-headed, I had to clutch the back of a chair to steady myself.

If I stayed three years, I'd inherit *150 million dollars.*

I'd own this mansion and the grounds, all the furniture, the pool, the garage, whatever was in the garage, along with an un-fathomable 572 acres. I'd hold the deed to caves and trees and an entire cemetery and wetlands, my very own nature preserve, with an ancient oak tree that was so old and stately, it had a name: Sylvan.

I'd have staff to maintain it all.

I'd have a "nonliquid" portion, too. God only knew what that was.

There would be no limits to what I might do.

This was insanity! Could it truly, possibly be *my* insanity?

For the first time since I'd laid eyes on the forbidding fortress on the hill, I hungered to stay in it, tonight and for countless nights to come. Get to know every inch, claim it, love it. Cameron Manor offered the attainment of inconceivable dreams. I briefly entertained the fanciful notion that somewhere in the ether, Mom had found a magic wand to wave, granting me every wish she might have had for me. If so, her wishes were a damn sight bigger than mine. Downright gargantuan.

The house was hushed, the windows closed, the soft push of air-conditioning the only sound until I turned and my cry of delight shattered the silence.

The room for which I'd been searching was connected to the area in which I stood, and it stretched the length of the pool. I love to bake and grow things—passions I inherited from my mother—and the heart of Juniper Cameron's home was warm, welcoming, a generous, dreamy affair of white countertops with gold veining, white cabinetry, and elegant, enormous appliances.

The floor-to-ceiling windows had clusters of potted herbs arranged before them on milk-paint blue stepladder benches. Dozens more pots dotted the counters; there was rosemary, basil, thyme, lemongrass, sage, saffron crocus. Rope lighting was tucked above crown moldings embossed with acanthus leaves; warm under-cabinet LEDs lent luminosity to polished quartz surfaces. The floor was burnished hand-scraped dark wood. Copper pans gleamed, suspended above the sparkling island that looked to be twenty feet long with seating on three sides. The range was eight burners with red knobs; there were two enormous refrigerators, three dishwashers, and a pantry behind a pair of frosted glass doors.

I stood, transfixed, gazing from counters to island, appliances to potted garnishments and back again, picturing the room filled with friends talking and laughing. I imagined Este visiting, the two of us learning new southern dishes together, spending an afternoon by the pool with an icy pitcher of margaritas and salt-rimmed glasses, music playing, followed by a night out at the Gossamer or the Shadows. Dancing without a care, because my bills were paid and my thoughts weren't obsessively fixated on home, where my mother lay dying, slowly and terribly, without dignity yet with seemingly inexhaustible grace.

My God. Could I really be this dead woman's last living heir?

Surely tomorrow someone would figure out they'd made a terrible mistake and I'd be swiftly dispatched back to Indiana with my duffle, my mother's ashes, and the bitter, all-too-brief taste of an impossible dream scalding my tongue.

Shaking myself from a stupor, I refocused on my mission. I couldn't process one thing more. I hurried to the fridge, heaped biscuits and chicken pot pie on a plate, heated it in the microwave, grabbed utensils, then, keeping my gaze fixed straight ahead because I was now fully on visual and emotional overload, retraced my path to the stairs, where I grabbed my duffle and raced up to find a room to call my own for the night.

I would only be able to absorb the house in small pieces at a time, and it seemed, for a change, time was on my side. According to James Balfour, I had three years to explore it, a lifetime, if I chose to stay, at which point I might paint the exterior sky blue or a delicate spring green.

I was still pretending I hadn't yet made up my mind to accept, but the moment I'd seen the light, airy room where I could bake to my heart's content, that I could fill with friends on holidays, even one day with children of my own, a thin pamphlet of dread had been shoved aside, reshelved behind thick volumes of giddiness and wonder. So easily did the house seduce me; my soul for a kitchen.

The bedroom I selected was directly above that space, also overlooking the pool, with a pair of French doors that opened to a cast-iron, jasmine- and bougainvillea-draped balcony with a small table and chairs where I might have coffee in the morning beneath oak branches nodding gently in the breeze. I concluded that I must have chosen the master suite of the house. It had its own sitting room, a spacious bathroom, and an opulent walk-in closet with a marble-topped dresser in the center, a lighted makeup vanity, and a wall of trifold mirrors with a pedestal upon which one might turn and assess one's outfit—all for a woman who could count her outfits on one hand and unpack using half a drawer.

I shook my head, dazed, and, after finding a light I could leave on low, hurried back out into the bedroom where the underwater lights from the pool reflected a blue dance of water on the ceiling.

I locked the door, tenderly placed Mom's ashes on the dresser, and ate swiftly. Mr. Balfour was right; it was comfort food and amazing. Then I dug my toothbrush from my duffle and brushed my teeth. After hungering for a shower all day, I skipped it to fall into bed, still smelling of Kellan, so I could get my crying out of the way and wake in the morning, rested enough to attempt to make sense of my current situation.

Within minutes and without tears, I was deeply asleep.

I woke in the middle of the night with no idea where I was, recalling my location at the precise moment I realized my mother was sitting on the edge of the bed, staring down at me with an intense expression. She was a younger version of herself, brimming with good health. I'd seen photos of her at this age and always found it hard to believe she'd ever been so vibrant and strong. Her warm golden eyes were clear, not bloodshot from illness and medications; her long chestnut hair, streaked with copper that shimmered metallic in the sun, so like mine, was lustrous and thick, not threaded with gray, and I was struck by how alike we looked. It had become difficult to see the resemblance by the time I started middle school. Mom had always seemed to wisp through our days, paler and frailer than everyone else. It had made me fiercely protective of her.

I blinked, knowing the illusion would vanish, but she was still there, so real I could smell her scent, no perfume, just the way Joanna Grey always smelled, a hint of lilac and something earthy from gardening, wed to something zesty from baking back in those days when she'd still been able to stand in the kitchen with her beloved recipe books, humming and improvising ingredients, depending on how much money we'd had that week for groceries. "Mom!" I cried.

"Zo, my darling!" Smiling, she opened her arms, and I surged up into them, hugging her tightly.

I knew then that I was dreaming, because we don't get second chances for goodbyes. People die, and we get left behind with broken hearts and fractured souls. Still, dreams offer comfort that can be carried into the day, and I was starved for the comfort of my mother. Burying my face in her neck, I inhaled deeply, luxuriating in the moment, all senses engaged until I was no longer smelling the scent of Joanna Grey but a foul putrefaction, as if the cancer had metastasized to her skin, rotting flesh, and I was choking, retching, revolted by the odor.

Her arms tightened painfully around me, crushing the breath from my lungs so viciously I couldn't even cry out, and although I couldn't see her face, I knew she wasn't my mother and never had been, that she wasn't even human. What held me in its gelid, viselike grip was a fleshy pod roiling with greed of such staggering proportions it sucked the oxygen from the room, leaving only flat, life-stealing air. I began to suffocate, my chest working like desperate bellows, mouth wide and straining. What clutched me had no morals, no scruples, no conscience. It hungered for everything, all the time; it was parasitic, saprophytic in its sinister nature, determined to attach, break down, devour, and multiply.

What held me didn't fear the darkness. The darkness feared *it*.

It could eat the darkness and still be hungry for more.

It could eat *me*, leaving no trace that I'd ever existed.

And I suffered the strangest premonition then that, if it did, somehow, inexplicably, no one would ever notice I was gone. I'd never be missed. Not even for one moment.

I clawed frantically toward consciousness. *Wake up wake up wake up, Zo!*

Then I was sitting bolt upright in bed, arms clutching nothing, the stench of rot in my nostrils, mouth wide on a breathless scream, alone in the room. Thumping a fist to my chest, I finally managed a long, desperate inhale.

I heard something then. Or thought I did. But the faint, mocking sound was so impossible I knew it could only be nightmare residue wed to the strangeness of my situation and location, kicking my imagination into overdrive.

For, deep within the walls of the house, I could have sworn I heard someone laugh.

7

When I was thirteen years old (we lied and said I was fifteen), I began cleaning houses with my mother.

Her eyes glistened with unshed tears the morning I got in the car with her for the first time, and I knew she desperately wished her daughter was off enjoying a carefree summer in the Blue Ridge Mountains, not donning a makeshift uniform to go to work. But money was tight, and we never knew when we might have to move again.

Had she given me the choice of cleaning houses or hunting treasures in the forest, scavenging whatever the season offered our table—nuts, berries, mushrooms, tender dandelion leaves; free food delights me to this day—I'd have chosen to clean. Not only did it allow me to finally contribute to our modest income, but houses fascinated me even then, unfolding intimate stories, some safe, others ugly, some happy, others tragic; harboring secrets in drawers, backs of closets, and forgotten pockets.

Before long, I knew which spouses were unfaithful, whose children struggled with grades, hid drugs beneath their mattresses, wrestled with self-image, were being bullied.

I became emotionally invested in those fathers and sons, mothers and daughters, reading diaries it wasn't my right to open, uncovering secrets that weren't mine to know and most definitely weren't mine to do something about, like leaving a phone number retrieved from a pocket on the lid of a washer (once I figured out who got home from work first) or displaying a used condom (swept from beneath the bed of a woman past menopause) atop a wastebasket and failing to bag trash when I left, or moving a concealed diary to a nightstand, hoping a parent might read it in time.

Small things, really, and if certain family members hadn't been keeping secrets in the first place, my actions wouldn't have kicked up a storm. But Adeline was cutting herself, and Keith was having yet another affair and thinking of leaving his wife. How could Mrs. Holden help her daughter, or Mrs. Miller fight for her marriage, if they didn't even know there was a threat?

The third time Mom moved us because of something I'd done, I stopped interfering. That was when I began making my unbreakable rules: *Never care about the people whose houses you clean, or any employer.* They certainly didn't care about us. We weren't even people to most of them. Merely faceless fulfillers of a function.

You're not responsible for fixing their families or ensuring they stay together, nor can you predict good will come from the things you do, Mom had said. A long pause, then sadly, *Do you really feel we're so broken, Zo?*

Her question cut to the quick. We were wonderful, and she was the best of mothers. I was loved and cherished, never hungry, never harmed. Our life was good.

Still . . . we were so unlike the families that lived in those houses of constancy and permanence. It was always just the two of us, slipping quietly into town, melting away in the darkness. As a child, I'd pretended we were good witches, forced to flee a wicked warlock, scrubbing away our tracks with twig brooms scented with cinnamon and clove. I'd needed the fantasy. Easy to begin to feel invisible when you're taught as a child to erase all trace of having been anywhere.

Mom made me feel seen while she was alive. Since the day of

her demise, I'd been wafting about, unnoticed as a ghost, lacking even the solace of a house to haunt.

In time I would understand that on the night I stepped across the threshold of the Cameron ancestral home, I couldn't have been more primed to be seduced by all the house at Watch Hill had to offer had I been raised, intentionally, to succumb. Which was certainly not Joanna Grey's intent.

More than merely four walls, an impossible dream of a life, *home* has always been an irresistible word to me.

WHEN I AWAKENED the next morning, I had seventeen text messages from Este, each more frantic than the last.

Since Mom passed, I'd gotten into the habit of turning off my ringer when I went to bed, desperate for those rare, few hours of sleep I might get. Silencing my phone was a luxury I never had while she was alive. I'd learned to sleep featherlight, lest she need something in the middle of the night or, God forbid—once the cancer had metastasized to bone—stumble and fall on her way to the bathroom, breaking something so badly she'd never walk again. Now to sleep was to temporarily die, feel nothing, a state for which I hungered with every atom of my being, fully aware that the moment my brain kicked awake, the crushing desolation of grief would once again saturate me to the bone.

I was shocked to find I'd slept a solid eight hours, and even more startled to discover that, according to my texts, the police were on their way to my short-term rental in Frankfort, Indiana, to break down the door and see if I was alive.

If it were anyone but Este, I wouldn't have believed it—Chief Beckett hated doing welfare checks, referred them to social services whenever he could—but Este had a way of persuading people to comply with her wishes. She'd saunter in, tall, charismatic, and commanding. Even I had fallen prey to her machinations a time or two, accused her of casting spells to get us to do her bidding. She'd cut me a startled look and said, "I would *never* do such a thing, Zo. The person with the strongest will wins in any situation. You just have to want what you want more than anyone else does. Passion is the currency of the universe."

It didn't hurt that she was gorgeous, with a British Nigerian mother and a Scottish father, blue eyes that ran the gamut from cloudless azure when happy to storm-filled ultramarine when impassioned by something (which was 99 percent of the time), and a fascinating mishmash of an accent. Este was as unpredictable as my life was routinized, could be a total pain in the ass, and I adored her. Most of the time, like any sisters, blood or chosen.

I'm fine. I'm in Louisiana, I texted.

WTF?!!!

I'll call you in a few days and fill you in. She was never going to believe what had happened. I didn't. Given time, maybe I would. Assuming it wasn't all snatched away any second now.

My ass. Talk.

When my phone vibrated, I thumbed it to voicemail. I'd been avoiding her since the day of the fire. Bonding deeply over the challenges the world had thrown our way, we prided ourselves on our strength in the face of adversity, and I'd been anything but strong the past few weeks, weeping at the slightest provocation, battling grief and depression. I despise spreading a mood around if it's not a good one. People have enough problems; they don't need mine. Este and I were similar in many ways, but our lives had diverged sharply since high school. She'd graduated college three years ago, had already begun to establish a reputation as an artist of considerable talent—as she'd informed me so grandly at the age of nine that she would—whereas, until yesterday, I'd been buried in the debt and rubble of my life, unable to see a way to dig myself out. Her star was rising; mine had sunk to the bottom of a pit of wet concrete. I'm still hiding from people. Give me a few more days.

It's been two weeks! That's all you get. Where in Louisiana? Why? And how long are you staying there?

I thought about it a moment, then—avoiding the why—replied, Not sure yet. Maybe indefinitely.

I'll be there this afternoon!

I sighed. Once Este made up her mind, I was as likely to divert a meteor from its path. She'd find a flight, get a cab, and be on my doorstep in a matter of hours if I didn't deflect her with an alternate plan.

How about Friday? Can you get away? Come for the weekend?

I can always get away. Address?

Town called Divinity. Place is Watch Hill.

Address?

I frowned, puzzling. I don't know that there is one. Fact was, the house didn't need one. You won't have any problem finding it. Ask anyone in town, they'll point you to it. I snickered, imagining the look on her face when she glanced up and saw the house for the first time. Wondered if she'd shiver with the same sudden chill.

You can't come before 6 p.m.

Why the hell not?

Long story. I'll tell you when you get here. 6. No sooner.

Although I wasn't remotely convinced the inheritance was genuinely mine, on the off chance it might be, I wasn't about to jeopardize it.

I began to put my phone down, but it lit up again.

Did they find a safe? After the fire?

I blinked. What?

Your mother told me that if anything ever happened to her, there was a fireproof safe in her closet. She wanted you to have it. Do you?

When did Mom tell you that? I hadn't known about the safe, but Este did?

Years ago. I dropped by but you weren't home. She was in a weird mood. She actually offered me tea, like I was a real person and everything. This I could hear Este saying dryly. Our mothers so despised each other, they'd been icily civil to us, at best. Did it survive the fire?

I was still struggling to wrap my brain around the fact that my mother had told Este something she'd not told me. Did you have tea with Mom? I asked, trying to imagine the bizarre event.

Eyeroll emoji. How is that even relevant?! Do you have the damn thing?

It survived the fire. What do you know about the safe?

Nothing, just that she wanted you to have it.

Three dots for a long moment, then,

Has anything strange happened to you since Joanna died?

I equivocated, Strange how?

Answer the question.

We can talk when you get here.

Bet your ass we will. Something happened. But you're okay?

Yes.

Not freaking out about anything?

Not at all.

It was a small, necessary lie. If she thought I was freaking out, she'd be here this afternoon, and I needed time to process my swift and strange reversal of fortune and, with any luck, stop crying uncontrollably at unexpected times. Not at all.

Friday then. 1 pm.

6!

CU☺

6! I mean it! It's important.

That was Este. No rules. She lived audaciously. If passion was the currency of the universe and you got as good as you gave, it was no wonder her life was so rich and colorful, and mine so impoverished. I'd done the right things, the necessary things, stoically and, I hoped, with a bit of Mom's grace. The only passions I'd ever indulged were my one-night stands.

Nor had I ever seen an ounce of explosive passion in Mom. Love? Yes. Deep and unconditional. Quiet joy, frequently. Wild, unfettered energy? Never. Placid mom, placid daughter. Hunter women were explosively self-possessed. Grey women were tidily self-contained. Once I'd also have said Grey women held no secrets from one another. Yet Mom had told Este something she'd never told me. It bothered me more than I cared to think about, so I shoved the thought away, focusing, instead, on the here and now.

As I sprawled in the softest sheets ever to caress my skin, atop the most luxurious mattress on which I'd ever slept, in the finest home I'd ever glimpsed (excluding the hideous, off-putting exterior), I vowed that once I signed those papers—and yes, I *would* sign them; I had no life to which anyone but a fool would willingly return—I would choose my dreams and pursue them as fiercely as Este did. Mom would want no less for me. If heaven, as such, existed and she was there—which of course gentle, good Joanna Grey would be—I imagined she was beaming with joy, delighted by my unexpected reversal of fortune, ecstatic at the abundance of opportunity with which my life was suddenly rife.

Thoughts of Mom jostled to mind fragments of the almost forgotten nightmare. Hugging her, only to realize it wasn't my mother at all. The throat-thickening stench of decay, the greed and evil of the entity that had clutched me. The odd, muffled laugh I'd imagined I'd heard from within the walls of the house.

"Absurd," I snorted, as I tossed back the covers and pushed up from bed. I'd been exhausted, emotionally and physically, in an undeniably strange house and stranger situation. Of course I'd had a bad dream.

My choices for the day staggered me: Shower in a luxurious spa bathroom or take a morning swim? See if there was a car for each of those bay doors in the garage, and use one to go sign papers that would make me a millionaire 150 times over, or stay put and explore the house I was allegedly to inherit? Find Juniper Cameron's office and search for genetic testing that proved we were related, or go down to Divinity to look for a job? Should I get a job or look into nearby colleges?

At the very least, I decided, I should allow myself the three days until Este arrived to acclimate and ponder my options. I had a future to plan, dreams to dream, and, in the sweet, golden light of morning streaming in the window above the pool with the cushioned chaises upon which I was determined to spend at least an hour this afternoon, not one of them was a nightmare.

LAST NIGHT IN the gloom, Cameron Manor had seemed to loom vast and menacingly around me as I, a tiny dot on a map I'd never seen, fumbled my way blindly through it.

In the soft, dewy light of a Louisiana morning, it felt completely different, seeming to stretch invitingly in all directions. *Come see me, explore me, I'm all yours!* it exclaimed brightly.

Inconceivable.

Despite my skepticism, I was game. When I stepped from my bedroom after the most indulgent shower I'd ever taken, finally washing the drugging scent of Kellan from my skin, and the staircase beckoned up rather than down, I yielded to the temptation to explore without purpose. I was mistress of my day for the first time in longer than I could recall and determined to savor the luxury for however long it might last.

As I ascended the stairs, I noticed eight sizeable stained-glass panels set into the roof of an atrium of sorts that capped the stairwell far above me, with what appeared to be manual cranks attached to the frames. Each of the loden and gold panels featured a symbol with three branches of intricate spirals, rotating counterclockwise, that seemed of archaic origin, and I made a mental note to ask Mr. Balfour about them. I was eager to know historic details of the manor, in case it really was my history. The idea that I might have roots stretching back centuries was quietly intoxicating.

When I reached the third floor, I skirted the balustrade, trailing my fingers along the railing, trying to acclimate myself to the idea that this was all soon to be mine—this lovely banister and the decidedly awful wallpaper and the gilt-framed portraits of staid Camerons in antiquated attire. I strode down a long corridor with half a dozen closed doors on either side, which ended in a wide parlor at the front of the house, with fireplaces at each end tall enough to stand upright in; a necessity, I supposed, in centuries before modern heating. The room was furnished more casually than those I'd glimpsed last night, with an eye to comfort, all thick rugs and overstuffed chairs and a plush sectional. It was the perfect place to curl up with a book on a rainy day.

Beyond a west-facing wall of windows, yet another vine-draped, cast-iron balcony spanned the width of the parlor. I opened the door and stepped out onto the narrow terrace, breathing deeply of the sultry morning breeze, staring down at the town of Divinity through the limbs of a pair of colossal oaks bracketing the front entry to the house.

I'd thought the view spectacular from the ground, but three stories up, through a fringe of gently swaying silvery moss, I faced an even more impressive vista. With a high-powered telescope angled the right way, I might examine the minute details of each building, peer into the windows of the homes. Puzzled at the uncharacteristically voyeuristic turn of my thoughts, I glanced over my shoulder and realized I must have subconsciously noted the large telescope on a wheeled base tucked in a far corner, nearly swallowed by a voluminous fall of drape.

My ancestor—if indeed she was—had been a peeping tom. No doubt she'd watched Devlin Blackstone swim nude, too. *Good for her about Devlin*, I thought, smiling faintly. Spying on the town seemed as disconcertingly controlling as her rules regarding visitors, but I decided to allow that, perhaps, at a hundred years of age, she'd had few other pleasures. Or perhaps she'd had reason. Or perhaps she'd not done it at all, but angled the telescope toward the stars.

"You don't want to get in my way this morning, James," a woman said sharply below. "I mean business. Step aside and let me in. I have important matters to discuss with her."

I glanced down and blinked, surprised. I'd been so distracted by the view that I'd failed to notice the drive had turned into a parking lot while I'd slept. Twenty or more cars were parked at hasty angles around the fountain, and dozens of women were jostling on the stairs, ascending to the porch where, apparently, Mr. Balfour stood sentry, refusing to allow them to pass. At the head of the group was a reed-thin woman with shoulder length ice-blond hair, wearing an exquisitely fitted blue suit and heels, pearls at her neck and wrists, expensive sunglasses perched atop her head, designer purse tucked beneath her arm while I, barefoot, in jeans, fidgeted with the hem of my T-shirt, deciding I might rotate my only two dresses for a while. As no one was looking up and likely wouldn't, I melted back a smidge, wondering if "her" was me.

"No one is going inside, Althea," said Mr. Balfour. "No one is discussing anything with her. I told you, you're to give her time—"

"We don't have time! The scholarship fund hasn't been approved, and the deadline is Friday. Ten of Divinity's brightest young graduates still don't know if they can afford university come fall," Althea interrupted.

"To hell with your scholarship fund, Althea," a brunette woman in a peach dress clipped. "The Coventry Women's Clinic takes priority. The opening is Tuesday, and we don't even have the budget to turn the lights on." Tone softening, she added, "No disrespect to Juniper, James. We all know how ill she was in her final months, too ill to be bothered with paperwork of any sort. We're just committed to ensuring her charity work continues."

"How do we even know this *alleged* heir will continue funding Juniper's charities?" Althea demanded. "What about the loans, the entrepreneur of the year awards? What if she just takes the Cameron fortune and runs? Will she care for Divinity as Juniper did? How *could* an outsider? Does she understand the duties and responsibilities that come with the estate?"

"I wasn't about to go into that kind of detail last night, Althea. Ms. Grey traveled a long way and was having difficulty absorbing the terms of her inheritance. She lost her mother a few weeks ago and is still grieving deeply. She needs time, and I mean to see that she gets it. Juniper chose me to handle Ms. Grey's acclimation period as I see fit. That, too, is spelled out in her will."

"Which you still haven't permitted us to see," Althea hissed.

"Nor will I. A last will and testament is a private matter. If you,

Ms. Bean—bearing absolutely no relationship to the deceased, nor were you counted among her friends—choose to contest it, there is a legal arena in which you might do so. I assure you, you won't win," Mr. Balfour replied coolly.

"What about genetic testing? Surely that's been done. When will we see the results?" Althea demanded.

"The same time you see the will," he retorted flatly. "Never."

Althea swiftly switched tactics. "The loss of her mother is yet more reason Ms. Grey would benefit from the warmth of women around her. We'd be of far more use to her at this delicate time than an elderly attorney. A *man*, at that."

"Yes, James, get out of the way and let us in! Let *her* be the one to decide whether or not she wants company," the champion of the Coventry Women's Clinic pressed.

"Absolutely not, Janie," said Mr. Balfour. "Two weeks. You will leave her—and me—in peace for a fortnight. Find ways to delay the openings and scholarships, and I assure you, they will merely be delays. If Ms. Grey doesn't feel up to making the necessary decisions by then, I'll see to the funding myself, via the estate. Now, leave, the lot of you, before you do what you intended and frighten her away."

"She's an outsider," Janie said, determined to push, "and a complete unknown. We don't want her here, and there are far more who feel the same than came with us today. Isabel and Archie can step in without missing a beat."

"If you think for one moment the Alexanders are the solution to our problems, you're more delusional than I thought," Mr. Balfour rebuked her. "She's a blood Cameron, and Juniper spent the final decades of her life and a considerable fortune finding her. Leave now, before Ms. Grey awakens."

I frowned. "Blood Cameron" was an odd turn of phrase.

"I'm not going anywhere," the Coventry Women's Clinic advocate huffed. "I'll set up camp on the lawn if I must."

"You'd hardly dare. Come nightfall, you'd race back down that hill," Mr. Balfour growled.

I frowned. What happened at nightfall? Devlin Blackstone was the only thing I could think of that was crepuscular, to purloin Mr. Balfour's word, and I could scarcely see a woman fleeing him. Rather, she'd race toward him.

"We aren't even certain," Mr. Balfour continued, "that she'll accept the terms of Juniper's will."

Althea rolled her eyes. "If we could be so lucky. There's not a fool alive that would turn her back on Juniper's money. That impoverished bitch is in debt up to her eyebrows, and she won't leave unless we make it clear just how unwelcome she is."

"But she *is* welcome, and *Juniper* is the key word there, as the one who chose Ms. Grey. The matter is final and incontestable. End of discussion," Mr. Balfour said flatly.

Althea demanded, "Arrange a proper reception so we can meet her tonight, and we'll leave. For now."

"My rules, my way, in my time, as Juniper willed it. Don't push me. She didn't keep me at her side for half a century for my legal skills alone." There was a pause, then he added quietly, "As well you know. Unless you wish a reminder."

The air seemed to grow strangely heavy, as if abruptly charged with the oppressive tension of a gathering torrential storm, heat lightning arcing, hot and wild, at the front. It was enough to make the hair on my arms stand on end. I rubbed at sudden goose bumps, watching in bemused silence as, one by one, the women turned, got in their cars, and drove away. How strange! Even venomous Althea left in silence, betraying her ire only by the piss and vinegar in her stride.

Clearly, Mr. Balfour held serious sway and power in this town. I was surprised to find I was trembling.

I was an outsider. Again.

No friends. Again.

Underdressed. Again.

Which shouldn't matter, but the right clothing had a way of making a woman feel as if she were wearing a suit of armor. I'd watched the girls in high school with all the right clothes; they'd been *untouchable*. I sincerely doubted Althea Bean (and, really, what kind of last name was that? At least I wasn't Zo Pea) woke and dressed each day in a suit, heels, and pearls. But when she decided to drop in unannounced on the poor heiress ("impoverished bitch," she'd called me!) who, as far as she was concerned, had stolen the inheritance from its rightful heirs, she'd come dressed for battle. She wasn't on my front step so early in the morning for approval of a scholarship fund. If Mr. Balfour hadn't prevented their entry, if I'd opened the door barefoot, with wet, uncombed hair and no makeup, to find that pack of women on the step, it would have made me feel as small and out of my depth as she'd intended. Temper flared, white-hot, startling me with its intensity, as the dragon in my belly snorted fire, demanding I take instant, aggressive action to defend myself and *check that bitch*, which was just weird. I was steady, moderate Zo. My way was to analyze obstacles, nuance difficult situations, not lash out. Yet adrenaline was surging through my body, and I positively *itched* to start a fight.

Stilling myself, I breathed, slow and measured, for several moments until my hands unclenched. To my astonishment, I saw that I'd fisted them so hard my nails had pierced my palms. Grief clearly intensified *all* emotions, not just sorrow, and I would need to be on guard against it.

The fact was, Ms. Bean's behavior was understandable. (Ah, *there* was pragmatic, see-it-from-everyone-else's-point-of-view Zo.) Well, maybe not entirely understandable, but local resistance to my presence certainly was. I'd been too stupefied by the sudden, surreal reversal of my fortunes to consider some folks in Divinity might be less than thrilled by my arrival, resenting that a complete stranger—and a young one at that—had been bequeathed the scepter and mantle of their beloved century-old matriarch. Clearly, Juniper had been vital to Divinity, funding countless endeavors, championing education and fledgling business ventures. Townsfolk were bound to be curious, resentful, wary.

"Forewarned," I murmured as I stepped back into the parlor and gently closed the door behind me. *Is forearmed*, Mom used to say.

I hurried back to my room to finish drying my hair and apply a bit of makeup. The clothing I couldn't do anything about. Nothing I owned was on Althea's level.

Except the steel in my soul.

8

AFTER FORTIFYING MYSELF WITH COFFEE and a generous portion of Lennox's creamy chicken pot pie casserole, followed by two fluffy biscuits smothered with peach jam, I phoned Mr. Balfour. Having lived on whatever was cheapest and quickest to prepare for the past few years—translated: packaged and highly processed—I found home-cooked food to be a sorely missed treat. When the attorney didn't answer, I left a message, asking if he had time to meet me at the manor this afternoon.

My mind was a murky jumble of thoughts, but one was crystal clear: it was imperative I head the intractable Ms. Bean off at the pass, firmly and tactfully. Mobs, even smallish covens of well-heeled women, had a tendency to escalate, unredressed. Some of my most difficult patrons in restaurant work had been the well-dressed, seemingly mannered ones. I'd learned not to judge any book by its cover, working in the service industry.

I wasn't a person to do things halfway. On the rare occasions I committed to something, I committed 110 percent. If—no, *once*—I accepted this inheritance, my every move would be watched, my motives second-guessed, my decisions subject to ruthless scrutiny, which made it crucial I start out as I intended to proceed: firm, fully invested, and capable, or if incapable of something, open to instruction on the matter. Stepping into the vacancy left by Juniper Cameron with anything less than competence and conviction would never fly here. The beneficent matriarch had been a force of nature and nurture. I hoped we were related, not merely for the financial legacy but that of character.

I knew nothing of my ancestry. The possibility I'd sprouted from fine, strong roots conferred a tantalizing sense of familial pride. I was grateful that, although I was only twenty-four, I'd lived a life of hard work and responsibility. Had I lived the kind of childhood I'd once envied, I'd not have been half as well suited for the challenges I faced.

As I was stepping through the back door to the rear courtyard, Mr. Balfour texted:

Does 1 work for you? I don't know which bedroom you chose but Juniper's suite is on the south end of the first floor. I do hope we've not intruded but Lennox took the liberty of procuring clothing and whatnot for you when she learned of the fire, and you'll find it in a closet there. We suffered a similar loss and know how time-consuming it can be to replenish.

"Time-consuming," he'd said, with his genteel southern manners, when the accurate word was *impossible*. I had no doubt he knew to the exact penny the appalling extent of my debt. Was there a single detail he and his wife had failed to consider? My recent concern, that I'd appear the poor relative I was, and feel lesser for it, had been addressed before I'd arrived. How would I ever get used to living like this—my needs anticipated and met before I even comprehended them myself?

1 is perfect. How kind and thoughtful of Lennox, thank you. Thrusting the phone in my back pocket, I stepped out onto the patio of cream and smoke pavers hemming the pool, delighted to find them warm beneath my bare toes. Up north, it was thirty-eight degrees and drizzling this morning; I'd checked. Then I'd done a small happy dance in the shower, celebrating the fact that I was

here, not there. My emotions certainly were . . . effusive today, my happiness giddy, my ire combustible.

Only yesterday, I'd been hoping the attorney had booked me into a hotel with a pool so I might soak up some sunshine before returning home. Now, beneath a sunny, cerulean sky, I stood in a spectacular garden courtyard—sandwiched between the rear of the manor and the wisteria-draped garage that matched the house for its formidable width—which boasted a resort-style pool with six fountains, four fire bowls, two Baja shelves with sparkling white chaises, a hot tub large enough to seat a dozen, a winding water slide, a lovely outdoor kitchen beneath a vine-draped pergola, a dining area, and a large seating cozy with cushioned sofas and a fire pit.

All of it, allegedly, mine.

I *never* had to check out and go back home.

I'm not much of a curser. Mom drilled into my head that I was given a brain, it was my responsibility to use it; that resorting to tired imprecations betrayed a lazy, undisciplined mind. But the fact is sometimes all you can do is shake your head and say, "What the fuck? Did I die in that fire, too, and this is heaven?"

I didn't, and it wasn't. I was here, and Mom wasn't, and she would never get to see the magnificence that was Watch Hill or watch me become more than either of us had ever dared dream I might one day be. Heart aching with grief, tears filled my eyes.

"Whuf-whuf-whuf."

I glanced behind me to find Rufus perched on the back of a pillowed chaise, head cocked, studying me with eyes of orange flame.

"I lost my mother in a fire," I told him miserably, sniffling, "and I miss her so much it feels like my soul is hemorrhaging."

"Whuf."

Wiping my eyes with the back of my hand, I forced myself to gather my grief and pack it away. I'd promised myself to corral it, permit only certain, specific hours of the day for weeping, and, by and large, I succeeded. "I suppose you want in."

"*Whuf-whuf.*"

"I thought owls hooted. What's with the whuffing?"

"*Hoo-hoo.*"

I blinked. "Some of them say 'pretty girl.'"

Pumpkin eyes regarded me, unblinking.

Snorting at my fanciful notion that the fierce dark owl, which didn't look remotely domesticated, might echo me like a well-trained parrot, I said, "Come on, I'll let you in."

The midnight raptor thrust off with powerful talons, soaring high before swooping low to skim the length of the courtyard, gliding effortlessly, with the barest twitch of a wingtip, to circumvent trees and shrubbery, fountains and statues, before alighting in a cubby above the door of a three-story greenhouse at the southernmost tip of the expansive garden.

I hurried to join him.

THE HOUSE MEANDERED in an unfathomable maze, and I swiftly concluded my guess at the square footage was woefully inaccurate. I estimated the greenhouse alone at five thousand square feet. I'd permitted myself only the briefest of peeks inside, as I watched Rufus glide up to settle on the limb of a jackfruit tree. If I entered, I'd lose the entire morning wandering around, staring open-mouthed at the abundance of exotic trees, foliage, flowers, and herbs. I'd glimpsed kumquat trees, as well as lemon and lime, hemming brick pathways; caught the scent of countless herbs and spices mingling together. Somewhere inside the lovely glass-roofed conservatory, a waterfall cascaded over stone, pooling into an unseen basin, adding humidity to the already humid clime. A waterfall—inside the house! I fancied, if the basin were a small pond of sorts, on a full moon night, I might immerse myself in those waters, salting them with my tears.

After closing the door to the greenhouse, I made my way back to the main stairs of the manor, picked the middle of three southern corridors, and headed off in search of Juniper's suite, hoping her office, with the all-important genetic testing, would also be in that direction.

My disorientation grew with every step. Breadcrumbs would have helped, but what I really needed was a stack of Post-its and a Sharpie. I made a mental note to grab them, assuming I ever found a study in this place, so I could tack one to the entrance of each corridor, noting which rooms could be found in that direction, until I got the lay of the land, assuming I ever did. Part of the problem was the seemingly endless interior rooms with no windows but multiple connecting doors, which twisted and turned into side corridors, making it easy to wander in circles without a view of the yard to get my bearings. Another part of it was that those interior rooms were only dimly lit by the same amber wall sconces, and I had, as yet, no clue how to work the Lutron lighting system. I'd poked tentatively at one of the computer panels on the wall but found the myriad options mystifying. We didn't speak the same language, technology and I.

I opened door after door: a room of hundreds of folding chairs and tables, shelves of linens and tabletop décor for entertaining, another room filled with spring and autumn outdoor decorations, yet another of Christmas garlands, artificial trees, a hundred or more large red trunks of, I assumed, ornaments and jumbo lawn decorations, including an elaborate Santa on his sleigh, and nine life-size reindeer. God, the Christmas party I could throw!

There was a room I could only compare to a petite grocery store, stocked with toilet paper, paper towels, bottled water, dish soap, laundry soap, and other household essentials. Another stuffed with linens of every kind. A closet filled with boxes of expensive perfumes, designer scarves and bags, haute couture ties, all with elegant gift boxes, ribbons, and cards placed neatly beside them. She had a gift closet. Who even did that?

With each door I opened, my astonishment escalated. This wasn't a house. It was a small town, boasting its own private boutiques.

Then I was through the maze of interior rooms, staring down a high-ceiling corridor (with more doors on each side I resolved not to open) that ended in a pair of tall doors with ornate brass and crystal handles. There was something about those doors, the elegance of them, their imposing placement beneath an elaborately carved arch, the polished, dark wood, and, in the center of each upper panel, an etching of two Trinity knots merged together that whispered, *You will find Juniper Cameron here.*

I knew in my bones that this was *her* hallway. She'd walked this corridor thousands of times; she'd lived and slept and dreamed at this end of the house, and it seemed those dreams wafted still in these walls. She was here in the faint scent of spicy roses blended with a subtle perfume that was crisp and clean. (I would later learn that for more than seventy years, maids had been placing a fresh vase of ivory and blue roses in both her suite and her office each morning, and they continued to do so after her demise; that her favorite cologne was Gra Siorai, created only for her by an exclusive French perfumery.) She was here in the solemn hush of the hallway, in the regal crown moldings and elaborate wainscotting between doors, the tasteful blue and cream herringbone carpet in the hall.

Hand reflexively opening and closing, I felt abruptly apprehensive, an interloper where I had no right to be, and realized I was swiftly becoming like the townspeople who held her in such high regard. But how could I not? She had so much, she'd *done* so much, she'd cared for this town for nearly a century. How could I live up to her legacy when I wasn't even certain I could find my way back to the room I'd slept in last night?

Mr. Balfour thought I might have chosen the suite that lay beyond those doors as mine.

Never.

I'd stay in my modest (yeah, right, but in comparison, certainly) bedroom on the second floor, which I'd found so opulent and over-the-top last night that I'd believed it to be the master suite. There was wealth, and there was *insane* wealth. I was treading in the realm of the insane.

I realized I was breathing shallowly, relaxed my hand, squared my shoulders, took a deep breath, and marched down the hall toward those intimidating doors.

I nearly jumped out of my skin when a door to my left flew open and two maids stepped out, pushing a cart piled high with freshly laundered bedlinens, towels, and pillowcases, canvas pouches of dirty laundry hooked to the sides. "Good morning, ma'am," they said as one, with nods that conveyed deference.

"Good morning," I said warmly. "I'm Zo Grey."

"We know, ma'am. I'm Betsy," said the older, more matronly of the two, "and this is Alice. Pleased to meet you, ma'am."

"You don't need to call me ma'am."

"Yes, ma'am," Betsy said with another small nod.

"You can call me Zo."

"No, ma'am."

Okay, that hadn't worked. "Is this a southern thing?"

"Yes, ma'am," Alice said, hazel eyes twinkling. "If you weren't the heir, we'd call you Miss Zo, but as the heir, it's ma'am to us, and all the staff."

"Did Juniper insist on that?"

"Oh, no, ma'am," Betsy said with a laugh, tucking a stray gray curl beneath her cap. "And she knew she'd never break us of it. It's a matter of respect. Welcome to Cameron Manor, ma'am. If there's anything we can do to help you settle in and get comfortable, please let us know."

"We saw you selected one of the north bedrooms," Alice said. "Would you like us to move your things to her suite, ma'am?"

"No," I said hastily. "I'm quite comfortable where I've settled, thank you."

"Very well, ma'am."

As they turned and began down the hall with their cart, I asked, "How many members of staff are here during the day?"

Turning, Betsy said, "There's old Clyde Baird that staffs the south parlor to oversee deliveries and whatnot, with the assistance of two houseboys you'll find on the south porch. Six maids arrive at nine thirty in the morning, departing at four in the afternoon. Juniper liked the early hours to herself, but if you'd like us to work a different shift, you've just to say so. There's a crew of two to six gardeners, depending on seasonal needs; a horticulturalist who sees to the greenhouse; two men who tend the pool, ponds, and fountains; and a part-time mechanic who keeps the cars running smoothly. Then, of course, there's the crew that tends the land. A team of maids comes quarterly and on a holiday schedule to do a deep-clean of the house, baseboards and light fixtures and such. The staff increases threefold during holidays, but for now it's the skeleton crew."

The skeleton crew: a mere fifteen to twenty-one people. "Thank you, Betsy."

"You're welcome, ma'am."

I watched as she and Alice vanished beyond a door to clean a bedroom that was, no doubt, never used, dazed and dismayed by the extravagance. How was a woman who'd barely kept her head above water most of her life supposed to grow accustomed to such excess, such . . . wastefulness? *Was* it wastefulness when it provided what I hoped were good jobs with benefits for so many?

It was no wonder Juniper had insisted I live here for three years. It could easily take me that long to fully comprehend her world, decide if I could fit into it, if I wanted to. Her legacy was turning out to be far more complex than I'd imagined.

I turned back to those double doors that both invited and intimidated.

"She chose me," I whispered. For whatever reason, Juniper Cameron believed I was her heir. I would never be able to fill her shoes if I didn't believe it, too. Hopefully somewhere in her suite were the papers that proved it.

I hurried to the door, ran my fingertips over one of the engraved symbols before closing my hand around the cool crystal knob, and pushed open the door, then paused a moment, reluctant to enter. Not that her suite wasn't inviting. To the contrary, it was the loveliest, most welcoming space I'd seen in the manor so far, light and airy and feminine.

The herringbone carpet continued into the suite, but transitioned from navy and cream to an aqua and ivory pattern that was no-pile yet plush beneath my feet. As opposed to the rich dark mahogany throughout the manor, the elaborate woodwork here was gloss-white, the furnishings coastal and breezy, with floor-to-ceiling windows on virtually every wall. What remained between was dressed with a pale, shimmery wallpaper that seemed almost crystalline, refracting light. Upon closer inspection, I realized that was because the fabric was actually dusted with tiny, sparkling crystals—like I said, *insane* wealth.

I forced myself to stride briskly through the foyer of the suite, past the table holding a large vase of blue and cream roses, to a bedroom where a tufted velvet bed faced an ornate fireplace and, beyond that, a door to a bathroom with lavish marble murals on the walls of the shower and above the deep jetted tub. Beyond the bathroom was a serene spa with a hot-rock sauna, a waterfall feature spilling down a gleaming silver wall, and two massage tables. I couldn't fathom the luxury of having a masseuse come to my house. I stepped swiftly into that mind-boggling bathroom, searching high and low, every drawer, each vanity top. (I mean, really, the woman had either pilfered my trash or swiped my hair for answers. That could work both ways.) To my astonishment, I found not a single brush or comb. How was that even possible? The woman had to brush her hair. But no: not a single strand of gene-laden locks. Feeling incredibly foolish, but driven by an obsessive desire to know, I crawled about the floor, seeking forgotten nail clippings or stray hairs that might have drifted into an untidied corner. But the suite had apparently been meticulously cleaned and stripped of all trace of genetic material. I mean, really—no brush? Not even a toothbrush? The trash can was empty, as I was fairly certain at that point it would be. Next, I went to the shower drain. Spotless, emitting the faint smell of bleach. I searched the massage table, the blankets, and came up empty-handed there, too.

Knowing I'd be disappointed, I ruffled her pillows, stripped back the sheets. Not a speck of anything.

No television, either; no trace of technology in the suite. And no study.

The closet was the size of my north bedroom, with opal carpet, sea-green wallpaper, custom drawers and shelves and glass cabinets all around; the transom ceiling was hung with four petite crystal chandeliers. It must have been recently emptied of Juniper's clothing, as only a small corner of it was in use. On a dresser island was an envelope with my name on it. I hurried over and withdrew a brief note from Lennox that said *Welcome, Ms. Grey! I guessed you at a size four but after a few months of our cooking, a six might better serve, so you've doubles of everything. Enjoy! All you see is yours.*

The last phrase reverberated, gong-like, in my head. That was exactly what I was having such a hard time accepting: that any of this extraordinary wealth, even the tiniest portion, was actually mine.

I drifted slowly toward the clothing with a mixture of trepidation and something uncomfortably close to reverence. Walmart was my mall. Here were labels bearing the names Dior, Versace, Chanel, Hermès, and Armani, with tags still on that made me gasp with shock and ever-pragmatic horror. There were suits, dresses, and evening gowns, with coordinating shoes, scarves, and purses displayed on shelves beneath them.

Near a pile of department store boxes that I assumed contained whatever "whatnot" was, I found designer workout gear, jeans by brands I'd never heard of, and (oh, thank you, Lennox, for something I understood!) soft flannel shirts and hiking boots. A stack of tees, sweatshirts, underwear, bras, half a dozen nightgowns with matching robes. Socks, tennis shoes, boots, sandals, flip-flops, hats, gloves, jackets.

Plucking a Chanel dress from the rack, I held it in front of me, eyeing myself in the mirror with wonder that vied with deep unease. My new wardrobe far exceeded the armor for which I'd hoped, and I had no doubt Lennox had chosen it to ensure I was prepared for a potentially fractious confrontation with portions of the town, but this dress alone would have paid our rent for a year. I'd never worn anything that cost more than thirty or forty dollars in my life. And there were *two* of everything. With the exception of exchanging texts with Este, nothing about my morning was comprehensible. Beneath pleasure lurked anxiety. I'd read news stories about lottery winners whose worlds went straight to hell after they struck it rich.

"Tools," I murmured, returning the dress to the rack. If I thought of the outfits as useful implements, it was easier. Exiting the closet, I saw two bellboy carts tucked discreetly to the side and made a mental note to come back and transport the items later.

I'd meet Mr. Balfour in my other dress this afternoon. I needed time to wrap my head around slipping into something that cost more than my car.

Abruptly, I couldn't leave the south end of the manor fast enough, but as I made a beeline for the door, I discovered a second envelope propped against the vase of flowers with my name written on it in bold yet feminine handwriting. I picked it up and turned it over to open it, only to find an old-fashioned, scarlet wax seal embossed with the initial *C* where the folds of the envelope joined and a message penned beneath on the back of the creamy vellum: *Do not open this until you've been in the manor seven full days and nights.*

I frowned. Was this from Juniper? Did it contain the genetic testing that would tell me how we were related? *Why* shouldn't I open it for a week? Or more specifically, "seven full days and nights," which struck me as a rather bizarre way to define a week. Technically, that was more than a week. I'd arrived Monday night. That meant it didn't count as a full day and night.

Furthermore, who would know? Was I being watched? I rubbernecked, checking every corner of the suite's foyer for cameras. None that I could see. Would opening the envelope constitute a breach of the estate's contingencies? Was this a test?

Irritated by yet another mystifying, controlling dictum, clutching the envelope, I hurried out the door, figuring it might take me so long to find my way back, I'd scarcely have time to change for my meeting with Mr. Balfour.

I divined a logic to the manor's layout on my return, realizing it made use of the interior, windowless rooms for storage purposes, while those on the perimeter with windows were used for habitation. So long as I didn't get diverted to the middle, it was navigable. I peeked into a stately two-floor library of burnished wood with tall, arched old-fashioned windows, multiple guest bedrooms, a small kitchen, and two more parlors of sorts. Having bypassed the interior maze, I was back at the main entry of the house in under five minutes, unfortunately sans Post-it notes and Sharpie. Still, I felt reasonably certain of my ability to retrace my steps to Juniper's suite when I was ready to fetch my new wardrobe, so I considered the morning, so far, a win.

I WAS SEATED in the parlor near the front foyer at five minutes to one, composing my thoughts, when Betsy ducked her capped head in to inform me Mr. Balfour was waiting for me in the south reception room.

"Why didn't he come to the front door?" I asked as I followed the sturdily built, bustling woman to one of the southern corridors I'd not explored.

"None but family uses the main entry," she replied, moving briskly down the corridor, not missing the opportunity to whisk a dustcloth along the lip of the wainscotting as she went.

Which meant it had only been used by a single person for a very long time, and emphasized the insult levied by Althea Bean assailing the main entrance. "I heard Juniper had a daughter."

The back of Betsy's head bobbed affirmative. "Two, ma'am."

Mr. Balfour had only mentioned one. "What happened to them?"

"The second was stillborn, leaving Ms. Cameron unable to conceive," she said, turning down an offshoot from the main corridor, where she stopped abruptly and pressed her palms to a section of wall that sprang open. Gesturing me to follow her through the faux wall into yet another corridor, she continued, "The first died in her twenties. That would have been in the early seventies, ma'am."

Juniper had lived alone for the past fifty years in this sprawling fortress with hidden doors. I would be pressing my hands to walls for days to come. Once I knew where they all were, I'd find them charming. Until then, I'd feel even more ill at ease than I already was. "What about her husband?"

"She never wed," Betsy replied.

My brows rose. Seventy or eighty years ago, being pregnant and unwed was scandalous. But while poor and unwed made a woman an outcast, rich and unwed had probably only gotten her called eccentric, "an independent thinker" ahead of her time.

"As generous and kind as Juniper was," Betsy went on, "not a person in Divinity would say a word about her decision not to marry. Besides, it's always been the Lady of Cameron Manor, never a gentleman, since the house was originally built, and they rarely wed."

Juniper's direct line had died out with her daughters. Which meant, way back, the lines had diverged. I'd have to begin my search a century in the past. "Did Juniper have siblings?"

"I'd have to ask Gran, see if she recalls anything of those days, but she's only seventy-six. Her sister, Ava, is eighty-nine and may recall more, if she's having one of her good days."

Surely there were records of the Cameron family tree, if only names scribbled in a Bible somewhere. "Can you tell me where Juniper's office is?"

"Third floor, southwest wing."

"Above her suite?"

"Approximately."

"You wouldn't happen to have a map of the house or floorplans, would you?"

She laughed gaily. "As if that would help."

"What do you mean?"

"Some things you just have to get a feel for, ma'am. Cameron Manor's one of them. She has her quirks, that's for sure. I can give you a bit of an overview. If you stand outside, facing the front porch, north is to your left, south to your right. The front of the house is west, the rear east. The manor was designed so entertaining and business meetings could be held separate from the private quarters. The north half of the house is private residence, the south devoted to storage, business, and entertaining."

I frowned. "Then why are Juniper's suite and office in the southwest wing?"

"Weren't always. Had the wing converted decades before I was hired on. Heard she wanted to be closer to the comings and goings of visitors, feel more connected to the town. To the rear is the southeast wing, which is reserved for parties and whatnot, and if you don't know where the hidden doors are, you'll not find your way from the front wing to the rear. The original master suite of the manor is in the northwest wing, but it's not been used for a long time, nor have the floors above it." Betsy shivered. "We tend to steer clear of that portion of the house."

"Why?"

She glanced over her shoulder at me, lips compressed. "Juniper instructed us not to clean there but once a year, and skip the rooms damaged by fire."

"What fire?" Was this "the charring" Mr. Balfour had mentioned? Wondering if it was a safety issue I needed to address, I made a mental note to inspect the northwest wing sooner rather than later. It must have been a recent loss, I mused, for I couldn't see Juniper permitting unrepaired fire damage in her pristine home for long.

"We're here, ma'am." She paused outside a doorway and ushered me through. "Will you be wanting dinner served this evening? And if so, what time?"

"No, thank you. Lennox did a lovely job stocking the fridge. But I'd like to talk with you more. Will you be here tomorrow?"

She shook her head. "I've a week off. Taking Gran in for hip replacement."

"The week after, then. Wishes of a speedy recovery for your gran."

"Yes, ma'am. Thank you, ma'am."

"Are you certain you couldn't get comfortable calling me Zo?"

"Afraid not, ma'am."

Sighing, I watched Betsy pivot and vanish down the corridor, then turned and entered the reception room.

"You didn't like Lennox's choices?" Mr. Balfour's smile faltered when he caught sight of my attire, a simple black dress and sandals.

"Your wife has exceptional taste," I assured him as I approached a seating cozy comprising two sofas at right angles with armchairs forming the other two sides of the square. "I'm looking forward to trying things on later tonight." Warmly, I added, "Please tell her I've never had better chicken pot pie in my life, although my mother would be crushed to hear that." It wasn't true. Mom's was better, but I liked Mr. Balfour. He'd championed me this morning, spared me an unwitting ambush.

A flush of pleasure stained his cheeks as he rose from the sofa, and I could see, even after fifty years of marriage, Mr. Balfour was still very much in love with his wife. "I'll be sure to tell her that," he said. "I trust you slept well?"

"Better than I have since Mom—yes, thank you." I avoided saying those words, as more often than not, they brought a swift burn of tears to my eyes. "After I let Rufus into the conservatory, I did some exploring. The house is lovely. Overwhelming, but every bit as gracious and inviting as you said."

"*Overwhelming* has always struck me as nothing more than unexpected change wed to unfamiliarity, both of which quickly fade. Although, at times, discomfiting, I find change exciting, invigorating, and hope you do, too. Does this mean you've decided to stay with us?"

My breath hitched halfway up my windpipe and lodged there. This moment would define the rest of my life, and my choices were at opposite ends of the spectrum. Stay and inherit abundance beyond my wildest dreams or return to a life of drudgery and debt.

In that breathless, suspended moment, an image arose, unbidden, of children, and how amazing it would be to fill the manor with a family of my own. I could see them racing up and down the corridors, discovering the eccentricities of the house with gales of laughter. What a childhood Cameron Manor would offer! With secret doors and rambling oaks to climb, a fabulous pool in which to swim, forest and caves to explore, and of such importance to me, a fine education all the way through grad school if desired, the ability to chase their dreams without hardship and struggle. Life here promised stability, constancy, community. Roots, permanent and strong. It wasn't merely my own path that would be enriched, but that of all future Grey generations.

If I returned to Indiana, I wasn't certain there would *be* future Grey generations. I couldn't see myself bringing babies into a world where I had to work constantly just to keep our heads above water. That was a hard life for a child. I knew; I'd lived it. Nor was I the type of woman a rich man might marry and save, not that I wanted one to do so. I'd never once imagined my wedding day, a thing to which it seemed most women I knew had given far more than fleeting thought. Este had hers planned right down to the last detail. She didn't want kids, but she definitely wanted a husband. I longed for children, but had never bothered to flesh out the man in the picture, I suppose because there'd been none in my world. Given Juniper's solo life, perhaps I really was a chip off the old and illustrious Cameron block.

Here, I could have as many children as I wanted, give them an incredible life. I could fill these halls with their laughter, and my arms with the love of a large family. I could make my own tribe and never feel orphaned and alone again.

I saw no point in delaying the inevitable. I'd choose this a thousand times over and be grateful to the end of my days. "Yes, I've decided to stay," I told him firmly.

His blue eyes danced. "I can't tell you how delighted I am to hear that. I have a copy of the settlement papers for your attorney to review before you sign."

I had no attorney, but with five thousand dollars a month, I could afford one, and would, for my peace of mind.

"If you've need of an attorney, I'd not hesitate to recommend any in Divinity, but for the sake of impartiality, you should select your own. I'll have an account set up at Rutherford's Savings and Loan down on the square this afternoon, with your first three-months' stipend. The living allowance will be deposited quarterly."

My shoulders lifted imperceptibly as a crushing weight eased. Fifteen thousand dollars meant I could begin calling creditors tomorrow to set up payment plans. "Thank you, Mr. Balfour." Settling into an armchair adjacent to him, I opened with small talk. "I noticed symbols in the stained glass above the stairs."

"Ah, yes, on the old windows. They used to crank those open before air-conditioning to ventilate the house. The triskelion is a Celtic symbol; you'll find many of those in and about the manor. The Camerons left the Highlands of Scotland to resettle here, as did many of the older families in Divinity, though they're wont to say they never truly left the Highlands, rather brought it with them, importing odds and ends and even one of the pubs in town, lock, stock, and barrel. The crosses of Divinity Chapel were hewn from the stone of Ben Nevis and shipped all the way from Lochaber."

"And the symbol on the doors to Juniper's suite?" Mom never told me a thing about our ancestry. It was dizzying to think I might have Scottish roots and that, here, I could finally learn about the Greys, where we came from.

"I've not seen it."

When I described it for him, he said, "Sounds like the Serch Bythol. Another Celtic symbol, of Welsh derivation, I believe."

I made a mental note of it—*serk beeth-ohl*—so I might look it up later, then tackled my primary objective. "I got the impression Juniper had been ill for quite some time."

"Indeed."

"It occurred to me there might be matters she was unable to handle in her last days that require immediate attention. If so, could you help me address them?"

Beaming, he exclaimed, "Absolutely, Ms. Grey! And may I commend you? Few so recently bereaved would spare a thought for such concerns. I'll bring you up to speed on pressing issues, and together, we'll dispatch them swiftly. I'll just draft a temporary provision to allow you to make time-sensitive decisions prior to signing the settlement documents."

SEVERAL HOURS LATER, with scholarships approved, funding for the Coventry Women's Clinic deposited into the necessary accounts, and expiring loans extended, along with a plethora of other matters I hadn't fully absorbed, I finished tucking the last of my new wardrobe into the closet above two stacks of unopened whatnot boxes. Those, I felt, would only overwhelm me further should I try to explore them. Beyond the French doors of my bedroom, dusk was falling, so I decided to return the cart tomorrow. Not only did I prefer to navigate the manor in the light of day, Juniper's suite made me uncomfortable in a way I didn't understand. Possibly, it was too over-the-top luxurious for me to ever feel at ease in. It was comforting to be back in my smaller, cozier bedroom. With the door shut, I could pretend for a time that the enormity of house and legacy didn't exist.

The envelope I'd found leaning against the vase was, indeed, from Juniper, and Mr. Balfour had stressed emphatically that I follow her instructions and not break the seal. Now I withdrew it from my pocket and propped it carefully on one of the closet shelves. Then, after eyeing it a moment, I opened a drawer and placed it inside, removing the settlement papers, which I planned to read tonight, and putting them on the shelf in my line of vision instead. Seeing the envelope every time I walked into the closet would irritate me. Some of Juniper's contingencies, I understood. Others just seemed heavy-handed and controlling. Her limits on guests and the denial of a housemate would rankle me eternally. Este could paint here as easily as in Indianapolis. I could convert part of the garage into a studio for her. Or have one built, I thought, brows lifting in astonishment at the thought. I had money. I had land. I could build a studio if I wanted to! The idea was stupefying. I could, I decided swiftly, at the very least treat myself to a new smartphone so I'd be able to take photos and fully use the internet again.

"Fish out of water," I murmured, reaching for my cell to call Mom and talk to her about how insane all this—

God, how many times is that going to happen? I thought miserably as I stared at my phone.

When it rang, I jerked, answering it reflexively, then scowled, because it was my landlord, Ray Sutton, who I'd been avoiding all day. He'd begun calling shortly after noon, left nearly a dozen voicemails. We'd never gotten along well, and I had no desire to talk to him right now.

"'Bout goddamn time you answered your goddamn phone!" Ray roared.

"Mr. Sutton, please calm—"

"Skipping town ain't gonna save you, missy! I'm gonna sue you for every penny you make for the rest of your sad-sack life. You're gonna be working forever to pay me back, or I'll have your ass thrown in jail!"

Surmising he didn't have insurance, I held the phone away from my ear with a sigh. There was little point trying to interrupt him. Mr. Sutton was off the wagon more than he was on it and, with an alcohol-fueled temper, would rant until he ran out of steam. I'd expected he might tear into me about the fire and was surprised he'd waited so long to do it, but this display of fury was excessive, even for him.

I began to hum softly, trying to tune out his crass invectives and threats. Whenever he finally paused for a breath, I'd tell him what the fire chief had told me the day of the fire: Mom hadn't cooked in over a year—the most common reason for house fires—so the likely cause was faulty wiring or a defective appliance. Carrying insurance on the structure was *his* responsibility, not mine. I should be suing *him* for not maintaining his rental property in better condition.

Holding the phone a sanity-preserving foot from my ear, I opened the French doors and stepped out onto the balcony. The night sky was exquisite, indigo and scarlet. The ever-present wind on Watch Hill tousled my hair and caressed my skin. Closing my eyes, I inhaled deeply of the fragrant breeze, seeking my placid, calm center, which had been so elusive of late.

I was here, not *there* in chilly Indiana with Ray Sutton screaming at me face-to-face. I was safe. I had money. I wasn't going to jail nor would I be—

Abruptly, I clapped the phone to my ear and exploded, "*What did you just say?*"

"I said you burned my house down, you crazy bitch, and you're gonna pay me every penny you owe me! Plus interest!"

"Before that."

"I got proof! They found accelerant, and *you*, missy—"

"Who found what accelerant?"

"You a goddamn moron? Fire chief. Gasoline. I told 'em you got motive out the ass. Burned my house down to get rid of that waste of a mother of yours. Everybody knows she wasn't dying fast enough, with you going deeper and deeper into debt every day. Well, you've gone and done it now, missy, you picked the wrong—"

I heard nothing more. Crimson rage exploded inside my skull, obliterating sound, darkening vision. The dragon in my stomach roared with bloodthirsty savagery, shaking herself so violently that scales clacked together like heavy iron plates. I felt as if I were shivering and boiling at the same time. I wanted to say hateful things to Ray Sutton. I wanted to tell him the truth about what the town of Frankfort thought of him. I wanted to slice into his soul and tell him *he* was the reason he'd lost his son to an overdose at seventeen, that gay wasn't a perversion or wrong, that Mackie Sutton had possessed one of the kindest, gentlest souls I'd ever known. Had Ray been standing in front of me, I'd have gone for his jugular with my teeth and nails.

Waste of a mother. Not dying fast enough. Accusing me of murdering the woman I'd loved more than anything in the world.

Accelerant.

The word reverberated inside my head as I struggled to comprehend it.

Because he'd lost his son, because I knew why Ray drank, and because I try to be the woman I expect myself to be, no matter how ugly life gets, I thumbed the phone off without saying another word, blocked Ray's number with shaking hands, and immediately dialed the Frankfort fire department.

"Tom Harris," I demanded sharply when a man answered. My heart was hammering so hard, I felt woozy.

"He's out for the next few days."

"This is Zo Grey. Ray Sutton just called and told me they found accelerant at my house. Do you need my address?"

"You kidding, Zo? It's me, Tommy Jr. You used to wait on us at Cracker Barrel. Mom's in the hospital again. That's why Dad's off, but I know he means to call you soon as he can."

From talk at the diners, I knew Tom's wife, Dottie, was battling breast cancer, and whenever she was admitted to the hospital, Tom, who'd shaved his head in solidarity, never left her side.

"We don't get fires burning that hot around here," Tommy Jr. continued. "Found gasoline and a damn-hell lot of it. Dad wants to know if you had gas stored in the basement. If you didn't, somebody sure wanted your house gone. Ray's got no insurance, stands nothing to gain, or we'd be looking at him."

For a moment I couldn't speak. Finally, I managed, "Your father said a safe survived the fire. Can you ship it to me?"

"No can do. Only Dad can release stuff. You have to talk to him. I'll have him call you."

I said a quiet thank-you and hung up.

Then I closed my eyes, slipping back to the afternoon of the fire, standing in the street, staring, blankly, at the charred remains of my world.

Seeing it, this time, as arson.

Burned too hot, too fast, Tom said to me that day. *Didn't stand a chance.*

We didn't store gas in the basement. We didn't have gas anywhere on the property. No accelerants of any kind.

I opened my eyes, staring blankly into the night, my hands curled into fists. Grief was hard enough to deal with. Now I had white-hot anger on top of it, and far more questions than I'd already had.

My mother hadn't died in an accidental fire.

Someone had killed Joanna Grey.

9

I KNOW WHERE STUBBORN, STOIC pride comes from.

It's a mask for shame.

Didn't matter how much love there was in my world, each time I started a new school, I was secretly ashamed of my clothing, of not being able to afford extracurricular school events, having no escort for father/daughter dances, being different in countless mortifying ways. Then, to make it even more complicated, I was ashamed of being ashamed, as if by feeling this way I was insulting my mother. Only Este had seen past it all to the real me. My outspoken friend, who was judged all the time from every side and fit nowhere, never judged me, and we fit together perfectly.

Glancing over at Devlin, I was glad I'd refused to let pride affect my decision when he'd knocked on the front door shortly after nightfall, asking if I'd like to go for a drink.

I'd wanted to hide in my bedroom, concealing my turmoil from the world, speaking to no one, pacing frantically, alternating between grief and rage. Quell my bloodthirsty inner dragon, try to divine who could possibly have wanted to burn our house down and kill my mother. Handle any and all problems privately, as I always did.

Instead, I put on makeup, brushed my hair, and slid into a new pair of designer jeans that fit like a glove, a silk top, and (Jimmy Choo!) sandals and forced myself to go out with him.

The truth was, I was afraid I might lose all hold on sanity if I stayed in my room, alone, with only dark thoughts and explosive emotions for company. Or worse, venture to the garage, take one of the cars to New Orleans, and hunt the man I wanted to vent them on, one superbly equipped to handle it, a man I had no intention of ever seeing again, especially since I so intensely hungered to, and hunger was a double-edged sword.

The first four times Mom and I had to evacuate a town so abruptly that we were forced to leave everything behind, including my precious few toys, I'd sobbed in the car, brokenhearted—not to mention terrified, channeling every ounce of Mom's panic. To this day, I couldn't bear to hear the song "Sweet Child o' Mine." She'd sung it to me over and over as we'd raced through the night, trying to soothe me. Much later I discovered just how many of the lyrics she'd changed, wisely leaving out the whole "oh, where do we go now?" part. Wasn't *that* always the question.

By the fifth time we abandoned the small number of things behind that I had ever so briefly called mine, I was impeccably detached. Implacability was easier on us both. We were a closed loop of emotion, Mom and I; her griefs and fears mine, mine hers. Battening down our hatches protected each other.

The possibility that some malicious pyro had randomly picked our small, dilapidated house to torch didn't resonate with me. I didn't know much about arsonists, but in movies, they tended to choose high-profile targets and strike at night, not in the middle of the day. There was ego, often showmanship involved. What challenge was there in burning a tiny, low-rent home in an isolated rural community?

Had the past caught up to us at long last? Was my father still alive? *Who*—the thought caused even more of a sick burn in my gut—had we been running from all these years, and why? Was it really my father? Was he still alive? Why didn't Mom ever tell me? Why hadn't I pushed for the truth as I aged?

I knew the answer to that. She'd been so delicate by the time I was a teenager that I was unwilling to burden her further with questions. I couldn't bear to be the cause of additional suffering. Over the years, as I'd grown increasingly exhausted by my juggling act of responsibilities, resignation had settled into my bones, as sharp and bitter as any Midwest winter's chill. Life was what it was. There was no time for questions, only action. Dangerous stuff, resignation. It drained the life from you so subtly and insidiously, you began to forget how you once felt. Ergo my aggressive one-night stands, to remind myself I was alive. I *could* choose something for myself, and it could be all mine, and only about me.

Now all those questions besieged me. When it was too late, Mom was gone, and I couldn't see her death as anything other than intentional. Someone out there in the world had deliberately set fire to our house, causing my mother to die a horrific death. Whether arsonist or villain from our past, that person had *murdered* my mother.

"How was your first night in the manor, Ms. Grey?"

Devlin's voice rolled over me, deep and velvety. I glanced over at him behind the wheel of the car, strong and hot as Hades in jeans and a collared shirt with the sleeves rolled up past his tattooed biceps, the fabric white against his dark skin. His hair was longish, some of it falling forward, the planes of his beautiful face a fascinating study of shadow and light, and I wanted to tell him to pull over this very instant, rip off his clothes, and dump all my grief and fury on his body, in the hope that it would clear my mind a bit. "It was good, but if you call me Ms. Grey one more time, I'm getting out of the car and walking back to the house. Call me Zo, Devlin. God knows, no one else will." Exasperation laced my words.

"Zo, it is then, fierce lass. Short for something?"

"Zodecky." Pronounced ZO-da-kye, emphasis on the first syllable and inevitably butchered by anyone who read it from a list. No one had ever called me fierce in my life. Devlin had done so twice. Had I changed so much since Mom's death that people could sense the overload of emotions I was feeling? How embarrassing.

"Zo-d'kai," he murmured, and I shivered when he purred my name; it had never sounded quite so beautiful, so sexy when anyone else said it. "Mean something?"

I didn't tell him there were two more syllables. A five-syllable name inevitably got butchered, so I'd done a hack-job on it myself in grade school, insisting on just Zo. Teachers would say, *Z-o-e?* I'd reply flatly, *No. Just like the word* no. *A Z and an O.* Zo was a strong name; powerful. It was *Oz* backward, the mighty wizard. Once you added the *e*—in my opinion—the name became softer, more approachable. No point in approaching. I made that clear from the first. Zo—just exactly like *no.* Do *not* get to know me. Do *not* ask to be my friend. We won't be staying long.

When I'd asked Mom where my name came from, she'd shrugged and said she liked the way the syllables flowed, which was a fine way to knit together a name.

"Not that I know of," I answered Devlin. "Where are we going?"

"The Shadows. Live music, fine spirits, reminds me of a pub I used to frequent in Edinburgh. Like to dance?"

I did, and since I was most definitely *not* going to have sex with Devlin Blackstone in Juniper Cameron's insanely expensive Mercedes, against the supplest leather seats I'd ever touched, which would feel divine beneath my bare ass while he thrust deep inside me, I hoped dancing would purge some of my volatile emotions. Mom had instilled her wide and varied love of music in me. Many were the times, before she'd gotten so sick, we'd had silly dance-offs to her favorite glam-rock bands. "Love to."

"Great," he said with a smile that made me stare blankly at him for a moment. "Ready to meet some of the more interesting townsfolk?" he asked as he parked the car in the crowded lot.

"Why not?" I couldn't picture the stiff, bristly Ms. Bean and her vegetable coven hanging out here, with their perfect suits and perfectly coiffed hair, and I definitely couldn't get any more irritable, emotional, and aroused than I already was.

I was about to be proved wrong on all those counts.

The Shadows wasn't at all what I expected, and I was surprised such a place existed in a town of Divinity's size. The club sat alone, a few miles beyond the outlying homes and businesses, down a long lane of dueling oaks that formed a leafy, moss-draped tunnel over the drive. The rectangular building was three floors with a shallow fourth that looked mostly decorative, sporting classical cornices and dormers, and I could see why it reminded Devlin of Scotland. It brought to mind the Hotel Monteleone, with its elaborate architecture and tasteful lighting, but here the spotlights splashed up the side of the limestone facade to drench the windows crimson, illuminating the cornices with the same fiery glow, effortlessly marrying elegance to "something wicked this way comes." The windows were high, arched, and framed with wrought iron scallops. It was the kind of establishment I'd have expected to see in a European city built long ago, when craftmanship was an art form, pagan holidays were observed, and women were still burned at the stake as witches.

When we stepped inside, I gasped, prompting another of Devlin's devastating smiles. "Juniper had a hand in the design of this place. Its prior incarnation wasn't nearly as impressive."

The coffered ceiling was a foot and half deep with ornately carved framing, the wood painted metallic gold, the sunken panels between charcoal. Glittering chandeliers hung before enormous double-arched windows. The bar was dark leather and wood, the room lined with tufted leather seating and tables on a honey-oak floor.

"When was it built?" I asked.

"It was begun in 1938 and finished two years later. Somewhere in the manor there's an album with newspaper clippings, blueprints, and old photos."

"But Juniper would have been, what—only twenty or so at the time?"

"Nineteen. The old-timers like to say she came out of the womb carrying a briefcase and blueprints. When she was twenty-two, five years after Roosevelt's Rural Electrification Act of 1936, she lobbied to bring power to the town, and ultimately funded Divinity's first electric co-op."

Designing buildings, founding power plants, having babies, never marrying. Big shoes to fill. "Is there anything Juniper Cameron wasn't responsible for in this town?" I said dryly.

"Last I heard—contrary to popular belief—the sun didn't rise and set on her command," he said, just as dryly, and we both laughed.

"Glad to hear that. I was beginning to worry."

"Main floor's a bit of dining and drinking, second floor is for music and dancing, with rooms for private parties off the side."

"And the third?"

"That's Caelen and Kenzie's apartment. They run the club, live above."

I'd half expected to hear that I owned it and heaved a small sigh of relief that I didn't.

"But you own the place, Zo, so if you want any changes, you've only to let them know."

Of course I did, I thought irritably. "Do me a favor."

"Ask away." The intense, heated look in his dark eyes offered anything, anything at all.

"Don't tell me if I own anything else in this town. I need time to deal with what I already know about."

He laughed. "As you wish. What's your poison?"

"Bourbon. Rocks. Top shelf." Why not? I owned the club, I thought, with testy disbelief.

When he headed for the bar, someone grasped my elbow tightly from behind. Pivoting, I drew upon every ounce of my willpower to keep my features impassive, as Ms. Bean had no idea that I knew full well what she'd attempted to do this morning.

Althea's smile was bright beneath eyes so cold I swore I saw a sheen of frost in them, a snowflake or two dusting her eyelashes. Her shoulder-length ice-blond hair was carefully lacquered; her fitted, sleeveless black dress revealed arms paper-smooth and white as snow and, above a choker of pearls, a similarly blood-less, pale neck. Diamonds flashed as she fluttered her free hand in the air, exclaiming, "You must be Zo Grey! I'm Althea Bean. It's *such* a pleasure to meet you. There are *so* many people I'd like you to meet, you simply must come with me." She'd not relin-quished her grip on me when I'd turned, merely adjusted it, and now her fingers dug painfully into my arm.

Smile overdone, features tight, the venom Althea radiated was palpable. Since I was already in a shit mood, I locked eyes with her and probed. Forewarned, I reminded myself. I'd take every shred of information about this woman I could get. My inner calm wasn't accessible, but my ability to gauge people's emo-tions, to catch a hint of their soul in their eyes, felt sharper and more potent than ever. I expected to be buffeted by waves of avarice, anger, resentment.

I sluiced in so easily, it rather stunned me, and got something else entirely.

Althea Bean was frightened.

Deeply, intensely afraid of something or someone.

Surely not me. Then who? Or what? Gently, I probed deeper . . . Ah, there was her anger, rising, uncoiling like a—

"*Stop* that!" Althea hissed, smile vanishing.

Wait, what? I gaped in disbelief. There was no way she meant what it sounded like she meant.

"Mind your manners! We don't *do* that to each other in Divinity, Zo Grey! I don't care if you are the Cameron heir!" Turning sharply, she stalked off without another word.

"What the hell did you just say to Althea?" Devlin was beside me then, placing a drink in my hand. "I'd have wagered that droves of flying monkeys couldn't keep that avaricious woman away from you."

For a long moment I couldn't reply. The idea that someone had actually *felt* me pushing into their head, as I thought of it, through the windows to their soul, was beyond my comprehension. But then, lately, everything was.

"I didn't say anything," I finally managed to mutter, which was entirely true. Yet somehow she'd known what I was doing. *Felt* me doing it.

Upon reflection, I wondered if she'd been doing it to me, too. I'd gotten an itchy, uncomfortable sensation between and slightly above my eyes, which had never happened before.

Until that moment, I hadn't credited the knowledge I believed I acquired probing gazes as . . . indisputable fact, rather like that ghost in the cabin we'd rented in West Virginia that I knew Mom saw, too (yet the single time I'd brought it up, she'd shut me down hard and fast). I think a lot of people do that, brush up against the weird, admit they "seem" to feel something, even avoid the room that sends an inexplicable chill up their spine, yet refuse to ponder it overlong. Mom had always taken a strong position against the paranormal, stressing science, math, the physics of normalcy and reality. She'd taught me there was only one kind of magic, and it was the most powerful of all: love.

Still, we'd left West Virginia shortly after I mentioned the ghost.

Now, I'd met someone who felt what I was doing to her, who'd somehow known I was taking a peek inside her head, and she'd said, *We don't do that to each other in Divinity, Zo Grey!* implying others in town had the ability, too. What the hell? How was this even possible?

I was abruptly reluctant to meet anyone's gaze, lest they go poking about inside *my* head. I found myself on the cusp of an uncomfortable moral conundrum that cast me in an unfavorable light. *Do unto others* was a credo Mom had instilled in me.

"The band's about to start," said Devlin, placing a hand on the small of my back and guiding me toward the stairs. The heat of his big hand through the thin silk of my shirt sent shivers of sexual awareness to places I needed to not be thinking about. As we moved through the crowded bar, I watched woman after woman and more than a few men turn to follow my companion with hungry gazes. It wasn't just me. Devlin Blackstone was a difficult man to ignore. Once you looked at him, you wanted to keep looking, if only to find an imperfection that might make it easier to look away.

The staircase, with tufted leather walls and a ceiling of black so sooty it looked soft as suede, gave me an idea what to expect from the second floor. Still, I stopped and stared when we topped the final riser. Color me provincial, but I never got to go bar-hopping to fancy clubs with friends, and even if I had, small-town Indiana was hardly nightclub central. I've heard if you want a room to look smaller, you should paint it a dark color, but the opposite was true on the second floor of the Shadows. The area devoted to music and dancing was cavernous, every inch of it black, exquisitely embellished with gold and crystal accents. Normally, I'd find a room of unrelieved black oppressive, but the variety of textures and the eclectic glitter of crystal and lighting made it sophisticated, mesmerizing.

The floor was matte black; the lower half of the walls gleaming, tufted obsidian leather; the upper half folds of shimmering onyx velvet. The ceiling, also inky, soared to an intricately coffered vault, the arched, sunken panels matte black against gloss obsidian trim. There was a line of medieval-looking candelabras containing brightly burning torches strung down the center, stretching from the back of the room to the stage, which was raised and looked as if it had been transported from a centuries-old theater. The perimeter was rimmed with circular snugs beneath old-fashioned chandeliers that had large, incandescent globes and were just peculiar enough to seem steampunk, and the seating curved around tables of such high-gloss black, they rippled like dark mirrors, offering curiously liquid reflections of people and of drinks in glittering cut crystal. The bar was a study in ebony and glass, the shelving faceted crystal, refracting the luster of lights in dazzling and unexpected ways. It was atmospheric, elegant, and edgy as fuck, delivering on the wicked promise of the blood-stained facade. I couldn't help but wonder if they held a Halloween bash here. If not, perhaps the new owner might suggest it.

When the LED lights came on, I gasped.

The coffered vault ceiling emitted subtle beams of light,

splashing pinpoints of pale gold across the black-velvet interior, intensifying the myriad reflections in crystal and tabletops tenfold. As the dance floor began to glow a deep, inky blue, a gust of fog billowed across it. I felt simultaneously as if I were inside an old castle and standing in a verdant field beneath a starry sky on a cloudless, sable night. Cobalt spread through the room, working up the walls and into the ceiling, then, while the band set up and tuned, the color scheme morphed slowly to forest green, then violet, subtly shifting the ambience of the room each time.

"Juniper had a fondness for artistic lighting and put a lot of money into it, here and at the manor," Devlin said, watching me.

"She certainly didn't let age prevent her from embracing new technologies." A lot of the older folks I knew back home found them befuddling and irritating. Hell, I did, too. I hadn't even been able to figure out the manor's lighting system.

"Her heart was young and her mind sharp until the end. All that passion and energy trapped inside a dying body," he said, shaking his head, and I realized he'd cared about the old woman. "We all loved her," he said, reading my expression. "She had a way of bringing out the best in people, seeing possibility where others saw only obstacles. She didn't just think outside the box; she invented entirely new ones."

For a woman who'd spent her whole life tightly confined within the boxes of obligation and demand, it was yet another tantalizing aspect of Juniper's inheritance: I need never be constrained by debts and duties again. I, too, could find possibility where others met obstacles. I could change countless lives for the better. I knew what it felt like to need that helping hand. I could repay people like Mae, who'd spoken up to get me a job I'd never shown up for (hopefully making oodles of paperwork for Mr. Schumann).

"Come," Devlin said, taking my hand. "You're about to be deluged, and I suspect you'd prefer a table between you and the town when they descend."

By the time we reached one of the half-moon leather booths and slid in, people had already begun falling into a queue and heading our way.

The next twenty minutes were a blur of faces and names, greetings and well-wishes. I met the Elders and Alloways, the Somervilles and MacGillivrays, the Rutherfords and Mathesons, Napiers and MacLellans, the Galloways, Kincaids, and Logans. I took special note of Isabel and Archibald Alexander, a mixed-race couple in their early forties—the alternate heirs, according to the Beanhead—who projected only warmth and gracious welcome; not that I dared probe their gazes for more.

There were no icy Altheas; all seemed openly curious about me, glad I'd come out tonight, and kind, if a bit reserved, which I understood completely. This town had a great deal at stake in me. I'd have been horrified that night if I'd had any idea just how enormous those stakes really were, but I didn't, so, blissfully ignorant, I basked in the relief of discovering the entire town of Divinity wasn't against me.

At long last, the line petered out, revealing a final couple I was delighted to see—Mr. Balfour, escorting a woman who could only be his wife, so proudly did he usher her forward. "It's lovely to see you out and about, Ms. Grey. You've made my night," Mr. Balfour said, eyes dancing. "May I present my better half?"

Of an age with her husband, Lennox Balfour was dressed much like me in jeans, a silk blouse, and low heels, and she wore her long white hair parted in the center, loose about her shoulders. Her eyes were the warmest spring green I'd ever seen, framed by decades of laugh lines. Energy and vitality radiated from her trim frame, and bangles clinked together at her wrist when she shook my hand. Around her neck, she wore a shimmering crystal wrapped in silver filagree with matching crystal earrings.

"I can't thank you enough for everything you and your husband have done for me, Mrs. Balfour. Please, sit," I invited.

Flushing with pleasure, Mr. Balfour gestured for his wife to slide in first, then followed suit. I noticed countless avid gazes turned our way and realized that, as far as he and the town knew, his job was on the line. He'd worked for Juniper Cameron for over half a century, but now there was a new heir and no guarantee he had a future working at her side. My arrival was tethered to *everyone's* applecart and could upset them all. God, what power Juniper Cameron had held in Divinity! And to hear tell of it, never once abused.

I noticed that although the Balfours greeted Devlin, it was without warmth and, aside from an initial glance his way, they kept their gazes on me. Even when he spoke, as we made small talk, they didn't look at him. I told myself not to read too much into it. It would take time to ferret out the nuances and complexities of the relationships here.

The band began to play a haunting Scottish ballad sung by a woman with a voice so pure and resonant with emotion that although I didn't understand a word of it, I was moved nearly to tears.

"It's called 'The Sorrow of Anwenn' and is, as you intuited, quite sad," Mr. Balfour told me. "That's Meribeth Logan, our local librarian and chanteuse. The Killians perform next."

"Is it Gaelic?"

"Yes," Lennox replied. "Divinity was settled over three centuries ago by a group of Scottish families seeking a new life, adventure, freedom to live and worship as they wished. They found all that and more here, yet never forgot where they came from. We're passionate about our heritage, honoring the old stories and ways. You'll find a great deal of history preserved about town, and many of our traditions on display, from bagpipes to kilts to our annual festival."

Mr. Balfour said, "They'll be playing a reel next. You must dance with us, Zo. I'll not brook refusal."

I had an oddly disembodied moment then, where I felt cleanly split in two and frozen by it. There was Zo whose mother was dead, murdered in a deliberately set fire, filled with grief and rage and no small anxiety over the many sudden changes in her life. Then there was Zo sitting in a trendy nightclub, wearing clothing that would have paid months of rent, filled with curiosity and excitement and a kind of disbelieving hope that she might, one day, be happy again, that dancing and enjoying herself wouldn't feel like such a betrayal of Joanna Grey and the countless questions that needed answering.

"What would your mother rather see you doing right now?" Mr. Balfour posed the question gently. "Grieving or dancing?"

Arrow through my heart. He'd seen right through me. *Live, my darling Zo. Live. Thirty days of grief, not one day more.* According to Mom's edict, I was permitted only two more weeks of weeping and woe.

"We lost our daughter, Erin, in the fire that burned our home," Lennox said quietly. "She was seventeen, getting ready to leave for university, brimming with dreams and plans for her future. The whole world was waiting for her, and she was going to conquer it."

Wincing, I said heavily, "I'm so sorry." They understood loss. And the loss of a child! To give birth, to nurture, shelter, and cherish, only to have that child stolen from you—hell itself could offer no greater torment.

"Though we knew there was nothing we could have done to save her, we punished ourselves for a long time." Lennox took my hand and squeezed it.

Mr. Balfour cast Lennox a look of such deep, abiding love, it melted my heart. "I nearly destroyed our marriage over it," he told me gravely. "Almost lost my best friend and soulmate because I couldn't let go of it, couldn't give myself permission to live in a world where I would never see Erin smile again, watch her become a doctor—that was her dream—or walk her down the aisle to entrust her to a man who couldn't possibly deserve her. Never hold their grandchildren in my arms. Dance, Ms. Grey. You'll have plenty of time for grief. It never wanders far. It's always there, a thought away, should you wish to hurt yourself on it."

Walk her down the aisle to entrust her to a man who couldn't possibly deserve her. I couldn't imagine life with such a father, or any father at all, for that matter. It was official: I adored James Balfour. Touched by their story, ceding the wisdom of their words, when Devlin took my hand, I stood and followed him to the dance floor.

As we moved to the center and the band began to stir, the tables emptied and the dance floor filled.

Of course Devlin was a good dancer. Undoubtedly, with that beautiful body of his, he exceled at anything requiring dexterity and grace. He was an exceptional partner, whose flirtatious patience was limitless as he taught me the intricate steps of one Scots dance after the next.

I lost my worries on the dance floor. There's something about being in a crush of people committed to carving out a few hours

of happiness for themselves, with no thought of yesterday or tomorrow, that builds an infectious energy and makes forgetting
easy, as you give yourself over to a communal conspiracy to feel
no pain. Mom used to say many people waste their lives in a
liminal no-man's-land, stranded on a bridge between their tragic
past and their uncertain future. The more they glance back, the
more afraid they become to go forward. And there is, she'd told
me, but one escape from that bridge. *Live now, my darling Zo.
That's all we have anyway. The past is baggage lost at the airport;
don't present your claim check. The uncertain future is nothing but fear
about things that will likely never come to pass.*

The songs were high energy with racing, frantic tempos, and
I realized why Mr. Balfour and his wife were so fit. They burned
it up on the dance floor, vying with Devlin's frenetic footwork.
At one point, Mr. Balfour, Lennox, and Devlin got into a com-
petitive showdown that had the crowd watching with fascination.
I'd not have been surprised to see sparks flying from their heels.

It was exhilarating and just what I needed. I wasn't the best
dancer out there, far from it, but I wasn't the worst, and I was indisputably the most committed and abandoned. With each song,
more of the unbearable tension quit my body. If I'd learned one
thing from caring for a terminal loved one, it was that sometimes
you had to relinquish the weight of the world for a time to have
any chance at all of shouldering it again the next day.

When the music shifted to a slow, haunting ballad, Devlin
slid his arms around me, pulling me close.

Danger there. I was young and strong, and felt as if I was
finally awakening after a long, terrible winter. Divinity was the
promise of spring, new life, second chances, and I was ravenous
for it all. Rather than sating my sexual appetite, a single night
with Kellan had served as a bellows, stoking it hotter still.

"You've the makings of a worthy partner," Devlin said, his eyes sexy and hooded and full of unsaid things like: *in countless ways.*

I basked a moment in the frank appreciation of his gaze. He was regarding me with more than carnal interest, which was all I'd ever been looking for in the past, and it made me feel both flattered and uncomfortable. This was ground upon which I had no idea how to tread. Ground you walked on every day—you *stayed.*

"I had the finest instructor on the dance floor." I evaded the subtleties of the compliment, smiling.

"I've a suspicion you need little instruction in anything. Once you understand your gifts, you're going to prove a natural."

"My gifts?"

"You're a blood Cameron. Comes with gifts," he said, staring down at me with an expression I couldn't decipher. "I've a feeling you might surprise us all."

There was that phrase again. I hoped I was. I wanted Juniper's legacy; all of it, her estate, her strength, her goodness. "What kind of gifts?"

I was buffeted then by . . . an emotion. Rubbing up against me, as close as his body was to mine. As if he'd said inside my mind, *Seriously, you're going to pretend?*

"What did you do to drive Althea away?" he asked.

He couldn't possibly know. Absolutely no damned way. "What do you think I did?" I equivocated.

Smiling faintly, he said, "Och, you want the words. Fine, then. I think you used one of your *gifts.*"

"What kind of gift?" I countered.

"The one where you lock eyes with me, lass, and see how deep into me you can look. You can be a bit rough if you wish. Try."

My jaw dropped as my brain stuttered over his words, echoing them again and again, trying to process that he'd said it. He had to be kidding. I had *not* come to a town where multiple people could not only read others the way I could, but spoke openly about . . . well, psychic stuff. Paranormal, extrasensory perception.

"Don't sell yourself short, lass. There are things we grow up believing because we've been taught to believe them. Things we think are impossible because we've been *told* they are. Then there are those things we feel in our bones. Despite the lies heard by our ears, our bones know the truth. Don't you feel, somewhere deep inside you, that there's more to life, to *you*, than you were given to believe? That perhaps, even, you were intentionally misled?"

Eyes narrowing, I growled, "Treading on dangerous ground there, insulting my mother."

"No father?"

I sliced my head in a tight, pissed negative.

His eyes narrowed. "I imagine your mother must have felt she had good reason for the way she raised you."

Anger vied with curiosity; my desire to know more won. "Are you implying my mother had this . . . this . . ."

"Deep sight," he supplied.

"Too?" I finished. There was a name for what I could do. Others knew it and could do it, too.

"Not implying. It's in your bloodline. Those of us who possess the ability begin instruction at a young age."

"If what you're saying is true, and I'm not saying it is, why would she conceal it from me?" I'd tried to talk to her once about how I got deluged by emotions, even images, if I looked too deeply into someone's eyes. She'd told me to stop imagining things. *Focus on the real world*, she'd said. *The one that actually exists. The one where I need you to go pull carrots from the garden for dinner.*

"Try it on me. Test this thing you don't believe is real."

On the off chance he was serious, on the off chance this "ability" of mine was something that truly existed and others could do it, too (refusing to ponder that my mother might have known and not only never told me about it, but flat-out lied to my face), and because I was insatiably curious about him and he'd given me permission, I locked gazes with him and probed.

Lust. Desire. He was feeling things that made the blood in my veins catch fire. I didn't get thoughts or clear images, just the enormity of his hunger wed to fierce strength, energy, and the timeless patience of something endlessly old, undeterred by waiting however long was necessary for whatever it was he wanted. According to Mom, "old souls" were people who'd lived many lifetimes. Although they didn't retain any memory of past lives, they did retain the lessons learned. Born with experience embedded in their very marrow, at a young age they displayed maturity, resilience, and wisdom others lacked. Devlin felt like a very old soul to me. Beneath it all was deep, powerful, unwavering emotion. He was true, constant, an undeterrable arrow to a committed goal.

Then a perfectly smooth blank wall. "Enough," he said.

"You felt me there," I said, stunned.

"Althea felt you, too. Dinna fash yourself for doing it, she'll tread lightly with you in the future. As she should."

"What is *with* this town?"

"What do you mean?"

"It's . . ." *Freaking me out!* "Strange." In countless ways.

"Is it? Or is it merely the first place you've ever felt as if you might fit? Where you might discover yourself? Become who and what you were always meant to be. Fear has no place in power, and you, Zo Grey, have great power. Be aware, be cautious, don't probe another's eyes in this town without invitation, *never* without invitation, and you'll be fine."

Then the music shifted up-tempo again, he threw back his head and laughed, and I shivered. He was so darkly beautiful and different from any man I'd ever met, and this town was so damned strange. Devlin and Divinity were stirring things inside me I couldn't begin to comprehend. I felt as if I were awakening from a deep fugue state, and the world, which had always seemed . . . well, gray as a Midwest winter, drab and bland, was far more vibrant and intense than I'd ever dreamed.

"Ah, I've been waiting for this one. Cut loose, Zo. You've mastered the reel. Make sparks fly. Best me. *If* you can, wee one." He flung the challenge with a devilish grin.

Pipes were joined by guitar, then the richly harmonic voices of many men chanting, and finally, the resounding crash of bass drums punctuating the chant.

"Wee one, my ass," I growled.

"You're a pup. You can't play with the big dogs out here. Or can you?"

When he spun me sharply away from him, I went flying across the dance floor. "Best me, Zo Grey," he shouted across the distance, and a maddened kind of exhilaration filled me. As the floor shifted to crimson, between the drinks I'd had, the onslaught of more company interested in me than I'd entertained in my life, and the bizarre turn of conversation, challenged by a man so unusual, so strange and strangely beautiful, goaded by the exotic-sounding guttural chant that kept increasing in tempo—*cummer gae ye before, cummer gae ye, gin ye winna gae before, cummer let me*—I let my inhibitions fall with a surge of competitive spirit so intense, it startled and surprised me. I'd spent my life meeting expectations, doing my best to succeed at whatever tasks were on my plate, but I'd never felt such a fierce desire to *win*.

Watching him like a hawk, I matched him, move for move. I danced with all the fury and grief and pain and passion in my soul. I danced like I'd fucked Kellan, without a single hold barred. I danced as if my very life depended on it.

Crimson slid across the floor, up and up, staining the starry walls with flame. I was moving so fast, the room blurred into a brilliant fiery smear as I remained utterly fixated on his feet, on making mine do the same. I was oblivious to all that was happening around us until Devlin shouted, "You've cleared the floor, lass, but you still haven't bested me," and I realized the others had fallen back into a circle to watch us.

I had no idea how I was supposed to best him, doubted my feet could move any faster, then the townsfolk moved together in a circle around us. Joining hands, they began to dance in a counterclockwise fashion (which I would later learn was "loupin' lightly widdershins"). It felt almost as if the frenetic tempo of their unified rotation was channeling energy to me, that I was dancing at the center of some kind of vortex that was pulling visceral power and adrenaline from the townspeople gathered round, funneling it to me, filling me with a frantic, primal drive, waking me up, making me feel intensely, almost painfully alive. Then abruptly my feet were going even faster, and Devlin was the one working to keep up.

The song seemed to go on forever as, faster and faster, we danced. The chanting waned, and the song became one of screaming guitar, frantic pipes, driving bass, with only the occasional guttural grunt. I felt as if my feet must be smoking in a room that was suddenly unbearably hot, so hot, I was dripping sweat as crimson flames licked up the walls to the onyx ceiling high above. The drum ratcheted up, intensifying to deafening crashes of thunder, pounding, pounding, like the ominous, inflammatory drums of war, goading me to dance better, faster, longer.

On and on we danced.

On and on they circled.

Not once did the bastard miss a step. Not once did he fail to match me. But, at least, I consoled myself, I'd taken the lead for a time.

When, finally, the song ended, I felt *incredible*.

Intoxicated, drunk on life, strong and centered, focused, a vessel overflowing with abundant energy, exquisitely aware of every inch of my body, each beat of my heart, every scent and sight in the room. Never had I felt so . . . electrified, connected, acutely aware, and . . . hungry, so very damned hungry, for everything.

Cheers broke out, then Devlin was beside me, taking my hand, dragging me from the dance floor into one of the dimly lit side rooms, shoving me back against the wall, locking eyes with me, and saying roughly, "Kissing you now, Zo."

"Yes," I said breathlessly, and before the word had even left me, his mouth was crushed to mine.

The dance had stirred a sexual frenzy inside me, and I kissed him back, matching his lust as I'd matched his steps, tearing at the buttons of his shirt, grinding against him.

No, no, no, a distant voice shouted in my head. *Do not shit where you eat!*

The common colloquialism from back home jarred me to my senses, and I forced myself to break the kiss, thrusting him away.

"No," I said, pressing a shaking finger to his lips. "Not doing this with you."

"Why?" he demanded in a rough voice.

"It's too much right now," I said, shoving off the wall and walking quickly past him, putting distance between us. Turning my back to him, because merely looking at him at this moment, with the tempest I was feeling, was too much temptation.

"'Right now' implies you've not a closed mind to it. To us," he said to my back.

"There is no 'us,' Devlin. I want to go home. I'm tired." It was true. Abruptly, I was exhausted. The dancing had both invigorated and oddly drained me.

"Don't give me your back, woman. Look at me."

I spun irritably.

He said nothing, merely cocked his beautiful dark head, regarding me for a long moment with those unusual, patient coppery eyes.

His shirt was half open, and I got a bit stuck there, so I yanked my gaze to his chin, but then his mouth was in my line of vision and I wasn't nearly done kissing it. I jerked my gaze to his eyes, narrowing mine, trying to decide if he was probing me.

"You'd feel me. Want me to show you?"

"Yes," I said testily. If any of this was true, and it seemed to be, I wanted to know if the itchy feeling I'd gotten with Althea was what it felt like. If I was going to be living in a place where others could do it, I needed to know when it was happening.

"You invited me in," he said carefully.

"Meaning?"

"You might wish to put some guards up. Ken you how to do that?"

"I've never had to."

"Then I won't. I'll teach you how to protect yourself first."

"A gentleman."

"Try not to sound so surprised."

"You must have dated every woman in this town." *Fucked* was what I really meant but wasn't about to say. To do so would betray a covetousness to which I had no right.

"Not one. And they rather despise me for it. I don't shit where I eat."

I blinked.

"It's a southern colloquialism."

"Northern, too. But *I'm* where you eat."

He sighed. "There is that. Come, I'll drive you home."

Home, I thought, as we turned and headed for the stairs.

It was such a seductive word.

But then, everything about Divinity was.

"IT'S TOO LATE," the man said quietly into his cell phone as he watched the couple in the black Mercedes drive away. "They broke the rules. It took the entire coven, all twelve Highblood families, but they awakened her fully tonight. Ripped her straight through the next six steps. She's empowered. Ignorant as fuck, with no clue what she is, but empowered, and you know how dangerous that is. She's both walking prey and nuclear bomb. I have no clue what they think they're doing. Trying to save their asses, I suppose, and they'll sweep up after the mess, if there's aught left to sweep. She could go either way now. Insanely risky, if you ask me."

He listened a moment. "I'm not sure I can. She's blood Cameron, from the nine houses, and she's fully awakened." Another pause. "Fuck you! You know I want the same thing. But I'm Half-blood. It's dangerous enough for me, being here. It was one thing when she was a sitting duck—"

He broke off, then snarled, "Fine. But no way I'm doing it. I may know someone who's willing, for the right price."

I woke the next morning, after a restless night of lucid, disturbing dreams, with the music of that incendiary reel playing in my head in exacting detail, each instrument, every voice, and especially the crazy-making beat of those relentless, lust-inciting drums.

I felt as if I'd dreamed the song, on repeat, all night. Rolling over in bed, I grabbed my phone and googled the lyrics, as best I could decipher them.

After a few minutes of video-surfing, I found it. The closest version to what I'd heard at the Shadows was by the Dolmen: "Witches Reel," although the band's drumming didn't compare. Last night, each thunderous crash had felt as if it was reverberating in my bones, rattling my soul, jarring me painfully, luminously awake and alive.

I'd certainly felt witchy dancing to it, I thought with a wry smile, then grief slammed into me. I'd been too exhausted from physical exertion (and more than a bit inebriated) last night to cry and had passed out the instant I'd slipped into bed. Anger wasn't far behind this morning, assaulting me with such ferocity, it would have doubled me over on the verge of puking if I'd been standing.

My mother had burned alive, and I knew how it felt. Somehow, I'd experienced it with her, though likely at a tenth of how hellish it was for her to endure. *How* had I experienced her death? Was that terrible moment we'd shared yet another mysterious facet of our "bloodline"? If Mom had been able to probe people like I could, she'd not only concealed the truth from me, but tried to make me believe I was imagining things. Had she *ever* planned to tell me? Was my strange ability, or "deep sight," one of those "things about the Greys" she'd promised we would discuss before she died, believing we had plenty of time?

She'd been taken far sooner than either of us had expected, ruthlessly murdered. The thought of my frail, gentle mother dying even more excruciatingly than she already was from cancer—by someone's deliberate design—was enough to make a mushroom cloud of bloodlust obliterate all capacity for linear thought. I pounded my pillow with a fist until my arm was trembling, then buried my face in it and wept until it was soaked with tears.

When the storm finally abated, I lay there, wondering how such a gentle, temperate woman could have given birth to the firestorm that was me lately. If Joanna Grey had ever felt a dragon stirring in her belly, you'd never have guessed it. More like a graceful, soft-eyed doe who ran and ran because the hunters were after us, always after us, and she'd hobbled me with blinders, telling me nothing, permitting their identities to remain a complete mystery to me. Instead of educating me, she'd taught her fawn to flee in ignorance, and we'd darted fearfully from town after town, erasing all trace of ourselves, over and over again.

No more.

Grief had consumed me from the moment I'd lost her. Now I felt the first stirrings of another emotion, one far more disturbing.

Anger.

At my mother.

For raising me in ignorance of what were clearly countless things I needed to know. For sharing nothing of our past, which had patently terrified her. If that past had managed to find its way into my present—it was a threat to which she'd left me blind. Unless, I mused, the safe, which she'd never once mentioned, held information she'd wanted me to have so badly that she'd told my best friend about it. Fact was, if I'd known it existed, I'd have snooped, and Mom knew me well enough to know that.

Impatient, I phoned the station again. When Tommy Jr. answered, I asked if Tom could give the package to Este, so she could bring it down to me Friday.

"Dunno. I'll talk to him. I know he's got to fill out a bunch of paperwork in order to release evidence, follow protocol."

"It's not evidence," I protested. "It's personal stuff."

"*Anything* recovered at the scene," Tommy clarified. "I'll have him call you as soon as possible."

Irritated, I thumbed off. I understood the pain of caring for a loved one with cancer, but I wanted that damn safe, and I wanted it now.

If I was to be doe or hunter, I wanted to be the one holding the crossbow.

A heavy duty, compound bow capable of ending life cleanly with a single arrow.

Despite my anger with my mother, she was and would always be my world, and whoever had burned her would also burn, I vowed so fiercely it disturbed me, made me wonder: Could I actually do that—kill someone deliberately?

It disturbed me even more deeply that I had no ready answer. The way I felt at the moment, yes, I would kill the person that had killed my mother; sight up from deep cover and take the bastard down.

Sighing, I pushed up from the bed, padded naked into the shower, and turned the spray on hot.

I'D FORGOTTEN TO let Rufus out last night, I realized as I hurried down the stairs thirty minutes later, but someone had. I supposed Devlin must have done it while I'd changed last night, because the Stygian owl was perched in his cubby outside the greenhouse, waiting to be let in. I smiled up at him, glad he'd not been trapped inside all night. "Hello, you handsome thing," I gushed, wondering if he'd ever be willing to perch on me again when I'd taken such a wild punch at him the night we'd met. I'd like that, walking around with this splendid, albeit rather demonic-looking beast riding on my shoulder.

He cocked his head, regarding me with pumpkin eyes.

I opened the door to the greenhouse and stepped back so he could fly in, but he didn't move. Then, after a moment, he ducked his head to push something off the ledge.

A small, bloody fox landed with a limp thud at my feet. Throat ripped open from ear to ear, the juvenile was clearly dead.

The thought *Wow, good for you, a fox, what a kill, big boy!* collided with *Oh, the poor little fox!* in my head, and the latter won. Narrowing my eyes, I scowled up at him. "Kill to eat. I need no gifts. I can feed myself."

Rufus stared at me unblinking for a long moment, then pushed aloft and circled the garden twice before ducking into the greenhouse, where he settled on his perch in the jackfruit tree, still staring at me, round-eyed.

"If it was a gift, thank you. But please don't bring me things that don't need to die. I love animals. All of them. More than people," I added frankly. Animals were pure, instinctive beings, devoid of malice, incapable of lying. I could stare into an animal's eyes all day without being buffeted by anything unpleasant, or even particularly complex.

He blinked slowly, and I suffered the fanciful thought he'd

acknowledged my words. I had witches on the brain and was devolving into all manner of fantasy. "A bird is a bird is a bird," I muttered, laughing at myself as I tugged the door closed behind me. Nothing more.

Still, just as the latch began to click into place, I could have sworn he whuffed something that sounded suspiciously like *pretty girl*.

AFTER A BREAKFAST of cheesy shrimp grits and a pork chop, plus two more of those fluffy lard biscuits warmed in the microwave and smothered with jam (I might actually need the size six clothing at this rate), I decided to continue my exploration of the manor, starting with Juniper's office.

So up the main stairs I went. I nodded to the Lady of Cameron Manor as I passed, humming softly—that damn song I couldn't get out of my head. After purging myself of anger and grief this morning, my mood and step were buoyant, and I supposed my emotions were just going to be all over the place for a while.

My night at the Shadows had done something to me. On the rare occasions I'd gone to bars back home (rarely going to the same one twice, unwilling to risk encountering a prior lover), I'd been hunting a man to share my bed. Last night, rather than refusing surnames, I'd actively sought them, committed them to memory as best I could, along with faces, because I planned to return to the club. I planned, at long last, to *stay*.

In so doing, I'd experienced the first faint stirrings of how it must feel to be part of a community. Though Mom and I had lived in Frankfort longer than we'd lived anywhere else, I'd had no time to make friends. Any and all precious free hours were spent by her side. I knew my neighbors, but not really, and mostly through gossip, not interaction.

I didn't delude myself that entry into local life here would be easy, but it was my nature to work hard, and I'd seen more than enough receptivity to my presence last night to make me cautiously optimistic. I could envision a future for myself here, and I wanted it.

I also wanted that elusive genetic testing so I could heave a sigh of relief and believe I truly deserved to be here and that all of this—home, community, financial security—was indisputably mine.

With money, I could hunt my mother's killer far more easily than without. At that thought, I checked my phone for the dozenth time. Still no call from Tom. I wanted to know where the accelerant had been found and how much of it there was, if the job was professional or sloppy. I was willing to allow a 2 percent possibility a gang of delinquent youth had done it just to watch something burn (believing no one was home), and details of the burn would, I felt, clarify the nature of the arsonist. Professional equaled intentional, which implied our past had caught up with us. Sloppy? Hmmm. Wasn't so sure what that meant.

Cresting the final step to the third floor, I circled the balustrade and was about to turn left into the southwest wing directly above Juniper's suite when I felt a curious tug to the right. Pausing, I glanced in that direction, down the corridor that led into the wing the maids avoided but for an annual cleaning, which was at least partially fire damaged and had rested abandoned for nearly seven decades.

For reasons I couldn't fathom, my desire to explore the gloom-filled corridor that traversed the front of the manor, closed doors lining both sides of the hallway, was abruptly stronger than my desire to find Juniper's office, and I'd not have believed that possible.

With a will of their own, my feet turned right. I moved to the mouth of the corridor and craned my neck to peer down it. The air here, at the entry, smelled old and stale, stagnant, hazed with dust and smoke. The hall seemed to stretch deceptively longer than possible, given the size of the house. The amber sconces that glowed invitingly in other parts of the manor were extinguished here, and I realized fire must have damaged the wiring and that the electricity was shut off in this wing. The only end to the corridor I could discern was a sort of telescopic dwindling to utter darkness.

Fire. Was I really ready to look at parts of a house that were charred? Would I weep again?

"Sorry to be disturbing you, ma'am."

I jerked, whirling to find Alice behind me, wearing a frown.

"I'd not be going into that wing, ma'am. It's best avoided. Didn't mean to startle you but there's a man below said there's some sort of problem at the barn. I could send Clyde, but, well, he has a bit of a bad leg, you know. Well, you don't know, but now you do." Hastily, she added, "It doesn't keep him from performing his duties. We're just . . . Well, the last ma'am knew and made allowances, not that Clyde ever *expected* allowances or special treatment, nor would any of us be asking such things of you, merely that—"

"No worries," I said hastily, to save her from what had devolved quickly into nervous babbling. Good grief, how many carts I was tethered to! And all were, understandably, apprehensive about whether I'd be making sweeping changes. Hastening to alleviate her fears, as well as those of the rest of the staff, I said, "Any exceptions made by Juniper will continue. If

Clyde has a troublesome leg, we'll work around it. Nothing will change. The barn?" I didn't even know there was a barn, but there had to be a place to store the machinery used to maintain the land.

"Behind the garage, through the Midnight Garden. You can't miss it."

"Did he say what kind of problem?"

She shook her head.

"I'll take care of it."

"Thank you, ma'am. And thank you about Clyde. He's a good man. He'll not disappoint you."

PAST THE GREENHOUSE, through the south gate, behind the garage, through another elaborate cast-iron gate welded into a towering brick enclosure, lay the Midnight Garden, which so thoroughly dazzled me, I briefly forgot about the barn. Dozens of mighty oaks bearing the aged, circular wounds of amputated lower limbs, stretched tall and smooth as graceful dancers, leafy parasols held aloft, fashioning a nearly impermeable ceiling of green through which scant sky peeked.

I felt as if I'd entered a secret world, a verdant, elemental place, spanning acres, where I'd have been unsurprised to find fairies tending the flowers and nymphs guarding the mirrored surfaces of stone-rimmed, moss-edged pools. Birdsong filled the air; squirrels leapt and played in their leafy homes.

The moment I entered those fourteen-foot-tall brick walls, time ceased to exist. As if in this garden there was no past or present or future. The very concept seemed silly here; time was obviously malleable, not linear, and one could as easily slip sideways as backward or forward. I fancied I might be standing in any century, in any country, perhaps one yet undiscovered—so apart and separate from the outside world did the Midnight Garden feel.

Holy, I thought. There was something very old and powerful here. The soil seemed to teem with life and possibility, thrumming with such energy I fancied I could feel a gentle vibration in the soles of my feet, as if the ground within these walls possessed a . . . knowing, an awareness . . . while the dirt that lay beyond was lifeless, inert. Here, things seeded would grow into their most abundant selves. Here, magic might be done, spells worked with the soil, so rich and full of life did it feel.

In the far corner, past a long, narrow reflecting pool circled with yet more smooth, flat stones, was what could only be the Sylvan Oak, with an inviting stone bench beneath it. I moved toward it, awed; I'd never beheld such a tree in my life, possessing such presence. It was nearly a hundred feet tall, the trunk a good thirty feet in circumference, and its branches, many of which rested heavily on the ground before thrusting back up to the sky, were so thick, so wide, Este and I might stretch on our backs side by side on a single limb, staring up at the canopy. This tree had suffered no amputations, limbs rambling from sky to earth before vaulting skyward again, unscarred. Enormous fringes of silvery moss drenched branches covered with ferns, ivy, and feathery vines. Here, a flower poked a shy head from a crevice. There, an owl had made its home; there, cocoons stuck delicately to the tender underbellies of leaves. The shimmering strands of a vast web (with a rather terrifyingly large yellow and black spider in the center) spanned a dozen feet, limb to limb. The Sylvan Oak was its own untouched ecosystem.

"Aren't you majestic?" I exclaimed, moving to the trunk, pressing my palms to the warm bark, as if I might feel the centuries of life pulsing in the sap that fed its bright, giant heart.

And, for a moment, I could have sworn I actually *did* feel a heartbeat of sorts. I jerked reflexively, backing away, eyeing it uneasily. Surely I'd imagined that.

I considered striding aggressively forward and pressing my hands to it again, then reconsidered. Mom always said, *Only ask a question, Zo, if you are fully prepared for any possible answer.* I had no interest in encountering even one more oddity to deal with. My psychic abilities that were shared by others in this town, Althea's nearly immobilizing fear of someone or something, Mom's murder, the countless unusual characteristics of the manor—it was all more than enough to keep me on a kind of constantly uneasy edge. If this tree somehow had a heartbeat, I was having an ostrich moment; head buried in the sand, I'd rather not know.

I shook myself. "The barn," I muttered, wondering just what kind of trouble could happen in a barn. Surely not anything too dramatic. It was just a barn, after all.

Right?

Then again, nothing else in Divinity seemed to be just anything. There were layers upon layers to unravel in this place.

To my left, another cast-iron gate, the exit from the garden. I hurried through it, toward the sprawling, rectangular, metal-roofed structure beyond.

As I entered the outbuilding via the large double doors, I inhaled deeply of sweet-clover hay, leather and saddle soap, and something bright and lemony. The barn was enormous and gloomy but for shafts of diffuse sunlight splintering through weathered siding, with a poured concrete floor upon which hulked combines, tractors, and trailers. Dusty stakes of forgot-

ten tobacco hung on high tiers, and horse stalls ran the length
of both sides. The outbuilding had a partial second floor stuffed
to overflowing with bales of hay and sacks of seed and fertilizer.
Far above, at the apex of the steeply sloped roof, suspended from
timbers by thick ropes, hung ancient farming implements, clear-
ing room for modern equipment on the floor.

"Hello?" I called. "Is anyone here?"

When there was no answer, a chill of foreboding licked up
my spine.

Retreat, that chill demanded. But the senses I'd been raised
to rely upon—things like sight and sound—were unable to discern cause for unease, and with pragmatism ingrained in me at
a young age, I called again, "Hello!" and took a few more steps
into the dimly lit outbuilding, skirting a combine, to peer deeper
into the shadows of the barn.

I don't know what tipped me off, but something did. I decided later I must have heard a creak as the implement above
me shifted, groaning on its ropes. My head whipped up, and
I saw one of those archaic pieces of farm machinery, a sort of
heavy, antiquated hay raker, shuddering on its tethers. Then it
was plunging straight for me, its countless long, curved prongs
saber-sharp. I staggered back, whirling to evade it, and three
enormous black mastiffs sprang savagely at me, snapping and
snarling, foam frothing their muzzles. I whirled to go the other
way, only to find three more slavering mastiffs there. I was trapped
between them.

My gaze whipped back up, and I saw death on those shining
blades. Something inside me ignited, as time suspended and my
life flashed before my eyes, and I realized I'd *had* no life yet and
I was, by God, not dying in a barn, killed by a farm implement,
hemmed in by savage dogs.

The mushroom cloud I'd felt this morning was back, a thing of unspeakable breadth and violence, white-hot and radioactive, shot through with an endless cry of injustice that my time here would be cut so short, just when good things had finally started happening to me. The cloud saturated every atom of my being, smoking, searing, charring me from within, and just when it became unbearable, when I felt it might scorch my soul from my body, driven by basest instinct, I pushed at the cloud, trying to thrust it out of me, driven by the sudden conviction my inner nuclear bomb might obliterate me before the machinery did.

I pushed at the radioactive mess with all my might, trying to scrape it into one great ball of poison and eject it from my body—I shoved and *shoved*, consumed by fury at the thing that sought to end my life, that damned machine—then the cloud was gone and I was woozy, on the verge of collapse. The machinery was almost on me when, abruptly, the lethal implement veered sharply to the left and landed on the combine with a grinding screech of metal against metal and an explosion of fiery sparks. It flattened the roof of the combine like an accordion, crushing it to the cab, vicious saber claws slamming to the floor where they gouged up chunks of concrete. Then, shivering and jerking, it collapsed in a conjoined heap of twisted metal and went still.

I stumbled backward, sobbing with fear and relief, a hand pressed to my chest, then spun and raced from the barn as fast as my trembling legs would carry me.

Only when I was nearly back to the house did I think—where had those terrifying dogs gone?

For that matter, where the hell had they *come* from?

I WAS SITTING at the kitchen island, a cup of coffee cradled in my still-trembling hands, when Alice arrived. The instant I'd returned to the house, I'd accosted the nearest maid and asked her to send Alice to me in the kitchen ASAP.

"The man who came to the door," I said sharply. "Who was he?"

Startled by my tone, she said nervously, "Truth be told, ma'am, I'd never seen him before. Is something amiss?"

I itched to return to the barn and inspect the ropes responsible for securing the equipment to the roof timbers and determine: Cut or frayed? But there was no way I was going back out there just yet. Inconceivable that this chain of events—new heir to immense fortune gets summoned to barn; no one's there; heavy machinery nearly kills her; and, oh, let's not forget the mystifying appearance of slavering dogs—was coincidence.

I locked eyes with Alice, rules be damned, and probed. Genuine concern, worry for her job, but no idea who the man was. She was telling the truth. If she had any awareness of my invasion, she didn't betray it.

"Do men you've never seen before often come to the door of the manor?"

"It happens from time to time. The farm crew changes. Few care to labor in the fields around these parts anymore. Our foreman, Leith Donaghue, struggles to find good men. Though he runs background checks on new hires, the field hands can be a rough lot, ma'am."

"Do I own dogs? Are there any here at the manor?"

She looked at me blankly. "No, ma'am. Juniper didn't have dogs."

"Thank you, Alice. That's all."

She didn't move. "Was I wrong to come to you, ma'am?" she said, anxiously twisting her hands in her apron.

"Not at all."

Still she didn't move, and I realized she wasn't going to. My tone had worried her, and in future dealings with the staff, I would take care to modulate my voice more carefully. Each word I uttered carried enormous weight here. Though I'd spent my life in service, I was boss to this staff. It was a new role for me and would take getting used to. Alice would stand there, certain she'd done something wrong, until I offered her an explanation. Even then, I suspected, she'd fret about it the rest of the day.

"There was no one in the barn," I told her.

"Apologies for wasting your time, ma'am," Alice said in a strained voice.

"You did nothing wrong. But if that man comes back again, please let me know immediately."

"Yes, ma'am." With a duck of her head and a near curtsey, she backed hastily from the room.

Backed. What was I—the queen? I sighed. To them, quite possibly. This town had certainly revolved around Juniper as if she were their royal mistress.

There were a few conclusions I could draw from what had just happened. Someone (with well-trained, terrifying dogs) had made an attempt on my life. The man who'd come to the door had gotten me sent to the barn so the attempt could be made. The man who'd done the luring was not necessarily the one who'd done the attempted killing. He might have simply been the messenger. There might be a pair of them after me.

Did people so detest my inheriting Cameron Manor they were willing to kill me to get rid of me? The most obvious suspects were the alternate heirs—the Alexanders. They stood to gain the most. But I'd met them last night, and unless I couldn't read people at all without using my invasive ability, they'd struck me as fine ones. As a server, I'd gotten a feel for the tiniest of details, ticks, gestures, the subtle shifting of a gaze that offered insight as to whether I would get a good tip, get stiffed, or have to fend off a grab for my breast or ass. I'd not gotten a single cue from the Alexanders that alarmed me. Nor, however, had I spent protracted one-on-one time with them. I intended do so in the near future, preferably in a public place, with loads of witnesses.

One hundred and fifty million dollars was a lot of money. People killed for far, far less. What had I gotten myself into? Would a wiser woman walk away? And return to what? Indiana, crushing debt, incessant work, no idea who'd burned our house and killed my mother, and neither money enough nor time to search for those answers.

Icy resolve filled me.

Not the doe. Never the doe.

Mine was the compound bow.

I was not running. I would never run again.

IF THE SPIRIT of Juniper Cameron lingered somewhere in the manor, it was in her office. A sense of masterful competence pervaded the serene room where, for decades, she'd overseen the care of the estate and the needs of Divinity.

The room felt so calm, so good to me, that I stood in the center of it for a few moments, eyes closed, absorbing the tranquility. After the morning I'd had, I needed it.

I'd decided, after finishing with Alice, to resume my search for the genetic testing, partly because I wanted to shove it in Althea Bean's face, but mostly to get my mind off what had just happened. I couldn't tease at the snarl of ugliness just yet; I needed to decompress. It was a defense mechanism I'd learned caring for

Mom. Each time we'd gotten increasingly worse news, I'd gone somewhere, done something to distract myself, avoiding the topic entirely. It had sometimes taken me days to face and digest the latest blow.

An hour ago, death had loomed above me, flashing on lethal blades, and I had no idea how I'd escaped it or why the machinery had abruptly shifted trajectory, crushing the combine, not me. And that was the least of the many things disturbing me.

Shoving thoughts of the event from my mind, I assessed the room. Towering bookcases flanked the perimeter, broken only by a mammoth fireplace with an ornate, pillared surround. Books stretched up more than twice my height, the upper shelves accessed by an anchored, rolling ladder. The ceiling was coffered with inset squares of gleaming copper, etched with more of those swirling triskelions.

The room was soothingly dark, brooking no distraction from the manor beyond the heavy and, I suspected, sound-proofed doors through which I'd entered. Here, as in Juniper's master suite, there was no trace of technology, no flat-screen television, no phone, no fax. Polished mahogany, embossed ivory carpet, and walls of midnight blue wove a spell of peace and clarity. A vase of those spicy-scented blue and cream roses perched atop the mantel of the fireplace, before which the desk was positioned. The drapes were ivory velvet, pulled tightly shut, the lighting soft, the furnishings elegantly inviting, with a tufted sofa and matching wingchairs.

I moved to the desk and, after divining nothing of interest atop it other than bills, the standard accessories, and an exquisite stained-glass lamp, opened the drawers and began rifling. Twenty minutes later, with nothing to show for it, I moved to the file cabinets built into the lower shelves of the bookcases.

Blueprints and plans, ledgers and accounts, folders of business investments so complex I didn't even bother trying to decipher them. Endless files of legal documents.

No genetic testing.

Next, I began searching the shelves for the family Bible and got quickly fixated on an ancient-looking leather tome on a high shelf, which not even tiptoeing on the ladder made me tall enough to reach.

I eyed the enormous fireplace a moment, decided the thick mantel would support me, and might well grant me the few inches I needed to reach the book. Easing onto it, I found myself a scant inch or two shy of success.

But, I mused, studying the ornate surround, if I clung to the ornamental header, I could leverage myself up onto the plinth supporting the right column, which would give me another four inches, more than I needed.

Clutching the header, I wedged my toe into the nook between the fluted cleft and centerboard, and was about to step up when, abruptly, there was a loud click, and to my astonishment, a wide panel of books swung soundlessly back to my right, revealing a cavernous darkness beyond.

I wanted to smack myself in the head for so swiftly forgetting the concealed doors in the manor. I eased back onto the ladder, practically slid down it, and peered into the opening that, aside from a faint pool of light spilling from behind me, was black as pitch. Leaning forward, I fumbled along the wall for a light switch but found none.

As my eyes acclimated to the darkness, I could have sworn I saw the faintest outline of a woman standing in the dark room, staring straight at me!

Backpedaling, I demanded sharply, "Who's there?" When there

was no reply, I spun and darted from one window to the next, yanking open the drapes, ushering the light of day into the midnight room. As I'd hoped, shafts of sun streamed through the door, into the hidden chamber.

Squaring my shoulders, I stalked back to the entry, peered in, and shook off a shudder, exhaling with shaky relief.

A life-size painting perched on an easel amidst dozens of other portraits and photos positioned on tables and affixed to walls.

I entered the room slowly—finding a light switch!—then began perusing the tables. Here, tucked into a shrine of sorts, were the Ladies of Cameron Manor. There were hundreds of photos and miniatures, some hanging, others atop graceful consoles and pedestal tables, along with an assortment of knickknacks; here, a highly polished silver hand mirror with the engraved initials EJC, there, a fancy, jeweled hair comb, a fringed clutch, a pocket-sized book of poetry.

I had no idea where these women fell in succession throughout the years but could determine the approximate era of their reign by the clothing and format in which they'd been rendered. I studied their faces intently, seeking resemblance, assurance that I was one of them. But other than hopeful imaginings that my nose, indeed, resembled this one's, or my eyes seemed to slant the same as another's did, I found none of the certainty for which I hungered. Not one of them, not even the one who'd startled me, who I decided had to be Juniper herself, as she was clad in the most modern attire, had amber eyes or any other particularly defining Grey feature that I could, with firm conviction, claim as my own.

My benefactor appeared to have sat for her portrait in her early thirties. Young and willowy, with strong bones, high cheeks, and a quirk of a smile at her mouth, blond hair twisted back in a chignon, Juniper radiated strength, humor, and resilience. She was the kind of woman one would never call pretty—it was too small and common a word—although she was stately and handsome in the way of a fine seafaring ship or an elegant pedigreed racehorse. There were dozens of smaller photos of her, too, documenting the passage of years, ending with one in which she must have been nearly a century old. Blue eyes still twinkled with mirth, in nests of deep wrinkles, beneath a wispy cap of thin, snowy curls. Though her face had collapsed to soft jowls and sagging skin, her cheeks remained round and red and smooth. A darling Mrs. Claus. It was no surprise the townsfolk adored her.

Wondering if one day my photos might also find their way here (assuming I survived that long), and inspired by Juniper's graceful strength and resilience, I decided to tackle the morning's unpleasant event and phone Mr. Balfour for his thoughts.

I didn't see the door until I was walking out and caught the barest glimpse of it from the corner of my eye, so subtly and seamlessly was it set into the wall between portraits, framed by nearly nonexistent trim, sporting a low-set crystal doorknob.

I hurried over to it, turned the knob, and pushed, surprised to find the crystal icy cold.

When it didn't budge, I realized it must be a pull-door, so I tugged. Still didn't budge. Stooping, I inspected the bizarrely cold knob for a locking mechanism, but found none. I examined the frame and decided the door was definitely an outie, so I pulled again. It felt as if the thing was glued to the wall, and I wondered if it was decorative but couldn't fathom the purpose of a decorative door. It didn't look particularly artistic to me.

Irritably, I tugged again, then, feeling a bit foolish and pigheaded, braced my foot against the wall, and (half expecting to go flying backward once it gave, crash into the paintings, and make a godawful mess) yanked on the door with all my strength.

It may as well have been set in stone.

Sighing, rubbing my hands together to warm them, I made a mental note to ask Mr. Balfour if he knew anything about it. Though he said he'd never toured the entire manor, surely in their decades of working together, he must have been in Juniper's office a time or two.

I pulled the drapes as I exited but left the door to the concealed room ajar and the light on. Something about the hidden room made me uncomfortable, but I couldn't put my finger on what. Why was a room that was clearly a tribute to the women who'd governed the manor so private? Why weren't the photos proudly displayed in an accessible area of the home? It struck me as odd and of almost . . . sinister intent, a sort of "these are the ladies, but they must be hidden away." Then there was the door with the icy knob that wouldn't open, which I found inexplicably eerie.

As I was passing through the southwest parlor, my phone rang with the call I'd been waiting for. Perching on a sofa, I answered it swiftly. "Hi, Tom. How's Dottie?" When you've watched a loved one drown in the brutal waves of a terminal illness, that's the first question out of your mouth to someone in the same boat.

"As well as she can be," he said wearily. "Thanks for asking."

I knew that weariness well. After a bit of small talk about her treatment and my assurance that we'd stored nothing flammable on the property, Tom told me the gas was concentrated in the basement, that one of the ancient casement windows had likely been broken for access, and he was disturbed by the quantity of accelerant found in the debris.

"Fact is, Zo, the moment the fire started, we could have been blocks away and not had a hope in hell of putting it out."

"Any leads?"

"Not one. We don't get fires like that around here. Normally, I'd look at the owner, but Ray's mortgage was paid off, and he carried no insurance. He had nothing to gain and a lot to lose. I'll keep an eye peeled for similar fires in surrounding cities and towns, but apart from that, we got ourselves a dead case. No one to question, nothing to investigate."

"Ray called and threatened me. Said he was going to sue."

Tom snorted. "I'll have a talk with him. He's been off the wagon again for months. You know how he gets. You got nothing to worry about, honey; you were in an interview when it happened, and nobody, but *nobody*, would ever believe you'd harm a hair on your mother's head. You devoted your whole life to her. Ray's a bitter, angry man. I'll handle him."

"Thank you," I said quietly. "Would you mind giving the contents of the safe to my friend, Este, who's coming to see me this weekend?"

"Where are you? Thought you were staying at that studio."

"Louisiana."

"Sorry, Zo. Wish I could, but I got to document proof of release only to next of kin, or executor of the estate."

"But I don't know when I'll be back," I protested. "What about shipping it to me?"

He was silent a long moment.

"It could be *months* before I'm in Indiana," I pressed determinedly.

Sighing, he said, "Technically, I'm supposed to hand it off."

"Surely if you UPS it to me with tracking, that's sufficient documentation. *Please*," I added fervently. "Mom was my world. Don't make me wait months."

Another sigh, then, "I expect I can make tracking proof enough."

"Oh, thank you!" I exclaimed, releasing a breath I'd not even realized I was holding. I wasn't certain it would arrive at the manor without street numbers, so I gave him the address of the Balfour and Baird Law Firm (without telling him it was a law firm, making a mental to note to apprise Mr. Balfour that a package for me would be arriving there). Tom promised to drop by the station sometime tomorrow and take it to UPS himself, which meant it would be here by Saturday, Monday at the latest.

After thanking him and wishing him the best, I was about to thumb off when he said, "Count your blessings it wasn't one of your days off, Zo, or you'd have died in that fire, too. Neighbors said they heard explosions, then the whole place was engulfed in flames. Happened pretty much instantly."

I sat frozen, holding the phone to my ear after he'd hung up.

I'd been so consumed by grief, so overwhelmed by the sudden, drastic change in my circumstances, and so enraged that someone had intentionally set the fire that had killed my mother, that I'd failed to recall it *was* supposed to be one of my days off.

I should have been home that day, too. I would have been, if I'd not gotten fired. We'd likely have been in Mom's bedroom, with an assortment of whatever treats I'd been able to afford at the grocery store that week, talking or watching a movie. Had whoever'd doused the basement with gasoline also crept silently up the stairs and barricaded the door to her room? Would we have both died, clutching each other, screaming? Had whoever burned the house *expected* me to be home? Was that day the first of what were actually *two* attempts on my life? Was I the target all along, and Mom merely collateral damage?

That thought enraged me even more. How long ago had Juniper Cameron informed people in Divinity that she'd located an heir, mentioned my name? Althea Bean had known details about me. Had it been long enough for an arsonist to put a plan in motion? Was I being sighted up and hunted? If so, what next?

"Pardon, ma'am?"

Scrambling to collect my wits, I turned to find a maid I'd not yet met framed in the doorway, wringing her hands and shifting her weight from foot to foot.

Oh, God, what now? "Yes?" I managed.

"Sorry to disturb you, but Leith is wondering what to do with the body."

I had to replay the question through my mind several times; still I wasn't entirely certain I'd heard her correctly. "The body?" I said carefully, nearly inaudibly, in case I'd heard her wrong. Surely I'd heard her wrong.

"Yes, ma'am."

Well, that wasn't informative. "What body?"

"The one in the barn."

"There's a body in the barn?" I said, even more carefully, keeping my face impassive, which was a feat, given my dawning horror.

She nodded, clearly uncomfortable.

"A dead body? As in a dead *person*?" Seriously? What the hell?

"Yes, ma'am."

"I'm sorry. I must be missing something. *Why* is there a dead person in the barn?"

She shrugged, looking miserable.

I opened my mouth, closed it again. There'd been no one there when I was, at least not that I'd seen. Finally, I said, faintly, "Is this a common occurrence?" Had I inherited a haunted, murderous barn that, while it had failed to kill me, had succeeded in killing someone else?

"No, ma'am. This is a first."

Facts, I reminded myself—a technique I'd learned at repeated doctor's appointments where the news just kept getting worse and worse—divorce emotion, wed wit to facts. "Do we know whose body it is?" That should shed some light.

"Alice said it was the man who came to the door earlier, ma'am."

I gaped. "How did he die?" Savage dog attack? Another piece of equipment fell?

"I was asking for Leith, ma'am. He's not certain what to do with it."

"Yes, but how did he die?" I repeated, voice rising despite my efforts to project calm assurance and control.

"I'm sorry, ma'am," she said. "Leith didn't say."

I was silent a long moment, then said, "Would you mind bringing Leith here? Alice, too."

"Yes, ma'am."

Again, I got the deferential nod, the near curtsey, the backing away. I wasn't sure what horrified me more: that there was a dead person in the barn or that when the staff found dead bodies, they sent maids to ask me how to dispose of them.

When once again she was framed in the doorway, with an extremely uncomfortable-looking Alice in tow, along with a stocky, ruddy-faced man who could only be the foreman, Leith, I motioned for them to come in.

They filed into the room and stood side by side, facing me and looking as if they'd rather be facing a firing squad.

"I understand you found a body in the barn," I said carefully to Leith.

"Yes, ma'am."

To Alice, "Was it the man who came to the door earlier?"

"Yes, ma'am."

"You're certain?"

"Absolutely, ma'am."

I felt like the Inquisition, with all these nervous people and *ma'ams*. I felt also like the subject of one. As lady of the manor, this was *my* problem, and I was leagues out of my depth. I queried Leith, "Was he crushed by machinery?"

He looked startled by the question. "No, but a piece had fallen. The ropes gave. Hit the combine, damaged it badly."

"Were the ropes frayed or cut?"

"I didn't inspect them."

Feigning confidence that I certainly didn't feel, I said, "Please do so, then bring them to the house. How did the man die?"

"I didn't see any injuries, ma'am. I just wanted to know what to do with the body."

Warily, I decided to fish. "What are the options?"

He said tightly, "Bury it. Burn it. Sink it in one of the lakes. Call the coroner."

Okay, now we'd moved beyond horrifying. He'd listed the coroner last and hadn't mentioned the police at all. "Have you had to dispose of bodies on the estate before?" I said sharply.

"I'm only saying I'll handle it however you wish, ma'am."

"Have you had to dispose of bodies on the estate before?" I said again, not about to let him evade the question. Just what kind of place was this?

"Never, ma'am," he said heatedly, with an unmistakable sheen of accusation in his gaze. "There were no bodies needing disposing." I heard *Then you came along, and presto, we've got one. Things certainly weren't run so slipshod when Juniper was here!*

"I'd like you to call the coroner. I want to know who the man is, why he was here, and how he died. I take it he's not one of your hires?"

"No, ma'am. Never seen him before. Not from around these parts."

"Have the coroner call me when he's picked up the . . ." I couldn't finish the sentence. The same man who'd lured me to the barn to be killed had somehow met his own death there.

"Yes, ma'am," Leith said. "I'll place the ropes at the south porch door. Will that be all, ma'am?"

When I nodded, they had a bit of a Three Stooges moment, tripping over each other in their haste to leave my presence.

I sat motionless after they'd gone, flexing my hand in that old, impossible-to-break habit, as if reaching for assurance or comfort, but finding none, only an absence where I seemed to expect, or hope, for something to be. I'd often wondered if it was the unconscious, instinctive act of a little girl reaching for a father she'd never known, a strong hand to hold, something to make her feel safe.

Forcing myself to stop, I inhaled slowly and exhaled even more slowly, steadying myself. I'd only just gotten my brain wrapped around the fact that a man had set me up to be killed, possibly even tried to kill me himself, that there may have been (likely had been!) a prior attempt on my life in Indiana, that my mother had been murdered—and now I had a dead body on my hands and yet another question on what was rapidly becoming a long and terrifying list.

Who on earth had killed *him*?

Alisdair

A ROYAL WITCH'S FOOTFALLS AGAIN *shudder through the earth of Cameron estate, ebbing and flowing, nourishing and draining. To the music in her blood, the young Cailleach was made to dance by a coven powerful enough to awaken the moon in the midnight sky, abundant enough to inspire the lust and covetousness of every other coven in existence, a coven dangerously unprotected. It is not merely my enemy that concerns me but the fate and very soul of Divinity.*

She sees me but doesn't see me, and I must find a way to change that. There is much I could teach her, enough that, with the power I sense in her blood, she might stand a chance. Minuscule, admittedly, but a chance is a chance is a chance, whereas, contrary to her limiting beliefs, a bird is not always a bird.

Here in Divinity, precious little is what it seems.

The witch weeps, and despite what happened today, those tears give me hope. If I can reach her, she is there to be reached. Her heart is light yet . . .

Ah, the savage vicissitudes of fate! Blood was spilled on hallowed, knowing ground, before she was pledged, and she drew power to protect herself in the most perilous of ways!

She dances on a minefield of her own making.

Where is that stillness now, witch? You must find it again. It is all that will serve you, all that can save you.

Do not make the same mistake again.

It will bind you for life. At least, what little of it remains, should our enemy prevail.

THIS REALLY WASN'T NECESSARY, I could have come down to your office," I told Mr. Balfour as we settled into the seating cozy in the south reception room a mere twenty minutes after I'd phoned him, detailing what had happened to me in the barn, from the implement falling and veering, to the mysterious dogs, and finally apprising him of the body. Truth was, I'd hungered to get behind the wheel of the Mercedes, watch the manor dwindle in my rearview mirror, and escape for a few hours.

"You'll not be leaving the house without protection until I get to the bottom of this," James Balfour said firmly.

"Protection?"

"You now have bodyguards: two out front, two in the rear courtyard. They'll change shift at dusk and dawn. Sleep easy knowing whatever danger is out there, you have eight of the most dangerous men alive guarding you twenty-four seven. Ex-special-ops, mercenaries. Lethal when necessary. They follow orders. They'll die to keep you alive. The moment you exit the house, assuming you have reason to do so"—his tone implied strongly I should *not*—"they will be at your side. And, lest you fret, they are extremely well compensated by the estate. Should any of them expire, their families will also be well compensated."

Expire. Tidy word, that. I shivered at the tone in Mr. Balfour's voice, which was unlike anything I'd heard from him before: flat, implacable, coldly efficient.

"And I suppose they were just hanging around, on standby, in case they were needed?" I mocked.

He shot me a measuring look and laughed softly. "Yes, Ms. Grey, Juniper was concerned something like this might happen. I'm the fool that wasn't. She said I underestimated the lure of wealth, as wealth has never been my driving force."

"Who wants me dead? The alternate heir?"

"I'd be stupefied if this was the work of Archie and Isabel. They knew they were Juniper's alternates, yet I've not seen anyone more relieved than they were when she told them she'd located you. They have a wonderful life with four lovely children, in a beautiful home, in a peaceful town. Stepping into Juniper's shoes is akin to inheriting the crown. It changes everything, and that isn't a transformation they sought. They would have become, as you have now, the focus of countless eyes and myriad, time-consuming demands. They would have complied, given up jobs they love—she's a children's book editor, and he's an international tax lawyer—and done their duty, as duty runs deep in them. But they'd never have chosen it willingly, and that's part of why Juniper selected them. He who hungers for the crown rarely wears it well."

"Then who?"

A gusty sigh, then, "I'm bound by contingencies. There are countless matters I wish to discuss with you at length, Ms. Grey, but I am currently prohibited. Should I violate those stipulations, your inheritance is in jeopardy. It's possible that's all someone sought. Not truly to try to kill you, but to make us *think* they had, goading me to make a misstep and ignore Juniper's express legally binding wishes. Should I do so, your position as the Cameron heir can be formally contested. If that's what happened here—a charade that was never meant to result in your death, only to frighten you—virtually anyone in Divinity might go that far. You're an outsider, an unknown, and many here ascribe to the adage 'better the devil you know.'"

"You said 'currently.' When do these contingencies no longer apply?"

"The moment you read Juniper's letter, which can be opened no earlier than 12:01 a.m. Tuesday morning. I'm to inspect it Monday evening, to ascertain the seal is still intact."

I'd arrived Monday night, and it was only Wednesday. That gave me six more nights to wait. "Do you have any idea how bizarre and off-putting all these contingencies are?"

"I can well imagine. Your friend, Este Hunter . . . perhaps she could come in this weekend."

"And that's even more bizarre and off-putting. You know who my friends are."

"Juniper had a report compiled on you. I was given a copy to read so I might better assist you when you arrived."

"If I need security, why would you suggest I invite my friend into potential danger?"

"I can guarantee as long as you are inside the manor, you will come to no harm. I will personally see to Ms. Hunter's safe arrival and leave-taking."

"How is this house so safe, when there's not even a security system?" A lack I'd found odd, given Juniper's wealth. "Four guards can't cover every window and door."

"The manor has no need of a security system, I assure you. You'll have to take my word on it for now. You'll understand, soon enough. Stay, at least until you've read her letter and we've had our talk. Invite your friend, enjoy your time together, in the house or at the pool, or take the guards with you, should you leave." He paused, then said quietly, "*Please*, Ms. Grey. You won't regret it.

You were born to be the heir of Cameron Manor. The blood of—her blood is in your veins. Juniper wasn't wrong."

Narrowing my eyes, I decided to fish on topics he was surely permitted to discuss. "Did Juniper have siblings?"

"Three older brothers. They fought in World War II. Two came back in coffins. The youngest, Marcus, went missing in action. It nearly destroyed Juniper, losing all three of them in the space of two years. She was in her early twenties. I've wondered if the one who went missing perhaps suffered amnesia from a war injury or, for an unfathomable reason, elected not to return. If he survived and had offspring, that might explain you. You could be her great-great-niece. But even before that, in prior centuries, the occasional Cameron son or daughter went missing or wandered off. No idea how far back or tangential an offshoot you might be."

"There's a door in Juniper's office that doesn't open. Do you know anything about it?"

"I've been in her office many times and never seen such a door."

"It's in the concealed room."

His brows rose. "That explains why I've never seen it. I had no idea there was one."

"Why do you want my friend to come visit?" Locking gazes with him, I said forcefully, "Invite me in."

Inhaling sharply, his eyes flared with shock, and he stiffened, then slowly relaxed. "By your leave, Ms. Grey," he said, holding my gaze.

I don't get words or even linear images. I get emotion with a bit of context and the flash of a vision or two. James Balfour's motives were of pure intent. The only flash I got was a brief image of a seven-pointed star on a delicate chain. He genuinely believed Este could help me, that she knew things I needed to know. I couldn't imagine what . . . unless . . . perhaps Mom had told Este about far more than the existence of a mere safe. The idea that she might have done so evoked both hope and a deep sense of daughterly betrayal—that my mother might tell my best friend things she'd not told me. Was that why Este had so insistently been calling, trying to see me since Mom died?

"When you did that in my office the afternoon we met, I didn't think you knew what you were doing," Mr. Balfour murmured.

I hadn't really understood it at the time, not the way I did now, but I had no intention of admitting it. "Can everyone in Divinity do it?"

"Many. Certainly not everyone."

"What is this ability?"

"Contingencies, Ms. Grey. Please be patient."

"How did the man in the barn die? Has anyone told you?"

"Not yet. But the moment I know, I'll text you. Will you phone Ms. Hunter?"

So many bizarre and deeply unsettling things had happened to me in such a short time, I desperately needed to see my best friend to hash it all out. And if Mom had told Este things that she'd never told me . . . Well, there was that surge of hope and pissed-off sense of betrayal again. "I already invited her. She'll be here Friday." Two days from now, thank heavens.

A smile lit his face. "Then you'll stay?"

"Tonight? Yes. Beyond that, I commit to nothing." I rose, feeling I'd gotten all the answers from James Balfour I was going to get until Tuesday morning at 12:01 a.m. And yes, *if* I was still here, I would most definitely be awake at the witching-hour-plus-one-minute, ripping that damned letter open.

Rising, he said in a low, intense voice, "I make this vow freely,

Ms. Grey. I will protect you with each and every tool at my dis-posal. I pledge my life to guard the blood heir of Cameron Manor."

So formal, so serious. "I've arranged for a package to be shipped to your office in my name. Please bring it to me the moment it arrives. Speaking of, is there a street address for the manor?"

"One Watch Hill," he replied.

I'd half expected him to say 666, so forbidding was the exte-rior of the stygian citadel, so strange the events in and around the place. "Thank you. That will be all." I was surprised by how smoothly I issued the curt dismissal, but I was frustrated, on the cusp of angry, and I'd not gotten a single answer from him, other than information about Juniper's siblings, that I deemed worth a damn.

THOUGH DEEPLY DISTRACTED, I managed to set up pay-ment plans with my creditors and choose a local attorney to re-view the settlement papers. The latter proved simpler than the former. In Frankfort, I was destitute Zo Grey, who owed money to nearly every doctor and hospital in a hundred-mile radius. In Divinity, I was Ms. Grey-Cameron, heir to an unfathomable fortune.

Mr. Ian Laherty of Laherty, Logan & Associates assured me he would have a copy of the settlement papers sent to his of-fice directly from Balfour and Baird—no need to trouble myself bringing them down—and a full report, reviewed by all part-ners, would be delivered to the manor at eleven tomorrow morn-ing by him, personally, as he'd relish the opportunity to say hello and welcome me to Divinity. When I inquired about payment, he told me it was an honor for his firm to provide the service, and he hoped I might consider them for future business endeavors.

I sat for a time after we hung up, mulling the strangeness of my life (setting aside, for the moment, the murder attempts; I'm a pro at compartmentalizing), dwelling solely upon how bizarre it felt to be courted by businesses, rather than bullied, threatened, and treated like the shadiest of debt dodgers.

When I found the ropes at the south porch door, I studied them intently, deciding irritably that although they looked frayed, they might have been manipulated to *look* frayed, and I could draw no firm conclusions about them.

It was early evening by the time I made my way to the kitchen to find food. I'd not eaten since breakfast, and apparently a brush with death was a shot of steroids to my appetite, because I was desperately, shakily ravenous. I glanced out the window as I passed through the front foyer, hoping to catch a glimpse of the bodyguards, but there were no men stationed on the porch.

Hurrying to the kitchen, I spied all four standing out by the pool, wearing headpieces and carrying guns, one giving orders, the others nodding.

Candy, I thought, staring.

I have a sweet tooth for a certain type of man, and James Balfour had stationed four decadent pieces of candy outside my door. As if Devlin wasn't temptation enough. These men would hopefully be of short duration. Perhaps they rotated out and were replaced every few days. Or, I mused, I could request replacements and not feel guilty because this type of professional likely had a waiting list of high-paying employers. I had a feeling James Balfour would do anything I asked, so long as I stayed.

My gaze drifted from one ruggedly attractive man to the next, as I pondered which man I was going to—

What was *wrong* with me?

Not only was I behaving as if I had no intention of leaving, I was scoping out a potential lay! It seemed Kellan had awakened a fire in me that could only be put out one way.

Not. Happening.

Shaking my head, I hurried to the fridge, heaped pork chops and shrimp grits on a plate, added some creamed corn I spotted in a covered bowl, plus a scoop of green beans with cottage ham, snagged another plate upon which I piled biscuits, plucked a bottle of jam from the fridge, and without warming any of it, sat at the counter and began shoveling it in.

Only after I'd wolfed down half my food was I able to place my fork aside and contemplate heating the rest. I was obsessed with Lennox's lard-based biscuits, and they weren't nearly as good cold.

I realized, then, that I was in light shock. Too much had happened, too fast; my brain was on overload and no longer processing data properly.

It used to happen when I was young, if Mom moved us too often; a kind of emotional whiplash would hit me, and I'd detach from my feelings, focus only on my physical needs, which, of course, amplified them. It was a dangerous way to be, as it was precisely those emotions I was refusing to feel (why make friends/ why care/we'll only leave again just when I start to feel happy) that drove my physical needs, and as I got older, my needs grew more complex and generated greater fallout if not handled well.

I wanted to stalk out the back door, fire a look at one of those chiseled, hard men, feel his strong arms around me. I wanted a man to touch me with big, appreciative hands, to make up for the fatherly hugs and affection I never got, the security and support I'd lived without, as I'd slowly and inexorably become the parent of our two-person family. I wanted to cede all responsibility and just be a young woman, lost in the moment, adrift in the illusion of love.

Popping the plate in the microwave, I sat back down at the counter, closed my eyes, and drifted inward, greeting and acknowledging each emotion, letting the grief hurt, the anger inflame, the lust inspire, the confusion frighten. By the time the microwave dinged, I was a bit calmer and able to finish the rest of my dinner at a more modest pace.

God, I loved those biscuits. Because I was denying myself the candy beyond the door, I slathered another two with jam, added some of the candied pecans I'd spotted in a glass canister nearby (serious sugar rush there) and took the plate upstairs with me, to retire early behind a locked door and decide what I was going to do when morning came.

Stay?

Or go?

One hundred. Fifty. Million.

Possibly a distant Cameron niece with family roots in this town. That elusive thing for which I'd longed all my life—a home.

Courted. Not harangued.

And if someone wanted me dead, as Cameron heir there was no guarantee leaving would make me any safer. It might merely make me a sitting duck in rural Indiana, alone in a flimsy-walled studio. After all, my arsonist had been there, not in Louisiana— although, conceivably that person might have traveled to Indiana from the south. An apartment building could be torched just as easily as a house. Here, at least, I had bodyguards and a fortress that, according to Mr. Balfour, was somehow mysteriously inviolable.

At dusk, I stepped onto the balcony to watch the security guards change shifts, then Devlin passed through on his way to the garage. I eyed the three of them, wondering when I'd become such a frenzy of lust that having multiple choices for my bed, and resisting them, seemed an exercise in pointless self-torture. When Devlin glanced up at me, the invitation in his eyes unmistakable, I asked him to let Rufus out, gave him a perfunctory nod, and went back inside to gorge on the only sweets I was willing to permit myself. I resented feeling out of control and was determined to regain dominion over my wayward thoughts.

Thus, committed to celibacy until restored to my customary competence and calm, I passed another night beneath the sheltering and allegedly "perfectly safe" roof of Cameron Manor, succumbing swiftly to sleep, where I was just as swiftly engulfed by nightmares of fires and killing blades, thunderous drums and rhythmic chanting, doors that couldn't be opened, affording no escape, and portraits in shadowy rooms that leered with sinister intent.

NINE O'CLOCK THURSDAY morning found me standing on the main floor of the manor, at the entrance to the funereal northwest wing, peering into the darkness of the forsaken corridor. After showering, dressing, and seeing Rufus tucked into the cleft of his jackfruit tree (sans fresh kill), I had two hours before Mr. Laherty arrived.

I had no idea why I was so intrigued by the abandoned wing, but after breakfast, no closer to a decision about whether to stay or go (who was I kidding—I wasn't leaving, that would be *running*), I found myself standing at the entrance, flashlight in hand, lacking conscious awareness of having chosen to come here, as if the disenfranchised wing of the manor had lured me with a subliminal siren song.

As I took my first step into the hallway, a chilly draft of air surprised me. This corridor felt far cooler than the rest of the manor. I wondered if perhaps they set the air-conditioning to a lower temperature in the damaged wing, hoping to diminish the acrid scent of smoke. Squaring my shoulders, I began to march down the corridor, shining the beam of my light up, down, and all around.

After passing a dozen or so closed doors, I turned to glance behind me and was astonished to see the pinpoint of light at the entry was dollhouse-tiny, seemingly a half mile away. I'd not bothered trying any of the doors; now, curious, I turned the handle of the nearest one and pushed. It didn't budge, and fearing a repeat of the mysterious door in the chamber of portraits, I shoved against it with my shoulder, at which point it gave so effortlessly I lost my balance and flew in headfirst, sprawling to my knees on precariously charred floorboards. Slowly, delicately, I inched backward, heaving a sigh of relief when I regained the corridor. Resting against the jamb, I shined my flashlight in.

A nursery, badly burned, with a decrepit, sagging, charred crib, chairs, dressers, and end tables, and no windows. Creepy, a baby's room with no windows. It was on the interior side and felt dark and suffocating as a coffin. I felt strongly that all things involving children should be bright and airy and clean, with lots of windows and fresh air. I'd have chosen virtually any other exterior room in the manor for a nursery, and were they my babies, they'd be sleeping right next to me. Pushing to my feet, I closed the door and forged on. I seemed to be on autopilot, as if I would know my destination only when I found it.

When I reached the end of the corridor, I realized I'd expected to find a door to the turret, which seemed to be the focal point of my obsession. Instead, I found a curved wall with no visible ingress. The hallway simply ended in an unbreachable, unadorned wall of mortared stone, from floor to fourteen-foot ceiling.

Why affix a turret to the house with no access? Had it once been open, then walled up in later years? If so, why, and how did one enter the tower? Mentally reviewing the exterior of the manor, I realized I'd not seen a single window on the north turret, nor could I recall seeing a door. Not that my memory was 100 percent.

Frustrated, I followed the wall to the right, where I discovered a small wooden, iron-belted door tucked into a shadowed, weird-angled niche at the junction of corridor and turret. Hinges groaned when I pushed it open and shined the beam of my flashlight in.

Here, the house morphed drastically from bright and modern to drab, musty, and antiquated. Gone were the high ceilings and ornate moldings. The tunnel that greeted me had a wide-planked ceiling so low it barely cleared the top of my head, dark, paneled walls sticky with cobwebs, and floors of rough-hewn plank flooring. Unbroken by windows or doors, with no lighting, it was tight and claustrophobic. Nonetheless, I stepped inside and began to walk.

And walk. And walk.

I felt as if I trekked a mile down that dark, confined chute, following the thin beam of my flashlight, feeling uncomfortably as if the narrow, tight walls might close in on me at any moment, crushing me deep in the belly of the house, to rot and be forgotten. I had the impression of descending a slope, although I couldn't fathom how that was structurally possible within the design of the house, unless I was tunneling underground.

At long last, the passageway deposited me before a door similar to the one through which I'd entered, also narrow and iron-belted. This one, however, was made of highly polished oak and, within a frame of intricate knotwork, the surface was covered with carved triskelions and seven-pointed stars. The arch above it, fashioned from the same glossy wood, had a seven-pointed star at the apex, with undecipherable symbols clustered about it. There was no doorknob, so I pressed my palms to it and gave it a gentle push, not about to go sprawling headlong again, into . . . Who knew? At this point in my discombobulating trek, I'd not have been surprised to find an oubliette or a dungeon on the other side of the door.

Instead, I found a colonial kitchen.

Leaning against the jamb, I trained the beam of my flashlight from side to side, high and low. Gray swaths of dense cobwebbing clung to the timbers of the ceiling in heavy, billowing drapes. There were no spiders I could see; it was the kind of matted, thick webbing that could only accumulate over decades, perhaps centuries, of disuse. A simple wooden table with chairs sat before a massive stone hearth in which two beehive-shaped warming ovens occupied the side walls. An enormous black cauldron was suspended from the fireplace crane, with tongs and toaster irons protruding. There was a wooden counter between two tall cabinets; long-handled skillets and kettles hung from pegs on the log and mud walls. I felt as if I'd slipped back in time, and shivered, realizing I was standing in the doorway of the original cabin, the very first house ever built on Watch Hill. The air here was surprisingly fresh, cool, and dry, with none of the musty odor of the chute.

I moved inside, past sprigs of long-dead flowers tied with ribbon and hanging from cabinet knobs, vases of centuries-old thistles and milkweed pods, kettles and pans arranged on the counter, ready for meal prep to begin. There were dark bottles of oils and tonics, canisters of spices on virtually every flat surface, even plates, utensils, and mugs arranged on the table, as if the original Camerons had lived in the cabin while the rest of the manor was being built around it, then, one day, right before dinner, they'd stepped from this room into the main house and never returned. A thick layer of dust coated it all, as if decades had passed with the interior undisturbed.

But this should be a prize, I thought, dismayed. Not tucked away down a forbidding chute, draped with cobwebs and forgotten.

Grateful the ceiling was a few feet higher here than in the restrictive passage, I ducked beneath the gauzy webbing and moved through the kitchen into a small sitting room with another fireplace. I peeked into two narrow bedrooms, then arrived at another oaken, belted door that slid open with silent ease, revealing a room that was part apothecary, part library, and dripped the antiquated storybook charm of bygone times.

Abruptly, I hungered to dig this delightful jewel of a cabin from the charred belly of the dragon in which it languished and restore it to the sunlight. Seal the notched logs, patch the crumbling mud and stone between them, polish the cauldron, remove the boards from the windows, and hang fresh, lacy curtains. Give it a proper setting and open it to the town, celebrating the roots of Divinity. It would fit nicely in the Midnight Garden, were there space enough without disturbing the stately oaks.

The room was lined with open-shelved cabinetry and bookcases that held tomes of every size and shape. High-backed, upholstered chairs sat before the hearth. The mantel was covered with bottles, jars, and clay pots; there were cabinets holding more tiny, dark bottles, along with mortars and pestles. In the center of the room was a tall pedestal, upon which a thick, ancient-looking book was open. I hurried to it, thinking to find botanical drawings, perhaps recipes, or if I was lucky, a family Bible.

I heard something as I moved toward the pedestal and, in retrospect, would wonder why it hadn't spooked me, alone in that dark, forgotten cabin, but the gently whispered word merely caressed the nape of my neck with the sweetest of kisses.

Kyle-och.

When I shined my flashlight on the manuscript, I was surprised to find the pages blank. Then the oddest thing happened. Words began to form, as if being inked by an invisible hand wielding an old-fashioned calligraphy pen.

Light . . . the . . . candle . . . Cailleach.

I blinked. Repeatedly. The words were still there.

Laughing nervously, I glanced about, half expecting to find I'd missed someone standing in the shadows, playing a prank on me, having a grand laugh at my expense. I shined my light high and low, ahead and behind me, but there was no one in the room besides me. When I couldn't think of anything else to do, I turned my back to the book for a few seconds, then whirled to look again.

The sentence was gone. Now the pages were filled with writing on both sides. Thoroughly discombobulated, I began to read.

The Cailleach practice the Way of the Will through which they translate their desires into reality. Passed from one generation to the next, magic is a quality in the blood not all humans possess. The power of a witch lies in their ability to shape their destiny and that of the world around them. Some say, due to intermingling over time, all humans possess at least one drop of magic, but a single drop is very different from hundreds of drops, cultivated through centuries of careful breeding. That witch is the one other witches, even cold vampires, fear.

Cold vampires. Did that mean there were *warm* vampires, too?
With a snort of uneasy mirth, I continued reading.

*There's vast diversity in witching bloodlines. Some have
zealously maintained their purity for millennia, meticulously
curating partners for the sole purpose of power, while others
have diluted their heritage by marrying for love outside the
community. Halfblood (or Lowblood, but that term is no longer
used in most circles) witches require the aid of spells and rituals
to focus their power, whereas Highblood witches are capable of
magic without them.*

*There are nine Royal witching houses: four that follow the
light path, four that follow the dark, and a single gray. To these
nine houses, all witches must answer. Little is known about the
gray house. They are intensely private, concealing the secrets of
their power. They appear during times of cataclysmic upheaval
and are wont to take cataclysmic action. Some say the universe
itself holds its breath until those terrible witches recede to
whatever shadow realms in which they reside. They are the
most feared witches of all. There were once eleven Royal houses,
but twice in recorded history, the gray house demolished a house
for reasons unknown, eradicating the entire bloodline to the
final seed.*

*The pattern and purpose of the universe is the Will of the
Way, and supersedes the will of all witches combined. If the
natural order of the Way is defied, the universe will exact a price
to rebalance its scales, behaving at times more savagely than the
darkest of witches.*

*Light witches work in tandem with the universe, drawing their
power from nature, maintaining a respectful exchange of energy,*

aware and compassionate. They focus their will in accordance
with the grander scheme of the universe's way.

   Dark witches do as they please, defiant of the grander scheme
of things, employing antithetical arts to deflect or evade the
universe's retribution, draining power with impunity from the
richest of sources, including, when necessary, the richest source of
all: human life.

   About gray witches, little is known. Living alone or with
a carefully selected few, eschewing the laws of the witching
community, they channel their magic from shadow realms few can
access, where some of the most powerful light and dark witches in
existence have been lost.

The entry ended there. When I tried to turn the page, they
seemed to have been glued together. The ancient, thick tome had
only two accessible pages, and apparently they wrote themselves, if
and when they felt like it. I replayed that final observation through
my mind a few times, trying desperately to make sense of it, but
there was none to be found. Books didn't write themselves.

   Yet, even as I watched, the pages went empty, and another
sentence formed.

Light the candle, Cameron witch.

A short, fat white candle squatted to the right of the book.
Despite my rapidly diminishing grasp on all things sane and
logical, I observed there were no matches.

   The page blanked again, then, *With your will.*

   The situation so drastically exceeded my ability to comprehend, dwelt so far beyond the realm of things I conceived of as

possible, that I felt as if I were in a delirium, a fever dream where nothing was real, and nothing mattered. So I decided, with another uncomfortable laugh, to play along.

Closing my eyes, I pictured the candle in my mind, envisioning a flame, but somehow, it didn't feel quite right. The candle seemed insubstantial, not fully fleshed, so I added driblets of wax down the sides, blackened the wick, and gave it a little curl at the tip. After a few moments of solidifying the image in my mind, I relit the candle and opened my eyes.

Flame danced on the wick.

It was instinctive to swat it out with my palm. The candle extinguished, I could work on convincing myself it had never been lit. A trick of the eye, nothing more. And that waft of hazy smoke curling upward was merely dust I'd disturbed.

The pages went blank as a draft rustled through the subterranean room; the temperature plummeted, and my breath began to frost the air.

A drop of what looked like ink appeared on the page but was swiftly dashed away.

Then a single letter began to form, jerking and twitching, as if enormous effort was required to complete it (it vaguely resembled an *R*) but again, it vanished.

The book began to shudder with such violence atop the pedestal that the candle toppled off and crashed to the floor. The tome's convulsions grew ever more frantic; it heaved into the air, whumped back down, jerked right, jerked left, then collapsed to the pedestal before bucking up again, as if gripped by some fierce internal battle to manifest whatever it was trying to say.

Suddenly a single word appeared for a millisecond before it, too, was dashed away.

RUN

I didn't need to be told twice.

Despite my determination to be the archer, never the doe—given I wasn't entirely certain a bow could actually kill anything that might manifest in this strange room that housed a book capable of writing itself—I whirled for the door and ran.

PART II

Dichotomy—*a classification into two contradictory or mutually exclusive parts*—is a word which will come, in time, to define not only Cameron Manor, which I will soon discover is a temperate Jekyll harboring a sociopathic Hyde, but virtually every aspect of my life.

I will learn that there is a seed of light in everything that is dark, and a kernel of darkness in all that is light, and so the line between good and evil, which I once found so clear and easy to see, grows increasingly blurred.

And so we lose our way.

Past Zo would say that which doesn't kill us makes us stronger.

Future Zo would say there are times no one wants to talk about—because the horror is etched so deeply into our psyche, branded with searing agony into our marrow—when that which doesn't kill us fails to make us stronger. It leaves us broken on the scorched earth of a battlefield where the war has been lost and we stand frozen, mourning the slain, wondering if death isn't the only answer.

That's where future Zo is right now.

Where everything is gray and ash.

But, like the charismatic narcopath that studied you so thoroughly before approaching knew exactly which buttons to push, precisely how much pressure to apply, the perfect lover with all the right words, in those early days, everything about Cameron Manor was thrilling, uplifting, seductive.

We cling to those first, perfect moments long after we should, believing with desperate fervor that somehow, if we just do the right thing, we can get them back.

IT'S FUNNY—THOUGH NOT REALLY AT all, if you think about it—how abruptly and completely we manage to rationalize the inexplicable. If the mind fails to seize upon a plausible explanation (which would endure only the gentlest of scrutiny), we dismiss the inexplicable event and refuse to consider it again. Tell ourselves it was an aberration, an oddity, that we are not masters of the universe; there are stranger things in the night than you and I.

There are, by the way.

By the time I regained the main foyer, with the entry table and vase of cut flowers, the brilliant colors of the lady of the manor with her children, and the dazzling stained glass above the stairwell, through which golden rays of sunshine streamed, I'd nearly convinced myself I'd gotten so spooked by the claustrophobic chute and dark cabin that I'd merely imagined the unnatural events in the apothecary/library.

Mind you, I knew it wasn't true. But in the light of day, with a warm Louisiana breeze fluttering the curtains, the incident was easier to make somehow *smudgy* in my mind, and if there's one thing I've learned, it's that the mind will insist there "must be" a logical explanation until the bitter end. Unable to resolve the event to my satisfaction, I equivocated that there *was* a logical explanation—I just didn't know what it was. Yet. Perhaps an elaborate prank. A Halloween jest set up for last year's bash that had been forgotten. Perhaps Juniper had a strange sense of humor.

God, do we mindfuck ourselves.

At 11 a.m., I met Ian Laherty in the south reception room.

When I entered, he surged up from the settee, a burly lumber-jack of a man in a dark suit and tie, with flaming red hair, fiery beard, and brilliant blue eyes in his late thirties. I could more easily envision him—knowing now what I did of Divinity's Scottish heritage—hauling rough-hewn trees through a field of heather than working behind a desk every day.

"Such a pleasure, Ms. Grey," he said, pumping my hand so en-thusiastically, I felt as if I had sea legs and braced my feet more firmly. "I missed you at the Shadows, arrived after you'd already gone. Wife was devastated she didn't get to meet you."

We made a bit of small talk about how I was finding the house and the grounds, and the weather in Louisiana as opposed to back home. Then, settling into the seating cozy, we addressed business.

"Were this anything but the Cameron estate," he told me, "I would haggle over details that are little more than issues of con-venience and comfort, such as restrictions on guests—which inci-dentally means should you wed, your husband can't live here until your three years are up, though my partners and I believe there is sufficient leeway to build a separate house on the grounds—and your occupancy in the manor. Please be advised, you must remain in residence in the house for eleven months of each year. For the next three years, you can only travel for up to a single month annually, *cumulative*."

"Why such bizarre restrictions?"

"There's a common thread tying them together. Juniper's aim was to keep you here, undistracted by travel or out of town guests, because she felt, if she could achieve that, you'd see Di-vinity, fall in love with the town and estate, and relish taking the reins. As opposed to, say, moving friends in, gallivanting around the globe, and ignoring the town that was her life's work. Mr. Balfour told me Juniper compiled a report on you, but she couldn't divine your personality, motivations, work ethic, or ambitions, and she knew nothing of your heart. It frightened her to relinquish her empire to a woman she'd never met. She held on to what things she could through these contingencies, hoping to elicit a positive outcome for both her heir and the town. None of them are harmful to you. They're chafing inconveniences; ones I'd protest vigorously, were this any other case, but I must advise you, Ms. Grey, none of her requirements are contestable. If you wish to inherit, you must abide by her stipulations. All of them."

"Are there other contingencies of which I should be aware?" I asked, intending to read the entire thing, front to back, twice.

He shook his head. "They all tie into occupancy, to keep you focused on building a life here." He paused, then said, "My partners and I wouldn't hesitate to advise you to sign. But if you haven't read through it, you should. You'll find our report on the top."

He rose and handed me a hefty leather folder, emblazoned with his law firm's name and logo. "The settlement is straightforward and not nearly as long as it looks. The majority of the pages are legal documents to be completed for banks and various institutions with whom she—you do business. Forms to be witnessed and notarized. The bequest itself is only seven pages plus a lengthy addendum, detailing the specifics of the inheritance, followed by a sizeable stack of the aforementioned legal documents. I'll take no more of your time, Ms. Grey, but hope, should you require assistance in the future, you'll not hesitate to phone me. You'll find my office, home, and cell numbers in the folder. Please feel free to call me, day or night."

After Alice ushered him out, I sat for a time, acknowledging that, despite the inexplicable, disturbing things that had happened to me of late, I wasn't sure wild horses could drag me away from Cameron Manor.

Yes, there were wrinkles in the new fabric of my life. There'd been more, and far more painful ones, in the old fabric. I'd gone from pauper to princess. Gone was worked-to-exhaustion, numb, tragic Zo of the chilly gray Midwestern states, who'd never been respected by anyone.

In the fascinating, sunny, vibrant town of Divinity, I was Ms. Grey-Cameron, heiress to the greatest of legacies, treated with respect by almost all, able to pay my debts and, at long last, see a promising future for myself.

It wasn't a carrot at the end of that stick.

It was Paradise.

Note from future Zo: The devil never thunders in on cloven hoof, reeking of brimstone, holding an ominously glowing contract that must be signed in blood. She dances near, smiling contagiously, tiara sparkling, holding the keys to the kingdom.

I FILLED THE subsequent hours with trivial occupations, staying blithely distracted. My appetite had been insane for the past few days, so I raided the kitchen like a woman starved, sampling everything I found in the fridge, freezer, and larder. I found I adored pralines and red velvet cake and hated boiled peanuts. "Crawfish"—which we called mudbugs back home—were never going to happen unless camouflaged by gumbo spiked with sufficient andouille to render them ignorable.

I explored the whatnot boxes, discovering an array of jewelry, hats, lingerie, designer purses, and wallets that left me stunned.

I sat in bed clutching Mom's urn and sobbed violently for

nearly an hour, stuffing my nose completely, leaving my eyes so red and swollen, I had to ice my face with a bag of frozen peas.

After that, Mr. Balfour texted to tell me they'd identified the body of one Finnegan Harlow, who had texts on his phone from a blocked number, reiterating that the woman was *under no circumstances* to be harmed, merely frightened. The cause of death: end stage congestive heart failure, with functional deterioration of the organ so severe, the coroner expressed astonishment Harlow had lived as long as he had.

Still, Mr. Balfour insisted I either remain in the house or take guards with me, should I leave. He proposed a driver meet Este in the nearby town of Sheldon to escort her to the manor, giving me the address of a restaurant, Lafitte's, at which he advised they meet.

Shortly before dusk, I went to let Rufus out, stepping into the rear courtyard, only to be instantly flanked by a pair of towering men who dripped the same kind of presence I'd felt that night in Criollo.

"Ms. Grey, I'm Jesse," the man on my right said. "That's Burke. We're day shift, about to change off."

I glanced up—and, good God, *up*—to meet Jesse's gaze, and got hung there. He was power and menace, held softly.

His eyes said he'd seen war and survived it by doing things no man should ever be forced to do. A patient, resigned strength emanated from him as if, at some point, he'd accepted that he was both utterly necessary and utterly expendable and that, because of the evils in the world, he'd become the most lethal among them, in order to hold the line and light. My heart clenched as I stared into gray eyes raging with storms yet so very, very quiet, and I got the sudden image of a formidable, armored black crab squatting inside his skull, clutching a shining pearl in its claws, holding on to it with all its might, and knew it was the final vestiges of his humanity he guarded so fiercely.

"A pleasure," I said, and meant it, turning to greet Burke, finding similar eyes and tightly governed lethality. "I was just going to the greenhouse."

"We'll escort you," Jesse said, studying my face. "I'm sorry for your loss, Ms. Grey. James told us about your mother."

I blinked and realized, to my complete mortification, the door to my balcony had been ajar while I'd sobbed, directly above their station. These obdurate men who'd experienced the brutalities of war had heard me weeping like an orphan, lost.

A gentleness I'd not have suspected flickered in Jesse's gaze, and he murmured, "Pray the day you can no longer weep like that never comes."

Turning, he, with Burke bringing up the rear, began to walk to the greenhouse, and I trailed him, fisting my hands to keep from grabbing Jesse's arm and dragging him into the nearest shadowed alcove for frantic, explosive sex. A big man who'd suffered, sacrificing himself to protect those in need; his empathy, prizing my tears, slayed me, stirring my lust. But then again, lately, everything did.

At the entry, he turned, looked down at me, and said quietly, "I serve of my own free will and am here for whatever you wish of me, Ms. Grey. Nights are long, alone."

I imagined being touched with kindness and desire was balm to Jesse's soul, after the horrors he'd experienced, that in consuming passion devoted solely to another's body, he could forget his pain for a time. We were two of a kind in that.

"You're here," Devlin growled behind me, "to guard the blood heir. Not one thing more."

Chocolate, chocolate everywhere, but not a bar to eat, I reminded myself. "I'd like to spend time alone in the greenhouse. I'll be safe enough inside. You can watch me through the glass."

"Not comfortable with that, ma'am. Beyond the foliage, we'll lose sight of you," Jesse clipped.

I felt a flash of ire at Devlin for Jesse's retreat into formality. I'd enjoyed being Ms. Grey, not ma'am. Surrounded by too much testosterone for my peace of mind, I opened the greenhouse door, watched as Rufus soared out, flying low to vanish into the gloaming, then marched back inside the house at a brisk pace, bidding the three men good night over my shoulder as I closed the door, stealing no additional glances at them.

I passed another restless night in frightening dreams of dark chutes and archaic grimoires that could fly, and chased me about, cackling maniacally from between glued pages; of terrifying bonfires and skulking men of brutal, secretive ilk; of gray-cloaked, featureless beings who carefully observed, from the quiet corners of my mind, each fear I faced and how I responded.

When the morning light swept across my bed to banish the dust of shadowy dreams, I woke with a single shining thought.

It was Friday—Este would soon be here!

A gloomy thought eclipsed it.

Hours before she was allowed to be, knowing Este, placing my inheritance in jeopardy.

Oh, how quickly it had become *my* inheritance; a thing I would permit no one to take from me.

I DIDN'T BOTHER trying to accomplish anything that day. After letting Rufus in and gorging on a breakfast of the thickest rashers of maple bacon I'd ever seen, poached eggs, and fresh tomatoes with parsley and chives I gathered from pots situated

on decorative stepladders, I wandered the south wing, acclimat-
ing myself to the corridors and rooms, greeting passing staff,
pressing my hands to panels, and hunting for hidden doors. I
found two more that merely connected hallways in unobtrusive
fashion, harboring neither mystery nor concealed treasure.

I had no desire to return to the shadowy, perplexing northwest
wing, although I planned to coax Este into exploring there with
me tomorrow, to see what she made of the strange book, assuming it "communicated" again.

I put my worries on hold, including those about Mom's murder
and the effort to frighten me, focusing instead on the delights of
Cameron Manor, while anticipating my best friend's arrival. Este
had a way of viewing life from an eclectic, artistically fresh per-
spective that never failed to help me clarify my path. And if she
genuinely knew things, if Mom had divulged secrets to her that
she'd never told me . . . well, I'd try hard to focus on being happy
Mom had, at least, planned ahead.

When, by four, Este had neither arrived nor responded to any
of my texts about meeting at Lafitte's, I was growing concerned. I
texted Mr. Balfour to ask if he'd heard from her, as I'd sent Este
his number as well. He hadn't, but the driver was scheduled to
be at the restaurant at five o'clock sharp and would wait until she
arrived, however long that took.

By six, she'd neither appeared to meet the driver in Sheldon
nor called. I was nearly frantic with worry and contemplating
calling her mother—and, heavens, did I find that woman off-
putting—when, finally, my phone rang.

"Este, where *are* you?" I exclaimed.

"I might ask you the same bloody thing!" she snarled in that
strange blend of accents, tribute to both parents, belonging to
neither.

"What do you mean? Didn't you get my texts about meeting at Lafitte's?"

"I wanted to find you myself. I don't need a damn driver. Problem is, apparently Divinity exists only in precious few entries online, not reality. At least not *mine*. I've been driving in bloody circles for hours, trying to follow a schizoid GPS, and it's *pissing* me off. The app actually asked me to bloody well rate my enjoyment of its services, smack in the middle of a roundabout! Do you know how many times I ended up circling the idiotic thing? I *despise* technology. How do I get to you? Is that driver of yours really the only way in?"

"You can't find Divinity," I said slowly. It was pretty much a straight shot, as I recalled, not many turns, and certainly no roundabouts.

"Not a chance in hell," she seethed.

"I don't understand."

"Look, I'm headed for Lafitte's now. You can tell the powers that be I got their message. I'll be a good little witch. See you soon, babe."

Este was gone.

A good little witch? Este had no problem saying bitch or any other curse word. Her mom could curse fluently in eight languages, and they sometimes held laughing cursing matches to see who could outdo the other.

Sighing, I headed for the kitchen to find something else to eat while I killed time.

I'D NEVER UNDERSTOOD why women squealed when they first saw each other until tonight. My desire for food and sex rapacious, my emotions, too, were amplified, and I raced out the front door the moment headlights flickered in the windows of the front parlor. I'd been curled up there since letting Rufus out for the evening, flipping through the pages of *Southern Living*, trying to decide what my taste was, now that I could afford taste. "Este!" I squealed when she stepped from the black SUV.

Statuesque, with long, dark curly hair, Este oozed earthy sensuality in a short dress, and the driver couldn't keep his eyes off her. Men tended to have that reaction to Este. As voluptuous as I was lithe, with beautiful dark skin and luminous blue eyes, she turned heads wherever we went; inevitably, I was noticed as an afterthought, but it never bothered me. I was proud of my best friend, loved that she dazzled others the way she dazzled me. She'd had my back, been my champion all my life. We'd stayed in touch over the years, despite miles and towns between us, exchanging emails and eventually texts, and I'd lived a rich vicarious life through her exploits. Now, finally, I had an exploit to share with her.

She froze, staring at me, then past me, up and up at the house, then slowly from side to side, her expression stunned. "Holy *fuck*," she breathed.

Laughing, I ran to her and hugged her fiercely. We squealed and hugged, and when we finally separated, she stepped back and studied me in the low light of the gas lamps. "We have a lot to talk about."

"We do," I agreed. "Come on, I'll get your bags."

"We've got them, Ms. Grey," Jesse said, behind me.

"I've got them," Devlin said. "Return to your post."

"My job is to guard Ms. Grey. I don't take orders from you," Jesse said coldly.

I glanced at Este, who was staring with rapt fascination at Devlin, then Jesse, and back again. The look she gave me spoke volumes, and, laughing, I looped my arm through hers and practically dragged her up the front steps, not caring who brought the luggage, so long as it came.

"Bloody hell, Zo, what have you gotten yourself into?" Este said slowly, looking in the door. Then she glanced down at the threshold and demanded, "Invite me in."

I laughed. "When have you ever waited for an invitation from anyone? Este Hunter goes where she wants, when she wants, however she wants. What were you, all of ten when you told me that? I think you were planning to be Lady Godiva for Halloween that year," I teased.

"Not this time," she said in a strange voice. "Do it."

Snorting, I said, "Don't be put off by my seeming wealth, O Wealthy One. Come in, you idiot."

Este stepped through the door, flinched, staggered, and caught herself against the jamb, much as I had, looking as if she might pass out. She was motionless a moment, then shook her head sharply and said, "Did *you* do that?"

"What?"

She pointed down at the wooden threshold.

"No idea what you mean."

"You don't see it?"

"See what?" I peered at the oak stripping. "Oh, those. Stars and triskelions are everywhere in the manor."

"Do they all shimmer like that?"

I looked more closely. They engravings did, indeed, seem to emit a faint glow I hadn't noticed, but then, I don't look at thresholds when I walk through doors. There were other, fainter symbols, too, that I couldn't identify, which might have been brushed on with luminescent paint.

"Do you know what these markings mean?" Este demanded.

"No. Do you?"

She studied them a long moment. Then, warily, "They're a bit complex for me. There's something . . . I can't quite grasp, there's too many layers. Something . . . concealed. You have no idea what's going on, do you? Bloody hell, it's a damned good thing I'm here."

I felt abruptly chilled. "What do you mean? Do you know something about those symbols?"

She closed her eyes and sighed. Opening them, she said, "Find me something to drink. Tequila will do. Then we need a place to talk. Privately."

Jesse arrived with her bags then, Devlin beside him, and I said, "You can bring them in and drop them by the stairs."

"No!" Este snapped.

"No!" Devlin snarled.

"Rescind that, Zo," Este said in a strained voice. "Tell Jesse not to come in, but to leave my bags on the porch. Exactly that."

I glanced from Este to Jesse to Devlin and back. The three of them were watching me with an intensity I couldn't decipher, and I felt the same way I had in Criollo—staring blindly at weft and weave beyond my comprehension, while everyone understood the complexity of the fabric but me. Este was worried, Devlin furious, and Jesse unreadable. "Fine," I said finally. "Don't come in, Jesse. Just leave them on the porch."

"As you wish, ma'am," he said. The look he shot Devlin was sharp enough to flay skin from bone, and his gaze passed with palpable chill over my best friend, which was unthinkable, coming from a man.

"Good night, Jesse, Devlin," I said with a curt nod, anxious to pick Este's brain.

"Tequila. Lime," Este urged. "And find me something south-ern, sweet and sinfully fattening. I need fortification."

"Got plenty of that. Follow me," I said, and turned for the kitchen.

BEFORE LONG, WE were seated, cross-legged, on my bed with a tray of confections between us, a bottle of Don Ramón Lim-ited Edition, two shot glasses, salt, and a plate of limes. Though made for sipping, we shot the first glass of the four-hundred-dollar bottle of tequila we'd found in the butler's pantry. From Este's demeanor, I had a feeling I might need fortification, too.

She'd changed into comfy clothes, as had I—matching pink plaid pajama bottoms and oversize tees—and now, twisting her long hair back in a clip, she did a second shot, tossed her dis-carded lime on a plate, and said, "I've been dying to talk to you since the day of the fire, Zo. I promised your mother I'd get to you ASAP if anything happened to her. You drove me crazy, avoiding me."

"You promised my mother," I echoed.

"She called me one day, while you were at work."

"The day you claimed you dropped by and she asked you in for tea?" I said tightly.

She nodded. "I wasn't comfortable telling you that on the phone. I needed to see you in person to talk about this. Joanna in-sisted I come over that day, made me vow to tell you things if she died suddenly before you—" Este broke off and redirected. "Be-fore the cancer took her, but never to breathe a word otherwise."

"When?" I said, sounding wounded even to myself.

"A few years ago."

"Tell me everything," I demanded. "Don't omit a single word."

"I need to start a bit further back. Remember the day we met?"

"Every detail." It was the most momentous event of my young life. I'd felt an instant kinship with Este that I'd never experienced before, except with Mom. As if, finally, someone else in the world made sense to me, and I fit somewhere.

"I told you I was so glad you were a witch, too, that I hated not having any witch friends."

I snorted. "That was a joke. You also told me Billy Baker had one ball."

"That wasn't a joke, either. I saw him in the boy's locker room."

"What were you doing in the boy's locker room? You were nine! Wait, scratch that. I don't think I want to know."

"I had the worst crush on Simon Fields, so I decided to spy and got more than I'd bargained for. I was *so* not ready for penises at that age."

"I think I'd have been traumatized. But I was pretty sheltered."

"I was for a few years, till the hormones kicked in. Anyway, when I realized you didn't have any idea you were a witch—I didn't even know that was possible—I didn't push."

I said acerbically, "I'm not a witch, Este. Got no magic wand to wave, trust me."

If I did, Mom would be alive. Countless things would be different. It used to be a fantasy of mine, as I'd envisioned us sweeping away our tracks with witchy, scented brooms—that I would discover some secret, deeply buried power inside me and use it to rescue us from our nomadic, scurrying, frightened life, to banish Mom's endless illnesses. Countless were the nights I put myself to sleep as a little girl, fleshing out that fantasy. I'd blast our wicked warlock enemy to bits, sweep my mother off to a Constant House with capital letters; we'd have nice things and get to keep them, and no one would look down their noses at us ever again.

Este's gaze darkened to cobalt and ice. "Yes, you are a witch, Zodecky Grey. And there's nothing funny about what I'm telling you. Open your mind and listen to me, and you need to be deadly serious about this. Your mother certainly was."

My smile faded, and I eyed her warily. She never called me by my full name, well, my mostly full name.

"I'm a witch," Este told me firmly. "Born into a family of Cailleach who practice the Way of the Will."

Kyle-och, she'd said, and *the Way of the Will*: the same words the by-turns-talkative-then-taciturn grimoire had shared in the cabin beneath the manor.

"We're light witches who follow a strict code. When you used to accuse me of bespelling people to get my way, it horrified me because a light witch would never abuse her power that way. That's a dark witch's path."

I stared at her. "Oh my God, you're actually serious. You really think you're a witch. Like, with powers. Got a broomstick, too? Do you fly? Perchance drift lazily down from a roof on Halloween?" I mocked.

"Samhain," Este said with grim intensity. "The feast day has an ancient, rich history, and there is no 'think' about it. I *am* a witch. It's my way of life, and it's everything to me. And yes, I have a damned broomstick. Several."

Choking back laughter, I pressed, "So, that means you *do* fly? Kick your legs over the side and soar, crooning 'Come Little Children'?"

"Don't mock the Way of the Will. The path of the Cailleach is sacred, and it's an honor to walk it."

"Do something witchy," I goaded. "Prove it."

"We don't waste power," she growled, then sighed. "But we knew you'd need proof. Your mom said she strongly discouraged belief in the otherworldly or paranormal any time you expressed an interest in it."

Ow. My mom told Este that? Este—who'd met with my mother years ago, then kept a vow to *her*, at my expense. Whose best friend was she?

"Look at the bookcase by the door," Este told me. "The top shelf of books."

I glanced over my shoulder.

"What color are they?"

Shrugging, I looked back at her. "Brown, bound in leather, all of them."

"Look again."

The top shelf sported about two dozen thick volumes bound in candy-apple red leather. I stared, blinked, blinked again. Then stared at Este.

"What color would you like them to be?"

"Green. But not smooth leather." I upped the ante. "I like suede."

She smirked. "Easy. Done."

This time, when I glanced at the books, I gasped, leapt from the bed, and plucked one from the shelf. It was bound in supple, buttery soft green suede. I ran my fingers over it wonderingly.

The book turned purple while I was holding it, so shocking me that I dropped it and whirled. "How are you *doing* that?" Was she mesmerizing me, convincing me I was seeing different colors and textures? I hadn't drunk that much tequila—a shot and a half so far—and I wasn't a lightweight! I had a feeling I might be drinking much more, given the strange turn of our conversation.

"I have an affinity for transmutation. Color especially, but also substance, plus other abilities. Each witch is different. Do you like the gray walls of this bedroom?"

"No," I admitted frankly, aware I was in the minority. Gray was all the rage with interior designers. I'd never lost my obsession with houses, poring over real estate listings online while shoveling food in my face on break, imagining the life one might enjoy in them. Over the past few years, everything had gotten "greiged," the exact shade of the wintry Indiana sky I so despised: depressing mud-gray splashed everywhere, on walls, floors, furniture. It baffled me. I was a sunshine/blue-sky whore. Well, at least, I'd always wanted to be; yet another reason I found Divinity so inviting.

I said, "I think gray is a color that doesn't know what it wants to be, so rather than assertively being something, it's timidly nothing. I despise gray. Be a color, get a life." That it was also my last name didn't elude me. I'd felt as bland as my surname. Calm, placid Zo Grey. Never be dramatic, don't act out, don't want anything, never complain, others have it worse, hush, hush, sweet child of mine.

Casting me a wink, Este raised her hands and, murmuring to herself, swirled them through the air. Abruptly, the walls of my bedroom were the same soft green as the books, which beautifully offset the view beyond the French doors. I blinked, stunned, then said, "Will they stay green?"

"Do you want them to?"

I nodded. Yes. Maybe she could do the outside of the manor, too, while she was at it—God, *could* she? Change the color of the entire house? Did I *believe* she had that kind of power, that she was a witch? My best friend, whom I'd known since we'd met in elementary school?

Este murmured softly, gestured again. "I sealed them to per-manence," she said, then patted the bed for me to rejoin her. "I'll make reparation later."

"What kind of reparation?"

"All witches have to draw power from something to control and use their magic. Light witches draw from nature and return it in some fashion. Plant a tree, grow flowers, fertilize the earth, do an unexpected kindness, help an animal. We always return the gift."

"And dark witches?" I asked, unable to stave off curiosity, al-though I didn't believe any of this. Then again, I thought uneasily, glancing about, the walls were a completely different color. How did I explain that? I felt as if my mind were fracturing. Magic didn't exist. Witches didn't exist. *And that ghost you used to see in West Virginia?* an inner voice mocked.

"Dark witches draw from any damned source they want, the richer the better, and human lives are not off the plate," Este said coldly. "They abuse it. And don't bother to return it. They drain the world. We feed it."

I stared at her a long moment, then resumed my seat on the bed in silence. I was a cauldron of so many emotions that I was having a difficult time identifying them, but bubbling most prevalently on the surface was anger. My mother had confided in Este, not me. Why would she do that? Though I wasn't yet will-ing, even after Este's demonstration, to acknowledge that either of us was a witch (although my gut vehemently disagreed with my brain and was mounting countless persuasive arguments), they'd all believed it and they'd withheld that information from me. They'd had secret meetings to which I'd not been invited. How many times had my mother hushed a question of mine, yet confided in others? It cut, deeply.

"Oh, Zo," she exclaimed, "I've so hungered to be myself around you! It's been so hard!"

"Poor you," I said coldly. "You might have told me at any time that you believed we were witches. Was your mouth broken? Oh, definitely not. You never shut up. But you didn't tell me this."

Eyes darkening, she said sharply, "One, it's not a belief. It's a fact, and I'll happily give you more proof. I *can* convince you. You may not like the way I do it, but I can. Two, I didn't dare. When I told my mother about you after we met, she hunted Joanna down at one of the houses she was cleaning, and they had a talk. Well . . . not quite a talk. Our mothers had an all-out battle that night. Mom came home in full retreat mode, and nothing intimidates Dalia Hunter. She told me if I ever mentioned witches to you again, not only would she punish me, but Joanna would do unspeakable things to me, and Mom wouldn't be able to stop her. She was more upset than I've ever seen her. She said she'd never feared another witch, not until she met Joanna Grey, and once she met her—"

"Okay, stop right there," I cut her off sharply. "No one feared my mother. Ever. Mom was incapable of inspiring fear. She was sweet and kind and gentle—"

"*And* a Highblood Royal"—Este cut me off—"her blood magic meticulously curated from the most explosive lines. Royal houses, even the light houses, are obsessed with their bloodlines, willing to do, become, virtually anything to enhance them. Mom said Joanna Grey dripped power. She terrified my mother."

My mom, a Highblood Royal, from one of the nine houses the book had mentioned? Joanna Grey terrifying anyone was impossible for me to imagine. I tried to picture her with fierce emotion blazing in her eyes but couldn't. I'd never seen it. "Bullshit. Soft doe eyes," I spat. "That's all I ever saw on her face." And I was getting madder and madder about it. If my mother did have fire in her blood—fire others had seen—why didn't I ever get to see it? I might have been different, if she had been. Our lives could have been different. She could terrify Dalia Hunter, and we *still* had to run?

"Same, babe, same. That's all I ever saw on yours."

Stung, I said, "Then why did you like me?"

Her gaze softened. "I knew who you really were, and every now and then, I'd catch a flash of fire. Do you know that every man you took to your bed was a witch? That alone gave me hope that you would find a way to break free and become who you were meant to be. A very powerful *witch*," she said pointedly. "And"—she frowned—"I'm not sure I wouldn't have told you, before it was too late. I'd been wrestling with that lately."

Oh, kudos to her. She'd *considered* telling me. I shelved her "too late" comment for later. There was a lot I was shelving for later.

"How do you know those men were witches? What did you do, track them down?" I added a hasty caveat, "Not that I'm saying I believe you. But if I did, what house was Mom from?" Light or dark was what I wanted to know.

"No idea. She wouldn't say, and Mom couldn't tell; we can only sense power and the intensity of it, not which way it leans. As for your lovers, I asked you enough questions to identify them. Then I hit the same bars. Every man you selected had magic in his blood. Some of them were damned impressive. If you hadn't gone there first, I certainly would have. You have decadent taste."

Was that the something extra I'd always been hunting— magic in a man's blood? What I'd thought of as an indefinable edgy side, unpredictable and powerful. Did that mean Kellan was a witch? Had he known I was, too, assuming any of this was true? And, considering the amount of presence I'd felt in Criollo that night, were all the men I'd found to my liking witches? If so, why had so many gathered in a single place?

"Did the men think I was a witch?"

"They knew. Even as weak as you were, they could feel it. You felt faint to me at first, too, until I'd been around you awhile. Then I began to feel something . . . enormous in you, deeply buried, tightly leashed."

Enormous like the mushroom cloud I'd felt building in the barn, that I'd feared might destroy me if I didn't do something with it. Leashed, like a dog. Controlled. "Go on," I said tersely.

"Mom told me Joanna didn't take you through the stages of awakening your blood magic. Instead, she suppressed your power. That's why you felt so weak to other witches, and that's what our moms fought about. Mom says suppressing a witch's power is a mortal sin, worse than burning her alive. Your power needs to breathe, get out in the world and do things. Because if it can't, it suffocates, day after day. You're worn down by a constant internal battle you don't even know you're fighting. Your magic is desperate to be born, but something is blocking it. Nothing tastes particularly good; nothing angers or excites you. You feel empty, living in a state of incessant, mild malcontent, incapable even of feeling strong discontent. Incapable of feeling strong anything."

She'd just described how I'd felt my entire life. Bland, passionless but for my infrequent one-night stands, possessing a shallow heart. Eternally feeling uncomfortable in my own skin, like it didn't fit right, like I'd been buttoned into someone else's coat at the hatcheck; too small, cut wrong, restrictive and confining.

"Most suppressed witches go mad. Many kill themselves. Mom said because you were Highblood Royal, you'd either commit suicide young or be strong enough to survive it. But she never forgave your mother for doing it, and your mother never forgave her for criticizing the decision she'd made."

"Why would Mom bind my power? Assuming this is true," I added tightly. It was beginning to sound entirely too true to me. But accepting that would mean accepting that my whole life had been a lie. I could see nothing Este stood to gain by telling me such an elaborate falsehood. Still, either she was lying or my entire life was a lie; pick my poison.

"It *is* true, all of it," she insisted. "How else do you explain what I did with the books?"

I couldn't explain it, any more than I could explain lighting a candle with my will, so I evaded testily. "Let me get this straight. You're a witch. I am, too. My mom was. And your mom is, and so is your dad?"

She nodded.

"And everyone knew but *me*? And you all had cozy talks about it, and made this decision not to tell me? I'm sorry, but I'm having serious fucking problems with this on multiple levels!"

"I would be, too. I'd be angry as hell at everyone. It doesn't make it any less true. And can I say how much I enjoy seeing you pissed? You never got mad about anything. You never got much of anything about anything. You're no longer bound, Zo. This is wonderful! You're fully alive! Finally."

A little late, by, like, nearly twenty-five years, in my opinion, but hey, it was just my life, not that anyone else seemed to think so. They thought it was *theirs* to make decisions about, managing me, withholding information. If what she was saying was true, I'd spent my whole life as a shadow of myself, unable to feel, to engage and appreciate life. And it was my own mother who'd sentenced me to that fate. While talking to others about it!

Perhaps the most compelling argument in favor of what Este was telling me was how much I'd changed since Mom died. My world had gone from pale to vibrant; my senses graduated from bland to complex, observant of the subtlest nuances; my emotions had transformed from shallow to incendiary, my passions explosive, as if a sudden release valve had been opened—or a deliberate suppression removed. The dragon who'd awakened at the moment of Mom's death had never gone back to sleep. Was that my magic, my power? I shivered with a sudden chill and narrowed my eyes. "I take it you're telling me the moment Mom died, I was freed?"

"Yes. Have you been eating everything in sight? Emotions intense and shifting rapidly? Sex drive out of control?"

I gaped at her. Absolutely. "But why would Mom bind my power?" I said again.

Este shook her head, gaze sad. "No idea. That's part of what pushed my mom over the edge. Joanna offered no explanation. And first witch lesson: your mom didn't bind your power, she suppressed it. There's a difference. Binding is done all at once. Suppressing has to be done day after day after day. Joanna refused to say a word about who she was or why she'd suppressed your magic. If she'd given Mom a reason, *any* reason, Mom would have tried to understand. Instead, Joanna threatened her, and when she wanted to be, your mother was terrifying. You said something strange happened to you. What was it? Something witchy?"

I no longer had any intention of telling her anything about the cabin, the cryptic book that wrote itself, or the candle I'd seemingly lit with will alone. Not until she'd given me more answers and I'd had time to mull things over.

"If this is true, how could you keep it from me, all these years?" I said heatedly. "How could you be my best friend, believing it was true, and never say a word? Didn't you think I had a *right* to know? Just a simple, *Hey, you're a witch, and your mom won't let you have your power.* Just a general damned heads-up."

"I wanted to tell you so many times!" Este protested.

"But you didn't."

"But I wanted to!"

"Intentions. Road to hell. Paved with," I said flatly.

She snapped, "There are many ways to pave a road to hell, and sometimes you don't have any good choices. You don't understand the witching world, Zo. There are witches you don't go up against, ever, and your mother was one of them. Mom threatened me, your mother threatened me, and Joanna Grey was the most forbidding thing I'd ever encountered in this world, until today, Divinity, and this house. You don't know this and never will—because you're Highblood Royal, the witch other witches fear and obey—but mere Highbloods like me, we don't mess with Royals. Ever."

She locked eyes with me, then said, with quiet intensity, "Zo, you're *surrounded* by Cailleach. You live in a town of witches that outsiders can't find, not even Highbloods—at least I couldn't. Divinity is one potent pot of roiling power. As we drove down Main Street, I got drunk off the magic in the air. It's on the breeze, it's in the soil. It's intoxicating. I want to go stand outside and dance, naked, in the storm of it. I want to inhale it, absorb it, channel it into creativity. I've never been in the midst of so many powerful witches. The driver told me, quite proudly, that you're the heir to the Cameron legacy, that you've inherited all this." She gestured expansively. "The Camerons are an ancient Royal light house; they've been around forever. Juniper Cameron was their matriarch, and now that she's dead, it sure looks to me like they brought you here to take her place as the head of their coven."

She paused a moment before continuing. "I thought about this a lot on the drive, after Evander told me why you were here. About how lucky it was they found you right before she died, when they'd searched fruitlessly for an heir for so many decades. About how determinedly your mother hid you, suppressed your power, for *decades*. And it led me to a deeply disturbing thought. Zo, what if this town, this coven is exactly what your mother was running from?"

14

I finished brushing my teeth, spat irritably, and watched the residue vanish down the drain, wishing the countless emotions keeping me awake would vanish with it. Este had gone off in search of a room to call her own an hour ago, when I, feigning exhaustion, insisted I needed sleep.

After all she'd told me, sleep proved impossible. No amount of tequila was going to change that, and I'd tried. I was intensely, painfully awake, my mind brutally clear, my heart alive and raging. I hungered for the oblivion of sleep, to forget, to briefly die and hope tomorrow I felt more mistress of my feelings and fate, for clearly at the moment, and apparently for all my life, I'd been mistress of neither.

I padded back into the bedroom, where I stood a long moment, eyeing the green suede books on the top shelf. Este must have spelled those to permanence, too.

"Spelled them to permanence," I muttered, trying to fathom it. Could *I* spell things to permanence? What were my gifts? I hadn't asked. In fact, I'd made her stop talking about witches and Mom entirely. My trusty technique of boxing things up and parceling them out in small amounts so I might absorb them in palatable increments had reasserted itself to preserve my sanity. Just like old times.

My insistence on abject disbelief, I conceded grudgingly, was a defense mechanism. The things she'd told me bore an irrefutable knell of truth, chiming deep in my marrow. *This,* they proclaimed, *was what you always felt but never knew. This explains everything.*

Devlin had prodded at it the other night, when he'd asked if somewhere deep in my bones, I hadn't always thought there was something more. That I lacked vital information, perhaps had even been intentionally misled. For years, I'd told myself my impression of somehow being in the dark when others weren't sprang simply from being uprooted so many times without explanation.

But it ran much, much deeper.

I'd existed at odds with myself my whole life. There was daytime Zo, who did all the things; she worked tirelessly and took care of Mom, and never complained, and never let herself want anything. Busy bee, flitting from task to task, too preoccupied to think about how she felt—or how she seemed curiously lacking in that department.

Then there was midnight Zo, who lay awake pondering the endless, empty ache inside her, a great void of a canyon that shouldn't hurt but did, as if something necessary for life had been carved out of her. Midnight Zo felt as if she were standing face-to-face with an impenetrable fog that only on exceedingly rare occasions parted ever so briefly, affording a tantalizing glimpse of something bright, wonderous, and magnificent that filled her so completely that, for a brief moment, on those exceptional nights, midnight Zo felt . . . whole, alive, and *real*. I'd hungered for that fulsome state with every ounce of my being, without even knowing what it was.

Then the fog would thicken, again obscuring my vision, and I wouldn't be able to recapture what I'd just felt. At all. I was left with only a memory of a distant impression of something that had briefly felt glorious, and the sure knowledge that, for some reason, I could never have it.

Fact: my mom believed she was a witch. Fact: Este and her family believed they were, too. Fact: Este and Dalia believed my mother was a Highblood Royal and terrifying.

Fact: they'd all talked about this, and they'd all kept it from me.

I'd wandered, stupid and blind, for twenty-four years, and not only had everyone let me, they'd willfully, intentionally blinded me.

My entire existence was shifting on its axis, leaving me consummately explosive. I had a million questions for Este. And couldn't face even one of them right now.

Did I believe I was a witch?

Yes.

Was I curious, even eager to explore it?

Absolutely.

Did any of that matter to me right now?

No.

I was too angry. It was one thing to grow up feeling emotions. You learned, along the way, with the help of mentors and parents, to manage and temper them.

I'd had no teachers, because I'd had no strong emotions.

Now I did.

And I'd had no instruction.

Anger was suffocating me, drowning me, choking me. The only way I knew to vent this thing, on those rare occasions I'd felt it—unnamed and volatile inside me—was through sex.

My best friend. My mother. Conspiring with Dalia to keep me in the dark, to keep me a placid automaton.

If I was a witch, I had *power*. And it had been denied me. I had magic. And was never permitted to know it. I'd been given no choice.

I loved Este. Always had.

But I sure as hell didn't know her, and apparently never had.

Nor had I known my own mother.

One of the books shot off the bookcase and fell to the floor, landing at my feet, open.

"What now?" I muttered irritably. Clearly, all the books in the house had a tendency to communicate, if and when they felt like it. Rather like my best friend and mother.

Sinking to the floor, I pulled the book onto my lap and read.

A man marches into battle, boldly dividing to conquer. His techniques are often brutal, ergo visible, ergo possible to combat.

A woman divides so subtly, so delicately, the soldiers don't even know they've been divided, as they stand, defenseless, separated by invisible fences.

And so the war is won.

Pissed, I turned the page. It was blank. As were the rest of them.

"I hate you," I told the book, fully aware of how childish I sounded, but decided I deserved the right to say something so childish, because I never had. I hadn't been permitted to *have* normal child feelings.

It occurred to me that it might have been really stupid for Mom to suppress my power, only to leave me with said power exploding yet grossly emotionally stunted, when she died. It occurred to me I had a lot to learn, and fast. Self-discipline would be crucial. I'd always prided myself on discipline but was beginning to realize it was easy to discipline yourself when you were an emotional iceberg, not a volcano.

There was little doubt what the book was telling me—and, yes, I'd just thought *what the book was telling me*—because having accepted I was a witch, and I privately had, although I wanted more proof, there seemed little point in denying anything else bizarre that was happening. "Call a spade a spade," I muttered. Things were what they were, and I would only make myself vulnerable by denying them. *Light the candle, Cameron witch*, the grimoire had said.

I frowned, wondering how many things I'd failed to notice and understand. Like the shimmering symbols etched at the threshold of Cameron Manor—a spell of some sort. Este hadn't been able to cross it. That was why she'd insisted I invite her in. That was also why Mr. Balfour believed I was safe inside the manor, despite the lack of a security system. Was it also, in some capacity, related to my transient faint at the threshold the night I arrived? What else didn't I know? Were the triskelions and the Serch Bythol also engraved spells, and if so, what effect did they have?

I'd invited Jesse in because of my blinders. Este and Devlin had both freaked out. Made me rescind it. I wanted to know why.

Apparently, Juniper was a witch, no less than the Grand Poobah of witches around these parts. And everyone believed I was a chip off that block. Was I?

My mother had divided us all with invisible fences, to further whatever war she'd been fighting—a war that, to me, was equally invisible.

I wanted to burst into tears but couldn't. My heart was frost, and my tears would be shards of ice.

It was so much easier to grieve Joanna Grey than to be angry with her. I hated feeling this. For the tiniest sliver of a moment, I hungered for the days I'd felt little to nothing. Because what I felt most of all, right now, was so goddamned alone and angry.

A solitary soldier, hemmed by invisible fences.

I DON'T KNOW if I ever used to dream while I slept. I certainly never remembered any. Perhaps the countless demands of life with Mom left me so exhausted that I slept too deep for the Sandman to find me. Or perhaps the moment my brain kicked on, pragmatic Zo admonished, *Vanish, useless dust. You serve me not. No time for dreams.* Or perhaps dreams, too, had been stolen from me: Zo can't have any magic, and she's also not allowed to dream. She might want things. Become a real live person. Better shoot that possibility down hard and fast.

Since entering the walls of Cameron Manor, I'd not only been dreaming richly, but my dreams were so lucid, presenting with such tactile detail, they felt inseparable from reality upon awakening, and emotional nuances of dream residue clung to me throughout the day.

I dreamed I strode a forest unlike any I'd seen, unlike any in existence. A hushed, primal place where generously spaced trees stretched out bare late-autumn branches of such rambling girth they met the gloaming in a canopy above my head. It was so velvet-dark, I'd have been unable to see, were it not for a forest floor carpeted with thick drifts of silvery-yellow leaves that gleamed radiantly, as if lit from within by phosphorescent midribs and veins.

I felt so free, untethered by worry or care, that I flung myself into the thick piles of luminous leaves, plunging my arms deep into fallen mounds. I made leaf angels, I laughed, I rolled. I knew I was somewhere sacred, and although I also knew it was a strange, wild place, untamed and unpredictable, I felt it was safe. At least for me.

Then, as I spread my arms in yet another sweeping arc, I encountered a *thing* beneath the leaves that responded to my touch, shifting as if disturbed, emitting a rumble from deep in its chest.

Something alive.

Without seeing it, I knew what it was.

Not a mere dog, that boon companion to man, but a hunting hound, one capable of great cunning and great savagery.

I also knew that until the moment I touched it, the beast had slumbered. Deeply, perhaps for time unmeasured. In dreams, concepts like eternity seem wholly plausible, and this beast, to me, felt eternal.

Abruptly a dozen hounds emerged from the lambent forest floor, shaking off illuminated leaves, dark, sinuous shadows rising to form a crouching ring around me.

Supine was prey. Pushing up to my knees, I glanced from hound to hound, eyes narrowed, assessing. Friend or foe? Why did they slumber in this forest? Were they hunters? Was I the hunted?

I surged to my feet, adopting an aggressive stance.

I am formidable, my eyes said. *I am indomitable. Do not test me.*

Closer they crept on tightly coiled haunches.

I awakened with a violent start and no answer to my question: Ally or adversary? Only a nagging feeling that by coming here, perhaps in the simple act of taking my first step across the threshold of Cameron Manor, I'd done what Mom had devoted her entire life to keeping me from doing.

Let sleeping dogs lie, my darling Zo, she'd say, whenever I asked about my father. *They have teeth. They have claws.*

"Fuck that noise," I growled as I got out of bed. "I do, too."

"WHAT WAS MOM'S message?" I demanded without preamble when I found Este in the kitchen the next morning, prepping coffee.

She glanced over her shoulder, brow furrowed with concern.

"I felt your anger all night. Either you or the house, I couldn't decide. Maybe both."

"You think the house is angry?"

"It has . . . presence."

"Do you dislike it?"

"I don't know yet. The kitchen is damned hard to resist. The pool and courtyard are divine. There's a feeling of expansiveness inside these walls, almost a . . . kiss of infinity, as if you could open doors to find more doors and yet more, and it might never end. But there's . . . something . . . something . . ." She trailed off, frowning. "I don't know. The jury is still out."

I'd gotten that same taste of infinity but attributed it to never being in a house so large. I felt confident that, once I'd explored every room, the discomfiting sensation would ease. "Mom's message," I prodded.

Fiddling with the machine, she said, "It wasn't like that. She just told me if she died unexpectedly, before—er, not from the cancer, I needed to get to you ASAP, tell you what you were, and help you awaken your power. Teach you the craft."

I said disbelievingly, "Nothing else? Like, maybe, why we were running all my life or from whom? Nothing about my father? Or who I am?" Maybe my *real* last name? Because I was pretty sure that was a lie, too. She'd named me after what she'd turned me into: something too timid to be a color.

Este shook her head. "Joanna wasn't big on disclosure. Her sole concern was that she would die and you would have no idea what was happening to you when your power awakened."

I sank onto a stool at the island, deflated. "That's *it*? Seriously?"

"Aside from making me promise to tell you about the safe," she said, sliding a steaming hot cup of chicory coffee in front of me. "Look what I found." She pushed a small stoneware pitcher forward, smiling. "There's a fridge in the butler's pantry stocked with lovely old-fashioned glass milk bottles, filled with real milk."

Thinking that I couldn't wait to get my hands on the contents of the fireproof lockbox, and they'd damned well better explain a lot, I peered into the pitcher. "Real," meaning straight from the cow. Usually, the sight of thick, clotted cream would delight me. Mom and I had a milk cow once. I'd named her Daisy. I'd loved that cow, curled with her on the grass, sleepy in the sun. It had been the *best* summer in the foothills of the West Virginia mountains. We'd made our own cheese and ice cream with fresh peaches, warm from just being picked. Mom taught me to make butter by shaking cream in a jar until it began to clump and turned. She'd shown me how to wash the curds in cold water with a soft spatula until they congealed, salt the butter lightly, and press it into a mold, then we'd slathered it on biscuits and cornbread with jam, and I'd thought we were queens, the luckiest of people, and so very rich. I'd thought we might get to stay. Daisy had convinced me. She was alive, and in our care. Surely, we were staying. Then the cow was gone, and so were we.

The sight of the cream turned my stomach.

My mother, who'd suppressed and made me doubt my fundamental nature, had discussed it openly with my best friend.

Este moved to stand behind me, put her hand on my shoulder. I bristled instantly. "I'm not the enemy, Zo. Truly, I'm not," she murmured.

I didn't yield an inch, shrugging my shoulder to get her hand off it.

Sighing, she sank into a seat next to me at the island. "Your mother loved you more than life itself, Zo. She'd have done anything to protect you. Although she never gave Mom a reason for suppressing your magic, she did invite her in for a brief glimpse of deep sight."

Invite her in . . . deep sight. Oh, yes, more proof I was a witch, and everyone knew things I didn't. Just dumb, blind Zo, stumbling about.

She continued, "Mom said that whatever Joanna was afraid would happen to you had her so terrified that she truly believed concealing your heritage from you was the only possible way to give you a chance at life. She was convinced Joanna was doing it from the deepest, most unconditional love. That's why Mom never spoke up. If she hadn't been convinced of that, she would have. She'd have defied the heavens themselves, had she believed your mother was doing it for any other reason."

I nearly wept then. God, these *emotions*! How did people deal with feeling so intensely all the time? How distracting!

In this, Este was right. All I'd ever felt from Mom was deep, unconditional love. I might have only been capable of shallow emotions myself, but I could feel the burn of that woman's love at all times, unwavering, warm and secure as a cloak around me, and if at all possible, eternal.

"You were her world. The only thing that mattered to her."

She'd been the only thing that mattered to me, too. It occurred to me that probably wasn't a healthy way to live. But then, little about how we'd lived had been.

"You believe you're a witch, don't you? Things happened, didn't they?" Este said quietly.

I nodded stiffly.

"Good. I have an art showing to prep for in Indy on Monday, and have to fly out stupid-early tomorrow morning. Before I leave, you have a great deal to learn. Let's begin."

MANY HOURS LATER, I sat on my bed staring at a fat brown leather journal embossed with an owl and Celtic knotwork, tied with a leather thong. Dressed and ready, I was killing time, waiting for Este to finish showering, stoically refusing to open the book. At least, I consoled myself, this one had actually been written and wouldn't mysteriously write itself. I hoped.

My brain was on overload.

Mom and I began putting this together for you many years ago, Este told me when she'd given me the journal this afternoon. *I think Mom always planned to tell you before it was too late, if Joanna didn't.*

There was that phrase again—*too late*. Again, I'd not asked. Overload.

We'd spent most of the day by the pool, ducking back into the kitchen for food and drink before returning to the sunny courtyard where my bodyguards kept a watchful eye from a distance. During those hours, Este told me so much my head was spinning with it all. She knew it was overload, ergo the journal.

It's easier to absorb by reading than hearing it. You'll want to go back and reread, gleaning more each time. I'm only giving you the basics right now, details are in the journal, she'd said. *Unfortunately, in no particular order. It was more difficult to write than we imagined. Difficult to decide what was most important to teach you first.*

Is it full of spells? I'd asked.

Babe, you don't need spells. You're Highblood Royal. The craft is will-based; that's why it's called the Way of the Will, or the way of intentions. We each have varying degrees of magic in our blood. We focus that power with our will, shape it, try to make it grow into reality. With a lesser degree of magic in the blood, words, spells, even enchanted objects become necessary to focus and amplify the witch's intention. Even then, it doesn't always work. Sometimes it works but not the way you meant it to. Spells are tricky, they have teeth. You must always respect that, and be extremely precise with your intention. If deep beneath the intention you believe you're shaping lurks another less savory one, you can spell yourself into a serious mess.

Did you ever do that?

She'd laughed. *Massively and more than once, especially during puberty, when my hormones were crazed and I had no idea how to handle them. Fortunately, Mom was there to rescue me. With the degree of magic your blood contains, will alone is enough, or it will be, once you've trained. That's why Royals are so feared. While most of us have to work hard to affect reality, to bring our vision into the world, the truly dangerous Royals, with undiluted blood and decades of practice, have merely to draw power from a source rich enough, and think their intentions into existence.*

She'd shuddered. *Don't get me started on the gray witches. When they battle another witch, every witch out there runs and hides.*

Este herself was a craft witch, she'd told me, which meant her power was in her hands. She was driven to create, and painting was the way she'd chosen to focus her power. If she didn't create for a long enough period of time, she began to feel physically ill. I remembered the times she'd shut herself away in her studio, painting feverishly, for weeks on end, coming out with twenty-five new pieces, each more brilliantly realized than the last.

But that's not magic that you're doing, I'd said, *That's painting.*

Remember Tilda Schomber, who couldn't get pregnant and wanted desperately to have children? When she commissioned a painting from me, I worked a fertility spell into it, Este had said, smiling. *It was some of the most potent magic I've done. I adore Tilly and poured my whole heart into it.*

I'd gotten chills. *She has three kids now.*

She's a fantastic mom. If someone with health problems commissions a painting, like Doc Fields with his liver issues, I layer a healing spell into it. That's why all my paintings are two in one: the actual painting you see in the daylight and the one that glows at night, from the luminescent paint I layer into it, laced with magic.

I'd said in a low voice, *Could you have healed my mother?*

Her eyes darkened. *Not a chance. Nothing could have healed Joanna Grey.*

Why not?

She'd sighed. *Complicated. Let's tackle that later.*

Later. I'd accepted the deferral, mind whirling.

What's my power? What kind of witch am I? She'd described sacral witches, skull witches, heart witches, craft or hand witches. There were the elemental ones: fire, water, air, and soil witches. And darker ones: war, pestilence, famine, and death witches. Where did I fit?

She'd stared at me, gaze troubled, then said quietly, *I don't know.*

"Great," I muttered now, smoothing my dress, flexing my leg and absently admiring the line of my calf in high heels. I'd rarely felt pretty; there'd been no time for it in my life. I did tonight.

Your power will present itself, Este told me. *By seeing what presents, we'll know what you are. Highblood Royals often have multiple talents, sometimes two or even three aspects.*

"So, I might be a death witch *and* a war witch. Lovely," I growled, as I pushed up from the bed. "Or maybe pestilence plus famine. Fan-freaking-tastic."

Mentally, I scooped up the entire mess and boxed it. Este had also asked me to try to imagine being her, at nine, threatened by both our moms. Asked if I could have defied both Joanna and Dalia at that age.

No, I'd told her wearily. *I do understand.*

Then understand, also, that the longer the lie went on, the more impossible it became to tell you. I will always have your back. I will always be your biggest advocate and champion. I will battle beside you through anything. I love you, Zo. I couldn't lose you. And once I was older, and considered defying them, I was pretty sure I'd only blow up our whole world. At the very least, you would hate me; at the worst, Joanna would have whisked you off somewhere I'd never be able to find you again. Life is messy, Zo. But you're free now. Please don't hate me for it. I was only trying to hold on to us, to our friendship, praying for the day I could help you become who and what you were always meant to be. When we could be sister witches forever. I lived for that day.

Never hate you, I'd told her, *always love you,* and we'd hugged and made plans to go out tonight. Hit the Gossamer, then the Shadows. Be young and wild and free, party like rock stars. Be passionately alive and thrilled to be.

It was long overdue, and I was more than ready.

15

ASSUMING I TRULY WAS A Highblood Royal, the only thing regal about tonight was that clubbing with bodyguards was a royal pain in the ass.

Not only did it severely curtail who I might dance with, and how close, but it was impossible to conceal that I had security, which added to the deference I inspired merely by being heir apparent. Men took one look at my bodyguards and looked away.

Este, on the other hand, had no dearth of partners, but that woman had dressed to kill and was, as usual, slaying.

I smiled over the rim of my margarita, watching her on the dance floor as men vied to edge out her current partner. Este was unabashedly who she was, no filters, no apologies. People were drawn to her confidence every bit as much as to her statuesque beauty, if not more so, and I loved watching her shine.

The Gossamer was young, eclectic, and fun. The music was all over the place, which I appreciated because my taste was, too. It was totally different from the crowd I'd met at the Shadows. Here, in the cerulean and chrome nightclub, the mood was sexy with a razor's edge: modern, inclusive, and diverse, as opposed to the elegant, Old World, exclusive, Celtic atmosphere of the Shadows. Thankfully, no one queued up to meet me; I was so not in the mood for that tonight.

What if this town, this coven is exactly what your mother was running from? Este had asked. Despite being open to having fun, I was on guard, senses alert, studying everyone. Fun, however, was proving hard to find as the few men willing to partner me had to put up with being stared down by four sets of stone-cold eyes, hulking close enough to slit my partner's throat if he so much as breathed wrong. Inevitably the men wilted and slithered away beneath the stress of the mercenaries' regard, leaving me alone but, for a novel change, not feeling underdressed or like an outlier.

I owned the Gossamer, Jesse had informed me on the way down. If something didn't meet with my approval, I had but to say so, and it would be changed. Perhaps, I thought, with a snort of laughter, I could tell Este I didn't like cerulean and have her transform it to pink.

I was drunk enough that the heady power of owning this club and so many other things rather appealed to me, which I found moderately disturbing, given that I didn't know my lineage. We'd been alternating shots with margaritas since we'd arrived a few hours ago, and I was definitely in my happy place. Well, as happy as I could get, given my totally fucked-up circumstances: murdered, lying mother and all, coupled with a few million un-answered questions.

"Could you *not* have simply stayed home?"

I spun to find Mr. Balfour standing behind me, looking ut-terly exasperated and, in black tie, utterly out of place in the Gossamer.

"What are you doing here?" I asked, frowning.

"Panicking, frankly," he said flatly. "I abandoned my wife at the opera the moment I heard you'd left Cameron Manor."

"The bodyguards called you?" I'd specifically told them not to and wanted to know where their loyalties lay. I was, after all, the one paying their bill. Oh, God, was I buzzed! Anger, so much anger in my gut right now. It was making me feel . . . borderline obnoxious. That was so far from the Zo I knew, it was nearly incomprehensible.

"I got a call from the parent of a clubgoer."

"I thought there was no real threat," I said pointedly.

"That we know of." He sighed heavily. "*Must* you be out? I'm sure Este has more to tell you, to teach you," he said meaningfully. "She did *tell* you things, right?"

I nodded, gaze cool. "I have questions."

"Tuesday. Not one minute sooner."

Bristling, I said tartly, "From what she's told me, I think you need me."

"We most certainly do," he replied, just as tartly. "Which is why I will not, under any circumstances, do one thing to jeopardize your ability to remain with us. Do you understand?"

Cold eyes bored into me. Cold like the mercenaries' eyes. There was more to James Balfour than a kindly old man, I realized then. "You're a witch, too," I said.

"Hush! This crowd is mostly Paleblood."

"Paleblood," I echoed.

He leaned in and said close to my ear, "Without magic in their blood. Pale. There are many like you and me in Divinity, but far more who are not. We do not advertise. Ever."

"How—"

"Stop. I'm leaving now before I say more than I should. I want you to leave, too," he said sternly.

"Is that an order? Do you think you *can* order me?" I was just drunk enough to get pissy about his tone.

His gaze and voice softened. "My dear Ms. Grey, that is a most fervent request. I will never order you. I will support whatever you choose to do. I merely hope you'll choose wisely until I can . . . bring you fully into your own. Until then, you are at risk from many things, from many sources."

"But you do definitely intend to help bring me fully into my own? After Tuesday?" I demanded. Este was leaving tomorrow. I hungered for instruction, I needed to learn everything I could about myself, and fast.

"I already pledged as much to you the other day. I will do everything in my power to make you equal to the crown you wear, to protect you and see you thrive. Here, in Divinity."

Then he was melting into the crowd, and gone. *Here, in Divinity,* he'd said, emphatically separating that phrase from the rest of his words, and I'd gotten the feeling he'd chosen his words carefully to bear the unspoken warning: *But if you leave this town, all bets are off.*

I wondered then if choosing to walk away wouldn't be far more problematic and fraught with danger than I'd begun to imagine. If Este was right, and Divinity *was* what Mom was running from, Mr. Balfour could just as easily prove foe, not friend.

I wondered, too, if what I'd felt the night I'd stepped across the threshold—*but of course, all roads lead here*—hadn't been the first real truth I'd ever known.

Then Este's hand was in mine and she was tugging me to the dance floor, laughing, her eyes brilliant with mischief. "Come on! I requested a song. You have to dance with me. I'm invoking 'no holds barred.'"

We'd done that a few times in Indy; taken turns forcing the other to go a little nuts. No holds barred meant we danced, oblivious, doing whatever the music made us feel like doing. No style, no method, only madness. Men usually decided we were lesbians when we did that, and tonight, I felt the impish desire to announce brightly, *Nope, just witches*, and cackle eerily.

"Do I know the song?" I asked as she tugged me through the crowd.

"Dunno, but you'll like it. And the bodyguards will clear us a good circle so we can make waves," she said, laughing.

A single drumbeat began to pound through the speakers of the club, steady and driving, and it had the same incendiary effect on me as the drumming of "Witches Reel."

I am my mother's savage daughter, a woman's strong voice proclaimed, as Este began to dance.

Joining in her laughter, I gave myself over to it, not caring what anyone thought of me. Oh, yes, I was my mother's savage daughter. And I would not lower my voice, either.

I love music, and the words of this particular song spoke to me on such a deep level, I was stunned. This was what I'd always been missing. A kind of . . . earthy mysticism that I could almost feel but never quite touch, lurking out there beyond my grasp but not completely beyond my vision. Unseen, yet always felt, even to my dimmed, leashed bones. I was delighted to see the song was having the same effect on every woman in the club, and within moments, the dance floor was filled with only women, shoulders back, tossing their hair, eyes blazing with pride and ferocity. For a few minutes, I was so blissfully united with such raw, conjoined feminine power, it was more intoxicating than any libation, as if we were all filling a cup from a shared cauldron of pain, grief, trial, and tribulation, and alchemizing it into a tonic of strength, joy, hope, and power.

That's what we women do. From the hour of our birth to the birth of our daughters to the dying of our grandmothers and mothers, we spin pain on our looms into a joyful fabric, for what would be the point of doing less?

Then the song ended, and the world went back to its normal strange state, rife with self-denial and trivial concerns, and Este was dragging me through the crowd again, insisting she had to pee, while my bodyguards elbowed their way behind us, struggling to keep up.

Like the Shadows, the Gossamer had many side rooms, and as we had no clue where the bathroom was and it was dark in the club, Este began opening door after door. At the fourth door, she gasped and froze, gaping with such an expression—of shock, astonishment, and . . . lust?—that I crammed myself into the opening, avid to see whatever she was seeing.

Devlin.

Oh, God, he was stripped to the waist, his arms full of a beautiful half-naked woman, his face buried in her neck. The shapely brunette was writhing against him, head flung back in ecstasy, moaning. I don't think of myself as a voyeur, but two gorgeous people having sex is pretty much guaranteed to rivet me. Feeling light-headed and suddenly short of breath, I stared, crushed in the narrow opening with Este.

Just then, Devlin lifted his face from the woman's neck, and I couldn't quite process what was happening; I grabbed Este's arm, clenching it much too hard, and gasped, "What the hell?"

Devlin looked straight at me, burnt umber eyes blazing, and I heard him in my mind, saying clearly, *I'd rather it was you, fierce lass. But you said "not now,"* Zo-d'kai. And in my mind, he said my name the same exotic way he'd said it in the car, but fisted around a groan of tortured lust, and I shivered, feeling fevered and chilled at the same time.

Then he dropped his beautiful, dark head forward again, and I watched, shocked and aroused, as he resumed what he'd been doing.

Este yanked the door shut and spun, leaning back against it, breathing heavily, a hand to her breast.

"Wait, was he—"

"Hush." She pivoted sharply away from the door. "Bathroom, then let's get the hell out of here! We don't talk about this till we're home, in private," she barked over her shoulder.

Nodding dumbly, I followed.

"I ALWAYS THOUGHT if I ever saw a vampire drinking some-one's blood, I'd be grossed out," Este said, dropping cross-legged on my bed beside me. "That was *so* not the case."

"Devlin's a *vampire*? His fangs were *real*?" I exploded, plumping pillows to wedge behind my back. Hot as Hades to begin with, the man was even more intriguing to me now. A vampire? Seriously? They existed!

"Definitely real. Have you ever touched him?"

"No!"

"I didn't mean slept with him. I meant touched him in any way. Was he icy or warm? This is important."

I'd shaken his hand, danced with him, kissed him, felt the heat of his palm burning through my silk shirt at the small of my back. Wanted to feel much, much more. "Definitely warm. But he never had fangs before. I would have noticed."

She peered at me intently. "*How* have you touched him?"

"I shook his hand the night we met," I said, a bit too defensively, even to my ears.

She snorted with laughter. "Oh, babe, you've gone there. Who wouldn't? How far?"

"I only kissed him, and only once."

"Well, take my advice, and don't do it again," she said, sobering. "That man is a warm vampire. Their fangs only present when they feed or, if they're very old and powerful, when they're feeling aggressive or aroused."

"Warm vampire?" I echoed. *Cold vampire*, the grimoire had offered, and I'd wondered if that meant there were warm ones, too. Apparently, yes.

"Did you think witches were the only paranormal creatures that were real? Myths, legends, stories, they all possess a degree of truth. Particularly the ones you find in every culture, in every country."

"So," I said slowly, "there are cold vampires, too?"

"A cold vampire is dead, but undead, a completely different creature, with a completely different origin. However, you should know, they're known to hang out around powerful witching communities. They'll serve as lackeys for a chance at a witch's blood, which can sustain them far longer than Paleblood. A warm vampire is a fully alive witch who has repeatedly drunk the blood of more powerful witches to extend his or her own life. After a period of time, the drinking of blood becomes necessary to sustain their immortality. A cold vampire won't die if deprived of blood. He or she is already dead. They'll just suffer hellishly. But a witch who is a warm vampire *will* die if they don't drink regularly."

"Then Devlin is a witch, too."

She nodded. "I've never seen a warm vamp before. I'd only heard tales. If there are any in Indiana, well . . . I sincerely doubt something so exotic would stick around BFE."

Bumfuck, Egypt, i.e., the middle of nowhere, which was what we called Frankfort and basically anyplace in the Midwest. "And?" I prodded.

"They're usually quite powerful in their own right, but hunger for greater power. Drinking the blood of more powerful witches not only extends their life, but increases the magic in their blood. Supposedly, some are capable of shifting shape, and they're rumored to have the ability to turn invisible, like the eldest of cold vampires. They guard their secrets as closely as the gray house. The magical increase they get is not passed to their progeny, and is theirs only so long as they continue drinking. There were dark days, in ancient history, when Royals were abducted and drunk to death. Now such a thing would see an entire bloodline wiped out in retaliation. If not by the Royal house offended, then by the gray house. No one wants to incur gray wrath, not even vampires. God, was that *sexy* or what?"

Disturbingly so. I'd never been a fan of vampires. I'd thought, like Este, I'd find their means of sustenance bloody and gruesome, and how could that possibly be sexy? But with Devlin, blood on his mouth and that primal, lust-filled look in his eyes, his ripped, half-naked body, his arms full of pale-skinned woman, it had been disconcertingly intimate, erotic, an unexpected, massive turn-on and, clearly, the woman had been enjoying the hell out of herself. I wondered how it would feel to be naked in Devlin's arms while he drank my blood. How much did he take? How much did he need to survive and how often? A few drops or—*Whoa, Zo, I admonished myself, sober up, and back that truck up.* "Is there a way to tell that a witch is also a vampire?"

She shook her head.

"But Devlin is a light witch, right?" I pressed. Oh, shit, I was definitely intrigued.

She cut me a hard look. "I know that look in your eyes, babe, and I'm telling you, don't go there. Warm vampires are different. Rules the rest of us obey are bendable to them. And how would I know? I can feel Devlin's power, not his lineage. But I would assume if he's here in Divinity, so close to the ex-matriarch, he's a light witch. I do know he's going to want your blood. You're the new heir. He'll try to seduce you. If he hasn't already," she said, arching a brow inquiringly. "Juniper may well have been feeding him. I can't see any other way that gorgeous man would be hanging around."

Well, that was deflating. He wanted my blood, not me. He lusted for the power and longevity it granted, not me. I hadn't even gotten my brain wrapped around the existence of witches, and now I had vampires to deal with, too.

"That doesn't mean he's not attracted to you," she added hastily. "I'm sure he is. I mean, how could he not be? You're the whole package, babe. But he'll want your blood. This is in the journal, Zo. It's actually in the first part of it because Mom and I knew you'd be prey for warm vampires. *Read* when I leave. Promise me you'll sit down and study that journal."

"I promise," I said, suddenly weary. Not physically, but mentally and emotionally exhausted. And much too buzzed. "How did you know Devlin's a witch? I mean, what gives it away?" I needed to know who was a witch in this town and who wasn't. Were Althea and her vegetable coven? If a person could employ deep sight, did that mean they were definitely a witch? Had I been descended upon, a few days ago, not by merely a group of angry women, but angry *witches*? I lacked the most basic skills and was seriously out of my depth.

"That's one of the many things you should have been taught as a child. We can feel each other. The lovers you chose. Why did you pick them?"

"I got a feeling from them of something . . . *more*. I couldn't explain it, even to myself. I just knew it when I found it."

"And when you met me the first time?"

"I felt like you were the first person, besides Mom, that really felt right and made sense to me."

"Exactly. That's what we feel. Did you feel that when you met Devlin?"

I recalled the shock of recognition, of familiarity, when I'd shaken his hand. I'd also felt it in spades my first night in Criollo, which meant the restaurant had, indeed, been packed with witches. Waiting for the heir's arrival? Had that many witches already known who I was, that I was coming, and when? Had I been a walking target that night? What if I'd chosen a witch other than Kellan? Might that witch have tried to kill me? I shivered. Just how many times had I had an unwitting near miss with Death recently? "Yes. It's subtle, then?"

"Not once you have your radar attuned for it. You get to the point where you can walk into a crowd of a thousand people and know instantly there are three witches among them. Finding them is a different matter. You have to focus and narrow it down. Like everything else in the craft, it takes practice. There are notes in the journal about this, too. I'm sorry, but it really pisses me off that your mother didn't teach you this when you were a child. Mom and Dad raised me in tune with all the odd things I felt, explaining them as I grew, teaching me to stretch and grow my power. You've got a lot of catching up to do."

It pissed me off, too. But then everything did lately. I wanted to protest that Este couldn't leave in the morning. I needed her to teach me. But with Juniper's rules about guests, her staying in residence simply wasn't an option.

"I'll come back next weekend," she said, gleaning my thoughts from my face.

"You can't," I said sourly, and told her about the contingencies.

"I don't like this, Zo. They're controlling you, isolating you."

"I have a feeling we're going to be renegotiating these edicts. For some reason, they seem to need me."

"Some reason? Babe, this town is a sitting duck without a Royal to guard it."

"Sitting duck how? Guard it from who?"

"Any other magical bloodline out there that wants it. Not just here, but globally. There are practitioners of the way in every culture. The nine houses we've been talking about are merely those in this country."

"I don't understand. Why would another bloodline want Divinity?"

She sighed heavily. "Oh, Zo, we need to talk about the social structure of the witching world. Power is their aphrodisiac."

"Even light witches?"

"Even. You'll find most witches who stay tightly plugged into the community, who participate and strive for position and sway, are every bit as power-hungry and success-driven as Palebloods. Some of the most heinous witch hunts and executions in history have been enacted by witches themselves. Mom and Dad broke away when they were young, raised me apart from it. Many witches go off on their own, eschew the protection of a coven for a solitary life without the drama. Some even turn their back on the craft itself."

"How many witches do you think are in this town? You said you could feel them when you walked into a room."

"A room doesn't equate to a town. I feel astronomical power here, but couldn't begin to make a guess. In the club tonight, excluding the bodyguards—"

"They're witches, too?" I exclaimed. No wonder I'd felt such a magnetic pull to them all!

Nodding, she continued, "There were seven other witches. The hot Jamaican bartender, the woman in Devlin's arms, and three on the balcony. I didn't spot the other two. The town is majority Palebloods, as we call them, who were probably carefully chosen, lured here with a job offer or investment opportunity. Someone, likely a town committee, selects the families they feel suitable to settle here. It's the ultimate in a planned community."

"But why not have a town of just witches?" I asked, frowning.

"There are far fewer witches in existence than Palebloods, and there's strength in numbers. People without magic have a great deal to offer. They bring loyalty, commitment, willingness to defend a way of life they value—and I imagine life here is pretty idyllic."

"But why," I said slowly, "would my mother have run away, then? Why take me from such a place?" For that matter, who was my father, and where did he fit in? Was it truly my father who'd been pursuing us, or someone else?

Este hesitated a moment, then said, "I may have misspoken last night. This town might not be what she was running from. There's another possibility." She lapsed into silence, frowning. Finally, she said, "I have to throw this out there because I'm leaving tomorrow. And you must be aware of all the possibilities to be on guard."

"What's this unsavory thing you don't want to tell me?"

"It's possible you're not a Cameron at all."

"What?" I exclaimed. "Are you sure I'm a Royal?"

"Before you'd been awakened, I couldn't feel you fully, but you are definitely a Royal. As was your mother. However, like I said, I have no way of knowing—nor does any witch—what house you're from. We can feel your power, but we can't tell if it's dark, light, or gray. Only that you're Royal. It's the sheer quantity of magic that emanates from you that gives you away, once awakened."

"If I wasn't awakened, how could Juniper have known I was a Royal?"

"Any witch she sent hunting would have felt your mother's power and known her child was Royal."

"But why would Juniper bring me here, if I wasn't a Cameron?"

"This town is a prize. Juniper's fortune is staggering. She left a kingdom, resting on the laurels of enormous wealth, with an insanely powerful coven to protect whatever Royal seizes it. If she'd been searching for a Cameron heir for a long time and couldn't find one, but knew she was going to die in a matter of weeks or months, she'd have done anything to assure the future of Divinity. Any Royal would be able to hold it. She may have simply managed to locate one of indeterminate heritage that she could pass off as a Cameron and been willing to accept you to protect her life's work, wagering that the reward of such a staggering 'inheritance,' plus narrow contingencies to shape you in your early years, would bring out the best in you. That if you weren't a Cameron, in time, you would become precisely the Cameron Divinity needed."

"I thought you said no other witches could find this town. How could there be a threat?"

"Royals can," she said with a grimace. "Word of Juniper's death circulated fast. We heard of it back home within hours. Once other houses knew her legacy was unprotected, it was ripe for the taking. Any Royal house could swoop in, make a brutal show of force, and after sufficient brutality, Divinity would pledge to the new house. A town like this, without Juniper, is prey. That's why Mr. Balfour had to get you here and awaken you quickly. I guarantee, the other houses had their most powerful witches inside the boundaries of Divinity within hours of Juniper dying. Everyone was waiting for her to go. She was over a century old, and it was widely known she had no heir. Not even all the witches in this town united could protect it against a Royal and their Highblood coven."

"Mr. Balfour said Juniper had selected an alternate. The

Alexanders are Highblood, but not Royal. How could they have hoped to hold the town?"

She shrugged. "A Hail Mary? Desperate measures in desperate times, perhaps to buy more time to continue hunting for a Royal. This is critical: you must never let anyone here know you might not be a Cameron."

"Why not? Wouldn't they still be grateful for the protection?"

She shook her head. "Yes and no. Depending on which house you're from. Your mother was willing to condemn you to a half-life. What was she trying to escape that she was willing to go to such extremes? What was she trying to prevent by suppressing you?"

"Not following."

"Zo, your mom may have been from one of the *dark* houses. Fleeing it. Trying to save you from it."

I said nothing for a moment, then, "But surely Juniper wouldn't have brought a dark witch to Divinity."

"None of us can tell whether your power is light or dark, or even gray, although I seriously doubt your mother would have chosen that last name, if you were. Grey is nearly as common a surname as Brown or White. Juniper may have deemed it worth the risk when she found you, wagering fifty-fifty odds you were light. Perhaps even better odds, hoping, if you were dark— because you'd never been awakened—time in Divinity would bring out the light in you. Being born into a dark witching family doesn't guarantee you will choose to follow that path. It's your choice. Even a death witch can choose to follow the light path."

"So," I said slowly, "not only am I a witch, I might be a bad one?"

What she'd said about me being a gray . . . She'd doubted my mother would have "chosen that surname." Of course not even my last name was truly mine. We'd been running and hiding all our lives.

"Everything is choice," Este said intensely. "*You* choose. No one chooses for you. We are *not* what we are born. We are *not* our power. We're what we choose to do with it."

We sat in silence a few minutes. All my life, I'd hungered for answers, and now that I was finally getting some, they weren't as savory as I'd imagined.

"I'm not saying you're not a Cameron," Este said. "You might very well be. But you must keep an open mind to all possibilities until you find proof of who you are. Because if you're a dark witch, you'll tend to . . . well, gravitate that way. Especially as no one is training you. And I really hope they start soon. Then there's the fact that you've been awakened, but your power hasn't been formally pledged to a house. That, too, leaves you open to going either way. God forbid you spill blood, unpledged."

"You mean kill someone?" Not that I had any inclination to (other than Mom's murderer) but I wanted to understand what she was getting at.

"God, no, don't do that, either!"

"What would happen if I did?"

She shuddered. "Just don't, Zo. Inadvertently or otherwise. If someone attacks you, don't fight back, not even to defend yourself. Run, until you're pledged."

"Why?"

"The dark houses would make an aggressive play for you, which, from them, means aggressively seductive. They're pros at intuiting which buttons to push, making you think you *want* what they're offering, that the power and beauty of their night will always outshine our day. But, worse, the gray house could lay claim to you, regardless of your true birthright."

"What do you mean, 'lay claim'? I could say no, right?"

Este's gaze shuttered. "Just don't spill blood, Zo. We don't talk about the gray house. They have an unpleasant way of sidling in and observing if you do, and you rarely know they're doing it until it's too late."

"Too late how?"

"Witches have a bad habit of vanishing when a gray appears. Often, many witches. Entire covens. Never to be seen again."

"But they're just witches, right? Like other witches?"

She sighed. "Hard to say. I couldn't tell you the name of a single witch from the gray Royal house. No clue if it's patriarchal or matriarchal, led by king or queen. They keep it that way. Enough on this subject," she said sharply. "They're an abyss; if you look in, they look back. They're not like the rest of us. Their purposes are different. They serve a different code entirely. They *are* something else entirely. Pray to the great Cailleach you never encounter one."

16

THREE O'CLOCK SUNDAY MORNING—THIRTY MINUTES after Este headed off to bed so she could catch a few hours of sleep before leaving for the airport—found me standing on the third floor of Cameron Manor in the inky, charred northwest corridor, arguing with myself.

Here, the house was dark as a full lunar eclipse, and chillingly eerie. Surely, there was a better time to do this. I had less than forty-eight hours before I could open Juniper's tell-all letter, which had damned well better tell all, and I'd devoured enough gothic novels to know the monsters came out at night, not in the middle of the day, and bad things happened in dark houses when erstwhile heroines went blithely chasing after this strange noise or that odd light, so what was I thinking?

That I couldn't get that dratted grimoire off my mind, wondering what else the tome might offer, were I to solicit it.

Este had burdened me, in the brief time she'd been here, with so much information that one would think I wouldn't actively seek more. I hadn't even told her the fire that burned our house had been deliberately set, about the seeming attempt on my life and the body in the barn or the historic cabin and inexplicable book. I'd been too busy trying to absorb all the information she was throwing at me to share any of my own.

But honestly, lurking beyond that was a deep, unshakeable wariness that stilled my tongue. I'd planned to tell Este everything down to the last detail when she arrived so I could pick her brain. I'd thought we'd be exploring the dangers of my new life together. Then I'd discovered she'd known what I was *all my life* and never told me, and distrust was seeded in my heart. I couldn't shake the feeling that there was something else important I needed to know, something critical. My best friend, whom I'd trusted blindly and completely, had never told me I was a witch; what else might she be withholding? At this moment, I trusted no one and nothing but myself. Not even, necessarily, whatever Juniper might disclose in her letter. How could I, after discovering those closest to me had been lying to me all my life? Why wouldn't strangers lie even more readily?

Perhaps the book knew something of my mother. That might seem a ludicrous thought, but this was a book that wrote itself, which was so far beyond absurd, ludicrous no longer applied. Perhaps it contained within it a lineage of all witches, and could tell me who I was, or at least offer a salient clue.

Run, it had commanded. But why? Initially, it seemed it was trying to help me understand what I was. Then opposing forces had battled for control of its pages and the right to communicate. Desperate to learn more from either narrator (who struck me as somehow more impartial than the people around me), I was just anesthetized enough by alcohol, and fueled by brewing anger, to feel irritably reckless, nearly indomitable.

Armed with two flashlights and a battery-operated lantern I'd looped over a shoulder, I cast a bright enough halo that I felt reasonably assured I wouldn't be completely wigged out once I entered the inky chute.

But, God, the manor was oppressively cavernous at night! In the dark, it was easy to imagine, as Este had said, that the house expanded infinitely. Were I to walk too far, or fail to pay strict attention, I might stray into some witchy no-man's-land from which return might not be as simple as merely retracing my steps but cost me a debt in blood, or a piece of my soul. Really, there was a turret with no ingress, a door in Juniper's office that didn't open, concealed panels in the walls connecting wings; Cameron Manor was far from predictable.

And I was a witch. How incomprehensible was all this?

As I paused, stoking my nerve, I envisioned the macabre fortress from the outside, recalling my gut impression of it the afternoon I'd first seen it, and laughed aloud at the idea that here and now, in the middle of the night, I, newly indomitable Zo Grey, stood in the blackest of pitch, about to enter the even inkier, heavily fire-damaged, most terrifying part of the house.

I had balls these days; I'd give me that. Or a perilous dearth of brain cells.

I realized then that laughter before battle is a suit of armor. Mood leavened, squaring my shoulders, I strode confidently into the entrance of the smoky, icy corridor, only to be startled by a sudden intensification of the darkness around me, a thickening of the air itself, as if the mouth of the corridor resisted my entry. I had to *shove* forward, pushing into it, and nearly tumbled headfirst to the floor when the eerie resistance mysteriously ceased.

My confidence quickly waned. The hallway got icier and strangely narrower the further I walked, began to feel oddly skewed, tilting precariously out of square. Shivering, I felt as if the walls had shifted crushingly close, the floor slanting. A time or two, I stopped to stretch my arms out and measure the width, to find the corridor hadn't changed; only my impression of it. Somehow, the house was making me feel claustrophobic and unbalanced when there was no reason to be. After a time, I glanced back but could see absolutely nothing. Not even the faintest glimmer of light behind me. It was as if I faced a solid black wall. I briefly debated retreating to my room, but the view behind felt somehow more menacing than that ahead, so I resumed walking.

And walking. I had no idea how the hallway could possibly be so long, but the northwest wing seemed to suffer some spatial anomaly with which the rest of the manor was unafflicted. Several times as I strode past seemingly endless closed doors, I could have sworn I heard a . . . rustling slither.

Still, I felt no sense of mortal threat, and I could conceive of rats perhaps having nested in this abandoned wing and making such a noise. As my life was so surreal anyway, I refused to be deterred from my mission. The doors, after all, remained closed. Nothing terrifying was shambling or exploding out, not that I was about to turn a knob to peep into a single one of those rooms. I think a part of me rather hoped something would come out and confront me, so there might finally be a tangible, identifiable threat in my life to face off with.

Finally, I reached the pale gray stone of the turret. I was in the narrow dark chute, walking for what seemed an hour, then, finally, at the door to the cabin.

This time, I paused to study the etchings, committing to memory the symbols, to look up later.

Then I pushed open the door and shined my flashlight high and low, assessing the cobwebby kitchen. Finding it unchanged, I marched determinedly through to the apothecary/library, looking neither left nor right.

The archaic grimoire lay open on the pedestal, emitting a faint greenish glow.

"Hello," I said, feeling foolish, but something herein was sentient, and I thought I'd do well to greet it.

As I stepped forward, a sentence inked itself.

Greetings, she with mystery and magyck in her blood. Why have you come?

"I have questions."

What are you?

"I am—" I broke off, on the verge of saying *a witch*, and switched instinctively to "Cailleach."

Yes.

"Do you know who I am?"

You just told me. Beyond that, all is choice.

"I mean which house, light or dark?"

All is choice.

"Am I a Cameron?"

The words remained. Nothing new was written. I tried three more ways of asking questions about my heritage, but the words simply remained.

Finally, I demanded, exasperated, "Who was my mother? What was Joanna Grey's real name?"

Abruptly, the pages were filled with words, and stepping closer, I began to read.

There are countless misconceptions about binding a witch's power. It can be done but carries a steep price. If a witch binds another's power—a heinous act undertaken only in the direst circumstances—both will die. An accident will swiftly befall the pair, and their demise will be gruesome and painful. Often a

*witch takes his or her own life rather than passively submitting
to whatever gruesome fate the universe has in store.*

   *If thirteen witches work in concert to bind a witch's power,
only the bound witch dies, but each of the thirteen will soon
suffer grievous injury and loss. Sliced into thirteen wedges of pie,
retribution is a more palatable just desert, but getting thirteen
witches to agree on any topic is nearly impossible: the ingredients
of a simple potion, the roundness of a full moon, even the color of
an entirely black cat can give rise to heated debate.*

So, I thought with a snort, witches were just like everyone else,
opinionated and prone to disagreement.

*A witch can suppress another witch's power, even prevent it
from being awakened, but if continued for an extended period
of time that too will result in the oppressor's death. Using power
to suppress the power of another drains the life from the body,
eventually sickening the witch with myriad incurable diseases,
and although it may take decades if the witch is Highblood Royal,
death will come, and their life will be tragic and illness-ridden
until it does.*

   *The suppressed witch will also suffer; at best, a flameless
candle, capable of only shallow passion, chafingly aware on a
subconscious level that they are a mere shadow of who they were
meant to be; at worst, their sanity fractures, driving them to
terminate an existence they are unable to bear.*

The entry ended there. A chill slithered up my spine, and I
stared blankly. Read it again.

My mother was sick all the time because she was suppressing me.

Doing it was draining the life from her.

My mother *knew* why she was sick all the time. She'd *chosen* it.

I was the reason my mother was dying. And if she hadn't burned, I would have been the reason she died.

She was willing to die to keep me from being a witch, at least while she was alive. Why? What would keeping my power from me until she died accomplish? It didn't make any sense.

More words appeared.

If the witch succeeds in suppressing the victim's power until they either bear a child without their power fully awakened or turn twenty-five, the magic will be vanquished from the suppressed witch's bloodline forever. The victim and all progeny will be Paleblood for all time. In such savage fashion, some of the most powerful Royal descendants of all time have been destroyed, and the world deprived of their gifts.

Oh, my God. A fist of razor blades clenched my heart.

There are times when suppressing another witch's power is claimed to be an act of love.

There is never an excuse for it.

Individual power is part of the universe's way. Each person is granted a fair measure of it, theirs to use, squander, or abuse as they choose, not someone else's to control.

How many times had Mom encouraged me to have babies, *lots* of babies, no need for a husband, get started right now! It was the surer bet, to get me pregnant at eighteen or twenty, no need to wait until I was twenty-five to eradicate my power, my birthright.

I would be twenty-five on November 1, All Saints' Day, born one minute after midnight, Mom always said with a faint, wry smile.

Before it's too late, Este had said. And twice, she'd broken off when talking, saying *before—er, before the cancer took her.* That was bullshit. This entire masquerade had hinged on Mom surviving her "myriad illnesses" until I turned twenty-five.

Or got pregnant. Este also said she thought Dalia would tell me before it was too late—meaning before I turned twenty-five. I guess if I'd gotten pregnant, I'd just have been screwed. I was suddenly grateful I'd condomed-up on those occasions I indulged.

Hand to my throat, breath rapid and harsh in my ears, I staggered back.

Este *knew*. She'd known all my life why my mother was dying, as had Dalia. They'd known from the day they met her why my mother was always sick.

And never told me.

It was bad enough that Este had withheld from me the truth about what I was, allowing my mother to suppress my power, but I'd just learned the information she'd concealed would have *saved my mother's life*, if she'd told me while I was young, before Mom had developed not one, but *three* rare forms of incurable cancer. Before this moment, this horrific revelation, I'd had no idea that Mom suppressing my power was what was *killing* her.

My entire existence dwindled to a single emotion, one of such anguish, grief, and rage that I nearly doubled over, keening and howling.

If Este had only told me the truth when we'd first met, I could have prevented it!

My mother would still be alive. I wouldn't have this aching, enormous hole in my heart that nothing would ever fill again.

The page blanked, and once again, the book began to write, but the ink was dashed away. The temperature in the room plummeted so sharply that my breath frosted the air, and tiny icy crystals formed on the sides of the pedestal. I watched as the tome repeated the same battle for dominance I'd seen last time, a desperate war between would-be narrators for control of the pages. Clearly, neither narrator wanted the other to communicate with me.

The book heaved and whumped back down, releasing a cloud of dust from the pedestal, and I sneezed. It shuddered violently, exploded abruptly into the air, wildly fanning more pages than it could possibly have, then slammed back down, open.

A single sentence manifested in crimson ink for all of three seconds before it vanished, but not before that sentence was burned, scarred, seared with horrifying permanence into my mind.

YOU KILLED MAN IN BARN YOUR POWER EXPLODED HIS HEART YOU DID THAT!

Gasping. I stumbled back.

YOU KILLED YOU KILLED YOU KILLED

Filled the entire page with bloody slashes of crimson ink.

DO IT AGAIN

The laughter of many layered voices filled the small room, echoing off the walls.

The words vanished.

DO NOT DO IT AGAIN, MUST PLEDGE—

The tome snapped closed and went still and dark.

As did something inside my heart.

A GOOD FRIEND would have let Este get those few hours of sleep before heading to the airport.

I wasn't feeling like a good friend. In fact, it felt like quid pro quo to wake her up and make her life miserable. I mean, wasn't that what she'd done to me by honoring our mothers' demands over the life of her alleged best friend, and the life of that friend's mother?

Everyone knew everything, except me, and it was the very people who claimed to love me most who'd been lying to me all my life!

Whirling, I stormed from the cabin. This time, the darkness didn't feel suffocating or dense, it felt comforting as a rich, velvety cloak. I barreled through it, my eyes blazing as fiercely as the halo of light I cast.

Leaving the abandoned, charred wing proved far easier than getting there, as if the northwest corridor was eager to expel me. My exit was void of mysterious rustlings, nor did I encounter any of that gluey resistance as I stalked from the wing into the house proper.

I had no idea which room Este had chosen, but knowing her, she'd stayed on the same floor as me, so I loped down a flight of stairs and began opening each door I passed, ducking my head in. I spied a bathroom light shining though the jamb of a mostly closed door in the third room, noted a mound in the bed, and stepped furiously into the room.

When the mound didn't move, I flipped on the overhead light.

There was no mound in the bed; it was pristinely made and tucked. Nor was the bathroom light ablaze beyond the jamb. I was so angry, I didn't care that either the house was dicking with me or I was losing grasp on the basics of reality. Just pivoted and stormed off to continue my search for the woman who'd never told me that she knew why my mother was dying.

And that her death had been *preventable*!

Had I really killed that man?

Was the book lying to me, too? If I couldn't even tell when people were lying to me, how would I know if a book was?

"Oh, God, that's my reality now. One where I have to wonder if books can lie to me!" I seethed. Everything I'd believed, my whole life, wasn't true. How do you move forward from that? How do you build a future for yourself when you don't even know the truth about your past? Who *was* I?

A good witch, a good witch, a good witch, I willed fervently to the universe. One who hadn't already killed a man without even knowing it.

Who were my two narrators? I deemed it safe to surmise one was malevolent, but which one? One had told me to "pledge." One seemed to be goading me to kill again. They didn't like each other and didn't want the other to talk to me.

I found Este in the kitchen, sitting at the far end of the island. Her head whipped up when I walked in, her calypso eyes wide, concerned, and wary.

She should be wary. I knew the truth now, the terrible truth she'd concealed from me all my life, claiming to be my best friend, saying that she would always have my back, battle at my side, forever sister witches. "My *ass*," I hissed.

Rising from the stool, hands spread in supplication, she said in an intense rush, "Zo, babe, I don't know what's going on, but this house is seriously messed up tonight. I've been feeling such rage emanating from the walls and . . . something so dark and . . . insanely *hungry* that I couldn't sleep, and I went looking for you—"

"You knew why my mother was dying all along, didn't you?" I demanded, stopping at the opposite end of the island, fisting my hands so hard my nails gouged my palms. I deemed it wise to keep the twenty-foot span of marble between us, because at the moment I itched to pick a physical fight. To launch myself at her, hammer out my pain and betrayal with my fists. While others had learned, over years of familiarity with intense emotion, to temper anger, I had no experience, no tools to tame the dragon snorting fire in my belly.

She searched my gaze a long moment, then said quietly, "Who told you?"

"How the fuck does that even matter?" I snarled disbelievingly, slamming my fists into the counter. "*You* didn't. For decades you didn't. You let me work my ass off to support Mom, let me bleed out what little heart I was *allowed* to have, let me live small and lifeless, and you never *once* told me that Mom didn't have to die! That our life could have been *completely* different!" I was shouting, I was so angry, punctuating my words with violent gestures.

"Zo, you need to calm down," Este exclaimed. "And stop gesturing so wildly with your hands! You can't do that with your power awakened."

I roared, "What I *need* is to know in what reality my *supposed* best friend thought it was okay not to tell me my mother was dying every damned day of her life because of *me*! It was one thing to not tell me I was a witch. Entirely another to make such a life-altering decision for me. You had the ability to keep my mother from dying, if only you'd told me when we were kids, before she got so incurably ill! Who were you being loyal to? What was all that crap about always having my back? You telling me the truth could have saved her life! You knew," I raged, circling the island toward her. She backed away, which pleased me, and I was fairly certain in a dim sort of fashion it shouldn't. "You knew that if she managed to survive until I turned twenty-five, I'd never have known what I was. I'd have lived a bland, miserable half-life *all my life*, buried in debt, grieving her, working three jobs, never having children because I'd never have let myself bring them into such a difficult existence. And you know how much I want children, but no, you—"

"I would have told you!" she shouted back.

"I might have gotten pregnant at any time! You didn't know that I wouldn't! Who were *you* to decide you could wait until closer to my twenty-fifth birthday?"

"Listen to me, you have to calm down. It's imperative—"

"Fuck you," I thundered. "I don't have to do anything anymore. No one controls me and never will again. I am not your bitch to leash and lie to, and I will never—"

"Zo, you can't let your emotions have rein. It's too dangerous. You're unpledged."

I had no idea how to subdue the storm raging inside me. I'd been lied to, crushed, and devastated by the two women I loved most. *I* was the reason my mother's life had been such a living hell, and the choice she'd made—which everyone had known about but me—was the reason *my* life had been. My emotional squall had gained such momentum that it was sweeping me along, a hapless victim of its wrath. And frankly, it felt good to vent it, to let it out. It felt as if I had decades of bottled fury. "I can do anything I want," I snarled. "I'm free. And that's what you didn't want, isn't it? Because I'm a Royal and more powerful than you. Admit it, you *liked* being stronger. You enjoyed being mightier than poor, stupid Zo Gray-as-the-goddamned-color, who worked and worked, and never complained while everyone talked about her behind her back and controlled her, and you went off and became a successful, famous artist. While my life just kept going further to hell in a handbasket."

Not fair, Zo, a faint voice said inside me, *and you know it. Este isn't like that.* But I couldn't see my best friend standing there, beyond my haze of crimson fury. She was, at that moment, a traitorous enemy who had lied to me all my life. Who had watched my mother die.

"That's *not* true," she retorted. "I lived for the day you'd be free. I love you, Zo. Listen to me, I *love* you!"

"Love doesn't lie," I said in a terrible voice. "Not when it means someone's mom dies because of it!"

"Sometimes it has to! I was controlled, too, by both our moms! Do you have any idea what your mother threatened me with?"

"I don't care," I spat. "Everything is choice. Isn't that what you told me? Or did you lie about that, too? Or maybe it only applies to others, not the illustrious Este Hunter, who was raised by loving parents, always knowing that she was a witch? I may not have been capable of intense love, but I know this much— love nurtures, it creates. Love does not deceive."

"Yes. Focus on that," Este said intensely. "Focus on love, Zo."

I couldn't. Fury was scorching my heart. At my mother, Dalia, my best friend, at the whole damned world. "We had to run all my life because you never told me the truth. Do you know how many middle-of-the-night dashes we made and how terrified I always was? If you'd told me when we were young, our lives would have been completely different. All the bad things were preventable; our constant running, me having to work three jobs all the time, Mom's illness and death—all of it. If only one of the two women I loved most in the world had told me the truth. *You're a witch, your mother is suppressing your power, and it's killing her in the process.* That's all you had to say. A *single* sentence."

"I was afraid of her, and, Zo, right now, I'm afraid of you, too," Este said with quiet intensity.

"You should be! You ruined my life while claiming to be my best friend."

"I *am* your best friend," she said desperately. "You have to understand—"

I didn't have to understand anything. I understood all I needed to. Mom didn't have to die. I'd been defanged, declawed, neutered, and lied to by everyone I loved. I'd been given no choices at all. It cost my mother her life.

The incendiary rage inside me turned abruptly icy, as if all my fury had congealed in that instant into a lethal killing frost, and I knew, just like I did in the barn, that if I didn't expel it, I would end up being the one harmed. Este's lips were moving, but I couldn't hear a word she was saying. Blood was thundering in my ears, deafening me. The lethal cold grew and grew, expanding in my center, spreading outward, and I knew if it reached my skin, if I allowed it to fill me completely, I would either explode or become something so entirely unrecognizable to myself that I wouldn't even care that I'd become it. This . . . black, cold monstrosity was not me, but it was consuming me swiftly, and it was instinct to scrape it all into one big mass and *shove*—

"Zo, don't! For the love of all that is light and sacred, resist! You can *do* this! I can teach you. Breathe, Zo, breathe!"

It was too late to teach me anything. The time to teach me was long past. She'd had that chance. They'd all had that chance, and none of them took it, so they didn't get to claim it now. She should have told me the truth when I was nine and Mom was young and healthy. That was the time to teach me.

I shoved with all my might to be free of the dark miasma, but it wouldn't budge. It wanted to be inside me. It wanted *me*. *Yes, yes*, it was whispering, *we are power, and united, no one will ever be able to hurt us again.* I needed something to help evict it. Closing my eyes, mind racing frantically, I tried to remember what Este had told me about using power, that it took more than thought in the beginning. But I had no time for spells or objects. I needed—

Energy to help me eject it, a rich source of energy, equal to this horror that was gaining strength inside me with each passing moment and beginning to feel utterly seductive.

I stopped shoving and reached outward, opening myself, seeking a source from which to draw. The moment I expanded, searching, I felt as if the world came vibrantly alive in a way that I would later learn most witches experienced at birth. They come into the universe knowing the wonder of that intimate connection, because their first awakening is performed before they even leave the womb, by loving parents who don't lie. I was astonished to discover that every physical thing in the kitchen and far beyond it, from the tenderest blade of grass to the animals in the forest past the Midnight Garden, the two bodyguards in the courtyard, and my ex–best friend, to even the chairs and table in the kitchen, all held a degree of tangible, usable energy, many far richer than others.

Eyes squeezed tightly shut, I focused and drew, trying desperately to take only what I needed, and only from sources I was willing to sacrifice, but I was clumsy and untried. The moment I commanded, energy surged into me with violent swiftness, as if helpless to deny my will. I gathered that rich, golden energy, corralled the heinous offense within its radiant light, and shoved frantically with all my might. I pushed so hard that when the monstrous thing finally began to give, its volatility caused a ricochet effect as it erupted from my body. I went flying backward from the island and slammed into the wall so hard, the back of my skull hit with an audible crack, my vision went dim, and I saw stars.

Blessedly, though, with a final, mighty thrust, the darkness vacated, with much screeching of timber and a thunderous crash and a woman's distant scream, then seemed to simply vanish.

A word from future Zo: the darkness we create—it never simply vanishes.

It damages. It takes. It carves. It lingers and haunts you.

I'd made that darkness. *I* put it out there in the world, and I'd taken sloppily, savagely from the world while doing it. My inability to control emotion had given birth to a terrible thing, and I despised myself for it.

Gingerly, I felt the back of my head to ascertain I wasn't bleeding and opened my eyes.

And despised myself even more once I saw what I'd done.

"IT'S OVER," THE man said quietly into his phone. "It's not quite what we were after, but Zo Grey will never be the Cameron heir."

After listening for a long moment, he replied, "There's no longer a need to kill her. Divinity won't accept her now."

He paused, then said with a soft laugh, "Indeed, for this, they may well kill her themselves, and so long as she is unpledged to a house, they can."

17

I STOOD MOTIONLESS, STARING ACROSS the kitchen, past the jagged, dark chasm in the floor, upon which a marble island had once stood, at Este.

Eyes closed, neck bloody, shirt drenched crimson, she was pinned to the opposite wall at the far end of the kitchen by a massive splinter of wood. Her long dark hair was tangled around the splinter as if she'd been trying to dodge it when it struck her.

I opened my mouth, but nothing came out. Silently I screamed her name, silently I screamed, *My God, what have I done, what have I done?*

I'd demolished the kitchen. There was no way across the chasm to my best friend; it cleaved the room from wall to wall and had taken most of the appliances, stepladders, and pots with it.

I whirled, racing for the back door, leapt out, dashed down the courtyard—holy hell, what had I done to the *courtyard?*

No time to look. At the far end of the kitchen, I grabbed an outdoor end table, smashed the window, frantically knocked out jagged pieces of glass, and hoisted myself over the ledge.

I was sobbing by the time I reached her. "Este! Este! Este!" I cried brokenly.

Slowly, she opened her eyes and smiled weakly. "Oh, bloody hell, Zo, you ruined the kitchen. It was my favorite room."

I gaped. "You're *joking?*"

"Get this damned splinter out."

I eyed the massive spike of wood lodged deep in the wall. "How?" I asked blankly. I wasn't that strong.

"*Will* it out. After that gigantic tantrum you just threw, it should prove no problem for you. And here I was, thinking I should have stayed up and begun training you. Clearly, you don't need my help."

"My God, Este, are you okay? You're bleeding everywhere!"

"I'm only stuck by my hair, you crazy, badass witch." She smiled again, very faintly. Her gaze was wary, studying me carefully.

"But you're bleeding all over—"

"Grazed my neck. Unpin me, for fuck's sake!"

I closed my eyes, seeking a source of energy but this time delicately, beguiling aid. Beyond the Midnight Garden stretched a lush field of wheat. I drew carefully, with love, summoning only minute atoms from individual shafts and, after a moment, opened my eyes to watch, dumbfounded, as the splinter gently levitated back, withdrawing from the plaster before crashing to the floor.

As Este dragged her hair free of the hole and scraped it over her shoulder, I grabbed her and hugged her fiercely. "Oh, Este, I'm so sorry! I never meant to hurt you! I swear I didn't!"

We clung to each other for a long moment then she drew back and said, "Believe me, babe, I know that. If you'd meant to, I'd be dead. If you didn't love me, if beneath your love you'd held a single iota of a deadly thought, that stake would have gone straight through my throat." Her gaze darkened with fear. "Zo, I don't know how you did that. You shouldn't have been able to. I thought you'd been awakened when your mom died but still had six more stages to go through, carefully and with guidance. But someone has forced you through *all* the stages. If I'd known that, I'd never have gone to bed. I'd have spent every minute teaching you to *not* do something like what you just did. Babe, you're *fully* empowered, unpledged and completely untrained, and I have no bloody clue what they think they're doing but you're *insanely* dangerous in the state you're in."

"You mean bad," I said woodenly.

"I mean untrained. Unpledged. If you'd killed me—" She broke off, compressing her lips.

"What?" I demanded.

Sighing, she said, "You don't come back from that. You can't kill unpledged. It changes you. And to kill someone you love? Damn, woman. Even the gray would think twice about whether to use you. You'd have carried my death; that kind of thing makes a witch darker than dark."

"How *exactly* does it change you?" I demanded. Had I killed the man in the barn or not? Which narrator had been speaking— the instructor or the liar?

"Just be very, *very* glad you didn't."

I was sick of nonanswers, but she was bleeding, and I pushed her hair back to see for myself just how "grazed" her neck was. When I did, I was horrified.

"Este, we have to get you to the hospital!"

"No hospital," she said wearily. "I'm going to teach you how to heal me. With all that terrifying power you have, you can. That's how you'll make reparation for what you did to this kitchen."

Sighing heavily, I groaned, "It didn't stop at the kitchen."

Her eyes went wide. "What? Where?"

I glanced miserably at the courtyard, tears filling my eyes.

Her gaze followed mine. "Oh, Zo!"

Everything in the courtyard was dead. Each tree, every flower, all the shrubs, blackened and dead. There were no more mighty oaks strung with fairy lights and bottles spinning on jute cords. They'd collapsed to charred piles. There were no planters with lush flowers, no magnolias, no wisteria tumbling down the side of the garage, no bushes, no tufts of decorative grass. It was as if a wildfire had ripped through the garden, destroying everything in its path, and I prayed it stopped there, that I hadn't also destroyed the sacred garden beyond. The charred earth was littered with creatures of the night, and I hoped with all my heart that Rufus was far away, high in the sky, surveying his nocturnal kingdom, not among them.

"I took life," I said brokenly. "Am I damned?"

She hugged me fiercely. "Never think that! You think that, you go there. This was *not* your fault. It's the fault of whoever awakened you, knowing you had no training. This one is not on you, and don't you dare carry it!"

I heard a kernel of truth in her words, but it made no difference to my heart. Come dawn, I would bury each of the blackened skeletons, the bats and the squirrels who'd nested, slumbering; the birds; the snakes tucked into thickets of brush; the voles; and the cat I'd had no idea lived with us, digging their graves, trying to divine what reparation I might make that could ever atone for what I'd done.

Had I *really* killed the man in the barn?

If so, according to Este, it was already too late for me. And, according to her, not only did I need to conceal from the townsfolk that I may not be a Cameron but also that I may have killed unpledged. Peril, peril everywhere.

I was a witch. I no longer suffered an ounce of a doubt on that score.

And a damned powerful one.

And quite possibly, a very, very *bad* one. For the briefest of moments, I felt another surge of fury. If only Mom had told me, if everything truly *was* choice, we could have learned to be good, couldn't we? She was kind, I was kind—surely we could have gone light! There was *nothing* two people who loved each other couldn't accomplish with conscious choice and discipline.

Swiftly, I locked my fury tightly away. I had no right to strong feelings anymore. The luxury of emotion, like everything else about my life and my future as a witch, would have to be earned. I would never again slip into such terrible darkness, I vowed fervently.

If the choice is me or damaging someone else or the world, I pledged fiercely, *I will sacrifice myself next time. But there won't be a next time.*

Ah, the vows we make with such utter conviction.

I've begun to wonder if the universe uses them to test us.

Alisdair

It BEGAN IN INNOCENCE, AS *do many of the world's great atrocities.*

I should know, I was witness to countless acts of evil, and often the perpetrator of them before I was condemned to this hell, forced to be eternally near, yet eternally separated from Rhiannon, who endures her own hell at our enemy's hand.

But I digress.

Zo Grey's story is still unfolding; there is an older one that must be told. I may be condemned to eternity, but my enemy has no such immortality, only cheats death again and again. One day, somehow, I will stop this. I will prevail.

It is a tale that begins centuries in the past.

The child had no idea what she was.

Nor did those who raised her.

Abandoned, of unknown lineage, the child's world was a dirt-floored, thatch-roofed hut with a single room, two sleeping lofts, and the ever-changing wonders of fields and brooks her da toiled in, in exchange for the protection of their feudal laird.

Much debate would one day be raised about whence she came—by which time she was already infamous—but the humble peasants who'd ached endlessly for children of their own, only to prove barren as the most miserly of drought-parched fields, suffered no such concerns. It was a blessing the bairn was found upon their doorstep on a dark and stormy night, one so calamitous they'd not have heard her squalls but for a momentary lull, during which a single heartbreaking cry pieced the night.

Whisking the wee soaked babe into heart and home, the pair questioned none of it. (Excepting once in hushed whispers that she might well be their laird's unwanted by-blow.) Not the finery in which she came swaddled, nor even the fat pouch of gold that would have changed their fortunes forever, had they not tucked it carefully behind a stone in the corner of their hut, up high, near the roof rafters. The love of a child could not be bought and paid for, only gifted, as the wee one had been gifted to them.

One day, they vowed, the gold would be hers, ensuring her a fine husband and life of ease. But until that day, she would learn the unvarnished, ofttimes harsh truths of the seasons and the soil, the value of filling a larder, the warmth of love uncorrupted by foolishness and frippery.

It began in innocence and with good intentions, as a great many evils do.

The child was seven, a young lass of incomparable loveliness and amiable demeanor, when her mother fell from the roof, which she'd been repairing whilst her husband was traveling to pay their annual tithe. Her mama landed badly, and the angle at which her neck was turned upon the flagstone, the pool of scarlet haloing her head, filled the child with terror that death was near.

As she knelt, wailing with grief, watching her mama's face pale to snow, eyes glazing, Death, indeed, appeared; the great Arawn, Celtic god of the Otherworld, long cloak flapping, as if arriving upon a wild storm.

Screaming, the child flung herself at the dark man, demanding he not take her, in a voice that brooked no resistance, a voice none had taught her, a voice that sprang from blood and bone.

Death demanded, Are you certain you wish this?

Yes, *the child shouted.* Leave her alone! Restore her to me!

There is a price, *Death said.*

I don't care! *the child screamed.*

Death smiled. One day you will.

With that, the dark man was gone.

When her mama pushed up from the stone, looking shocked and confused, sporting naught but a small abrasion of scalp, the child flung herself into her arms, and they clung together, sobbing with relief.

Upon learning, the next day, that the village midwife had stumbled over a broom, striking her head upon the corner of the hand-hewn table her husband had gifted her upon their wedding day, snapping her neck, mother and daughter did what villagers do and took freshly baked loaves of bread and a leg of glazed mutton to the grieving widower. They murmured fervent thanks as they journeyed home, for their own good fortunes, and gave it no further thought.

As her mama was forever chiding her abundance of imagination—fairies did not frolic in the babbling brook, gossiping of near and distant human deeds, nor did birds sing the sorrows or joys of the seasons to come (despite their daughter's predictions being uncannily accurate)—the child decided, muddled by panic and mindless fear, that she'd only imagined the dark man.

Until the night he came again.

PART III

In the peaceful, intoxicating lulls between horrors, I would experience joys at Cameron Manor that I'd never known.

Such as the simple contentment of staying in one place, knowing I was where I belonged.

I'd ached for the pleasure of living in a Constant House, getting to watch the march of seasons play out their infinite, ever-changing expressions, year after year, savoring the rich, variegated nuances, on the same terrain, with the same faces. Enjoying the same seasonal traditions, with the same group of friends, in a life that wasn't eternally shadowed by running, illness, worry, and fear. Putting up the same Christmas decorations (owning Christmas decorations!) and hosting an annual party for the same neighbors.

I've long believed the intimate knowing of a single thing is worth far more than a casual knowing of many things, conferring a sense of rootedness that is priceless.

In the halls of Cameron Manor, in the town of Divinity, I would find all that and so much more.

Only to have it all taken from me.

19

I USED TO THINK I never lied to myself. Perhaps, for the first twenty-four years of my life, I didn't, because I lacked sufficient emotion to suffer the need to evade any of it. I think self-deceit springs from deep, troubling emotions we can't bear to face, so we tell ourselves a modified version of the truth, wherein we cast a more palatable reflection in the mirror of our hearts.

I'd nearly killed my best friend. Had I harbored a hint of true malice toward her, she would have been dead.

I might have killed the man in the barn. The jury was still out on that verdict. I'd twice sought wisdom from a dually narrated book, and I lacked the ability to discern truth from lie. Perhaps both narrators had ulterior motives. For a woman who'd pursued a single agenda her entire life—keeping her mother alive or, at least, in comfortable misery—it was disconcerting to discover others had multiple and, to my way of thinking, selfish agendas, designed to solely benefit themselves. Even Este had selfish aims: obey our mothers' directives while being my best friend, love me while knowing I was being controlled and lied to, and she was lying to me, too—or in the kindest possible light, withholding crucial information under duress. How did one manage to live with such inner conflict?

And my mother—God only knew what her motives were.

To survive in this strange new world with intense emotions and lethal powers, I was going to have to start thinking like everyone else, or I'd never see the next hazard coming. Or, worse, I'd become the hazard myself. Ergo it was time to start thinking selfishly and self-protectively.

Joanna Grey had raised me to be unforgivably naïve.

For some reason, she'd been willing to give her own life to keep me that way.

I suffered no doubt that she loved me. Which meant she'd truly believed it was the only choice she had.

Which begged a single damning question: What was she so terrified I might otherwise become?

AFTER ESTE LEFT, with much hugging and more than a few tears (she was right, healing her shallow though sizeable wound proved far easier than the destruction I'd wrought), I strode into the courtyard to survey, absorb, and punish myself for my carelessness, aware that, despite my love for my best friend, I now felt an equally deep wariness of her. I wasn't certain I could soon forgive her for not telling me the truth many years ago. I had too many emotions to sort through and inadequate tools with which to resolve them.

Beneath the waning light of the moon, I gathered the ashy remains of animals in a large wicker basket, using the pool net to scoop out crisped bats and owls (not one of them a Stygian!) from the once sparkling water, while thanking the heavens above I'd stumbled across no skeletons of bodyguards. The power I'd summoned had come in such a swift, violent rush, I'd had no clue from whence it sprang.

Then I sat for a time on the sooty pavers as dawn slowly began to gild the obsidian horizon beyond the garage. I was hoping Devlin might step out, being crepuscular and all, but perhaps as a warm vampire, he'd already gone to ground somewhere. Assuming, like cold ones, warm vampires also eschewed the sun and passed their daytime hours in subterranean crypts. Had he appeared, I'd have hammered him with questions.

God, I lived in a world of witches and vampires, destroyed kitchens and courtyards, sentient books and bodies in barns and murders, attempted and successful!

I endeavored, for a time—as I watched the sun slowly spread the mounts of its fan into an ever-widening display of gold to pale pink to blue—to convince myself that I'd gone mad, broken by my mother's death, and none of this was happening. That, indeed, madness was preferable to my current reality.

I glanced into the basket of skeletal remains at my side and sighed.

Real, all too real.

Abruptly, the basket was plucked from the ground, and a voice said stridently behind me, "Return to the manor and clean yourself up this very moment, Ms. Grey. The matter will be handled."

I turned to stare up at Mr. Balfour. "What are you doing here?"

"Every wi—" He broke off with a muffled curse, then continued, "Every person of a certain ilk in Divinity felt what you did the moment you did it. I headed up the instant Ms. Hunter left for the airport with Evander. Your . . . inadvertent mishap shall be attended to. You need not spare it a thought. But I must insist you remain inside the manor and do nothing—and I do mean nothing at *all*—until Tuesday at 12:01 a.m., when you read Juniper's letter. Do you think you can, perchance, manage to pass the next forty hours in an innocuous fashion?"

"*You're* the one who told me to invite Este here," I replied churlishly.

"I did not, however, tell you to go clubbing with her nor, for reasons unfathomable, decide to go to war with her, nor take it out on the estate in such a highly visible display. Now, go to your room!"

I blinked, astonished. "Did you just tell me to 'go to my room'?" Not once in my life had anyone ever told me to "go to my room." I'd had no father, nor had I ever given Mom a reason to say it.

"I most certainly did. Once there, you will give yourself a manicure, a pedicure, try on outfits, read a book, take a bubble bath, indulge in the sorts of activities genteel, *temperate* women do when they endeavor to relax. You will do ineffectual, quotidian, harmless things. You will not explore the house. You will not seek answers. You will not test any of your . . . abilities. You will not, *for any reason whatsoever*, leave the manor. You will make yourself small—very, *very* small—and still. Do you understand?"

"I have to be pledged," I muttered. "I'm dangerous this way."

He opened his mouth and closed it again.

"Let me guess," I spat, caustically. "Contingencies. I destroy the kitchen, this once-lovely garden, I kill every night creature within it, yet still you espouse your damned contingencies."

"Don't forget the front lawn," he spat back. "Juniper said you'd be a lot to handle. I had no idea how perspicacious she'd prove."

I gaped. "I charred that, too? What about the Midnight Garden?"

He muttered, "Untouchable, even for you. Thus far, you have crossed no lines that are not uncrossable, and I will not lose you as the Cameron heir."

"What if I lose *myself* before Tuesday?" I cried.

"That is why you will go to your room this very instant, and do *nothing*."

"Why can't I be pledged now? Why can't my training begin?

I know I'm a witch. The whole damn town knows it, according to you."

Bristling, he said sharply, "If I had any idea what you were talking about, in this hypothetical world of yours, in which only those of 'a certain ilk,' and certainly not 'the whole damn town' knew things, I would tell you that a minimum of seven days must pass between the first awakening and the pledging ceremony, or the pledging fails and the Cameron torch will not light."

"Has that ever happened?" I asked, with a prick of unease.

His gaze darkened. "In this hypothetical world of yours, I wasn't alive then but, once, yes."

"What happened? "

"You'll get a different story from everyone you ask, and no one who was actually present is still alive. The only thing all agree on is that some type of gray house interference was at the root of it. Allegedly, they contested the pledging."

"Why?"

"That's where stories differ dramatically. I've never heard a version I believe."

"What versions did you hear?"

"Repeating unsubstantiated gossip is speculative libel," he said stiffly. "I only told you to underscore the fact that ideally, a fortnight is permitted to expire between the two events, to assure auspicious results, but a minimum of seven days and nights in residence at Cameron Manor is required. To attempt it any earlier would be pointless, futile, utterly ineffective—do you need additional adjectives, or have you grasped my meaning? Hypothetically speaking, of *course*."

"Well, hypothetically speaking," I clipped frostily, "I think this whole damn plan of yours is riddled with egregious flaws, unforeseeable, gargantuan potholes, and nonhypothetical cataclysmic potential. I might have killed my best friend! Do you understand that? It could have been her skeleton in this basket!"

He observed flatly, "It would hardly have fit."

I shot him a look that I suspected—were it laced with the full brunt of my staggering and terrible power—could quite possibly kill, and realized I was going to have to learn, quickly, to master even my most minute expressions.

"Purely a matter of physics," he said irritably. "A foolish, insensitive comment, and merely my first thought. And yes, that would have been a far larger problem. Still, not insurmountable. *Hypothetically*."

"I tell you that I nearly killed my best friend, and all you have to say is that it wouldn't have been 'insurmountable'?"

"You have no idea what's at stake. Do you think this kind of legacy, hundreds of millions of dollars, billions in global investments, the full force of . . . of a . . . a . . . town . . . standing eternally behind you, comes without struggle, without price?"

I snarled, "That I have to be evil?"

He stiffened ramrod straight. "The Camerons are a *light* house," he thundered. "We have always been. Proud and true, with a vaunted history stretching centuries into an illustrious past. You spring, *hypothetically*, from the most powerful light bloodline in this country and are counted among the dozen most powerful light houses in the world, amongst all systems of belief and practice."

"*Hypothetically*," I growled. "Definition: in a way imagined or suggested that is not necessarily valid or true."

Mom taught me young the importance of vocabulary, to work on it, use it to better myself. Others, she'd said, might look down their noses at us for our poverty but never our lack of eloquence. A well-spoken phrase at a well-chosen moment could silence even the harshest of critics. Here, I merely sought to point out that Mr. Balfour, along with everyone else, was quite possibly lying to me. And that *hypothetically* was, in my book, an exceedingly dangerous word.

His nostrils flared. "*Factually*, the Camerons are a light house and among the lightest in the world. As I'm quite sure the friend you nearly killed must have told you. Evil does not herein abide. Not on my watch."

"You're certain of that."

"Utterly."

"Invite me in," I ordered.

"By your leave," he snapped.

"Drop all your guards," I demanded.

He went still as stone. "That I cannot and will not do. If you are unable to read my heart with such guards as I deem necessary to hold, you are not who and what I believe you to be. Hypothetically speaking. There are parts of my life that will never be yours to peruse. They have naught to do with you. There is a sanctum of privacy within a man's soul that Juniper never violated."

I'd never thought I could despise the word *hypothetically* more. I wanted to rip into him savagely. That was what angry Zo would do. I would not be that woman. I met his gaze levelly and delved gently, with great care, reaching for his heart, not his mind.

It was strong and true. He loved his wife endlessly and deeply. He'd loved his daughter beyond reason. Part of his heart would never be intact again since he'd lost Erin to the fire. There was something . . . something else he'd lost, too, something barricaded behind unbreachable walls.

He cared for me. Very much indeed, I was surprised to find. He feared for me, worried for me, wanted only the best for me and from me. It was the closest to paternal emotion I'd ever felt, and it nearly undid me.

"But I screwed up everything!" I cried. "How can you feel that way about me?" That I shone, and had great value, would one day do much good, that I was an impeccable choice to lead this town and coven.

"Hypothetically," he said quietly, and with a note of weary resignation, "we had few choices. Forty hours and seven minutes. That's all the time you need sit still and survive quietly without harming yourself or anyone else. Then you can open Juniper's letter, and I can answer your questions. We will pledge you, although I would strongly prefer to wait the fortnight and spend that time teaching you. The Cameron torch will burn brightly again. You will be safe, always. We will not allow you to be lost. We will stand behind you, gathered round you, for so long as you live, while doing everything in our power to assure you a long and happy life."

His face softened. "It is our fault it had to be done this way. We didn't find you soon enough. You bear no blame for what happened. Let it go. The darkness we become—*if* we become it, if we *permit* ourselves to become it—transpires because we lose faith in ourselves. Easier to believe the worst of ourselves than to face the rigors of the battle necessary to regain lost faith. Do not tread that perilous, *emotional* path, Ms. Grey. Each of us is flawed. None of us are spared. To obsess over our flaws defies, and undermines, the very purpose of our existence. If you see only bad when you look within, you render yourself incapable of bringing good into the world. Ms. Bean is a prime, damaged example of that, and very nearly a lost cause. Check. Your. Emotions. Eschew blame you don't own. Stay still. You're nearly there. Now," he rebuked me firmly, "off with you. Shower.

You smell dreadful. The next time you view this courtyard, it will be precisely as it was."

I stared. "Is that possible?"

"In Divinity, under the right circumstances, with the strength of a Kovan, anything and everything is possible." He added, quickly, "Hypothetically, of course."

"I thought the word was *coven*."

"Hypothetically, a coven is thirteen witches. A Kovan is thirteen families of Highblood witches, comprising one hundred and sixty-nine. This will be the first time the Kovan unites behind you. There will never be a last. Of course, this is all—"

"I know," I muttered irritably, "hypothetical."

Neither of us, at that moment, had any idea how swiftly his latter assertion would be tested.

IN ONE OF the many whatnot boxes, there was a manicure and pedicure kit, with a dozen shades of tasteful pastel polish. I'd smirked when I'd seen it. What point in doing nails on hands that worked themselves to the bone every day or toes clad eternally in sensible shoes?

No longer smirking, I dug out the box, showered, exfoliated, shaved my legs, deep-conditioned my hair, dried it, then sat down to do my fingernails.

Terribly.

How the hell did women with a single dominant hand do this?

It took me four tries—polish and remove, polish and remove—but finally both my hands and feet sported identical iridescent pearly *light* polish, done reasonably well, or at least not crusting my cuticles anymore.

Okay, I'd killed three hours. Yay for me. I now had thirty-seven

hours and seven minutes to occupy myself with such utter triv-
ialities that I couldn't possibly feel one speck of strong emotion.

Too late for that. Strong emotion was frothing and roiling in
the pit of my stomach, fueled by incessant questions. Who was
I? What or who was my mother running from all our lives? Who
was my father, and how did he fit into all this? Was I even a
Cameron? (And right there, I very nearly lunged up from the
bed to go searching the manor from top to bottom for genetic
testing, yet this house had proved to hold multiple inflammatory
volumes, and with that thought, I eyed the books on the shelf
with a wealth of unease, praying one wouldn't abruptly fly off to
tell me something else upsetting.) Why had my best friend never
told me the truth?

Sighing gustily, I leapt from the bed, grabbed my purse, and
dug through it for a bottle I'd been given by a neighbor in Frankfort, Indiana, as I'd slumped, sobbing in the street. Mrs. Haw-
thorne, a harried mother of four children whose husband had
recently left her—and whose kids participated in every sport
under the sun, which she was constantly transporting them to
or retrieving them from—had slipped an arm around me as I'd
wept. She'd thrust the small bottle into my trembling hands as
we'd huddled together. Said it wasn't a weakness that sometimes
you just couldn't feel all the feelings, all the time.

I eyed it warily.

Not once in my life had I used a mood-altering drug of any
sort. Admittedly, there'd been times I'd stared at my mother's
endless bottles of pills, many for pain, many promising somno-
lence, wondering if I might get a decent night's sleep were I to
take one, but I was never willing to dull my senses, lest she wake
in the night and need me.

Now I read the label, searched the internet to discern precisely what the drug did, then shook out two small round yellow pills and tossed them back with a swallow of water.

A GABA potentiator, surely it would calm the dragon within.

I curled on my side, tugged the blankets over my head, and waited. Thirty-six hours, fifty-two minutes to go.

Eventually, blessedly, I slept.

And dreamed.

It was unlike any dream I'd ever had.

Far more lucid and tactile even than those I'd been having since entering Cameron Manor.

I was in a dark place, so black, so pitch, initially I thought I was dreaming I'd gone blind.

But eventually, eyes straining to define something, anything, far in the distance, I espied a pale orange glow. Dim, shadowy, cloaked and hooded figures circled a statue of something I couldn't describe, other than that it was giant, towering over them, and the outline of it, for reasons unknown, struck a chord of atavistic terror in my heart.

The figures were chanting, a fast and rhythmic staccato, over and over, but I couldn't make out the words.

I was startled to find I was crouched on my hands and knees in the darkness, as if hiding from someone or something. Indeed, I felt I was in forbidden territory where, if caught trespassing, a terrible price would be demanded of me.

It was so tactile and real: the stone floor rough and cold beneath my bare knees and hands, the acridity of bitter herbs smoking the air, an enormous cauldron emitting a coppery scent as it bubbled over a low blue flame. I was seized by the urgent need to know more, as if I must be here for a reason, as if perchance the drug had carried me beyond the confines of my mind into the ether (in which case perhaps I'd never dare take a drug again), so I began to inch forward, creeping with silent stealth, eventually dropping to my belly to squirm nearer. At last, the words were clear:

> Make her suffer, drive her mad
> Bedevil good luck into bad
> Sow fear to make the heir fight back
> Drown her light in blessed black
> As we beseech, so mote it be
> We troth our very souls to thee

"The heir," they'd said, and there was no mistaking who that was. I gasped. I couldn't help myself.

Instantly, the chanting ceased and the shadowy figures whirled as one in my direction, although how they could possibly have heard my soft gasp over their chanting was beyond me.

Wake up, wake up, wake up, Zodeckymira! I shrieked silently. *Pull back, pull back, flee!*

I wanted to know who they were. I needed to see the faces of my enemies.

They moved impossibly then, together as one, cloaked haunts whisking on wind. Even the statue seemed to ripple and undulate as if turning to look, and I knew I dare not linger. Abruptly, I sensed additional presences and whirled to find a thick gray mist moving toward me from behind and, within that oddly terrifying, icy fog, the shadowy outlines of hooded faces.

Dark before me, gray behind!

I thought of Mom burning, how heinously she'd been murdered, the agony of her suffering, and used it as a stake through my heart to force myself awake.

When I shot up in bed, gasping, hand to my heart, trembling from head to toe, the room was so dark that, for those first terrified few seconds, I feared I'd not escaped. But slowly, as my eyes focused, I was able to make out the shapes of furniture that told me I was, indeed, back in my room.

I glanced swiftly at the French doors, beyond which fairy lights twinkled and blue bottles clinked together on jute cords in tree limbs that had not been there this morning. I realized I'd slept so long and deeply that night had fallen, and I would be able to open Juniper's letter in roughly . . . I checked my phone . . . twenty-five hours.

The Kovan had apparently done as Mr. Balfour had promised. Erased the devastation I'd wrought, as if it had never transpired.

My first thought should have been, *Who are my enemies, and how do I continue to safely pass the hours I have left?*

Instead, they were of crepuscular hours and, of course, Devlin.

IT WAS 11:32 p.m. when I paused with my hand on the doorknob of my bedroom, fully intending to disobey Mr. Balfour's orders and leave my room (I mean, at the very least, I had to eat, which meant the kitchen was clearly within bounds, so why wouldn't the garage be?) to steal a last glance at myself in the mirror.

I wasn't lying to myself at that moment. I knew what I needed. Sex. Precisely twenty-four hours and twenty-eight minutes of it, and since driving to New Orleans to see the man (witch!—and I wondered desperately from which house) I truly hungered to see would constitute a violation of the rules far greater than venturing to the garage, which I felt was only a slight infraction of his express orders, Devlin it would have to be. I'd figure out how to handle the fallout from breaking one of my own inviolable rules once I was pledged. Devlin was only around at night. Surely I could manage to avoid him in the future.

If I could keep myself thus occupied until 12:01 a.m. Tuesday, I was certain I could stay out of harm's way and prevent myself from being the cause of any.

And if Devlin had to remain somewhere all day tomorrow in the dark, all the better. I'd stay with him. Tucked away with a man I'd judged with my deep sight as constant and true. Really, there was no other place for me to go, and I knew myself too well.

Here, alone, traipsing morosely between kitchen and bedroom, I'd eventually succumb to one of my countless anxieties and fears, going off to search the manor or seek tomes I dare not consult at this juncture—and I couldn't shake the feeling that the dream I'd experienced in such palpable detail had been more than a mere dream. That somewhere out there, a dark coven was cursing me, summoning whatever they worshipped to wreak havoc, to sabotage me. To prevent me from becoming the Cameron heir. And I could only construe that gray mist as "the abyss" Este had warned me not to gaze into. It sure as hell seemed the abyss was gazing into me, at least in my dreams.

A week ago? Ludicrous thoughts.

Tonight? All too frighteningly plausible.

Although the Kovan had repaired the damage I'd done, I was not yet pledged to them, nor, more significantly, I suspected, were they to me. Mr. Balfour had ordered, so they had obeyed. I supposed it would have been difficult to explain to the many Palebloods in Divinity how the immediate estate grounds had burned overnight but only to the perimeter, and none of the house. Wiser to repair it all before the oddity was noted.

I'd considered reading the notebook Este and Dalia had composed for me, but deemed that dangerous, too. Not only might I find something upsetting in their tutorial (aside from the constant reminder that the two women who'd penned it had lied to me for decades), but who could say one of the noncorporeal narrators in the house might not usurp its pages?

I trusted nothing. Neither written words nor spoken.

What was left to me?

The nonverbal language of the body, a dance as old as time, one that predated language of any sort. Given the immense difficulty men and women seemed to have communicating with each other, I thought drolly, perhaps it should have stayed that way. Silent but for grunts and moans.

I hungered to vent the enormity of my volatile emotion on a man's body. Pour it out of me, drench him with it. Distract myself, forget myself, lose all sense of time and place in the eroticism of a man's explosive lust. Stand up stronger, clearer, more controlled, for having released it.

Perhaps, as a witch, my passion would make grass grow lusher and flowers bloom, I thought with a faint smile. I found it difficult to believe the way I felt when I was having sex could possibly put anything but good into the world, were anything at all to manifest. Surely, like humans, for witches, sex was just sex, right?

Sighing heavily, I assured my reflection I looked pretty and desirable and Devlin would be thrilled to see me, turned the knob, stepped through the door, and fell flat on my face.

Groaning, I rolled over to see what I'd tripped on.

Oh, God.

I stared at it for a long moment. I didn't need to look at the return address to know what it was.

Still, for Mr. Balfour to bring it here was an act I deemed incredibly risky. Unless he'd already opened and resealed it, pilfering anything that might make me feel strong emotion.

My hand trembled only slightly as I reached for the sheet of Balfour and Baird letterhead atop the cardboard shipping box.

Contrary to what you think, I did not open it. I am your solicitor and champion, not oppressor. I trust you will do your utmost to contain your emotions. If you feel unequal to the task, text or call me. I will be there anon, and will guide you safely through.

I could nearly hear his heart-heavy sigh in the next line:

Young Zo, you remind me and Lennox so much of our children. Erin, too, was . . . a lot to handle. Some are born with more. Our daughter came with more in excess, yet her light far outshone her rebel ways, as does yours. Have faith in yourself. Never lose it. It cannot be taken from you. It can only be given away. The thieves who try to steal it know that. They count on you *not* knowing that.

I tugged the package toward me and sat for a long moment, cradling in my arms the box containing the contents of my mother's fireproof safe. Whatever she'd decided to protect from potential calamity, either to hide from me or to leave with me, I would find within.

Answers at last?

Clutching it to my heart, I surged to my feet, hurried back into my room, and closed and locked the door behind me.

Sex with Devlin would have to wait. And might prove far more necessary to maintain my grasp on temperance, depending on what I found within.

20

My beloved daughter,

Where there is love, there is no law.

No need for laws, and no law you wouldn't break.

From the moment I held you in my arms, I knew there was nothing I wouldn't do for you. No price I wouldn't pay to see you grow into the strong, loving, resilient woman you've become. I knew that I would give my dying breath to ensure that you would live, have children, and know happiness. And never, *ever* drink the poison I tasted far too young.

I've made countless mistakes. We all do, no matter how hard we try. Each time I ripped up your roots and dragged you to the next town, another piece of my heart broke. I hungered to give you the life you longed for, yet to give you any life at all, I had no choice but to do what I did.

I pray that, in spite of my mistakes, my inability to clearly foresee future paths, I succeed, and you do not fall prey to the horror and curse that is your "birthright."

If you are reading this letter, I died before you turned twenty-five.

I CLOSED MY EYES, ABLE to interpret that only one way: had I turned twenty-five and been rendered Paleblood forever, she'd have destroyed the letter, having accomplished her aim. Sighing, I opened them and resumed reading.

Because there is still hope, I can tell you little. The less you know, the safer you are. But there are some things you must know, which Este will tell you and help you with. I confided in her, so she and Dalia could step in if tragedy befell me young. Dalia has a copy of this letter (sealed, and it had damn well better still be sealed—that nosy, judgmental witch!) in case the contents of the safe fail to reach you. Dalia and I may not care for each other, but she will do right by you. I ruthlessly used deep sight on her to be certain I could trust her (it's not only unbearably painful but can cause lasting damage if done improperly or viciously), one of many things for which she never forgave me.

I sought to spare you a war you could never win. Now I hope to keep you concealed from that war until the day you are finally completely safe. There will come a day that certain things I've long awaited transpire. Someone will find you, bearing a letter from me that tells you all, withholding nothing.

You have reason and right to be angry with the decisions I made. But please understand, my darling Zo, I had few options, and sometimes—I pray this is a lesson you never learn—there are no good choices. You can choose only from the lesser of evils. You pay the price willingly, for love.

One of my gifts is far-vision. Unfortunately, those visions shift and change with the passage of time. I see too many possible paths to predict the outcome with certainty. There are precious few elements of which I am certain, the most important of which is—in the few futures where you succeed, I've concealed virtually everything from you.

I paused a moment, replaying that line in mind. The *few* futures? Meaning I failed in most of them? That was worrying as hell. "Thanks for the words of comfort, Mom," I muttered.

I despise keeping you in the dark.

"I despise you *doing* it," I told the page irritably.

But I despise a great deal about the choices I've been forced to make. Still, I would make them over and over, to ensure your safety.

Zo, my beloved daughter, you have made me inexpressibly proud. You are all that has ever mattered to me. I never understood love until the moment I held you in my arms. I thought I did. I loved your father. Adored that man, would have kept him forever. He is not from whence we fled. He died long ago. I allowed you to believe he was our villain because you needed a villain, and he was the safest choice. Still, the enormous love I felt for your father was a spark compared to the bonfire that rages in my heart for you, my darling, magnificent daughter.

You are, and have always been, my everything.

With love eternal,
Mom

PS: I know you. Not merely the paler, suppressed version but the true you. I carried you within my body. I knew you

before you were even born. Had you known about the
safe, you'd have broken into it years ago. With a single
ounce of information, one hint of a clue, you would hunt,
you would go to war. And although you hold within you
power deliberately, genetically amplified, it is a war you
cannot win.

After speaking with Este, I bid you, do *not* complete the final
stage of awakening. Get pregnant. Stay hidden until the child
is born. End this, now and forevermore.

"I don't fucking believe it!" The words exploded from me.
Emotions were erupting inside me, running the gamut from agony to disbelief to fury.

First: grief—enormous, for I was holding a letter penned in
my mother's hand. She'd touched this paper. She'd held it and
folded it and carefully tucked it away for me. She'd always had
beautiful penmanship, cursive, each character lovingly shaped,
her capital letters large and gracefully swooping into smaller,
more delicate arches and curves. I couldn't stop running my fingers over the pages, as if through them I might reach across the
veil between life and death, grasp her hand, and feel her fingers
twine with mine once more.

Mommy, Mommy, my heart cried. How completely we are forever that child for whom our mothers are Mommy: she who has a
Band-Aid for any and all wounds, body, heart, and soul; she who
alchemizes tears to laughter with kisses, hugs, and assurances
that "everything will be all right" and "this, too, shall pass"; she
who sweeps nightmares to dust, out the window, and far away,
with the broom of ancient, time-honored rhymes and songs of

good triumphing over evil and assuring us that heaven, indeed, exists.

Second: disbelief—she'd not told me a damned thing I could use. She'd chosen deliberately to give me no answers, unless a mysterious set of circumstances transpired and a second letter arrived.

Well, other than that my father wasn't the villain and that she'd loved him deeply. Rather big stuff there. I could stop despising my father and start wondering who he was. That he'd died long ago—was that the darkness so quick to spring to her eyes on the rare occasions I'd mentioned him? Had he not died naturally, but been murdered like my mother? Been taken from her?

What was this war she thought I couldn't win?

Had I, the subject of unlucky odds that defied calculation, eschewing the laws of physics, ended up in precisely the last place she'd ever wanted me to be?

Was Divinity the "whence" from which she'd fled? Or had she been running from something much darker?

Was I, even now, standing on the battlefield she'd long ago escaped?

I went utterly motionless, chills prickling every inch of my skin.

If so, I *still* wasn't willing to leave.

Third: fury—oh, my God, how well my mother knew me!

I would have broken into the safe.

I *would* hunt.

I *would* go to war.

If this was the battlefield, I wasn't yielding a motherfucking inch. This would-be queen would damned well be queen.

I bid you, do not complete the final stage of awakening.

"Too late for that, Mom," I whispered. I'd somehow been forced through all the stages. I was violently and brutally awakened.

And although you hold within you power deliberately, genetically amplified . . .

Amplified how, why, and by whom? Had I been bred for some nefarious purpose?

Who was my enemy?

I don't know how many times I read her letter, only that, eventually, I calmed a bit as I did, holding it, pressing it to my heart—these pages that had been touched by my mother— before finally placing it aside and, again, looking into the box.

One other time, aside from that brief sojourn during which we'd had my beloved cow, I'd felt we were rich. We'd leased a house the prior tenant had vacated quickly, leaving much behind (the one in West Virginia, with the ghost Mom claimed didn't exist). The landlord told us to keep whatever we wanted, and we'd been so grateful for every bit of it.

There'd been a quilt made of rich red velvet that Mom said we would use to fashion a lovely dress for me.

Instead, while she was away at work, I'd made a shirt for her. She was so beautiful in red, and the quilt was the perfect shade to complement her complexion and rich chestnut hair. (I think I convinced myself she'd be so beautiful in it, no man could resist her, and I'd get a father.) Mom taught me to sew young; we were forever making our own clothing out of odds and ends. I cut apart one of her oldest shirts to use as a guide, purloined thread and needle from the dollar store, found buttons on one of the many shirts left hanging in the closet by the prior oc- cupant. I'd stitched a label into the nape, with her name on it: Joanna Grey, with small hearts embroidered at each side. It had taken me well over a month, but when I was done, it was finer than anything we'd ever owned. I'd made it with all the love in my heart. She looked amazing in it, had worn it often and with great pride.

I lifted it now from the box and pressed it to my nose.

Ah, there, beyond the hint of smoke, the scent of my mother! Covering my face with it, I inhaled deeply, feeling invisible arms slip around me, as comforting as one of her hugs.

Beneath the shirt, various treasures that had disappeared over the years, much to my dismay—they'd been tucked away, saved for me as if she'd always known such a day would come. The stuffed cat I'd named Glinda. A soft, worn blanket I'd had as a child. Magnets from all the states we'd lived in, oodles of notes we'd left each other. Some of my baby clothes and, finally, one of those old cigar boxes at the very bottom. I lifted it out with trembling hands and carefully raised the lid.

Photos!

I had photos!

Clutching her shirt, I began to sort slowly through them, crying and laughing at the same time: the two of us kneeling in the strawberry fields (with red smeared all around my mouth because I'd always eaten more than I ever tossed into the baskets) in Illinois the summer I was seven. Me, curled with Daisy the cow, sleeping in the sunshine. Mom laughing as she paddled cream in the ancient blue hand-cranked butter churn we'd bought at a flea market for a quarter. Me, sprawled on a blanket on a rare summer's afternoon she'd taken off work to spend with me, floating on tire inner tubes down a lazy, wide creek. A close-up of Mom's eyes; I wondered who'd taken it, her gaze was filled with such light and love. I felt I could stare into her eyes for hours, basking in the love that had always glowed with amber light, no matter how sick she was, no matter how hard our lives became.

The next one gave me pause. More than pause. I froze.

Mom must have taken the photo, for the man was gazing at the photographer with such deep, abiding love, such utter adoration that I caught my breath and held it, wondering how it would feel to be looked at that way. As if the man would slay dragons for me.

He was handsome! Dark haired, green eyed, and tall, wide through the shoulders, with a devastating smile.

I flipped it over. I was not disappointed, as I'd expected to be, by the woman who'd told me so little thus far.

Your father, my darling Zo.

No name. No date. But, at long last, I had a picture of my father. I knew what he looked like.

I could, for the first time in my life, envision parents.

I'd had parents who'd loved each other.

I.

Had.

Roots.

Independent of Watch Hill. Independent of any connection to the Camerons. I don't think I'd realized, until that moment, how adrift I'd felt, knowing nothing of the man who'd helped make me. As if Mom and I had sprung alone from some terrible cataclysmic event, and no men were to be trusted.

But some of them could be. The look on my father's face made that abundantly clear. As if he'd have willingly died for her.

Oh, God, had he? What had happened so long ago that made

my mother run? Had she, in truth, sprung from a dark lineage, fallen for a light witch, and her family had done something to him?

My father. She'd loved him. A cold, dark part of my heart began to warm at the thought.

Aside from a thick crush of brown packing paper at the bottom, that was it. I placed it aside and sat clutching Mom's shirt, sifting through the photos again and again, weeping.

TWENTY-TWO HOURS AND nine minutes to go, and at shortly before 2 a.m., after having erased my tears and touched up my makeup, I was again at the door, assuring myself I was only going to the kitchen for food.

I entered the room I couldn't wait to see restored, as the manor's kitchen delighted me to no end, only to discover the Kovan hadn't bothered to repair the interior, and although the fridge was still neatly affixed to the wall, the floor directly in front of it was gone, leaving not even the narrowest of perches for me to make a madcap attempt (and I was feeling perilously madcap), and the icy draft gusting from the jagged chasm where once the island had stood gave me pause. Slowly, feeling strangely mesmerized by the void, I inched forward to the edge and gazed down. Had there been a nearby pebble, I'd have nudged it in to gauge the depth, as the chasm descended to utter blackness and seemed bottomless. I got the sudden, dreadful feeling I'd inadvertently done something awful, like . . . say . . . opened a portal to hell.

Despite the late hour, I texted Mr. Balfour.

> The kitchen?
> You were not to leave your room.

I don't get to eat?

I hardly see how you could, given most of the floor is missing. I bade the Kovan repair only the exterior. I will help you repair the interior. I have temporarily suspended maid service in that area of the house. None will enter the northeast wing. Invite no one in.

A pause, then,

I forgot about food.

Clearly. Is the chasm dangerous?

I would counsel against leaping into it.

I could hear him saying this dryly.

I have no intention of doing so.

Return to your room. I will have carryout delivered at the back door. I'll text you when it arrives.

Careful as always, allowing no one to enter the heavily warded manor. When I didn't reply immediately, he texted, Are you all right?

Not feeling nuclear at the present moment. I was certain he heard the dry mockery of my tone as well.

My assurance was a fair bit of a lie. Despite having treasures to clutch, photos of me and Mom, and of my father, too, I was still radioactive as a walking time bomb.

The box?

Thank you for bringing it.

But you're all right after viewing the contents?

I am.

Return to your room. Food will arrive shortly. Open the back door, retrieve it, and return to your room. You have less than

twenty-four hours. I'll have coffee and breakfast sent in the
morning. Text me if you need anything. Don't fret you might
wake me. I won't be sleeping.

Thrusting my phone back in my pocket, my brain ordered my
feet toward my room.

The squall in my heart turned them toward the back door.

I STEPPED OUT INTO THE sultry, jasmine-scented night, waiting for a pair of bodyguards to flank me, aware that, if this was Jesse and Burke's shift, I'd likely get another offer from the gray-eyed bodyguard/witch who deeply intrigued me—though Devlin, the warm vampire-witch, fascinated me more. I found the newly re-furbished courtyard empty but for me.

The first thought to take shape in my mind was sheer aston-ishment at the beauty that had been so flawlessly re-created while I'd been busy in my room. Illuminated by solar torches, strands of fairy lights, and the pale blue luminosity of the pool, the court-yard was once again a spectacular tumble of lush southern foli-age. There was no trace of char or ash. My power had wrought terrible destruction, but clearly, the power with which I'd been endowed was also capable of birthing magnificent life (even the blue bottles swaying on jute cords were back!), and I hungered to learn more about that facet of my heritage. How would it feel to make a tree? A flower? My God, how was that possible? Yet here I was, staring at the evidence that it was, indeed, and so much more! I wondered where the Kovan had drawn the energy to fabricate so much new life, and how it was replenished. I had so much to learn!

My second thought was much darker, and I froze, realizing the courtyard had been empty this morning, too, at dawn, while I'd collected skeletal remains. I'd just been too distraught to no-tice. Yet Mr. Balfour had insisted there would always be a pair of bodyguards, front and rear, and that I would never move about unescorted beyond the walls of the manor.

He certainly would have noticed their absence this morning, when he'd plucked the basket of bone and ash from my side, yet he'd made no comment about it. I might have convinced myself he'd dispatched them before approaching me, but why hadn't they been flanking me as I'd gathered the remains to begin with? And why weren't they here now?

I realized I was holding my breath and released it slowly.

There'd been no human remains. Of that, I was certain. I had *not* killed Jesse, my selfless protector, and his companion, Burke. Nor anyone else. Nor did I have reason to believe that what the grimoire had told me about the man in the barn was true. I couldn't believe James Balfour would lie to me about Finnegan Harlow's cause of death, claiming it was an ongoing, chronic condition if the truth were otherwise. Not after I'd looked so deeply into his heart.

Still, perhaps the coroner had lied to him?

I reached for my phone to text Mr. Balfour and ask where the guards were, then realized if I did, he'd know I was outside. I mentally stuttered a moment, wondering if by breaking a rule to keep myself from getting into trouble, I might not be inadvertently setting the stage for precisely what I sought to avoid.

Just as I was about to force myself to turn back for the door and return to my room, a voice issued from the darkness, from a place I'd have sworn no man stood, empty of all but night, an alcove beneath the wisteria tumbling from the roof of the garage.

"Balfour pulled back the guards and asked me to watch over you from dusk to dawn, lass," Devlin's voice said.

"I find that hard to believe," I told the empty alcove. "It's clear neither he nor Lennox care for you much. Why is that?"

There was a ripple in the darkness, as if night was gathering itself, stitching together first the faint outline, then the fully fleshed body of a darkly beautiful man wearing only jeans and bare, tattooed skin. He was inhumanly attractive, a force of nature, restrained, graceful, yet redolent of storm.

"For the same reason he chose me to watch over you." Devlin moved forward, stepping into the courtyard's low illumination, which graced the strong, chiseled planes of his face with the brush of a painter, silvery and dark, highlighting and concealing features of perfect symmetry. "Because I am older and far more powerful. Balfour cares for nothing more powerful than he. However, he will certainly avail himself of my aid when it suits him."

"He cares for me." I'd felt it. "And I'm more powerful than he is." At least, allegedly I was.

He inclined his head but made no reply.

I stared at him across the courtyard. "How much older?"

"Ages, dates, true names, places of birth, all can be used for ill in the wrong hands."

"Hundreds of years?"

He smiled faintly. "I'll cede that, lass."

I narrowed my eyes. "Centuries. You're telling me you've been alive for centuries." It wasn't a question. It was sarcasm. People didn't live for centuries.

"You saw me the other night. I've no doubt your friend, Este, filled you in on the details."

"Where were you born?" I demanded.

He repeated with light mockery, "Ages, dates, true names, places of birth . . ."

"You can at least tell me what country you were born in," I said irritably. Answers, I was desperate for solid ones anyplace they might be found.

He was silent a moment, then, "In what you would call Ireland."

"*I* would call Ireland," I echoed dryly.

"It has been known by many names: Eire, Hibernia, Ogygia, much as Scotland was once Caledonia or Alba. The precise naming of a place contains information."

"As in, it might betray which century or, even, millennium?" I said with a snort.

"Aye, lass."

"I refuse to believe I'm staring across the courtyard at a man who might be centuries or, even more inconceivably, thousands of years old."

He shrugged. "Believe what you will. Your choice. But then, everything is." He flashed me a look of such frank carnality, it was nearly the Look. "Such as, the moment you choose to share my bed."

Now he was sounding entirely too much like Este and the grimoire. Why did everyone keep telling me everything was my choice, when it felt as if nothing in my life, to date, had been my choice?

"*If*, not 'the moment,'" I corrected pissily, despite the fact that I'd come for precisely that.

His smile faded. Eyes narrowing, glittering, he stalked toward me, spitting his words out staccato fast. "Do you think me fool enough not to know what you came outside for, Zo-d'kai? You want honesty? Give me honesty. You came because you have a storm inside you, one you worry you can't contain, and you fear your potential for destruction. You came because—despite the enormity of power you possess—you feel powerless, lost, afraid of yourself, doubting who you are and who you might one day be. You came because your heart is shattered by your mother's death, your mind fractured by traumas and revelations. You came because you don't have anywhere else to go, orphan Zo. You *came*, fierce lass, to dump the violence of your emotions on some lucky bastard's body, and that lucky bastard is me. I read it in your eyes the moment you stepped out the door. I accept, asking nothing in return, and will keep you safe as long as need be."

By this time in his rapid-fire and fiery speech, he'd eliminated all distance between us. He stood a breath from my body, and I could feel him throwing presence, his energy, the immensity of the passion rolling off him. It was like standing in the midst of a full-blown lightning storm before the rain has begun, the air charged and crackling, something explosive about to happen.

"You came," he continued in a low, intense voice, "because you've not yet fucked since you've been fully awakened as a witch, and I assure you, it will exceed your wildest dreams."

I shivered. I would always shiver, I would soon learn, anytime Devlin said the word *fuck*, and I knew we were about to. *We think we want a man who sees us*, I thought, every bit as incensed now as I'd been when Kellan had seen into me so clearly.

"I *do* have somewhere else to go," I informed him tightly. Kellan was never far from my mind. That man had turned me inside out, met me measure for measure, left me hungering for so much more of him. "There's a different man I'd like to see. But seeing him would require leaving the estate. I'm willing to break *some* rules tonight, not all." Boy, did the bitch in me come out when a man saw me too clearly, I thought, as amused as I was mortified by it.

Devlin arched a brow and said softly, "Woman, I don't care why you fuck me so long as you do. Go ahead, make me feel like second choice, second best. It'll only make me work harder to prove you wrong. I like to win. And I'm good at it." Challenge blazed in his eyes as he stared down at me. "You'll never see me in the light of day. Come share my dark erotic night. Use me as you desire, for anything you desire, Zo-d'kai." He offered his hand.

"I thought you didn't shit where you eat," I said flatly.

"You might be the exception to everything," he retorted, just as flatly, with a flash of ire in his gaze.

Inevitable, I acknowledged. Sex with Devlin Blackstone had been inevitable since the moment I'd seen him. Even before I'd known he was a warm vampire and powerful witch. "You said you would teach me to put up barriers. What else will you teach me about the craft of the Cailleach?"

"Anything you wish that does not place either of us in jeopardy. You've but to ask."

Levelly meeting his gaze, I said, "Invite me in."

"I think that's my line, lass."

"That's true of warm vampires, too?" I was fascinated. "Not just cold ones? If I weren't in a heavily warded manor, you still wouldn't be able to come in without invitation?"

"All is choice, especially those matters that spring from ancient powers and rites. I invite you in."

I intended to push forcefully into that fiery burnt-umber gaze but ended up melting the moment I slid into the sheer heat, lust, and desire he was feeling for me. To undress me slowly, to taste every inch of my body with his tongue, his kisses. So many erotic images buffeted me, my knees went soft, as if saying, *Yes, yes, drop down, here onto the ground, right now, sink into the fragrant soil with this man, let go, let go, become something else, wild and free.*

Locking my legs, I probed deeper. Oh, yes, definitely a very, *very* old soul, one that brought to mind circles of enchanted stones and bonfires, runes chiseled by hand into rocks and potions mixed amid meetings in secret catacombs; of rounded mounds with slatted openings that caught the moon just so on winter's solstice; savage drums and orgiastic dancing on a hallowed night's eve; and as I'd sensed before, 100 percent devotion to that which he committed, an unwavering arrow to a goal, fiercely protective, fiercely loyal.

"Enough?" he said, coppery eyes glittering, a smile curving his lips.

More than.

I took the hand he offered, gasping aloud when his fingers twined with mine.

"You've no idea what sex is like, fully awakened. I'm honored to be the man who will be your true first time."

Okay, seriously melting. "Honored" to be the one.

I had no idea what sharing his bed would bring, but sensed that it might be redefining, life-changing.

I was a fully awakened witch, a powerful woman who *would* master her power, who would learn to make trees and flowers and birth new things, not harm them, about to make love for the first time, with full cognizance of what I was. Oh, God, had I really thought *make love*? I *never* used those words. It was always just *sex* and most definitely would be this time, too.

Devlin was an outlet, a diversion, a never-to-be-repeated event, and as far as I was concerned, a frank necessity right now to make it through the next twenty-some hours without imperiling myself or anyone else.

How sweet the lies we tell ourselves.

How convincing.

That night, and many beyond it, the damned vampire would get so deep inside me he grazed my soul.

Had he said later, in bed, *May I drink your blood?* I might well have simply replied, *Which thigh?*

But he didn't, because Devlin never asked for anything. He gave and gave, then gave more.

Such seduction.

Both manor and man.

The garage inside was nothing like I'd imagined beyond the ground level floor, which was almost exactly as I'd envisioned, with stalls of one luxury car after the next.

Beneath the ground floor, down a hidden staircase (each tread chiseled with strange markings I suspected wouldn't be quite so easy to navigate were I not being carried in the vampire's arms), was Devlin's home. He lived on the estate in a palatial underground abode. This, too, I would come to learn when I desperately needed them, had hidden connecting doors and concealed rooms.

Two floors beneath the main, his bedroom. He tossed me onto the bed, then was on me like a dark sirocco, sans dust, only heat and primal overload.

It was wild, the most visceral, raw sex I'd ever had, every sensation exquisitely heightened, in a place that felt hidden and tucked away and free. No holds barred, we burned up his bed— literally. I didn't know if it was him or me, but somehow, at one point, the sheets were actually ablaze, and we had to tear ourselves away from each other while he murmured something that extinguished the flames.

"Wasn't me," he growled.

"Well, I sure as hell don't know how I did it, *if* I did," I growled back, aching from the interruption. "Just keep putting it out if it happens again."

"Stop manifesting metaphor, and fuck me, woman."

I *had* been thinking we were burning up the sheets.

"You're thinking too much," he said irately.

"You're talking too much," I snapped back, and then we were both laughing, then we were on the floor and he was inside me again, and I wasn't laughing anymore.

Or thinking. Just dumping, venting, pouring all my anguish and confusion, my fear, my pain and grief onto his body, with anger, with violence, with frustrated rage as we ranged from room to room, from bed to chair to counter to couch, then finally with all the tenderness in my soul, because I hungered to feel some kind of tenderness in this strange, new brutal and frightening world in which I, orphaned Zo Grey, felt so damned alone and lost, stripped of my mother, bereft of my best friend, adrift with no idea who or what I truly was.

It was when I turned tender that he inhaled sharply and fell back onto the couch staring up at me, his gaze inscrutable. "Didn't expect that," he said roughly.

"Don't move. Let me do whatever I want. Do nothing. I want control."

"As you wish, Zo-d'kai."

God, every time he said my name that way, I felt I'd never heard it correctly before.

I was tender with Mom. Such a gentle woman, she brought out the gentle in me. I'd never been gentle with a man I took to my bed.

This time I poured wonder and reverence, appreciation, respect, honesty into my every touch. Just Zo. No games. I'd always promised no games in the past with my Look but it had still been just a game to me. A one-night stand, a finite event. I would rock their world while taking what I wanted, getting what I needed. All my tender was used at home.

But now, with Devlin, I dropped all pretense. I touched him with just me.

I would wonder about it later and decide it was because, since Mom was gone, I couldn't show that part of myself to anyone. I had no one to be tender with. And tenderness is a strength. It isn't pity, as some like to claim, or weakness, as others like to say, and it certainly doesn't pity or weaken the one receiving it. On the contrary, that kind of intimacy restores parts fallen away, stripped from us, or given away in reckless, unthinking moments; a little tenderness can gather and restitch the scattered bits of the soul.

That was when Devlin got to mine.

When, at last, I stopped, he gave back in kind.

Laid me back on the couch and touched me the same way. With infinite gentleness, as if I were made of delicate porcelain, tracing every inch of my skin, ending with my face, running his fingers butterfly soft over my nose, my eyes, brows, cheeks, and lips as if memorizing every line and curve, savoring them to the depths of his being.

Shit. Shit. Shit.

For the first time in my life, I wondered if I'd bitten off more than I could chew.

Thoughts of staying. Of a second time. Of . . . caring about the man in my bed blossomed in my—

Oh, damn it all to hell! My *heart*. The lightest, the gentlest of touches, that was the one that got inside me.

Easy to fuck.

But to make *love*?

Only the greatest risk of all.

MUCH LATER, I lay with my head on his chest, listening to the steady, powerful beat of his heart, lightly tracing my fingers over one of the archaic-looking tattoos on his arm. "Does it mean something?" I asked.

"It's this branch of the Cameron family tree's motto, in Gaelic. You'll find it around the estate in many places."

Devlin Blackstone sported the Cameron family motto on his skin. I wondered why. "What does it say?"

"'Where there is love, there is no law.' Some claim long ago, it used to be 'where there is clan, there is no law.'"

I inhaled sharply. My mother's words. An uncanny coincidence or much more? Was I truly a Cameron?

"Did Juniper give you her blood?" The words were out before I even knew I was thinking them. Why was he here? Why was he so committed to the Camerons? Why did Mr. Balfour dislike him? Was it truly so simple as Mr. Balfour resenting Devlin's greater power? Somehow, that didn't compute for me.

He glanced down at me. "On occasion. Not often. Why?"

"I'm trying to understand how you fit in here."

"Och, that's easy, lass," he said with a laugh. "We all benefit from tribe, a clan. There's safety, a sense of belonging, in numbers, even more so in the witching community, and the Camerons are one of the finest, if not the finest, light houses in the world. Easy to pledge to. Easy to stay. You'll see. Come," he said suddenly. "I want you to see something. I go often to watch, and it's nearly time."

"You mean leave the garage?" I was dismayed. Not only did I have no desire to stop having sex with Devlin, it somehow felt like "out there" was unwise and unsafe. I needed to, as Mr. Balfour had said, stay small and still, and while I'd certainly been neither, I was in a very private, tucked-away place where I felt it prudent to remain.

He smiled faintly. "We'll be back quickly. It's nearly dawn, and you'll pass the day with me until it's time to open Juniper's letter. Then Balfour begins teaching you and preparing you for the pledging ceremony."

A shadow flitted through his eyes as he spoke, and I said, "Is something wrong?"

"Not at all. Just not a fan of Balfour," he replied tersely.

"Why?" I pressed.

"We've butted heads a few times. He has his ways. I have mine." Then we were dressing, and he was tugging me back up the stairs and out the door, through a gate and yet another, into the Midnight Garden.

Here, the bright gibbous moon barely penetrated the dense overhead canopy, yet the thickly carpeted floor of the garden gleamed with a luminous silvery light all its own, rather like the lambent forest floor in the dream I'd had about the hounds hidden in fallen yellow leaves.

"Witches are deeply connected to nature. We all have our affinities for various elements and animals. You'll find yours."

"Was Juniper's an owl?"

"Aye, among others. She had affinities with many animals. Mine is the stag. There's a grand one on the estate with too many antlers to count. Sometimes I peg it at thirty-four or -five points, other times I'd swear he's got more than forty. He's a great, regal beast, and the number of decades I've watched him is impossible, given the life expectancy of a stag. He meets a doe in the garden shortly before dawn every night, and they leave together." He glanced down at me. "I wonder if he'll come with you here. He never appears if someone else is with me."

"You've brought others to see him?" The witch whose blood he'd been drinking at the Gossamer? Was this just a night like

any other for him? I despised the barb of . . . yeah, not even naming that word . . . that pierced my ego. I didn't feel that word.
Ever. Because I didn't make love, and I didn't go back a second
time.

Yet the searing, haunting intimacy that had passed between
us on the couch . . .

I was beginning to regret being tender. I regretted opening
that door. I wondered if he was regretting it, too.

"I brought Juniper several times; she would have loved him.
He didn't come. The stag has rich meaning in Celtic mythol-
ogy. There are legends about them appearing at pivotal times or
choosing certain estates to . . . protect and guard. They're seen
as a symbol of the fertility of the forest, the rebirth of nature, the
cycle of the seasons. And, of course, male virility."

"I get your affinity now." He certainly packed a punch of male
virility. We'd gone through multiple condoms, and I'd considered asking him to double up, as energetically as we'd gone at it.
"How do the stag and doe get into the garden with the walls?"

"Yet another of his mysteries."

As we moved deeper into that hushed, verdant place, he took
my hand in his, lacing our fingers together. I'd never held hands
with a man before. I'd done everything else a woman could do,
but never this simple intimacy. It was . . . almost frightening to
me, but it was also comforting, quietly intoxicating. To feel so
casually yet freely connected. Not about sex, about liking each
other. I shivered.

"Cold, lass?" he asked instantly.

"Not at all."

He paused and glanced down at me. "Tell me what you feel in
this place."

"As if it's enchanted. That there's power in the soil here that isn't beyond these walls."

"Aye. The dirt in the garden was imported from Scotland. Long ago, one of the first Camerons had the stones for the churches shipped, along with an entire boat loaded with Scottish soil."

"I find devotion to building churches in a town of witches unusual."

"We practice our ways; the townsfolk practice theirs. The way of the Cailleach is not exclusionary. Those who seek light, in all manners, are to be respected."

"Why did the Camerons leave if they loved their home so much?"

"The Cailleach will never be like those who persecute us, who thrive on being exclusionary and use it to torment others. Countless men, women, and children were tortured, convicted, killed." His gaze turned bitter. "So many fine people—diviners, healers, even heart witches, willing to die for their lieges—brutally murdered. The village would love them at first, care for them, as the witches cared for the inhabitants, without ever uttering words such as *Cailleach, demon spawn,* or *crone.* Then something would happen," he spat. "The winter would last too long. Their crops would fail. The milk might sour. Someone's child would die. And suddenly the healer, the one who lived alone or was different in any way they could latch on to was the one to blame for their troubles. Only by purging them and, often, their entire line or circle of friends from the village could prosperity be restored."

"Ergo, the safety in numbers," I murmured. "In creating a place like Divinity."

"Aye, far from the memories of those lost. A place with naught but possibility. Hush, I believe he comes." His voice dropped to a whisper, and he sounded deeply surprised.

He drew me back against a tree, and as we stood motionless, something moved behind the great sweeping limbs of the Sylvan Oak just as an owl hooted softly. I glanced up into the branches to see a pair of round vermillion eyes staring directly at me.

"Rufus," I whispered, delighted to see him alive, perched in the cleft of a limb of the mighty ancient oak.

Then the most enormous stag I'd ever seen, with a thick shaggy collar and too many antlers to count, stepped out from behind the tree and into a shaft of moonlight.

A graceful, equally regal-looking doe joined him from the other side of the tree.

They touched noses, then the stag turned to look straight at Devlin, after lingering just an instant on me. Devlin nodded to him, then stag and doe melted beyond the tree and into the night together.

"Why do you come?" I asked in a hushed voice when they were gone. Hushed because the moment seemed somehow magical, their meeting meriting reverence.

"I don't know," he replied, sounding slightly irritated.

I smiled faintly. Was Devlin Blackstone, beneath those tattoos and vampire skin, despite the countless centuries he'd lived and the wars he must have seen, perhaps even participated in, still a romantic at heart?

"He draws me. He ran with me once, long ago. Only once. Perhaps I come hoping it will be repeated."

"Ran with you?"

"I can take other forms."

"Tell me," I demanded.

He glanced sharply up at the sky. "Run with me now. Dawn is nigh."

Turning, we fled. I had no idea what might happen to Devlin if touched by the light of day, and no desire to find out. I felt . . . protective of him. Not a thing I'd ever felt before for anyone but Mom.

Damn, but the man had gotten under my skin.

Alisdair

She saw us together tonight.

It enrages me that I lack the tongue to speak words she might understand.

I would tell her to run, with greatest haste, and never look back! Do not even so much as idly reflect upon this cursed place again.

Already, the young witch is sinking, sinking, and I am powerless to cast her a line to save her from the quicksand sucking her down.

Darkness on all sides of her.

Light, too, but the handicap light always suffers is that the darkness doesn't fight fair.

There are rules a light witch won't break. There are rules broken, for which a light witch will be punished, and harshly, as she will soon learn.

There are no rules a dark witch heeds.

Sometimes you have to dirty your hands, witch—not let them be dirtied for you, with you too distracted by the distractions they've set into play.

By Dagda, I am right here!

Somehow, I must find a way to communicate.

Usurping the grimoire's pages has proved beyond my means for long. There are many who seek to control it. The air in the old cabin, *which should have been razed long ago, is thicker with interference than cobwebs!*

Ah, how innocently it began, and how quickly it became anything but . . .

The child was twelve the night Death came again.

Her da was carried home from war, the wound of a battle-axe deep in his chest, too grievous for any to heal. Her mama had taken one look and gone to fetch the village priest, while the men who'd brought him returned to their own families, nursing their lesser wounds.

Alone, weeping, this time when Death came, the young girl's voice rang with power and authority, for she had already once defied him, and her demands were the same.

Death demanded: Are you certain you wish this?

Yes, *the girl shouted.* Leave him alone! Restore him to me!

There is a price, *Death said.*

I don't care! *she screamed.*

His gaze considerably cooler, Death replied, One day you will.

Then the great Arawn melted into the shadows, returning to the Otherworld, far from defeated. For when Arawn came, someone went. Never did the Lord of Death return to his kingdom, Annwn, without a soul.

When her mama returned with the priest, it was to find her husband sitting at the table, eating bread and meat in bemused and wary silence.

Babbling, nearly incoherent, her mama assured the priest she must have mistaken her husband for one of the other injured men in the darkness, and hastened the man of the cloth from their hut.

But she knew it was her husband who'd lain at Death's door, a mortal wound cleaving his breastbone.

And she knew well how many others knew it, too.

Her gaze wary and frightened, she gazed down at the girl, recalling the day she herself had tumbled from the roof. She'd been certain she'd felt something strong and hard go soft and broken in her neck. She'd not permitted herself to dwell upon it overmuch. Blessings, miracles, these were matters too lofty to be questioned by the likes of her.

The girl, jaw jutting defiance, with a measure of what would soon become enormous arrogance, cried, I sent Death away, just like I did for you! And stop telling me that I imagine things. Look at Da—he's healed. *I* did that!

The crofters exchanged a look, then her da nodded. Turning to the girl, he said, You will ne'er utter a word of this e'er again. Tae any!

Ordering her mama to grab only what was absolutely necessary, he went quickly to retrieve the gold, for they would surely be burned as witches at dawn, accused of consorting with imps from hell and commanding demons to do their bidding, were they still in the hut to be found when the villagers came.

As they stole through the forest beneath a silvery moon, they encountered a neighboring crofter, a braw man and friend, who was at first astounded, then enraged and horrified to see her da up and alive, moving as if never harmed. For their great laird, the O'Keefe, had died that night, the killing wound of a battle-axe suddenly appearing in his chest when no such injury had been done him in battle. Before the eyes of dozens of witnesses, the O'Keefe had begun to gush heart blood, collapsed heavily to the floor, and died as an icy wind whipped the tapestries into a frenzy upon the walls. Such doings were clearly the work of devilish hands!

Da was forced to use his sword against the man to permit their escape. The crofter's innocent blood seeped deep into the ground as they fled, and blood spilled in such ways leaves a residue in the soil. Some places are tainted forever, and there are witches who deliberately seek them, using them to amplify their power for nefarious ends.

One would think the girl would have learned something that night, and one would be right.

But it was the wrong thing.

She learned silence, she learned stealth, she learned to begin seeking the lonely ones, the strange ones in the villages that soon became too numerous to count, as Death came again, and again, and her small family was forced to flee, again and again.

23

I REMAINED WITH DEVLIN THROUGHOUT the day, until nightfall, returning to the manor with just enough time to shower and dress
before meeting Mr. Balfour at 11:45 p.m.

I'd succeeded in bringing harm to no one and nothing, depos-
iting myself safely at the doorstep of the all-important deadline.

We women have a hard time concealing a truly spectacular
night from astute eyes. It changes the way we move, walk, hold
ourselves, especially when it's more than sex, when a deeper, true
connection takes place, a thing I'd never permitted in my life,
but it had happened despite my intentions.

Devlin was open, charming, disarming me with frank honesty
and humor at unexpected moments. I had to admit, I was fascinated by how long he'd lived, what he was. By becoming a warm
vampire, he'd opened the door to many new, extraordinary powers no everyday witch, not even a Highblood like me, would ever
possess, such as shapeshifting, a topic he'd resisted discussing
further.

Although I'd endeavored to scrub away the sensually satisfied,
unexpectedly romantic glow the past twenty-some hours, most
of them in bed with Devlin, had bestowed upon me, I must have
failed because when I walked into the south parlor, Mr. Balfour
looked me up, down, and up again, then met my gaze in silence,
without the faintest hint of a smile or warmth.

His was a weighty silence that spoke volumes.

You went to him, his eyes said, disappointment clear. *You didn't
lean on me, rely on me, a man who wants nothing from you in return
but to see you take your rightful place.*

For a woman who'd known no father, the look of paternal dis-appointment in his blue gaze was crushing. "He asked nothing from me, either!" I protested.

"Yet," Mr. Balfour said tightly. "There is no witch in this town who will not one day ask something of you."

"Why do you dislike him so?" I cried, exasperated. I adored Mr. Balfour, could feel his strength and true aim, just as I could Devlin's.

"Why is one mortal life and the power with which that man was born not enough for him? I don't care for *any* warm vam-pires. It goes against the grain of what I believe."

I opened my mouth to make a sharp retort, defending Devlin, then closed it again. I could see Mr. Balfour's point; I'd won-dered the same thing myself and had asked Devlin. It wasn't my place to belittle another's beliefs on life and death, their faith, their view of the proper order of things as they saw it. Although, for Mom, I'd certainly have cheated death any way I could. If I'd known my blood held such power, I'd have fed it to her daily, even if it had meant sneaking it into her food.

"He said it wasn't about the power," I told Mr. Balfour. "He loves being alive, watching time unfold. He knows that one day he will die. He's just not ready yet."

"You asked him?"

"That and many other questions."

"Did you give him your blood?"

"No. And he didn't ask for it," I said sharply.

"Ah, my dear Ms. Grey, he will. You brought the letter?"

I withdrew it carefully from the whatnot box I'd emptied, tucking it in with tissue paper cushioning on all sides, afraid the seal might somehow get cracked and I'd be disqualified from becoming the Cameron heir.

After seven full days and nights in this manor, despite the many terrifying, inexplicable, and disturbing things that had transpired in my life, I'd never felt more strongly that I was home.

This was where I was supposed to be. Here in Divinity, a part of the Cameron clan whose motto was "where there is love (or clan), there is no law." Talk about passion. Such loyalty and belonging appealed to me immensely.

And yes, it would be frightening. I would make mistakes. I would need to lean on people like Mr. Balfour to teach me not to, to show me how to make reparation for those mistakes I'd already made.

In a very short time, I'd come to adore it here. It felt . . . right. I was a sponge, ravenous to soak up all I could about who I was and might become. I'd not yet gotten to see much of the town and was looking forward to being out in it more. Getting to know the divine sprawl of a home the Cameron clan had created to keep their witches safe from harm, along with its denizens. To tend it, guard it, nurture it, devote my life to it.

Mr. Balfour's gaze softened. "Yes," he said softly. "That's why Juniper chose you."

"Did you just use deep sight on me uninvited?" I demanded, with an appalled gasp. I'd felt nothing. And from the brief bit of instruction Devlin had given me late this afternoon, I now knew exactly how it felt. Althea Bean *had* been trying to do it to me that night at the Shadows. Then she'd snapped at *me* for doing it to her. The nerve!

He smiled faintly. "No. It's blazing in your eyes the same way it did in Juniper's. You fell in love with us, as she knew you would. You see us, the value of our way of life, and you are ready, willing, and more than capable of becoming not just a part of it, but Divinity's keeper and protector." He paused a heavy moment, then added, grudgingly, "And if Devlin played any part in solidifying your feelings, I forgive you for disappointing me by going to him."

"I forgive you for being disappointed," I replied tartly.

He laughed, eyes dancing. "That is precisely how Juniper would have responded in similar circumstances."

Accepting the envelope I offered, he inspected the seal carefully and returned it to me.

"Do you know what it says?"

He shook his head. "Whether you choose to confide in me the contents of her letter is up to you." But his eyes made it clear he hoped I would. He rose slowly and said, "I trust you won't open it until one minute after midnight, and I shall leave you to it. Text or call if you wish anything of me."

With that, he moved to the door and stepped out into the night.

I glanced at my phone: six minutes to go.

It suddenly felt very important that I be in the right place to read the letter, but I had no idea where that right place was, only that I had six minutes to find it.

Had the kitchen not currently contained what felt like an icy portal to hell, that was where I would have gone. It was and would always feel to me (once restored!) like the happy heart of the home. The only other heart I could think of was the original cabin and, oh hell, no way. Not only did I doubt that the wing would permit me to make it there in under six minutes, it had begun to feel not like a jewel to be unearthed, but the dark heart of the house.

Nor did my bedroom seem right, or Juniper's suite, not even her office or— Oh!

The conservatory, to which I'd thus far given little more than a cursory look. Surrounded by lush foliage, elemental, calm, restorative, symbolic of the Cailleach's affinity for nature. It was the perfect place to—I hoped—at long last learn the truth of who I was.

Pivoting, I strode briskly through the house and into the kitchen, keeping my eyes averted from the chasm, which I despised myself for having created and loathed seeing, burst through the back door, hurried to the conservatory, and stepped inside.

Rufus greeted me from his perch in the jackfruit tree with a soft chuffing sound.

"Oh, I'm so sorry, I keep forgetting to let you out!" I exclaimed, holding the door ajar.

He made no move to leave; to the contrary, only settled more snugly into the foliage, and I laughed at my sudden fanciful notion that he'd noted what I clutched in my hand and chosen to remain, to learn along with me, at long last, who I truly was.

That notion didn't seem quite as fanciful when, as I made my way through the softly illuminated jungle of tropical trees and flowers, at last finding the waterfall with its small pool encircled by mossy stones, he followed me to roost on a limb above as I perched on a boulder in that lovely enclave.

Not the best light, but enough to read by. I checked my phone: 12:01 on the dot!

Hands trembling ever so slightly, I turned the envelope over and cracked the waxen seal.

Two pages of thick vellum were tucked inside. Unfolding and smoothing them on my lap, unconsciously holding my breath, I began to read.

My darlingmost darlings, Zo and Joanna!
     I have never felt such joy as I did the day it was
confirmed that the two of you are indeed of the Cameron
line and our Royal bloodline endures.
     Welcome home, my dearest ones!

My breath exploded from me, and I closed my eyes, blinking
back a hot burn of tears. Juniper's warm welcome was one my
mother would never hear.

Mr. Balfour had told me that Juniper slipped into a coma and
died six days after my mother. Yet this letter welcomed us both,
which meant it was written before Mom died.

Why, then, was the envelope addressed only to me?

Reaching for my phone, I shot a quick text to Mr. Balfour: Did
Juniper slip into a coma before my mother died?

He replied, Yes. She penned those letters in case she didn't survive.
It would have broken her heart to learn of your mother's passing. She
wrote a letter for Joanna, too, but instructed me to give it to no one but
her. I have it tucked away in a safe place.

I nearly had to stuff a fist in my mouth to keep from screaming.
If only Juniper had found us sooner! If only she'd told *no one* she'd
located heirs, because I was convinced it was her revelation of our
existence that had dispatched an arsonist to Indiana and incited
the dense gathering of so many witches my first night in Louisiana at Criollo. Someone didn't want us here so badly that they'd
taken measures to prevent our arrival. But I'd not been home with
my mother, so a second attempt on my life had, indeed, been
made at the barn. And it would likely continue. I'd quite possibly missed another attempt on my life at the Hotel Monteleone
restaurant simply by not taking the wrong witch to my bed.

May I see Mom's letter, too?

There was a lull this time, then, I will have to give that some consideration, he texted, loyalties clearly torn between past and present heir. Her instructions were precise. Is all well?

Yes. I was just startled that she mentioned both of us. I've only read the first few lines.

Very well. I'm here.

I returned my gaze to the thick vellum and Juniper's lovely, though shaky penmanship, some letters careful and well-formed, others wobbling.

I'd been searching for so very long, I'd nearly lost hope. But your DNA was a match, which thrilled me to the marrow of my weary bones. The genetic proof was indisputable: I am, my darling—and my hand trembles with such emotion as I write this, you must forgive my penmanship, which was once so fine—your great-grandaunt!

I shivered. I had roots, true Cameron roots!

You descend from my brother Marcus, who was lost at war. In finding you and your mother, I found a part of my cherished brother again. I confess, I spent most of the day weeping when the news was delivered, for I am an old woman, maudlin for days gone by, finally able to bring Marcus home, after a fashion, and after so very long.

I will never know his story, why my brother failed to

return from war. I suspect injury followed by amnesia, as wild horses couldn't have kept him away from his beloved home. It was the cruelest of torments to have no facts, no body to bury and honor. I don't know how you and your mother came to be in Indiana. There is so much I don't know that I wish I did, which I ache to have been part of, but any dismay and sorrow I might feel is eclipsed by happiness, knowing my brother lives on in the two of you, that the Cameron line continues, and my family is coming home to take their rightful place in Divinity.

The manor has been so lonely these past decades! I moved my suite to the south wing long ago. Living in the wing in which my brothers and I grew up, then sharing it with my daughter until she, too, died, had become unbearable to me. I needed more connection, more people around.

You may choose to refurbish it. I lacked the heart. I bid you, repair it. Make it magnificent and fill Cameron Manor with life again!

The view of Divinity is splendid from what was once my suite. I hope you and Joanna grace these hallways with all the love and laughter that once filled them. I pray you rebuild our line, strong and true.

You *must* succeed where I failed, Zo.

I nearly let our line die out.

I nearly left our clan unprotected, and for that I will never forgive myself. As with any royalty, there must *always* be an heir and a spare, preferably more.

I remembered the maid telling me that Juniper had lost a second daughter and been unable to have children after that. How heavy that must have made her heart! It was no wonder she'd devoted such time and so many resources to locating an heir.

> I beg you, fill this home with children, grandchildren,
> and greats, and ensure no one ever makes such a
> consummate, dangerous mistake as I did again. We
> Cameron women rarely take a husband. Don't feel you
> must. But do get on with things, as rebuilding our line
> is now one of your most important duties to Kovan,
> coven, and clan.

I paused there, pondering how greatly at odds my mother's and Juniper's desires were. Mom had begun urging me to have a baby around the time I'd turned eighteen, with my power un-awakened, so that all magic would be forever extinguished from our bloodline.

Juniper was urging me to have babies with all haste, with my power fully awakened, in order to *protect* our bloodline. They were such disparate positions, they were impossible to reconcile. Kill the magic on the one hand, protect it on the other. Why such dichotomous approaches?

Sighing, I resumed reading.

> So long as there is only one person to continue our
> bloodline, Divinity remains in peril. Forgive me for being
> so blunt—time is of the essence—but there is safety in
> the number of heirs. Because none dared try to take me
> down in the latter half of my life—Lord knows they did
> when I was young!—James doesn't fully apprehend the
> danger I know you are in.
>
> You are young, untried, and there are many from other

houses who will see you as a single, simple threat to be eliminated. Joanna is past childbearing age and ill. She will not be perceived as such. I left my legacy to you rather than Joanna because of her illness. Divinity needs a strong, young heir.

You have been in the manor now for seven days and nights. Long enough to have learned how precious are our home, our town, our people, our clan, our way of life, and our right to live free of persecution for our faith.

I'm *so* sorry I didn't find you sooner, in time to get Joanna the best of care. But I pray I've found you in time for the two of you to spend precious years here together.

My hand wearies from writing.

My body aches from living, and my heart is sore from watching so many go before me. A century of life has been both blessing and curse.

James swears I held on so long from sheer stubborn determination not to leave Divinity unprotected. He's right. He usually is. James is a fine, solid man with a heart of gold. You can rely upon him to help you settle in. Devlin is another solid man. You can count on him, trust him implicitly, as I do.

"Aha, take that, James Balfour," I muttered. "She mentions the two of you in the same breath, with the same regard." I wondered if the coolness between Mr. Balfour and Devlin had bothered Juniper as much as it did me. Then I wondered if, perhaps, they'd dared not show it in front of her. Maybe it was just me, since I was young and new. Regardless, I planned to nip that behavior in the bud soon.

Now that I've found Divinity's heir, I am at long last able to breathe easier, slipping, yielding, where once I'd have continued to battle the eternal footman who has turned down the lights and patiently holds my coat, bidding me go. I fear I am not long for this world and will not be here by the time you arrive.

If I am not, please do me a kindness and bring my favorite roses to my grave. Visit me from time to time to tell me of your life. Listen to this silly old woman, fancying spirits may get to linger! But if they do, mine will be listening and watching over you.

There's so much I wanted to tell you about your family, and your great-grandfather. About our rich heritage and your enormous power. About those who can be counted on, those who can be counted upon to be difficult; who to keep at a watchful distance, who to draw near; but I've dispatched others to those tasks, I've yet to pen Joanna's letter, and tiring as I am from exertion, I must draw this letter to a close.

I knew Marcus like the back of my hand; his heart was strong and true. You are his direct descendant.

I am entitled to say this. My heart swells with pride, glows with happiness, knowing you'll soon arrive, and I may not get to tell you this in person.

I love you already, young Zo.

You are a part of my brother, a part of me, descended from a long line of light Cailleach who bring infinite good into the world. You have roots and a heritage of which to be immensely proud.

You are blood Cameron, to the bone.

Welcome home! I can only pray I live to meet you.

If not, rule wisely, love well and as much as possible, and fill these halls with life again, my dearest, darling great-grandniece.

With love eternal,
Juniper

I was crying by the time I finished. I'd gotten a sense of Juniper from both her lovely home and the way everyone spoke about her, but only now did I feel I truly *knew* her. That we'd somehow connected through her letter, as if she'd reached across time and space to touch me so deeply. It left me aching with disappointment that we'd never met.

Juniper was my great-grandaunt!

I was a blood Cameron!

The burning question of my identity was finally off my plate.

I belonged here. I *was* the heir. Although the will alone had granted me the *legal* right to Juniper's legacy, this letter, penned so eloquently in her own hand, confirmed she'd had genetic testing done. Neither court of law nor dissenters in Divinity could prevent me from inheriting her legacy.

There are many from other houses who will see you as a single, simple threat to be eliminated . . .

Oh, how accurately she'd called it!

With that thought, I frowned, wondering why she'd risked telling anyone of our existence prior to our arrival. Then I realized she'd no doubt believed she had to declare the heir, as she wasn't certain she would survive until we arrived.

Were the heir not announced before her death, I could only imagine how fierce the resistance would have been. She'd made her choice clear, yet opposition still existed in pockets of the town.

I smiled, feeling as if an enormous weight had been lifted from my shoulders, replaced by a lighter though no less complex and overwhelming one—to assume my place as the head of coven and Kovan, to serve Divinity as well as my great-grandaunt had served.

My great-grandfather was Marcus Cameron, Juniper's brother! I was a light witch, not dark—yet another burning question I could remove from my very full plate. My father had loved my mother, I had roots, strong and true.

My smiled faded swiftly as I realized all those thoughts only raised another deeply disturbing question.

If not from my father, and not from Divinity, what in the world had my mother spent her entire life running from?

What was the war she'd thought I could never win?

I sighed.

Another letter.

A smidge more information.

Left, still, with burning questions.

Carefully folding the letter and tucking it back into the envelope, I pushed up from the boulder as Rufus whuffed softly above me. I glanced up into vermillion eyes that held mine longer than bird or beast ever had. I wondered if deep sight worked on an owl. If so, what did Rufus feel? Did owls think?

Holding that fiery crimson gaze, I expanded my witch senses to discover—

Ow!

"Holy hell!" I exploded. What had just happened? It felt as if I'd gone slamming into a solid wall studded with spikes at such velocity, I'd ricocheted off it.

Narrowing his eyes to slits, Rufus chuffed as if in rebuke,

thrust up from the limb, and soared to the top of the tallest tree in the conservatory.

"Guess not," I muttered, filing that away to ask Devlin about. Did animals resent our intrusion? Was it like that with all of them, or were owls just particularly testy?

I felt a sudden fierce need to proclaim to the world that, at long last, I knew who I was. Yet I had no one of my own to tell it to.

That wasn't entirely true, I mused. There was Este.

There was a time that pulling out my phone to call her and babble happily about this would have been effortlessly easy.

Not quite so reflexive now.

Yet she was all I had from my old life, and I couldn't bear the thought of us never being friends again. I strongly hoped that in time we would find our way back to the relationship I'd trusted and treasured.

I wasn't quite ready to call her, so I sent a text instead.

I AM the Cameron heir! Marcus Cameron, Juniper's brother, was my great-grandfather! I finally know who I am! Followed by a whole line of happy emojis and champagne glasses.

Merely typing those words filled me with such pleasure.

Three dots appeared. Then vanished. Then appeared and vanished several more times.

Then:

Did you find the genetic paperwork proving it?

Well, that was a bit . . . frosty, I thought, pricked. No, Juniper told me. She left me a letter.

So, you still don't have any proof.

Okay, that was downright icy. I stared at the screen of my phone for a long, stunned moment. Why couldn't Este be happy for me? I'd always been happy for her successes, begrudging none of them.

What are you saying? I fired back.

> Just that. You don't have any proof. You have the same thing you had before: someone's word. Why didn't she give you a copy of the genetic testing?

You can't ever be happy for me, can you? Her letter is more than enough proof, even in a court of law!

Three dots appeared and vanished, over and over again. Finally,

> Babe, I want to be happy for you.

Then TRY HARDER! I added angry emojis.

Flipping my phone to mute, I shoved it in my back pocket and stalked from the conservatory, wondering what had happened to us being forever sisters and always having each other's back.

24

Inhaling shakily, I gazed at my reflection in the full-length, tri-fold mirrors in my bedroom closet.

The pledging ceremony, to which Devlin would be my escort, was less than an hour away, to be held at the Shadows, on the outskirts of town.

When I'd shared Juniper's letter with Mr. Balfour this morning, I'd never seen him happier, gushing with delight, asking if he might make a copy of it to share with the Kovan. *In her own hand!* he'd exclaimed.

I wasn't a fool. Clearly, there was a slow but steady burn of opposition among the witching families in Divinity, and Juniper's letter was precisely what he'd needed to extinguish those flames.

We'll hold the pledging ceremony tonight, he'd said, beaming.

I thought it was better to wait and train me first.

He'd met my gaze in silence. In a short time, I'd become adept at reading the man.

It was because there was resistance, not because I needed training, I said dryly.

This is exactly what we needed. No one will protest now. Juniper's word is adamantine, beyond impugning. Not an ounce of reticence will remain once the Kovan sees her letter. Now, go get the papers and sign them. You've still not legally accepted the legacy.

I'd completely forgotten about that.

For the second time in two days, my hands had trembled with deep emotion, as I'd proudly signed the documents in all the necessary places: Zodeckymira Grey-Cameron.

"I'm Zo Cameron," I murmured to my reflection in the mirror. "About to pledge my life to the care and keeping of our clan."

Completing the pledging wouldn't solve everything—far from it. I had countless questions that needed answers. Who'd killed my mother and tried to kill me? What had Mom and I spent our whole lives running from? Who was my father, and what had happened to him? But with Juniper's letter, the questions that had been deeply gnawing away inside me, making me doubt myself, making me afraid of who and what I was, and undermining my confidence had been put to rest.

Juniper was right. The attempts on my life would continue. The early years of my reign wouldn't be easy, but I didn't think hers had been, either. She'd said "none dared try" in the latter half of her life, but that in younger days, she'd faced the same threats—uneasy lies the head that wears a crown.

My formal training would begin tomorrow, according to Mr. Balfour (James, he'd asked me to call him this morning, though he refused to address me as less than Ms. Cameron, stressing its importance with the Kovan) with the repair of the kitchen.

I felt as if I'd lived a year in the past week, five years in the three and a half weeks since Mom's death. I felt somehow so much . . . older, in a good way, and I hoped wiser.

How swiftly my life had changed!

I'd gone from pauper to queen; from unnoticed to the focus of everyone's gazes; from hunted, I vowed, to hunter (for with the resources of Juniper's legacy I *would* track down my enemies and quell them, and I *would* discover those responsible for my mother's death); from a woman incapable of feeling deeply and afraid to allow herself to feel anything, to a woman who was sort of, kind of, maybe . . . falling in . . . well, "falling for" Devlin was as much as I would allow on the matter; and finally, from a woman unawakened and hobbled by lies, vision dimmed by blinders, to a fully empowered witch.

"My God," I whispered. If Mom could see me now! I had position and power, home and clan, security, stability, all the things I knew she'd wanted for me. I could and would further my education, in the early hours or late evening, once my other duties were complete. Life wouldn't be easy, it never was, but it was certainly a far cry better than the life she and I had known.

I would continue to explore and ferret out the secrets of the manor, uncover the identities of my mysterious grimoire narrators, try, with Devlin, to solve the riddle of the regal stag and his lady who mysteriously met each dawn in the Midnight Garden.

I would come to know this town and its inhabitants intimately, divine what Althea Bean feared and why, who the shadowy coven was that sought to drive me away, which families in the Kovan could be trusted and which needed to be kept at a distance.

I would learn all I could about the power in my blood, using it to prove myself a worthy successor to my great-grandaunt, Juniper Cameron.

And I would also, I thought, a smile curving my lips, fill this manor with life.

"Quickly," I assured my reflection. I no longer suffered qualms about bringing children into my world, although I'd have to be careful, taking wise, protective measures for them until I became formidable enough that none dared challenge me.

Lack of a husband didn't bother me.

At least not now. Perhaps that would change in time. So much about my life had.

Perhaps, I mused thoughtfully, it was time to stop using condoms and let what may be, be. Fact was, I'd not have minded a child from any of the men I'd taken to my bed over the years. I'd always chosen well.

Smoothing my hands over my long chestnut hair, I assessed myself a final time. *Wear a suit, formal, powerful, and light,* Mr. Balfour had said. The cream Chanel would be perfect.

I'd done as he bade and barely recognized the amber-eyed woman looking back at me, dressed in a gorgeous ivory suit, wearing a diamond necklace and earrings to match. No one would ever look down their noses at this woman and her dented, battered car, make fun of her frugal nature or Walmart clothes.

From beyond the closet where I stood assessing myself, through the open balcony doors, I heard Devlin call my name.

Blood racing with nervous excitement, I quit the bedroom, hurried down the stairs, and did what I'd wanted to do since the moment I met Devlin Blackstone.

Invited him in.

ONE HUNDRED AND sixty-nine witches formed the Kovan.

There were double that number outside the Shadows, security for the pledging of the Cameron heir.

Mr. Balfour was taking no chances.

The air hummed with power, crackled with energy, sizzled with magic, and I caught my breath as I slid from the Mercedes and took Devlin's hand.

Part of me wanted to go still, close my eyes, open my senses, and bask in the enormity of power surrounding me, as Este had said (and that thought made me sad; never would I have believed an event of such significance would take place in my life without my best friend at my side).

Another part felt the weight of eyes on me, gazes assessing, measuring, and knew that, despite all measures taken to safe-guard heirs, a rotten apple or two often made it into the barrel. I moved swiftly to the door, with Devlin's arm about my shoulders, flanked by an impenetrable wall of bodyguards on either side the entire way.

"Anyone who seeks to harm you will have to get through me, too, lass," he said close to my ear. "Never going to happen."

I shivered at the tone. I'd felt the same from Jesse: Devlin's was power and menace, held softly. I had an ancient, warm vampire-witch at my side who could shapeshift into who knew what, and it conferred a deep sense of security. I wondered if that was why Juniper allowed him to live beneath the garage behind the manor. With her power, she'd not needed bodyguards but could certainly rest easier at night, knowing such a powerful ally was on the grounds. Balfour at her side during the day, Devlin outside at night. I, too, would enjoy the comforts of both.

The first floor was empty but for Lennox and James, who hurried to greet me.

"Stunning!" Lennox exclaimed, smiling. "You look divine in that suit, as I knew you would."

After exchanging pleasantries (with only me, not Devlin; Mr. Balfour and I were going to have a talk about that), James tugged me aside, brushing an imaginary speck off the lapel of my suit, eyes alight with pride.

"Are you ready?" he said quietly.

"I am." I'd never been more ready for anything in my life.

"The ceremony itself is simple. There is a standing stone, brought with the Camerons from Scotland, that has been raised from beneath the stage tonight. I will proclaim you the new Cameron heir to the Kovan and cut your palm, which you will then press to the stone. Upon completing your vows, the torch in the candelabra above the stage will light. I doubt you noticed the night you danced with us, but that is the only candelabra in which the torch wasn't glowing. It is the Cameron torch and it was extinguished the moment Juniper died. The ceremony takes mere minutes. Ms. Cameron, do you understand that you are binding yourself to protect the clan Cameron, the Kovan, and all the inhabitants of Divinity, for life?"

I felt a sudden chill at my nape. The moment seemed so . . . so . . . momentous and weighty that it felt nearly . . . ominous.

You still don't have any proof. All you have is someone's word, Este had said.

All you have is someone's word, all you have is someone's word, echoed over and over in my mind.

What if she was right to be worried about me?

Was it possible I was being lied to about, well, *everything*?

All is choice, everyone, including books, kept saying to me. Even Devlin.

Was choice still binding if you chose something you didn't know you were choosing? I mean, full disclosure had to be part of free will and choice in a karmic sense, didn't it?

What if, at this precise moment, everyone was lying to me *but* the woman who'd lied to me all my life?

That was my conundrum.

I studied Mr. Balfour intently and realized part of the reason I felt apprehensive was because I was sensing, with my normal, non-witch senses, that *he* was apprehensive. "What's worrying you?"

"This is the first and, I pray, only pledging ceremony I will ever oversee," Mr. Balfour replied. "It's a once-in-a-lifetime event, and it is solely my responsibility. If something goes wrong, I will be the one held culpable."

"How could something go wrong?"

"I have no idea," he said heavily, "and far too rich an imagination. I will not breathe easy until the torch is lit."

Nor will I, I thought glumly.

What was my fear?

Well . . . what if the Camerons were truly a house of *dark* witches? And I, dumb, gullible, easily-lied-to Zo, had missed countless red flags, failing to figure it out before pledging away my very soul?

Then why, I countered to myself, would the coven in my lucid-seeming trance of a dream have petitioned some terrifying being to *drown my light in blessed black*?

Well, gee, I thought caustically, *maybe because they need me to turn dark in order to lead their dark Kovan. Get with the program here, Zo.*

"I fear your imagination is equally rich," Mr. Balfour said dryly. "It's all over your face. What did your friend Este tell you about us, the Cameron line?"

"Only good things," I admitted.

"We can postpone this until you feel more certain," he said gently.

Still, again, I got the sense of . . . things . . . he feared. About tonight. "Is there something you're not telling me?"

"There are many things I haven't told you. Yet. There hasn't been time. But rest assured, I would never permit harm of any kind to come to you, Ms. Cameron. I assure you that all I have done, I've done to keep you safe. To protect you. To see you take your rightful place as the leader of one of the lightest, truest, most honorable Kovans in the world."

His words were resonant with a knell my bones recognized as truth.

If I could be lied to so easily, well—how could I live if that were true? At some point, I would have to take a leap of faith. Trust myself, my heart, my instincts. Or spend the rest my life afraid to believe anything or anyone again, all because my mother and best friend had lied to me for so long, they'd made me afraid to trust myself and my ability to judge character and situations.

I *did* trust my instincts.

I wouldn't allow Mom and Este and their fears to take that from me. I was feeling nerves, nothing more, and who wouldn't in my position? Squaring my shoulders, I said with firm conviction, "I'm ready to do it. Let's go."

Beaming, Mr. Balfour offered me his arm and escorted me up the stairs.

Alisdair

I EAVESDROP, AS I ALWAYS do, unseen and unnoticed, and am despairingly aware of what transpires tonight, and that the lies woven go deeper than even the icy chasm that cleaves the kitchen floor.

So many agendas, so many players, all jockeying for what? More power? Why? Power is not the stuff of which a worthwhile life is made. That can be found only in surrender to the Will of the Way, the universe's grander scheme of things, in which we are but tiny, myopic, selfish participants.

Be wary, young Cailleach! Run! The net around you closes swiftly.

Yet for the first time since your arrival, I feel a flicker of hope.

I'm no longer certain it will be my enemy who takes you down.

26

As we topped the stairs and stepped out onto the second floor of the Shadows, I gasped. The activated color theme, which I would later learn was used only for a pledging ceremony, made the dark, cavernous room appear a lofty, bright cathedral of obsidian and amber, bathed in warm honey-gold light, reflecting off countless mirrorlike surfaces and glittering cut-crystal facets.

Unlike the night I'd danced here to "Witches Reel," when the club had felt wicked and sexy, gusting with fog and lit by crimson flames, tonight it was bright and felt somehow holy. I'd never have believed such a dark room could be so brilliant, warm, and inviting, but the clever arrangement of reflective surfaces coupled with the genius of the lighting system offered a wide array of effects.

Yet another of Juniper's touches.

Devlin had told me she'd never wearied, never stopped participating, living, working, caring, until shortly before she died, when her body, at long last, grew too frail to be coerced into activity by the sheer force of her indomitable will.

I couldn't imagine living an entire century in a single place, being part of something like Divinity for so long. Dying wouldn't be easy when one loved one's home, one's world, so deeply and completely. How hard to leave it all behind, a century of rooted life!

The center of the dance floor was lined with rows of folding chairs, affording an aisle down the middle, leading to the stage, upon which an enormous standing stone had been hoisted from below.

Glancing up, I spied the sole unlit candelabra in the room—the Cameron torch that had gone out with Juniper's final breath.

It was my job to light it tonight, and, I vowed, I would.

One hundred and sixty-nine members of the Kovan rose from their chairs, turning to watch me as we entered the room.

As Mr. Balfour escorted me up the aisle, it felt oddly like a wedding march, and I supposed it rather was, as I was wedding myself to Divinity for life. I glanced from side to side, taking note of faces, realizing these, the Kovan, were the families that had come to greet me my first night in the club: the Elders and Alloways, the Somervilles and MacGillivrays, Rutherfords and Mathesons, Napiers and MacLellans, the Galloways, Kincaids, Logans, and Alexanders, and the Balfours.

As Devlin and Lennox veered off to take seats in the front row, I narrowed my eyes, wondering why, then, Althea Bean was present. Perhaps she'd married into one of the families and kept her last name. I wasn't particularly pleased to see her here and find she was part of the "inner circle" after all.

Then we were at the stage and Mr. Balfour was escorting me up the stairs as the Kovan resumed their seats.

Moving toward the giant obelisk, I was surprised to find I was trembling. Staring out at so many faces, all gazing expectantly up at me, I nearly swooned; the moment felt so . . . ponderous, enormous, and slightly . . . terrifying.

In that moment, countless fears coalesced in my mind.

What if I was wrong?

What if I couldn't read anyone?

What if I was too stupid to live and, in fact, *wasn't* long for this world?

What if I was some kind of . . . bizarre sacrifice necessary for this Kovan to—

Future Zo would tell you that my mother often said, *We make the biggest decisions of our lives with the most broken parts of ourselves, my darling. We can't help it, even when we try. Those broken parts are our needy babies, crying out for nurturing, love, and healing, and we will go to great lengths to silence their cries. The problem is babies can't see danger. They know only need.*

I had a lot of broken parts.

And this legacy, this town, this moment succored each and every one of them.

Mom also used to say, and the crassness of it drove me crazy, coming from a woman who was always so eloquent, *Shit or get off the pot, Zo.*

In other words: Commit. One way or the other. Stop vacillating. I nearly snorted, remembering it. I'd get so mad at her every time she said it.

Locking my legs to still the trembling, I turned to Mr. Balfour, who placed a hand on my shoulder and guided me to the right of the towering stone.

Quietly, he told me, "Like the crosses of Divinity Chapel, the Cameron Pledging Stone was hewn from the rock of Ben Nevis and shipped from Lochaber. It's engraved with many of the same symbols you'll find in and around the manor, and about town. After I draw blood from your palm, you will place your hand upon this series of symbols." He gestured to the stone, where the same symbols tattooed on Devlin's arm had been chiseled; they were stained with the faint brown of blood from past Cameron hands. "It's the Cameron clan motto in Gaelic, which says 'where there is clan, there is no law.' There have been dark ages when that motto was interpreted as a call to recklessness, to doing anything whatsoever to protect and defend the Cameron house. In truth, the meaning is far deeper, wiser, and more ancient. That where there is *true* clan, there is no need for law. True clan strives to achieve the best and bring forth the finest in each other, rendering law and punishment unnecessary."

His voice dropped. "Admittedly, there are still those who adhere to the other interpretation, but they are the minority here. Some also debate the word *clan* and claim it means *love* instead. Regardless, the meaning is the same. You are Cameron, and as head of the Kovan, you will strive to achieve the best and bring out the finest in Divinity."

"Invite me in," I whispered.

"By your leave," he whispered back.

We locked gazes and held.

This was it, all I could do, all I could trust; my deepest witch senses. And behind his gentle but fierce and intensely intelligent blue eyes, this man's heart was ride-or-die loyal to not only the Cameron clan and Divinity but *me*. It blazed inside him, so warm and kind and deeply caring that, had we been elsewhere, I might have burst into tears. Never had a man felt such a thing for me. His feelings were deep, fatherly, protective, a gentleness wed to something powerful, a peaceful bear who would turn savage to protect his cub.

If, at this moment, I was reading James Balfour's heart wrong, I was blind and couldn't possibly hope to navigate life.

Because I was reading his heart with mine.

And if I couldn't trust my own heart, I was fucked.

He smiled. "You're going to be fine. Are you ready?"

I nodded.

Turning to address the Kovan, he said strongly, "As the sole living descendant of Juniper Cameron and the great-granddaughter of Marcus Cameron—"

"Where is the genetic testing?" a woman demanded, rising.

It wasn't Althea, I was surprised to see, but someone to whom I'd not yet been introduced.

"Sit down!" Mr. Balfour thundered. "Both Juniper's will and her letter—which you all saw today—"

"A copy of," the woman snapped. "Copies can be manipulated. Nor have we *ever* seen her will."

The man seated beside her stood. "I agree with Megan. Where is the genetic testing? We've seen no true proof that this woman is in any way related to Juniper Cameron."

"You'll see proof when the torch lights," Mr. Balfour said coolly.

So, I observed wryly, all resistance hadn't melted away today as Mr. Balfour had hoped.

Althea Bean stood. "She is unacceptable!" she spat. "And unlike your inability to show us a shred of evidence, I'll give you cold, hard, *indisputable* facts."

Her eyes narrowed intently, focusing beyond me, at the rear of the raised platform upon which we stood. I jerked when something whirred and a white screen descended behind me, nearly filling the stage.

Then a brilliant light flickered on from seemingly nowhere, illuminating the enormous screen, with Mr. Balfour and me silhouetted in front of it.

I glanced from the screen to Althea, trying to figure out what she was using her magic to do. Her lips were compressed in a tight, vindictive smile as she withdrew several thick sheets of paper from a folder she clutched. Holding one aloft, she triumphantly informed the room, "I've not only made copies for each of you, but have the digital originals." Frowning with effort (clearly not a powerful witch, despite being in the inner circle, I thought snidely), she focused on whatever she was holding, and abruptly, the room gasped.

I turned to see the screen filled with a horrifying image and realized she was holding photos, using her power to superimpose the image on the screen for the entire Kovan to view.

Two corpses, blackened, wizened—but not beyond identifying—crumpled on the charred, ashy ground of the back courtyard at Cameron Manor.

Gruesome mummies, shrunken inside seemingly enormous black pants and shirts; clothing that was untouched by the fate that had befallen them. The life had been stripped, stolen from *them*, not their attire.

Hand flying to my throat, I gasped. My gaze flew to Mr. Balfour, filled with accusation. "You told Devlin you pulled back the bodyguards!"

A muscle worked in his jaw, but he said nothing.

Whirling, I sought Devlin's gaze. He, too, was standing, hands fisted at his sides, poised as if he was about to lunge for the stage, to use his body as a shield for me. "Aye, that is what he claimed," he growled.

"But that's Jesse and Burke!" I cried.

Another image appeared, two more corpses, charred in the front yard. The other two guards, men whose names I'd never learned, reduced to similar shrunken corpses inside pristine clothes.

A third image, and this one took me a bit longer to process, as it was a coroner's report. I had, indeed, been lied to about the man in the barn's cause of death; his heart had literally exploded, as if crushed in a fist of steely spikes.

Then the screen filled with all three images, side by side.

"She has killed," Althea snarled, "not once but *five* times, unpledged! You know it, James. And you've *covered* for her. But we're not about to let her or you get away with this. It wouldn't matter now if she were Juniper's own daughter! You know the price for what she's done! I am issuing a formal demand that the price be paid here, now, tonight. Yours is a price we'll collect later," she added venomously.

I stared from Althea to Devlin to Mr. Balfour and back again, with increasing franticness and fear. Had I truly killed those five men? Had I killed kind Jesse, Burke, and all those others?

"You have no proof that she actually killed those men," Mr. Balfour spat back. "And I have good reason to believe someone else did. Someone who was waiting, watching, and took advantage of an opportunity to make it look like she had committed the crime. For all I know, it may have been you who killed them, Althea. Although, diluted as you are, you'd require a coven at your back, a thing I'm aware you've covertly gathered for your purposes in the past. I know how many out there would rather see our town unprotected, ripe for a coup. Not only beyond the bounds of Divinity, but within the town itself. What better way than to frame the legitimate heir? Now, sit down and shut up! This ceremony will continue, and you *will* abide by—"

Everyone stood then, erupting in enraged shouts and roars. It was so deafening, it was difficult to make out what anyone was saying, but I could pick up enough to judge that although some agreed with Althea, others passionately sided with Mr. Balfour.

My God, the politics of it all! I could see it happening both ways. But surely if I'd killed, wouldn't I know it? Wouldn't it have . . . I don't know, made something in me feel different? I felt like exactly the same woman I'd always been, honorable, desiring to do good, be light, to care for this town.

I gazed imploringly at Mr. Balfour. "Tell me the truth. Did I kill those men?"

"SILENCE!" Mr. Balfour roared, and everyone froze.

Literally.

"Did you just freeze the whole room?" I said, gasping.

"Not me," Devlin said dryly. "I'm more powerful than he is."

Mr. Balfour cut me a sharp look. "It is sometimes necessary to silence this lot of fools in such fashion. Juniper didn't choose me to stand at her side all those years merely for my legal prowess."

Power sizzled and crackled in the air as he thundered at the Kovan, "You will hear me out. I have read Zo Cameron's heart with deep sight. She is true. I believe her to be the Cameron heir, and I believe her to be the rightful leader of this Kovan. Let us see if the torch agrees. Let us see if it lights for her. You must at least—"

He broke off, choking and gurgling as the electrifying sensation of magic being discharged intensified exponentially in the air.

I glanced, panicked, at the members of the Kovan, searching face after face, trying to decide who was attacking him. Many were staring, hard, directly at him. Dozens in fact. Were they all working in concert together? They might have been silenced by his spell, but I doubted any of their power had been stripped from them.

"A light witch who takes life unpledged dies," Althea shouted into the sudden silence, which I presumed meant whatever spell Mr. Balfour had employed had been nullified when he was silenced. "I demand justice. I demand this murderous, vile woman receive the mandated punishment for her actions. You know our laws! She must be killed, here and now!"

With her words, a stout, upright timber draped with heavy, knotted ropes for binding and surrounded by piles and piles of rough-hewn kindling abruptly manifested on the floor directly beneath the stage.

A pyre. For *burning*.

Who the hell had magicked *that* into existence? Althea's vegetable coven or the Kovan itself? The ancient grisly method of executing a witch sent an atavistic lance of terror through my heart, as whoever had erected it intended.

Seriously? They would burn me alive, like witches of yore? Was I to die like my mother before me? The Kovan would *kill* me on such flimsy presentation of evidence, without any sort of investigation?

I would have found that impossible to believe, but as I scanned the room, I realized with dawning horror that nearly half the witches in the room wore similar expressions.

Anticipatory, bloodthirsty, concurring silently with Althea's demand.

Some of the most heinous witch hunts and executions in history have been enacted by witches themselves, Este had said.

With a bone deep shiver, I fully, chillingly apprehended just how perilous the ground beneath my feet had become. I perched on ice thinner than glazing on a windowpane.

None of them knew me, really.

Other than James and Devlin, I'd barely spoken to any of them, aside from greetings that night at the Shadows. I was nothing to this gathering of witches. An outsider, a nobody. And there was a massively rich, enormously powerful legacy up for grabs, to anyone mighty enough to seize it.

How simple to dispose of me, poor, orphaned Zo Grey, with so few who cared about her and certainly no one magically endowed enough to go up against something as forbidding as the town of Divinity.

How easy for a Kovan of such power to kill me and conceal all trace of evidence.

"If she's truly a Cameron, she's even more dangerous than—" Althea choked and sputtered, grasping frantically at her throat.

Attacked. But who was doing it? I continued searching the room, trying to figure out who was working this dark magic.

"Zo didn't kill those men!" Devlin roared. "I, too, know the woman's heart. She's not capable of such savagery. On the contra—"

Holy hell! Devlin, too? Who was doing this?

Somehow, and I'd never have believed the Beanhead capable of such power, Althea surmounted whatever was being done to her and once again found her voice. "Kill her!" she screamed, lips peeling back in a savage, bloodthirsty snarl. "I *insist* she be burned alive! She has taken life and—"

Althea was once again silenced, but this time a loud, horrifying cracking sound exploded in the room. One moment Ms. Bean was screaming for my death, the next her head was lolling at a gruesome angle, falling sloppily toward a shoulder, eyes wide and staring.

She slumped to the floor in a meticulously coiffed heap, dead.

I stared, horrified. This was the way of the Cailleach? Who had done it? Every person in the room was suspect to me. I whipped my gaze from Mr. Balfour, to Devlin, then the rest of the Ko—

Oh, shit, shit, shit, shit, shit.

At the far end of the room, a thick gray mist was drifting in dense tendrils from the floor. Or had it been there for some time and none of us had noticed, too busy bickering amongst ourselves?

Gray had always seemed a passive color to me, one too timid to be a color at all.

Staring at that fog, for the first time in my life, I apprehended the true color of gray. It was gunmetal, a diamond-hard, knife-sharp, aggressive color that knew exactly what it was: a razor-edged chasm between black and white in which one might be forever lost, drifting in an all-obscuring fog.

I watched, mouth ajar, as the dense gloom rose and rose, tendrils morphing into whipping tentacles that stretched hungrily all the way to the cathedral ceiling, stretching up and up until they forged a solid wall of dark, writhing grayness. Within that wall formed a multitude of slithering entities that lurked just beyond my brain's ability to define them, as if fashioned of creatures humans knew on a deep, atavistic level but hadn't seen in millennia, beings we prayed in desperate hours, in troubled times, never to see again.

An icy multitude of voices thundered from the murky vapor: "She belongs to us. She is beyond your reach now."

Every member of the Kovan peeled back and away from the fog as fast as they could, hugging the perimeter of the room as that dense, oppressive, charcoal mass oozed toward the stage.

Devlin alone did not yield, but leapt up onto the stage and took my hand in his. "You will not take her!" he roared. His fingers, twined with mine, rippled strangely as if his very bones were changing, shifting. He growled low in his throat, as if resisting it, then his fingers solidified again.

Still the gray miasma moved closer, closer, until I could no longer see the Kovan beyond it. A solid wall obscured my vision, flush to the stage, staring down at Devlin, Mr. Balfour, and me, faceless, without eyes, yet I somehow felt the weight of infinite judging gazes.

Taking my other hand, Mr. Balfour snarled, "She did not kill those men, and you have no right to claim her."

"So you say. We believe otherwise," the voices said flatly.

Mr. Balfour said, "You know the politics of our community! You know how many would set her up—"

"*SILENCE!*" The fog spoke in a voice unlike any I'd ever heard, containing an even greater multitude of voices, layered upon one another into a resolute, implacable command. Impossible to defy, stealing the words from our lips, muting any possible reply.

I tried. I opened my mouth repeatedly, attempting to form words, but none would come.

Abruptly, I was furious. Both Mr. Balfour and Devlin had at least gotten a chance to speak in my defense.

Was I to be given none?

That was bullshit.

I was a Cameron! I didn't believe for one moment otherwise. And as such, I was the most powerful witch in this room.

Eyes narrowing, I reached deep within for Zo, the real, true, fully empowered Zo Cameron. I would have my chance to speak to this . . . this . . . stain of unyielding terror that was *not* going to take me. Not today, not ever.

I'd spent enough of my life gray. Bold though the shade may be, I was done being it. I was vibrant, colorful Zo Cameron, and that was who I intended to remain.

Gently, carefully, I reached for power, spanning the boundaries of the town, opening myself to each blade of grass, each tree, each flower, bud, and stem. I beseeched them to donate willingly but a single atom of their life force, thereby gathering billions of atoms of energy without taking too much from any living thing yet drawing more than enough to break the gray house spell.

Then I snapped, "I belong to no one but myself! I will not—"

I broke off abruptly, this time from shock as a cloaked, heavily hooded figure manifested within the towering dark wall and thrust forward, emerging from it to drop heavily onto the stage.

One of the gray house, come to speak? I wondered, stunned into silence.

Tall and powerfully built was the only impression I could gather from the voluminous dark gray folds of robe. It was male, although I'm not sure how I knew that; something about the presence the figure exuded, perhaps. The folds of his hood fell about his face, gaping open, yet where a face should have been was merely a blur, a smear of featureless grayness.

Mr. Balfour moved to stand as a shield in front of me. "You'll have to go through me to—"

As if a tightly focused, invisible tornado hit him and him alone, Mr. Balfour was abruptly ripped from the stage, tossed nearly to the ceiling, and flung across the room, where he slammed into the wall with a loud crack before crashing to the floor, far below, in a crumpled heap.

I stared in horror, willing him to move, if only a finger, to let me know he was alive.

Never had Mr. Balfour looked so frail, so fully his age, with brittle bones that accompanied three-quarters of a century of life. I glanced frantically at Lennox, who was standing, hands fisted, tears streaming down her face, mouth open on a silent scream.

My gaze whipped back to him. "James!" I cried.

He lay motionless, blood slowly staining the floor around his head.

I lunged forward, grief and fury boiling in my veins. Not Mr. Balfour. Anyone but him. That man and my mother were the only protectors I'd ever known. I would not permit both of them to give their lives for me!

"You sonofabitch!" I snarled. "You motherfucker, you *will* *restore him*! If James Balfour is dead, you will bring him back to life. As Royal heir to the Cameron house, I *demand* it!"

"*SILENCE!*" the gray fog thundered in that multitude of voices again, this time even more resonant, more laced with power.

Hands flying to my neck, I tried frantically to speak again but failed.

"I am not Death, witch; you cannot command me. We all belong to one of the houses." The figure spoke icily, and it was, indeed, male. "And you, Zo Grey, are ours."

"You!" Devlin snarled at the hooded man.

The figure seemed to find his response amusing. Sardonic humor laced his reply, "You and I are destined to eternally be on opposite sides, Blackstone."

Yanking his hand from mine, Devlin surged forward, then drew up short, as if he'd slammed into an invisible wall.

"You know better," the cloaked figure said, laughing. Something about his laughter nagged at me, as did his voice. "We may have sprung from the same ancient well, but the similarities end there."

"I will hunt you to the ends of the earth if you take her, Mac-Keltar," Devlin snarled.

"Good luck with that," the gray figure mocked. "You've tried before and failed. You always will. She is mine."

"No," Devlin said flatly, "she is not yours. It was my bed she shared last night."

Stiffening, the figure said with soft menace, "But never will again."

That voice. Where had I heard that voice?

The fog exploded, obliterating my vision of everything and everyone.

I felt it pressing in on me, thick, suffocating, and oppressive, and I drew again for power, but I was somehow . . . being blocked. I couldn't draw a damned thing! In fact, I was horrified to realize, I couldn't feel myself at all. No wonder the gray house was the most feared of all. No wonder the room had peeled back.

I vowed silently, then and there, if James Balfour was dead, I would hunt and destroy each and every witch belonging to that abominable house, if it took me a thousand eternities.

What had the gray house *done* to me?

How had they done it?

I was lost in fog, powerless. If there was an ounce of true witch within me, I'd somehow been completely severed from her.

I had the dim sensation of being gathered up in powerful arms, lifted, and drawn into a vortex of sorts, felt a chilling, biting rush of wind and pressure as if I was being moved in some impossible fashion across some impossible distance. Far off, though fading quickly, I could hear Devlin roaring.

Then I heard nothing.

Saw nothing at all.

Gray turned to black.

Black to blindness.

To silence so absolute it reeked of oblivion.

The world ceased to exist. I was nowhere and nothing.

A consciousness conscious only of its own consciousness, no body. A disembodied, drifting, blind mind.

Then the fog began to lift, ever so slowly peeling back, and my vision slowly returned.

I *was* in someone's arms.

The tall gray-cloaked man Devlin had called MacKeltar.

I stared up at the gray hood, at the smear where a face should be, and as I stared, the smear began to coalesce into features and I knew, abruptly, exactly where I'd heard that laughter, that voice before.

Gaping, I managed to utter a single disbelieving word. *"Kellan?"*

About the Author

KAREN MARIE MONING is the #1 *New York Times* bestselling author of the Fever series, featuring MacKayla Lane, and the award-winning Highlander series. She has a bachelor's degree in society and law from Purdue University.